MATE ME

IMMORTAL VICES AND VIRTUES: SHADOW SHIFTER BONDS

BOOK ONE

AURELIA JANE

KEL CARPENTER

About the Authors

Kel Carpenter and Aurelia Jane are the hilarious team behind the international bestselling book, Reject Me.

They pride themselves in being absolute weirdos, spending hours on the phone coming up with detailed worlds, and laughing about crazy ideas for torturing characters. While they believe they each have the personality of a rabid badger, people still seem to like them okay.

They share a love of coffee, snarky t-shirts, and tacos, and they've made some adorable tiny people with their equally weird husbands. Best friends and work wives, Kel has the audacity to live in Maryland while Aurelia lives in Texas, but they try to see each other as much as possible.

patreon.com/kelcarpenterandaureliajane

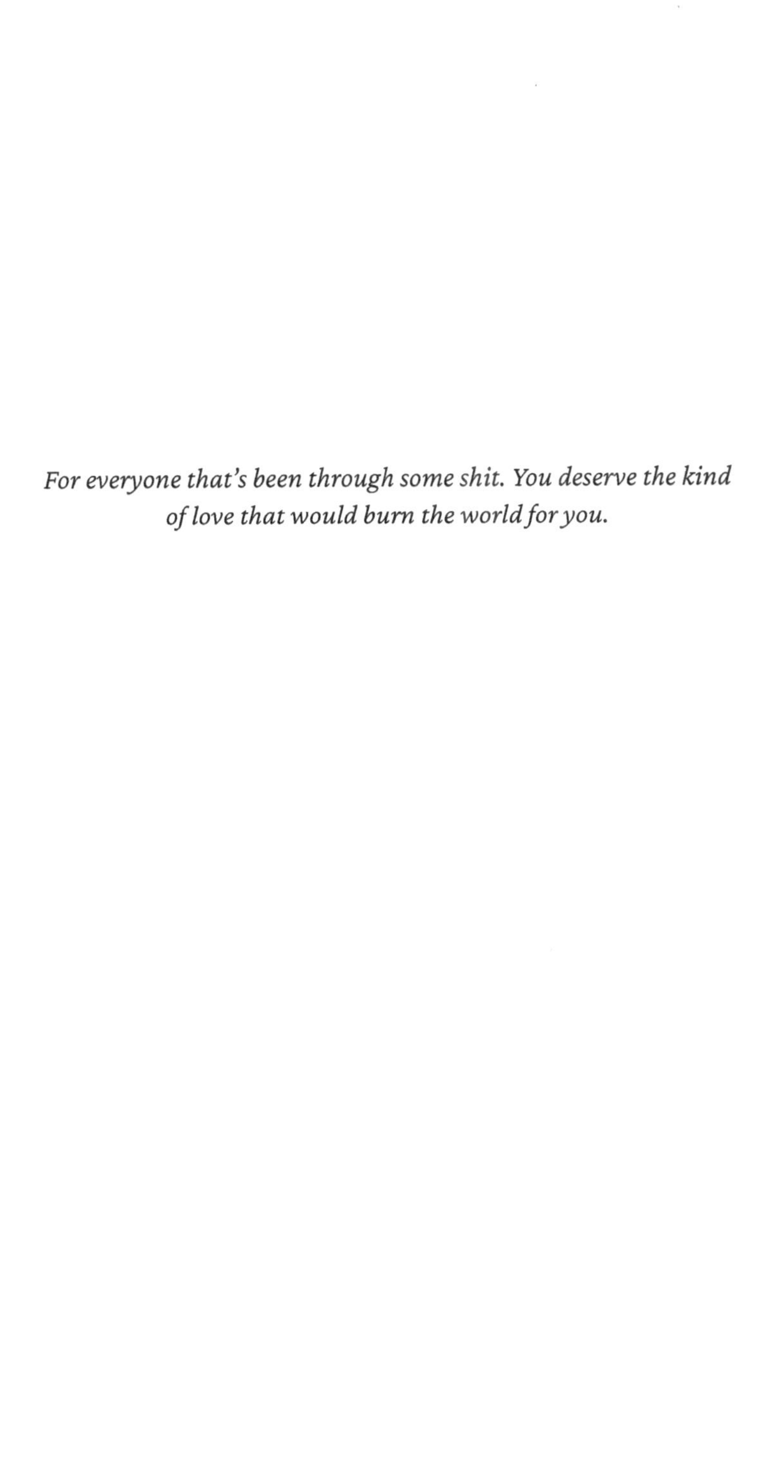

*For everyone that's been through some shit. You deserve the kind
of love that would burn the world for you.*

PROLOGUE

Gravel crunched beneath my knees; the thin shards of rock slicing into my flesh as I kneeled before eleven other primordials.

On my left, they forced Abyssian, my brother, to his knees. On my right, Pollux, my oldest friend. My only friend.

The eleven gathered before us, taking on delicate human forms as we often did when mingling with lesser beings. We only brought ourselves to this plane of existence during times of celebration. To feast and fuck and arrogantly grace mortals with our presence.

This time was different.

They were here for revenge.

They were here for me.

They had one item on the agenda.

Punishment.

Pious stood at the forefront of the group, and next to him, the traitorous woman who'd robbed me of my soul. He chained her arms, holding them behind her back as she cried out to me. I shut myself off and closed my eyes, dropping my chin to my chest while her pleas for forgiveness echoed across the plains.

My heart had become stone in the wake of her betrayal. Never mind her revelations of regret or the pain of guilt that was eating her insides. Never mind any of it. I foolishly believed a mortal woman would choose love—would choose me—above power.

I was mistaken, and now I would suffer for it.

"We stand here today to sentence one of our own. Caius, you were warned of mortals and their weaknesses. You were told what would come to pass, but you still chose to trust this woman despite all knowledge of mankind's selfishness. You cast aside your own, risking us all, and for what?" Pious spat. My head lolled forward, roughly shorn hair covering my eyes. I huffed a humorless laugh.

No, I had never been told what would come to pass.

I'd been told humans were power-hungry, untrustworthy, and incapable of true devotion.

I hadn't been told that the woman I loved would deceive me and steal half my soul.

In the background, a swirling abyss taunted us. I didn't have to ask what they planned to do. The portal to Tartarus was telling. That didn't stop Pious from rambling on. He'd always loved to hear himself speak.

"We sentence you, King of Monsters, to the realm of your own creation. It was made to be a prison, and now it will be yours."

Abraxia wept, incoherent words mingling with her hyperventilating cries.

"Silence!" Ix's commanding bellow shook the ground, her primordial powers leaking through her human form. She took Abraxia's bindings from Pious so that he could come forward, his attitude reeking of unmerited superiority.

I was beyond caring. Beyond shame. Beyond anything but the soul-searing pain that she had put me through, and she'd done it with their help.

"Pollux and Abyssian shall join you in exile—"

"Just shut up and get on with it," Pollux muttered.

"—As they supported you in this naïve wager."

"You can't do this!" Abyssian shouted and struggled at his invisible chains, but a minor fae god was no match for the magic of a primordial.

"Cast him out," Ix said. Two others came forward and I locked eyes with Ru'than. He was a younger primordial, but still ageless compared to mortals.

"Ru'than, don't do this. You know this is wrong," I pleaded. He'd always been a voice of reason. It had to be a unanimous decision to banish me. I knew him well, and I knew he was my friend.

Or so I'd thought.

He paused, his warm brown eyes softening, clearly torn. D'axi shoved his shoulder, chastising him in a low growl. "You know what he did. So finish this and do what you're told."

Ru'than's head fell, and he nodded softly. Together, they grabbed Abyssian and hefted him through the portal. My heart sank.

"Abyssian and Pollux were not part of this," I said, knowing none of it would change their minds. "This is between you and me, Pious."

"You chose your allies, Caius, and poorly, might I add."

"Fuck you," Pol spat.

"Fearless, aren't you?" Pious said, angered by Pollux's outburst. "Perhaps, instead, they chose poorly when they sought you as a leader, Caius. Nevertheless, they can suffer with you."

When Ru'than and D'axi moved to apprehend Pollux, the shadow shifter snapped, "No need. I will do it myself."

They stepped back letting him get to his feet. Pol regarded me and dropped one hand to my shoulder, squeezing it once before he stepped into the portal. I was lucky to have him. To have his loyalty and his friendship. Too bad he couldn't say the same about me. My actions damned him. Some friend I was.

"You can't hold my soul forever Pious," I ground out. "The power will destroy you, and when it does, my soul will return."

Pious laughed. "I don't need to hold it. A guardian can do that for me." His cruel smile caused Abraxia to choke on sobs, and I realized what she was there for. We were both being sentenced. Still, I couldn't bear to look at her.

An orb of pulsing white light appeared above his palm, and my betrayer paled as she fervently shook her head. The eleven gathered, muttering the words that would seal our fates, then he slammed the orb into her chest. She fell forward, screaming, hunched over with her face pressed into the dirt. The cloth of her dress burned, splitting right up the middle, and falling to the sides. Black runes carved themselves into her skin, up her back and onto her shoulder.

As the runes seared into place, I read them, falling deeper into hopelessness.

An unbreakable ward.

Passed on, from guardian to guardian.

For eternity.

Abraxia whimpered and Pious kicked her side, causing her to fall over.

Turning his smug face back to me, he raised his voice, giving his final declaration. "From henceforth you will be nameless. You will never be loved or revered—only feared. The world will come to forget Caius the Primordial ever existed, and the only name known to future generations will be when they pass down the tales of the Soulless One. Take your place where you belong, brother. Among the monsters."

That word snapped something inside of me and I stood up, pointedly glaring at Pious as I stepped toward him. "You are no brother of mine." Looking at the other ten, I saw Ru'than's soulful eyes filled with pain, but he still didn't speak up. I shook my head in disgust. "*None* of you are."

I turned my back on them. This wasn't the future I wanted. I wasn't even sure I would survive being separated from the earth and the light, but I would walk into Hell on my own two feet.

They wanted to call me a King of Monsters?

Fine.

Then that is what I would become.

The worst part about digging up a grave wasn't actually the smell; it was the unknown. The obvious expectation is that we'd find a body, of course, but it wasn't that cut and dry. For millennia other cultures had protected the entombed with a series of curses, trip wires, and other various booby traps. Add in the possibility that you might find a spelled corpse or a really pissed off vampire, and it equaled a fairly hazardous job.

I'd say I was used to it by now, but that was hardly the case.

Grave robbing was our family business. It wasn't as bad as it sounded. We weren't digging up bodies at random, or disturbing ancient burial grounds. Rubies, pottery, coins, pocket watches: none of that mattered. Items like that were no longer valued as currency in this world. What we were paid to acquire was either sentimental or enchanted. Usually the latter.

We were merely contractors . . . who dug up the dead.

Okay, maybe it was as bad as it sounded, but we did what we needed to do for survival. We lived in an unconventional world, which meant we had unconventional job prospects.

That was why we were spending our night digging a hole in a cemetery across the river from our home in The Crossroads.

The autumn air was crisp, laced with the scent of the rain we'd likely get sometime overnight. For now, only a few clouds floated in the dark sky. A full moon illuminated the graveyard, giving us so much light we didn't even need magic or lanterns.

I didn't want to take this as a rush job. Our buyer was eager, and that meant we needed to work quickly. I had a standard rule that I didn't mingle with the dead on a full moon, but when work had been slow, and our client was willing to pay handsomely, it was hard to say no.

Still, it made me feel uneasy.

"What do you think we're gonna find this time?" Nog asked, interrupting my train of thought. "Pile of dusty bones in tattered clothes, or something cool like a zombie?"

My cousin had a very blasé attitude about our line of work, and very little scared him—which wasn't a good thing. At nineteen, he had too little fear and too much confidence. It was a dangerous combination when he was a latent shifter and didn't have much in the way of strength or power.

"Hopefully we just find the lapel pin we were paid to locate," I answered, pushing my foot on the shovel as I continued to dig. We stood in a hole about five feet deep and probably about the same width, and we were almost finished.

"I wonder what it does," he mused with genuine interest in his voice. "I can never tell if they want something that was buried fifty years ago because they want it as a family keepsake or if they want it for some spell."

"Honestly, I try not to think about it."

"Why not?" He'd completely stopped shoveling. "Aren't you a little curious what people are up to?"

My cousin was the king of asking dumb questions.

"I try not to think about it because not all witches are good and those objects could be used for creating wards on people against their will, Nog," I answered quietly.

Awkward silence spanned between us.

I held no ill-will toward any species. I was half shifter and half witch, but I also knew very well what witches were capable of. As far as everyone outside my family knew, I had an intricate tattoo of weaving ancient symbols on my back, but it was far more complicated than that. It was a ward—placed on me the night I was born—by a coven of doomsday witches. The very same coven of zealots that had raised my mother . . . and killed her after she'd given birth to me twenty-seven years ago.

The magic beneath my skin made me a guardian, destined to protect a darkness within me I wasn't even sure I believed was there.

What I did know was that the ward had been passed down for centuries. My mother was a guardian, and her mother before her, and her mother—and each one of them was sacrificed in the transfer when they had a child at twenty-five.

Not me. I noped right out of that situation.

When I learned I was destined for the same fate, I escaped. I wandered aimlessly for weeks. Then my dad found me. He'd spent a decade trying to track me down, and now he spent his time tracking down a cure, for lack of a better word. My not having a baby only solved half the problem. At some point, I'd die. If there was even a grain of truth to the stories we'd been told, there had to be a way to pass on the duties of a guardian to someone else, but I'd be damned if I forced it on anyone.

My cousin's eyes shifted toward my back before he quickly looked at me again, then his lips twisted to the side as he fidgeted with his hands. "My bad," he mumbled. "You know we'll find a way to fix it."

"I know. I just want to get this hole dug and be on our way." Angling my shovel slightly, I sprayed him with some dirt. "So, chop chop before I cut your pay."

"All right, all right. I'm just stretching," he said, brushing the dirt off his chest.

"Mmm hmm." I shook my head.

A familiar laugh sounded, announcing my cousin Clara's arrival, late as usual. "You do an awful lot of stretching, Nog," she said with a snort. "There's a reason Reagan has calluses on her hands, and you don't."

"Oh, nice of you to finally grace us with your presence, dear sister," he said, bowing in mock respect and looking up where she stood at the edge of the pit. "Did you get lost, or were you busy with your fuckboy flavor of the month?"

"Stop calling him that." Clara rolled her eyes, flicking a strand of her straight black hair over her shoulder. "I'm here, aren't I? I made double today by taking a job with Crowley and his crew before coming to this one, thank you very much."

"Now that you're here, do you care to help out? You make ten percent from us, and you don't do any of the work," he grumbled.

"I am helping." Clara plopped down on the ground and leaned against the headstone while she pulled out yarn and crocheted a little doll. "I'm a modern-day insurance policy, Nog. You never know when you'll need me."

"Insurance? Hardly. Extortion is more like it," he argued. "We don't even know if there's a spirit in there. We pay you and you just sit around *'in case.'*"

"That's how insurance works, genius."

Nog looked at me while he gestured up to his sister. "Do we really need her?"

"You know we do. Two weeks ago a vampire popped out of a coffin and tried to use you as a snack," I said, shoving the blade into the dirt with force. "She's worth ten percent any day of the week, so stop bitching at her and dig so I can go home, for the love of the gods."

"Home?" Clara repeated lightly, changing the course of the conversation the moment she caught my slipup. "It's Saturday. You said you'd be at the pub tonight."

Dammit.

The truth was I had a date, but I never liked them knowing about it. They thought Ben and I had broken up months ago, which in fairness, we had. I just failed to mention when we got back together. We were casual, and I didn't want to make a thing out of it. My cousins meant well, but they butted in, showed up on my dates, had zero filter about their opinions, and frankly, it was embarrassing.

"Changed my mind." I shrugged, not looking up. "I'd like to make it an early night."

From the corner of my eye, I saw Nog lean on his shovel, tilting his head. "Nothing else planned?"

Don't make eye contact. I wasn't a great liar if I had to look at someone while doing so. Staring at the spot where I was digging, I scooped another mound of dirt. "Nope. Just tired."

"Reagan, are you hiding something?" Clara asked, putting her crochet down and turning toward me. "Are you feeling okay? Is the ward—"

Oh hell, I never should have said I was tired. My family constantly worried. No matter how much they tried not to show it, I knew they were anxious about finding a spell or some way to get the ward off me. Sometimes they treated me like I was glass, fearing that any outside force would cause me to shatter. I stopped digging and looked up at my cousin. "Poor choice of words. I promise. Nothing has changed with it." I forced a smile.

"No nightmares?" she pressed. "No hallucinations or voices?"

"Nope. I would tell you if I did." Wards could supposedly send people on a downward spiral the longer they carried them. Since I'd made it longer than any guardian that came before me, we could only assume it was a matter of time.

If I started to experience any madness, I wasn't sure I'd tell Clara, exactly, but I'd at least tell my sister. This was another reason I liked being with Ben. He didn't know about all this, so it was never a discussion. I felt like I was normal when we were together—even if I wasn't able to truly be myself.

"Yeah, would you actually tell me, though? Or would you just tell Sin and have her keep the secret from me? I know how sisters work," she countered. "You're not the greatest at asking for help."

"What is this, a therapy session?"

"That's not an answer," Nog added. Now they were teaming up with each other. Typical siblings.

I opened my mouth to answer, but a familiar sound echoed in the hole. My attention refocused the moment my shovel thudded against the wooden box. Saved by the dead. Brushing the remaining dirt from the surface, we saw the heart-shaped emblem we'd been told was engraved on top.

"Looks like it's the right one," I whispered, feeling for the clasp on the side.

The coffin wasn't even open yet, but the scent of death permeated the air. Clara waved her hand in front of her nose and made a slight gagging sound. "I'll never get used to that."

Nog inhaled deeply. "Smells like payday if you ask me."

"Ew." I walloped him upside the head. "Have some respect."

"I have respect! We all die. This dude isn't using whatever he was buried with, so I respect the wishes of those who pay us, Rea."

I shook my head in disapproval, but it wasn't worth an argument.

"You ready, twinkle fingers?" Nog taunted, grinning at his sister. Clara winked at him, and I held my hand out for the picture we'd been given, taking another look at the item. We only wanted to do the job once, and we needed to see exactly what we were supposed to be getting.

Round cut moonstone lapel pin. Silver. About the size of an old quarter. Simple enough.

"Okay, here we go. One, two . . ." I gripped the edge of the lid and pulled it open. Instantly, a blast of power exploded outward. Nog yelped as we were both tossed out of the hole and landed on our backs with a loud thud.

"Three," I coughed out, rolling over to get up when an animated corpse came flying out after us. I grabbed a shovel, cursing beneath my breath.

Nog screamed a high-pitched wail as it went after him, arms open like it wanted to wrap around him in a bear hug.

He didn't have a weapon, so all he did was swat at it like he was fending off a swarm of mosquitos. "Clara, do what you get paid to do!"

With a few long strides, I wound up, preparing to use the shovel like a bat. I swung, connected directly with the head like a baseball sitting on a tee. It popped right off, rolling on the ground until it went down the grave we'd just reopened. The body dropped in an audible clacking of bones, and Clara's laughs suddenly filled the air.

It only took a moment for me to put two and two together. Clara had powerful spirit magic. Though I'd never seen her reanimate a body like this before, it was clearly easy for her, and she'd do just about anything to piss off her brother.

"For fuck's sake, you swamp witch! That wasn't funny!" Nog shouted, dusting himself off.

She cackled louder, wiggling her fingers. "Twinkle, twinkle, asshat."

"I can't believe you," I grumbled. Shaking my head, I threw the shovel to the side and dropped to a knee beside the body. Rolling it over, I found the lapel pin that matched the picture. I removed it carefully and put it in an enchanted pouch.

"It was just a bit of fun," Clara argued in defense. "C'mon, when have you ever heard Nog scream like that? That was prime B horror movie quality just now."

"I'm docking your pay for that bullshit." Grabbing my satchel that was leaning up against a gravestone, I pulled it over my head and rested the strap on my shoulder. "Nog," I called, and he glanced in my direction. I tossed him the keys to the truck so he could get himself home. "Get this cleaned up and put the body back. *Nicely*."

"Wait, you aren't staying?"

Shaking my head, I wiped my hands on my jeans and showed him, palms facing out. "You spent most of the night talking. When your calluses look like mine, I'll stick around to help you clean up."

He griped, but I outranked him and he knew if he argued, he'd lose.

I started walking away, sensing that Clara was close on my heels. "So what's really up?" she asked casually, keeping pace with me as we made our way to her truck.

"You know how I feel about working on a full moon. I just want to get home."

"Do you sense any danger?"

My animal lightly stirred inside me.

I sighed. The loose connection between us was hard to read. We both felt uneasy, but not in the way my cousin was suggesting. "You know she doesn't. Otherwise I wouldn't have left your brother back there by himself."

"What exactly is it, then? Yeah, you hate working on full moons, but you've never said the specifics as to why."

When we got to her truck, I turned to her and held my hands out for her keys. The corner of her lips tilted down, and she reluctantly gave them to me.

"We dig up the dead and piss off spirits in the middle of the night, Clara. Story after story will tell you that nothing good happens on a full moon."

She smiled softly. "But look? All that worry for nothing. We're done now, and all is well."

I hummed noncommittally. She could be optimistic, but I had a feeling tonight wasn't going to be any different.

Narrator: it was actually worse.

CHAPTER 2

REAGAN

We weren't home for ten minutes before my cousin started grilling me. She'd spent the car ride practically burning a hole in the side of my face as she glared at me, trying to get a read. Apparently it worked.

"You're not still seeing Ben, are you?" Clara asked knowingly.

Damn her. She had terrible foresight ninety percent of the time, but her ability to sniff out my lies was unusually good.

"Weren't you going out with Crowley tonight?" I smeared peanut butter on some crackers and refused to meet her accusatory stare. Stuffing one in my mouth, I chewed and wished she would leave me alone.

"I cancelled them when I thought you might be lying about your plans for the night." She leaned against the counter and crossed her arms.

"You know I'm an adult, right? I can see whoever I want and do what I want in my free time." The words were slightly muffled, and tiny crumbs flew out of my mouth.

"You could do better than that backwoods shifter, Reagan."

I swallowed, and let out an exasperated sigh, turning to face her. "*I'm* a backwoods shifter, Clara. I live here, too, and in case you don't remember, my animal lives inside me but can't come out. I'm part witch with no real access to any threads of magic beyond your basic parlor tricks. I have strength, healing, and thank the gods I'm smart because that's all I have to offer in a world that values supernatural power, so please remind me why you think I can do better than basically everyone I've ever met."

"That's not what I mean," she continued.

"Then what do you mean, hmm?"

"I mean you could do better than Ben Flowers. It's not about being from The Crossroads or what powers he has, or you for that matter. I just don't trust him."

"Look, it's not like I have plans to settle down."

"So you are seeing him?" She narrowed her eyes.

"Let it go, Clara. I know you mean well, I really do, but just drop it. This is why I don't tell y'all anything . . ." I pinched the bridge of my nose and shook my head. "You know what? Never mind. I'm going to bed."

I left her in the kitchen and went to my room, slamming the door before packing my satchel with some moonshine and a DVD. Looking in the mirror, I almost laughed. I looked like—well, like I'd been digging up a grave. Stripping off the dirt-covered jeans and shirt, I kicked them into a pile in the corner by my small dresser. After re-braiding my hair, I wiped off my face with a washcloth and changed into comfortable leggings and an off-the-shoulder sweater.

I listened by my door and heard Clara in the kitchen, banging around pans as she began to cook. She always did when she was upset, and I knew our argument had probably frustrated the hell out of her.

Sighing, I turned to leave, but I had no plans on exiting through the front. Twenty-seven years old and I still preferred to sneak out my window rather than tell the truth about where I was going.

Clara had never liked Ben, and Nog piggybacked on whatever his sister said—unless it was about him, of course. She never even gave Ben a chance; just said she had a bad feeling about him. That wasn't enough to go on. She had notoriously bad taste in men, and her current boyfriend was no different.

After he picked me up down the road, Ben and I spent the night laying on a pile of blankets on the rooftop of his building downtown. It wasn't romantic. It was comfortable. Just drinking my special moonshine blend, eating pizza, and watching a movie on a portable DVD player he'd scored in a trade a few months back. He didn't even have to spell it. It still worked on its own, and that made it a fantastic find. I had a decent collection of films, and even though I'd seen it a hundred times, he indulged my desire to watch *The Princess Bride* yet again.

When the credits began to roll, he turned it off and we laid in silence. The St. Louis Arch stood in the distance, but without lights, all you could see was the outline. The smell of the river was faint, and I could almost taste the rain in the atmosphere. It wasn't here yet, but it was close.

Clouds rolled through the sky, blocking out the moon and showing her again. Stars glittered and peeked through in the same way. It was serene, and coupled with the moonshine, I was damn near falling asleep.

"Do you ever think about leaving The Crossroads?" he asked me, his tone casual and light.

My eyes widened. A sudden jolt of fear coursed through me, but I couldn't explain it. I sat up, turning to look at him. "Why? Do you?"

Ben propped himself up on his elbows and tilted his head regarding me. "Yeah, sometimes. Is that so bad?"

I could think of a number of reasons why it was bad. First and foremost, I valued my family more than anything, and my family lived here. Second, leaving would mean we'd have even less protection than we have now. It was dangerous at the best of times.

Once the world's governments collapsed, supernaturals established their own hierarchy. There were eight Houses that ruled, or maybe it was nine? I couldn't keep track of the way they formed and sometimes imploded in a very short time frame. We were situated in the largest No Man's Land in the middle of what used to be Midwest America. Others like it were simply open territory that the Houses either couldn't or wouldn't take over—but we were a little more put together in The Crossroads. Houseless, yes, but not as cutthroat, all while still being dangerous. On one hand, it meant we didn't have to worry about whatever political shenanigans the Houses were up to. We weren't involved in their politics or border disputes. On the other hand, it did make survival a little more difficult when powerful allies did not back you. Still, we managed to do okay for ourselves. Railroad tracks from all over converged in The Crossroads—thus the name. It was how we managed trade, and that was a great achievement for a city that had no authority elsewhere.

"This is the safest No Man's Land there is. Why would you want to risk leaving that?"

He shrugged, sitting forward and resting his elbows on his knees. "We only know what we've been told,

Reagan. I don't know what the rest of the world looks like."

I sighed, understanding more of what he was getting at. "Fair enough, but I do know my dad is out there saving orphaned kids before rogue organizations can capture and sell them off. That speaks volumes. It's safer here, even if we don't know what actually lies beyond the plains."

"I suppose," he said softly. "You don't ever feel trapped, though?"

I huffed a humorless laugh. "More than you know," I muttered.

"What's that supposed to mean?"

Pressing my lips together, I knew I couldn't go on. I'd already said enough.

Ben picked up a pebble and threw it. "Do you do this with all your friends?"

"Do what?"

"It's like you start to trust me, then you shut it down again. It's maddening."

"That's not it." I shook my head, looking down at my socks while picking at a string. "It's . . . the same as you, really. Wish I could see the ocean, the mountains, any type of different landscape. I dream about them, you know; dream about visiting my cousin at Mt. Rainier, but it's easier if I don't think about it too much because I plan on staying here."

It wasn't untrue. I wanted to see and explore. It just wasn't an option.

At times, especially moments such as these, I wished I could share more with Ben. Tell him I was a guardian. Tell him how I felt trapped every day of my life, forced into a role I didn't understand, carrying something that was destined to kill me or drive me insane. And I couldn't say a damn word. Sharing any of those details with him put everyone in danger.

It was safer to go through life when everyone suspected I was a latent horse shifter.

What no one knew was she was much more than that. An animal thought to be extinct long ago lived within me. We didn't lie when we said it was an equine . . . we just didn't elaborate and specify that she was a dark unicorn. If anyone found out, we'd be captured and sold to the highest bidder. They'd force a shift if they could, study us, and try to use our magic for personal gain.

I'd heard plenty of stories about how dragons had been kept in cages, drugged to prevent shifting, manipulated in experiments, and had their magical scales torn off to be used as currency.

No, thanks.

If I started to throw myself a pity party about staying in The Crossroads, all I had to do was remind myself of the alternative.

Instead, I pushed down my desires and tried to appreciate what I already had.

A gust of wind rushed through downtown, cutting straight through my sweater and sending a chill through my body.

"Come here," Ben said, gesturing for me to come beside him and get under the blanket. I scooted toward him and curled myself against his heat. He rested his chin on top of my head, and I closed my eyes. "You know I wouldn't leave The Crossroads without you, right? You stay, I stay."

It was a bittersweet sentiment. I wanted to feel that for Ben too, but I didn't love him. Not because he wasn't worthy of it, but because I didn't let myself get close enough to allow it. We were supposed to be casual. Nothing serious. No commitments. I'd even told him he was good to date other women if he wanted, but he never did. He hadn't ever told me he loved me, but I had started to suspect it was coming soon.

If he was going to cross the line into a more permanent territory, it was time to end things. It wasn't fair to drag it out. My conscience reminded me as much. *Yeah, yeah. Sue me for wanting to feel normal for just one more night.*

Swallowing the knot that had formed in my throat, I said, "You know I wouldn't keep you here, Ben. If you wanted to go, I wouldn't stop you."

"Are you saying you want me to leave?"

"No, I'm saying I won't hold you back. Besides, your mate could be out there somewhere—"

"What would you say if I told you I wanted you to be my mate?"

My breath hitched and my entire body tensed. This night had taken a drastic turn. Slowly, I sat up, trying to put some distance between us. "I . . . I would say I don't want to be mated. We weren't supposed to be that serious, Ben. Maybe we should—"

He jerked away forcefully, rolled over and stood up. Running his fingers through his hair, he looked at me with furrowed brows. "You don't want a mate, fine, but you always do this to me, Reagan."

"What?" I asked, squinting my eyes in confusion. I pushed myself up to stand, hugging myself and tucking my hands beneath my arms at my side as the wind whipped around us.

"You're hot and cold. Saying one thing, meaning another—"

"Whoa, there. Who's hot and cold now? I thought we agreed this was casual. That doesn't mean anything other than exactly what it sounds like. Hell, you just called me your friend."

Ben's jaw clenched, anger brewing inside him. "You misinterpreted that. What was I supposed to call you? My lover? My girlfriend? Friend felt like the safest word, so I didn't scare you off again."

I scrunched my eyebrows and thought for a second. Did I misinterpret? I wasn't sure. Maybe I'd misunderstood a lot of what had happened between us and that was what had led us to this fun encounter.

"I'm not trying to lead you on, Ben. I was clear from the beginning—"

"You were clear that you wanted to be with me. Every time we've been together, it's 'casual.' Then we broke it off, and you came right back to my door."

I felt like I'd been slapped. Is that what I had done? Is that why he thought this was more? I cleared my throat. "I came back because I enjoyed your company, and you enjoyed mine. I even told you to date other women."

"You said it, but you didn't mean it."

Well, that one I knew wasn't me. "Um, yes I did. If you took those words to mean something else, that's on you."

The wolf inside him vibrated with rage. Hot-headed shifters. I should have known better. I bent down to gather my things, tossing the satchel over my shoulder.

"Running away, like always." He shook his head and scoffed. "What would you do if you found a mate, Rea?"

I threw my hands out in frustration. "I'd reject them, *Ben*. I don't want a mate. When my dad lost my mom it nearly destroyed him. I don't want anything having that much power over me, especially some guy fate ties me to for no good reason."

Tingles of electricity reached my fingertips, and dark

shadows coiled around my arms. I had no real witch magic to speak of, but when I got angry, some part of me reacted to that lineage. It was like the emotion was trying to guide it, but I felt no attachment to it so I couldn't control it.

When Clara tried to teach me, I blew up a plant and set fire to a living room pillow. When I left the magic alone, it didn't do much more than make my fingers look like smoky Fourth of July sparklers.

He glanced at my hands, closed his eyes briefly and sighed. He flexed his fists and let go. "I'm sorry. My wolf is agitated. He's getting harder to control lately."

Crossing my arms again, I looked away, tears threatening to spill over. "I don't think we should hang out anymore. See each other. Whatever this is, it went too far. I, uh, I thought we were on the same page. If I hurt you, I'm sorry."

Maybe it wasn't right to apologize, but I genuinely didn't want to hurt him.

"Hey," he said softly, approaching me with slow steps. "I'm sorry, okay?"

Ben held my chin between his finger and thumb, turning me to face him. I looked up, seeing gold streaks across the blue of his irises. Something I'd never seen before, and I wondered if I'd ever really looked so closely.

I nodded. "Okay."

Then he leaned down to kiss me, and I stupidly let him.

Like a dumbass.

What the hell was wrong with me?

"Ben," I mumbled, pulling away and placing my hands on his chest, nudging to separate us.

I thought he was conceding.

I was wrong.

He moved so swiftly, I never saw it coming.

Strong arms wrapped around me, crushing me against him, and his teeth sunk into the exposed shoulder muscle at the base of my neck. Fangs pierced the skin, and I cried out as I registered what was happening.

The bastard was trying to claim me.

I shoved hard, feeling a blast of weak magic explode from my hands. The minor power coupled with the force of my shifter strength knocked him back. He stumbled, looking at me confused.

"What the fuck, Ben?" I shouted, wiping his saliva from my exposed shoulder. Blood streaked my hand.

Fur had erupted along the sides of his face, his eyes glowing. "You said 'okay'—"

"I said okay when you apologized! Not for you to try and claim me, asshole!" Grabbing my satchel, I packed up my things. Ben vibrated, struggling to control an unwanted shift, but I didn't care.

The door to the rooftop flew open, the metal clanging as it bounced off the wall.

"Told ya she'd be here," Nog said triumphantly as his sister appeared behind him.

I wanted to scream at both of them for following me, but for once, I was happy they did. I stormed toward the door, giving Ben my back. "I was just leaving. C'mon."

"Reagan, wait," he called, and I whirled around to face him. "I fucked up. So bad. I'm so sorry. I don't know what's happening to me right now. The urge to claim is strong. I can't explain it—"

"Goodbye, Ben." I turned away from him, even when I saw the pain in his eyes. Even if something in nature was pushing him to claim a mate, I'd just said I didn't want one and he did it anyway.

I held Clara's hand and tugged her into the stairwell.

Nog followed as we huffed it down twelve flights. When we exited to the street, a sudden dizziness began to take hold of me. I stumbled, and Nog caught me, holding my side.

"Reagan?" he said, worry filling his tone.

"I'm okay." I shook my head. Bad idea. The world began to spin. Cradling my temple, I said, "Less okay."

Clara grabbed my cheeks, trying to look at me head on, but she was out of focus. My vision began to swim. "Reagan, your pupils . . . shit."

My cousin no doubt saw the bite and blood on my shoulder, and magic began to swirl around her hands.

"Is that . . . did he. . . ?" Nog said, anger filling his tone.

"He tried," Clara answered. "I don't think he got to finish. The mark isn't deep enough to be complete."

"What's happening?" I whispered.

An invisible force pulled my body, weighing me down. I tried to reach for my animal, but I could barely feel her presence.

A loud thud sounded in my ears and pain exploded in my head as I unceremoniously dropped to the concrete sidewalk like a lead balloon.

My cousins shouted my name in panic, kneeling beside me.

"We've got you. We'll get you home," Clara said in a soothing voice.

I stared up at the sky as the clouds wisped across a blanket of stars, and a bright white orb came into focus for a brief moment, almost as if to laugh at my current state.

"Told you . . ." I mumbled, feeling my eyelids flutter as my consciousness faded.

Clara crouched beside me, stroking my head. "Told me what, Rea?"

"Nothing good happens on a full moon."

CHAPTER 3

CAIUS

The waves crashed softly on the shoreline, the rhythmic splash creating a sense of peace and calm in an otherwise chaotic world.

Time crawled slowly into the early morning hours, but the eternal night dragged on.

Darkness consumed Tartarus, never changing. There was no bright, burning star to warm the ground. No colorful changing of the seasons. After a while, the drab atmosphere grew on me. The longing for a vivid and lively environment eventually waned, though the anger I felt over my loss never truly did.

I couldn't remember the feeling of the sunlight on my skin. I couldn't recall the scent of spring, or the sound of songbirds.

I'd almost lost hope that one day I'd leave this place, but I still held onto a fraying thread.

I sighed, shifting my weight to my right leg, and crossing my arms. My actions caught Styx's attention. She'd come looking for me, knowing where I went when I needed to think.

"That's twice now you've sighed like that since I've been here. What troubles you, Caius?" she asked.

Styx was observant, always watching her surroundings and sizing up anyone around us. With bronze skin and dark hair, she was stunning, but it wasn't her looks that drew me to her all those years ago. It was the calculated gleam in her eye. She was as dangerous as she was beautiful. Kelpies often were. I'd found her here, banished for a crime, yet, unlike so many others, she didn't beg for forgiveness. She didn't apologize for what she'd done, and when I'd heard the story, I understood why. I respected her for it. She may not have crossed from Earth to Tartarus with me, but she became part of my court, and her loyalty was just as fierce as Abyssian and Pollux's.

She didn't exactly get along with everyone, but that wasn't a requirement to earn my trust.

Angling my head toward her, I pressed my lips together. "The visions."

"Did something new happen in them?"

I lifted my shoulder in a half-hearted shrug. "They're becoming more frequent. I can't get her face out of my head."

"We've searched for years and found nothing. If she was in Tartarus, we'd know." She took an extra moment, considering her next words. "I don't think it's anything more than a dream, Caius."

I shook my head. "It's not. I don't know who she is, but it's maddening. Something about her calls to me. Her beauty is . . ." I closed my eyes and inhaled deeply, almost as though I was trying to imagine her scent. "I've never seen anyone like her. She haunts me."

"You speak of her as someone would a mate," she said, a hint of disgust in her tone.

With a chuckle, I said, "Primordials don't have mates. No one could ever be our equal. That doesn't stop me from wanting to find her."

It was a sad and lonely truth to my kind. Even if having half my power stripped away demoted my status to a measly god, there were some aspects of my creation that remained unchanging, and I had accepted that truth long ago. Fuck love anyway. That's what doomed me to this prison in the first place. It still didn't stop me from wanting to taste the woman who'd plagued my dreams for years.

"Will you miss it?" she asked, jutting her chin out to the vast, dark ocean. "When the day comes for you to leave, I mean."

A small smile graced my lips. "Yes, surprisingly."

The realm was meant to be filled with the damned, and yet, in my rule, it evolved. Families were born here. Civilization formed. Industry thrived. Yes, the damned still suffered, but life was also *lived*.

The creators—the ancients—they had it wrong all along. At one time, I had been too. There was no black and white. No one was all good, and no one was all bad. This place showed that to me day in and day out. Gray was a beautiful color, and Tartarus was a testament to it.

Yet, none of that pride quelled my desire to escape and take back what was mine. Several thousand years was a long time to simmer in my anger and hatred while plotting revenge on those who'd put me here.

"This world is a better place because of your rule, my friend. Don't forget that."

"I can't. You won't stop reminding me." I smirked at her, then returned my gaze to the ocean just as a shadow of unease drifted over me, tightening in my chest. The rich scent of sweet apples and earthy oak reached me.

That was . . . new.

"Do you smell that?" I asked, and Styx raised an eyebrow in question.

"Smell what?"

Shaking my head, I did my best to brush it off. "Nothing."

I could feel Styx's gaze as she assessed my every move. A deeper part of me began to feel distress and I couldn't explain it. Emotions whispered, teasing the edge of my mind, but they were not my own.

Without another word, I made for the castle entrance where the sand and ocean met. Built into the rocky mountainside terrain of an active volcano, it looked more intimidating than inviting.

She followed, taking the steps two at a time to keep up with me.

"Caius, what's wrong?" she asked between heavy breaths.

"I'm not sure." I knew I couldn't hide that something was affecting me, but I couldn't give a real answer when I wasn't entirely sure what was happening myself.

We weren't halfway there when heavy beads of sweat dotted my brow and began to drip down my temples. I came to a stop, wiping it off with the back of my hand. The temperature here remained the same, and I climbed these steps daily. Never once had this realm elicited a reaction like this without a more intense physical exertion.

The response was almost . . . human.

Bursting through the doors into my throne room, I walked through the attached atrium and headed for a table. A pewter pitcher and goblet sat near a stack of parchment. Gulping water did nothing to cool me off.

Styx spoke softly to a porter, instructing him to bring in

the rest of my trusted court. He nodded at the command and turned to leave.

"Wait," I called, and he froze. "Summon Broca as well."

The young man nodded again, scurrying out quickly. Styx groaned obnoxiously, not trying to hide her displeasure.

"Tell me how you really feel," I said sarcastically, taking a seat at a large round table. Ivy and various medicinal herbs grew along trellises on the wall, creating a warm, inviting space amidst the rock. I could use some of those medicines right about now. My gut twisted again, and I grit my teeth at the discomfort.

Styx scoffed in derision. "She's not a soothsayer, and she speaks in riddles. Don't give credence to anything that old goat tells you. You never know if a glaistig is helping you or trying to screw you over."

Turning to her, I raised a brow. "You doubt her?"

She gestured vaguely. "To be fair, I doubt everyone. Pollux and I have that in common. I wanted to stab Oberon the day I met him."

"And yet you didn't."

"I'm still not sure I made the right choice."

My trusted companions, Abyssian, Oberon, and Pollux walked into the great room, an urgency in their steps.

"I heard that," Oberon said, flipping her off.

She turned to look at him as she stood with her arms crossed. "I sure hope so. I said it loud enough."

"You look like shit, Caius," Abyssian said, assessing me from head to toe.

"Feeling like it, brother," I muttered, rubbing the side of my temples as a momentous headache began to form.

The unsettling clacking of hooves sounded in the hall,

and Pollux squeezed his eyes shut before grumbling, "Why is she here?"

"Because I've been summoned, you twit." Broca's melodic voice echoed off the rocky ceiling. A glaistig, half goat, half woman, entered the room. She'd chosen to arrive in her human form, and she was a sight to behold. A cascade of red hair fell down her back in a loose braid, her wide green eyes scanning the room as she weighed her audience. She walked closely to Abyssian, sending him a wink as she brushed his arm. He looked away, muttering something unintelligible.

The moment her gaze fell on me, her features tightened. "She has reached you," Broca whispered harshly.

"Who has reached him?" Pollux and Abyssian asked in unison.

"The guardian." She spoke softly, almost in awe of what she was seeing with her magic.

"That isn't possible," I said, shaking my head in disbelief. It had been millennia since my imprisonment. How a guardian this far down the line could . . .

Our conversation may as well have been coded, and it provided no context for my court. The four of them exchanged worried looks before Pollux asked, "Caius, what's happening?"

His question was ignored, but I didn't care. Broca approached me slowly, her eyes shining with interest. "You feel it."

"What does it mean?" I asked, standing before her.

Broca's beauty morphed. Aged wrinkles creased around her eyes, and silver strands marred a sea of red hair. Graceful, soft hands were replaced with spindly fingers and gnarled knuckles. Her bones snapped; human legs shifting into her half goat form.

Styx and Oberon armed themselves, but I threw a hand out toward them, commanding them to stop.

The glaistig's palm slammed into my head, her sharp nails pressing into the flesh. White clouds covered the mossy green of her irises as she used her power. Thunder rumbled in the distance, shaking the mountain around us. With her head tilted back, she spoke, her voice deep and trembling with the strain.

> *A great battle, your future holds.*
> *Within the course the truth unfolds.*
> *The day will come when you must choose,*
> *No matter the choice, you will lose.*
> *Speak the words upon your breath.*
> *To give her life will cause your death.*

When she released her hand, I sucked in a harsh breath, stumbling and coughing as I tried to regain composure.

The words replayed in my mind as I tried to make sense of them, but the members of my court had no intention of waiting for an explanation.

Styx rushed Broca; fists balled at her sides. "What the hell does that mean?"

"Our world's future hangs in the balance," she said cryptically, not bothering to even look at the great fighter that stood before her. "I can't see anything beyond that."

"You didn't even tell us what you *did* see! You explained nothing. You spoke poetic gibberish," Abyssian ground out. "Fucking witch."

"I am not a witch," she hissed. "Don't be nasty, fae lord. You were more than content with me while in my bed."

Oberon smacked his forehead. "Really, man?"

"Not the time," he said, his jaw clenched. Styx looked at him with fresh disgust.

"Enough!" I growled. "Is the guardian trying to kill me? Is that why I feel . . . pain?" The admission was almost as bad as the physical manifestation of the pain itself.

She shrugged, returning her attention to me. "Do you think she's trying to kill you?"

"I told you not to trust this one," Styx spat, throwing her hands up in frustration.

"Answer me, glaistig."

"I do give you answers. You just don't like them." Her gaze narrowed, a slight tic twitching beneath her eye. "She cannot kill you. Your fate is of your choosing, my king. Soon you will understand the choices that lie ahead of you."

I cursed, running my hands through my hair, wishing I could understand more of what her prophecy meant, if it even was a prophecy. Desperation clawed at my throat. My heart pounded fiercely, and everyone heard it.

"What is happening to him, Broca?" Pollux demanded, storming up to her and placing the tip of a blade into the soft skin under the chin. "Speak now, or I'll take great pleasure in torturing you for the eternity I've been damned to exist here."

Broca cackled at his posturing, displaying yellow teeth as she laughed at him. Her form shifted once more, the features of a beautiful woodland spirit appearing in place of the haggard crone.

"Pol, look," Abyssian said in a rushed tone, grabbing the man by his arm and pointing toward me. Oberon's lips parted as he gasped, and Styx's eyes widened.

Everyone in the room looked in my direction, speechless at what we were all seeing.

Fire licked at my skin and my fingertips tingled. Portal magic. Access to a spell I hadn't conjured since half my soul had been locked away in a guardian's possession. Holding my hand palm up, a fine glittery mist formed.

"How?" I asked, feeling the power flow through my veins again. It breathed new life into me. I twirled my fingers, watching the magic snake between them, looping around in a rainbow of colors. Gods, how I'd missed it.

The cloying scent of apples and oak began to permeate the air, and my stomach tightened as a fleeting rush of desire pulsed in the recesses of my mind.

The elation was short-lived when a painful throb split through my brain, and a scream sounded in my head. Clenching my jaw through the ache, the torment and tension brought me to my knees, a loud smack filling the room when I crumbled to the floor, cradling my head in my hands.

Styx and Oberon dropped beside me, attempting to hold me up. "What's happening to him?" he yelled, looking at the glaistig.

I met her eyes, and the words she spoke reverberated off the walls before chaos ensued.

Her green eyes gleamed, and a cruel smile curled up Broca's red lips.

"The ward is breaking."

CHAPTER 4

REAGAN

The distinctive scent of eastern redbuds, oak trees, and fresh water flooded my senses. An orange glow colored the western sky, rapidly disappearing and highlighting a sky speckled with stars in its wake.

Standing near a creek, I turned around, taking in my surroundings. I didn't know where I was, or how I'd come to this location.

"Hello?" I called out. My voice echoed in the twilight, unanswered.

Not a sound. No animals scurrying or leaves rustling. There wasn't even a gust of wind, but my skin suddenly felt chilled.

Movement downstream caught my attention, and I looked over to find an old cathedral where there hadn't been one before.

A warm light flickered through a window; little silhouettes danced around the frame. A shadow coiled and moved like a finger beckoning me to come closer. My heart pounded. A whisper in my mind said *danger*, but my curiosity fueled me. Something about this place seemed familiar, and yet it felt new. I couldn't explain it, but I knew I had to see who was inside.

Peering through the glass, I saw the back of a little girl lying in her bed, tucked in on her side. Twin braids peeked out of the covers. A lantern lit the dim room, and an older woman sat down beside her. The bed dipped, the springs creaking with the added weight. Her red robe wrapped around her body and tied in the middle. With round glasses and mousy brown hair piled into a bun on top of her head, she looked pretty, but plain.

"Are you ready for a story?" she asked. Though I'd never heard the woman's voice, I remembered it. I knew her, yet I couldn't remember why.

The little girl nodded and rolled over, clasping her hands across her stomach. When I looked at her face, I gasped.

Large, dark brown eyes were framed by long lashes, and with a single, tiny beauty mark near the crease of her nose. The top of her pink lips curved into a familiar cupid's bow. I absentmindedly touched my own, tracing it with my fingertip.

An indistinguishable tattoo peeked out from her night-gown, arching over her shoulder just slightly.

I was looking at myself. I couldn't have been more than five years old.

A lump formed in my throat, robbing me of the ability to speak. I banged on the window, but neither of them stirred.

"It's time you knew," the old woman said, reaching to move a strand of dark brown hair off the little girl's face.

"Know what, Elda?" she asked, her small voice innocent and soft.

"What your purpose is." She inhaled slowly and began to recite the story. "Everyone has a purpose. Mine is taking care of you, because yours is protecting the whole world."

Little Reagan's eyes grew round. "The whole world!" she exclaimed in awe.

"Shhhh," Elda chastised quietly, even as a smile tugged at her lips. "I'll tell you why if you promise to be quiet. Can you do that?"

The girl nodded in excitement.

"In the beginning, there were twelve primordials of creation. Each of them were responsible for making our world and everything in it."

"Even cookies?" the little girl asked, forgetting herself.

"Especially cookies," Elda smiled gently before continuing. "For thousands of years they lived peacefully, coexisting with one another and the worlds they'd created, but the serenity didn't last. One of the primordials grew unsettled. He felt that the people were ungrateful for what he'd done in creating them, and that they needed to experience true strife to appreciate the gift of life." Little Reagan gasped and Elda lifted a brow. The girl's lips pressed together as she resettled.

"The other primordials disagreed, and rightly so. Light and dark exists in us all, and they knew that the balance would be altered if he was given his way. As time went on, his discontentment grew, and he was adamant that chaos should be unleashed on us all. He began making plans and the other primordials knew they had to do something, but a primordial cannot be killed. So the eleven bound together and imprisoned him. They put him in Tartarus, a realm of his making—"

"Wait a minute. If he's so strong, then how did they do it?"

"By taking away what made him a primordial. They removed half of his soul, stripping him of the power to create portals and life itself, ensuring he could never escape. But the eleven could not contain what they had taken. They were already primordials themselves, and they worried that if they took on his soul—it would corrupt them all. But a brave witch stepped forward and said that she would bear the burden and become a vessel. So they placed half his soul inside of her and charged her line with its safekeeping. She was the first guardian, and her name was Abraxia."

"But Elda, what was *his* name? The one they trapped?"

"He is the Soulless One, and nothing more. He remains locked in his realm, because of you."

"Me?" Little Reagan gasped. "But I'm only five." She held up her fingers to show. Elda nodded, clasping the girl's hand in her own.

"But you're also the guardian. The ward on your back keeps him contained, so as long as it's there and you're alive —he can't come back. You're a hero, Reagan."

"I am?" she asked with wonder in her voice. It churned my stomach, sickening me.

Elda nodded. "If anything ever happened to you, if the ward broke, the Soulless One would return and the end of days would be nigh."

I didn't stick around to hear anymore. Stumbling backwards, my butt hit the forest floor with a thud.

I hadn't heard that story in ages. It was troubling that the tale was familiar, but the scene wasn't. The room and the glimmer of it as a memory felt so . . . real.

Standing up, I brushed myself off when I heard a man's voice speaking in low tones. My heart rate increased, adrenaline shooting through my body. They couldn't see me, I reminded myself, and walked up to where I heard them speaking.

A tall man with a gray beard stood beside Elda. She looked older than she had only moments before. Traces of white hair streaked her bun, and the corners of her eyes crinkled more. They both looked into the trees warily, taking a moment to listen. Elda waved a hand, sending magic out. A stunning spell hit a squirrel, and it fell to the forest floor. The old man chuckled.

"You laugh, but she's getting better at sneaking around, Josiah."

"She's getting too powerful is the problem," he countered, crossing his arms. "I told you not to teach her magic."

"She's a witch. It comes naturally. Accidents are more likely to happen if she's untrained, and none of us wanted to take that risk. I just didn't expect her to excel at it."

"She's only half witch," he said, disgust laced in each word. "The other half of her is a beast. A disgrace to her line. Every guardian has always been a witch, but her whore mother had to go and fuck that creature." He shook his head. "I would be lying if I said I didn't take pleasure watching the life drain from her eyes the day she bore Reagan, but the fact remains that she still damned us. Without Reagan having full power as a mage, I don't even know how long she'll be able to contain the devil inside her."

"Nor do I," Elda said, sighing as she scanned the forest. "I worry she won't have the strength to make it until she's twenty-five. Twenty, maybe."

"We won't have to wait that long. I've already made arrangements."

Elda's eyes snapped back at him. "What do you mean?"

"She'll be old enough to bear a child within the year."

Her lips parted. "She's ten!"

"She's a vessel, Elda," he said, lowering his voice. "You helped raise her mother for the same purpose. We were too late with her, and I won't have it happen again with Reagan. The ward needs to pass on to someone with more witch blood. Charles is powerful. Coupled with what her mother's line has passed on, we can breed the shifter out of the offspring within a few generations."

"You cannot be serious." She shook her head. "This is . . . twelve-year-olds don't have babies."

Josiah stepped in front of her. "This is what must be done. We can't risk waiting until she's twenty-five to transfer the ward. Charles was meant to be her sire, but her mother ruined that. He was always meant to sire the next guardian. I expect you to tell me the moment she starts bleeding. When she has the baby, we'll take care of this problem and be back on course, just as the ancestors instructed."

Danger. The whisper in my mind got louder. It was angry. Filled with hurt and fear and betrayal.

A scream rent the air, and a deep rumbling shook the ground. Josiah and Elda's surprise was genuine, but neither of them were able to conjure a spell fast enough. In slow motion, I watched as a fiery ball exploded from the trees, bursting outward and burning everything it touched. Someone called my name in the distance, but I stood still, frozen by an overwhelming sense of terror I couldn't understand. My fingertips felt hot, and the pins and needles sensation rippled over my body.

I opened my mouth to scream, knowing I was about to be burned alive.

"Rea! Wake up, Rea!" The voice calling me finally registered as my sister's.

My eyes flew open, and my back arched off the bed as I gasped harshly, sucking in air as though I'd not been breathing. Sweat coated my body.

The smell of rosebuds trees and creek water had been replaced by a subtle scent of my homemade apple pumpkin candles. The forestscape had disappeared. I was in my twin-sized bed, in my room, safe at home. My latest mural adorned the wall opposite me. A castle built onto the side of a rocky cliff, with deep blue waves crashing against it. Looking at it now made me feel uneasy. I'd have to paint over it soon.

In the dim glow of an enchanted fairy light, my sister sat at my bedside. Her long dark hair was pulled back in a sloppy bun. Day-old makeup flaked around her eyes accentuating the dark circles that curved beneath them. Clara and Nog sat on the floor beneath the mural, their heads leaned against each other, their backs to the wall. My youngest cousin, Jo, was curled up in their laps. They were all sound asleep. Between Clara's index and forefinger, a metal crochet hook had stopped halfway through a loop. The soft flesh of her lip was red and angry, like she'd been constantly gnawing.

Sin brushed her hand over my forehead, soothing me with calming shushes. "You're home, Reagan. It's okay."

I tried to sit up, but my muscles were tense, refusing to move easily. "What happened?" I croaked, my throat feeling like I'd swallowed a mouthful of sand.

"You don't remember?" she asked, holding a cup of water with a straw and offering it to me.

I lifted my neck up and sipped, trying to think. What I remembered was my dream. That was at the forefront of my mind. When I shook my head slightly, a sharp pain pulsed in my shoulder.

"Ben bit you. Tried to claim you," she said.

The night came flooding back, and I sighed. "Yeah, now I do. He was acting weird all night . . . prick. How long have I been out?" I tried to move again, but pain shot through my back, and I hissed. My sister diverted her gaze, looking toward my window. My stomach sank. "Sin?" I prompted, an urgency in my voice.

"You've been out for two days," she said softly. "Nog, Clara, and I have been taking shifts to watch over you."

"Two days?" I choked out. "How? It was just a bite. I should have healed by now. He didn't claim me."

"Something happened to the bite, Rea. I don't know. No salve or potion has worked . . . the ward . . ."

Panic shot through me. "What about the ward?"

She shook her head. "It's not good. It's like it's infected."

"That's not possible . . ." I pressed my lips together to stop it from trembling. The ward was built to keep what I guarded safe, but it was also made to keep me alive. Scrapes healed instantly, colds and other illnesses were non-existent in my life. I'd taken a few big hits and bounced back within an hour. If what she said was true . . .

"Whatever it is has focused on the tattoo," she said carefully. "The entire infection is in the shape of it."

I groaned, and Jo stirred, stretching out his leg. "What is Jo even doing here? He shouldn't be sleeping on the floor."

"He was worried about you."

"Tell me you didn't let him try to heal me." While I'd never tell anyone, Jo was my favorite cousin, and he held a special place in my heart. At nine years old, he was incredibly powerful. None of us really knew about his mother. His dad just brought him home one day and said don't ask questions. From the moment I held him as a newborn, I was drawn to his calm energy. He never showed signs of being a shifter or witch, so we didn't even know what kind of supernatural he was. His healing magic was unlike anything we'd ever seen–but every time he used it, it took a toll on his body and made him more fragile than the rest of us. I just felt protective over him. He was small for his age, but his heart was bigger than anyone I'd ever met.

"You know we can't stop him. He tried to heal you, but it didn't work. Knocked him out pretty good, but he's refused to leave your side. I even put him in my bed, but he keeps coming back here and falling asleep," she said with a thoughtful smile.

"Dammit," I muttered. I felt immediate guilt that he'd spent energy on me. "Can you take him home? Let him rest there?"

She shook her head. "Tía dropped him off when she went to look for Dad."

"Dad's coming home?" I missed him, but I hated that he would be worried.

She nodded. "When you didn't get better within a few hours, we didn't plan on waiting. It took her a day, but she located him and they're on their way here. He'll know what to do."

Pain throbbed in my back, sending the discomfort into my legs. I shifted, moving myself to a sitting position and tilting my head so it rested on the wall beside me.

"It burns," I murmured. Sin held my hand I squeezed my eyes shut, trying to breathe through the stinging wave that surged over my body.

When I opened them again, I tensed, gasping at what I saw.

The opposite wall transformed from cheap wood paneling and a closet door to an oval of shimmering color.

The palette swirled, forming a picture. A scene. A place I didn't recognize.

"Do you see this?" I whispered, unable to look away.

"See what?" Sin asked, looking in the same direction. She shook her head. "Reagan, look at me. Stop and look at me," she said in panic, grabbing my face to pull my attention back to her, but I couldn't take my eyes off it.

I could make out a face in the cloudy wall. A man. I'd never seen him before, but my heart knew him . . . and it knew I should be afraid.

He was tall with strong shoulders. He didn't lack muscle, but he wasn't as bulky as most shifters were. Despite that, the shadows radiating from him communicated loud and clear that he was immensely powerful. A cruel smile curled up his lips, and his black eyes bore into mine, fire and flame dancing in them as though we were looking through worlds and seeing each other in real time.

My sister shouted my name again, but my voice was lost. Blistering heat lanced through my back, and I cried out, the scene before me disappearing.

"Reagan, what's happening?" she said, holding my shoulders and pulling me to her.

"It was him," I choked out.

"Who?"

"The Soulless One."

CHAPTER 5

REAGAN

It all blended together. Reality. Imagination.

I dreamed again of a place I knew yet had never visited. Faces I could recall of people I had never met.

A fever had taken me deeper into a place of nightmares. Whatever sickness I'd been plagued with was rapidly consuming me. The pain had intensified, and I felt weaker each time I woke up. I'd never been ill; not like this. The ward protected me, just as it protected what I guarded. If I was this unwell . . . the barrier would struggle to remain intact.

Fear coiled in my belly, but I didn't dare acknowledge it. That would give a voice to what lingered there.

Harsh, anxious whispers echoed in the house, bouncing off the plaster walls. The deep tenor of my father's voice was unmistakable. I had no idea how long I'd been out. My eyelids fluttered open to see my living room ceiling. They'd moved me to the couch at some point, no doubt due to the size of my room. It was a small space, and if they wanted to keep an eye on me, there was no way everyone would be able to squeeze in there.

"I can hear you talking about me," I mumbled, my scratchy throat giving a gravelly quality to each word.

"Hey," my dad said softly. "There's my girl."

"You're awake," Sin breathed, rushing to my side. My father followed behind her, worry etched all over his face.

"Hard to sleep with you two fussing at each other." I smiled weakly. "Where is everyone?"

"Tía took Jo back to their house to rest, and Dad wanted some time to check things out for himself without Nog and Clara bickering."

"Sounds about right." I tried to take even breaths between speaking. Everything felt harder than it should. "When did you get back?"

"About two hours ago. Sin caught me up." His eyes left mine, concentrating on my neck. A dark shadow passed over him.

"One thing at a time, Dad," Sin said, and I chuckled half-heartedly. Dad was an alpha. He never did things one at a time. I'd have to talk him off that ledge or Ben would end up six feet under. He deserved a swift kick in the balls, but he didn't need to die.

"Did you make it to visit Tía Sarah and Tía Abbey?" Shifting my body, I tried to sit up. Instead, a burning sensation shot through me, and I hissed. My sister dropped to her knees, helping me readjust.

"Yes. Don't change the subject," he said, crossing his arms.

"All right, all right. What's the damage?" I asked, both hesitation and hope filling every single word. Sin pressed her lips together in a firm, thin line. A crease formed between her brows as they pushed toward each other. The little bit of hope I felt was crushed, and she shook her head slightly. "That bad, huh?"

"How long have you been having the visions?" my dad started, crouching down beside the couch.

"The hallucinations?" I asked, wiping sweat from my brow. "That's never happened before. It's just the fever."

He shook his head. "Before you saw the man. I'm talking about the mural on your wall. That happened prior to the fever. Sin said you drew them from dreams."

"When did I say that?" I asked, somewhat alarmed that I had confessed anything without recalling.

"Last night, after you said you saw the Soulless One. You lost consciousness but you were talking in your sleep. You also said you saw him as though he was in that place you had painted. Not just like some ghost in your room."

"These are visions, Reagan. I need to know when they started," my dad pressed.

"What?" I shook my head and looked at him in confusion. "I don't know. I saw the castle on the mountain a while ago. It's nothing. Just a recurring dream."

"When?" he growled, the alpha command vibrating in the room.

His reaction made me jump, and I couldn't help but stutter my response. I thought back to when I first began painting it. "T-ten years now? Give or take some."

The color drained from my sister's face.

"We're out of time," my dad choked out, looking at my sister. He cursed under his breath. "I just always thought they'd lied to Rosa to keep her in check. It wasn't even the bite. That's just moving it up. It's been slowly breaking down for ten years."

"This was what Elda said would happen, didn't she?" Sin whispered.

"That what could happ—" My brain caught up, registering every detail in the conversation. My sister asked our father that question. Not me. Adrenaline rushed to my head, and the room felt wobbly. "What did you just say?"

"Reagan," he started, but a rage began to fill me, and I cut him off.

"N-no," I stammered, pointing my finger accusingly at Sin. "You said Elda. How do you know that name? She was in my fever dream, telling me a bedtime story. There's no way you can know that name unless . . ."

While Sin's expression was nothing but shock, my father's was more resigned. He closed his eyes tight, exhaling loudly. The non-answer was more than I could handle.

"She's real," I breathed in disbelief. My heart pounded and my palms grew sweaty. "Oh my god . . . How? And how do you know her? *How do I not remember?*"

My dad placed his hands out gently, motioning for me to remain calm. The alpha tone left his voice, replaced by a softer note. One asking for forgiveness.

"Yes, she was real. She was an elder with the coven that held you and your mother captive. She raised you both."

"Why do I remember her now? I know the story of the Soulless One. I know what I guard, but why not her?"

"I think . . ." He took a deep breath, glancing at my sister briefly before continuing. "Whatever infection is affecting you right now is allowing traumatic memories to surface. It's breaking the . . . magic that protects you from it."

I narrowed my eyes and grit my teeth against a wave of pain. The flashes of my dream where Elda spoke with Josiah resurfaced. "Explain to me what that exactly means."

Dad sniffed quietly, taking a minute before speaking. "Your mother had powerful magic, Reagan. Cloaking spells were her specialty. We were mates, drawn to each other no matter what. I never gave credence to the story of the Soulless One, but she assured me it was real. I should have listened." He pinched the bridge of his nose, pausing before he continued. "Before she realized she was living with a cult, she snuck out to see me like any other teenager would. We thought Elda suspected, but she had no proof. I figured she was trying to scare your mom when she began to warn her of visions and dreams. Elda said it was a sign the ward was weakening and would need to be reinforced. It never happened before a guardian turned twenty-five, but they were insistent on documenting anything that changed with her. It sounded like another bullshit way to control Rosa's every move."

I tilted my head, and the movement in my neck was stiff. "You think these dreams of Elda are the same thing they warned Mom about?"

"I never believed your mother was actually a guardian. Not until later." His eyes softened, and his voice lowered, but the fact he didn't answer my question didn't go unnoticed. "Your mother realized that coven's intent when she got pregnant with you, but they already pieced together you were mine. They took her. Disappeared without a trace. They masked her scent and blocked her from me so I couldn't even follow the mate bond. I knew they'd killed her when the connection broke. The only thing that kept me going was finding you and bringing you home safely."

"Dad, you've been searching for a way to transfer this ward since you brought me home. If you didn't believe she was a guardian, what made you believe I am?"

Sin and my dad met each other's gaze briefly before he spoke again. "I learned a lot when you came home. Had I believed your mother—truly believed it wasn't just a bunch of superstitious witches—then I would have gotten her out myself. I would have started my search for how to transfer it safely much sooner. It's my greatest regret."

I couldn't remember much of my childhood. I'd shared what I knew; fractured bits and pieces of my life before my dad found me, but it was all so fuzzy. All I had of my mother was a pendant I wore and the few stories my dad would share. My ability to retain long-term memories became stronger when my dad found me and brought me to my family. Of course it made sense that would happen. I was safe and loved.

I had so many questions, but one weighed heavy. If he knew about Elda, and she was real . . .

"What about Josiah?" I asked, raising a brow. My dad's eyes flashed with hatred, and it was at that moment I knew there was more truth in my dreams. I felt another rush of anger when I recalled the disgusting words he'd said to Elda. The ire mingled with shots of an icy burn that covered my skin.

"That parasite is dead," he answered through clenched teeth.

Before I could respond, a sharp wave of pain crashed through me. My entire body jerked, and I felt a horrible tearing sensation across my back. I cried out, doubling over. The world began to spin in dizzying revolutions, and the stench of decay filled my nostrils. I began to dry heave, the arching of my midsection increasing the pain.

"Reagan!" Sin yelled, grabbing a bucket and putting it under my face.

My dad hovered over both of us while he lifted my shirt slightly and inspected my back as my sister tried to soothe me with soft shushing noises.

"The infection is spreading," he whispered, then let out a string of curses.

Sin sat up slightly, looking at what my dad had just seen. Her eyes widened. "It's tearing open," she said in horror, standing up quickly. "What do we do?"

"I don't know. I can't transfer the ward. I have nowhere to move it." He thought for a moment, then looked at my sister. "She needs to shift so she can heal. It's our only chance."

"Is there even a way to let Eres out to protect her?"

"Fuck if I know anymore." He pulled a phone from his pocket and pressed a button before holding it up to his ear. "Celeste, I need you at Reagan's *now*. Bring the kids. The ward is breaking. We need to get her to shift, but the infection needs to be contained."

"What do you mean let Eres out? Who is Eres?" I coughed, tasting blood in my mouth.

"Tell her," Sin whispered. "You said we're out of time. She needs to know, Dad. Now."

My dad closed his eyes. Running his hands through his hair, fisting the ends.

"What aren't you telling me?" I said weakly, tears of anger threatening to spill over.

"It's not that simple," he began.

"Dad," my sister shouted. "Tell her!"

He sighed, long and hard, as though he was gathering courage. " Eres is your animal. I bound your magic when you were eleven, Reagan," he said slowly. "Both your magic and your memories. I left what you needed to know, and nothing more."

"That's not possible," I argued, wincing at my every move.

He shook his head, his eyes welling with tears. "I don't have that magic, no. So I did what I do best. I tracked down those that could. It took three witches to create the spell."

My dark unicorn stirred inside me, and a sense of internal discomfort tickled the edge of my psyche. Betrayal flooded me. "No . . ."

My sister cut in. "You were so broken when you came home, Rea. The nightmares. What that damned coven put you through." Sin swallowed thickly, but she held firm. "You lashed out so much. Fits of blind rage, and feral explosions of your magic. Even in your sleep. You were so . . . you couldn't control your power. It was going to consume you, and everyone around you. We had no choice."

"You were in on it?" I asked, my voice breaking as the tears flowed freely. Sin's lips parted, but no words came out.

"You almost killed her." My dad's admission startled me, and for a split second, I almost forgot the pain.

"I would never—"

"Reagan, you weren't yourself." He spoke in a gentle tone, one he used when he was trying to make me see reason. "We both knew you would never do it on purpose. You were reliving a nightmare day in and day out and you had no way to escape. It wasn't your fault."

"Eres . . ." I started, choosing my words carefully before I passed out again. "You can't bind a shifter."

"You can if the animal agrees," my dad said quietly.

Time stopped. The sound of blood rushing to my head echoed in my ears, and I tried desperately to swallow the thick lump in my throat. "You . . . *what*? You *spoke* to her?"

He held his chin up, but whatever bravado he had as an alpha was wavering as he spilled his secrets. "It's how I knew you were truly a guardian. She knows what you protect. Everything we saw you experience, Eres felt tenfold. She feels what you feel because she was living it *with* you, and she fully believed it was going to destroy you both. From the outside, we saw you shrinking in on your-self. It was only a matter of time before your mind shat-tered entirely. My choices were limited."

"I'm sorry," a voice whispered to me. A voice only I could hear; one that had been hidden in the deep recesses of my mind, unlocking another memory that had been closed off from me against my will.

Eres. My animal.

I jumped up without thinking, startled at hearing her speak to me after only ever feeling her general moods and presence. The moment was short-lived, and I dropped to the floor abruptly as pain racked my body. The world turned sideways as my cheek pressed against the cold tiles. I laid there with my stomach down and arms sprawled out. Consciousness threatened to leave me.

"You've always been there?"

"Yes."

"You lied to me," I said to her.

"No, I protected you," Eres responded softly.

As my sister and dad shouted in response to my graceful descent, the front door burst open, and my Tía Celeste came running in with Clara, Nog, and Jo at her heels.

Celeste and Clara dropped to her knees, sliding across the floor as she reached me. With palms out, a shimmering white light wisped around my cousin's hands. I heard the familiar flick of my dad's switchblade opening before I real-ized he was cutting the nasty t-shirt down the middle of my back.

My stomach roiled at the sudden stench.

"Dear Gods, Alvaro. It's rotting the flesh," Tía Celeste said, shock filling her voice. "Where is the safety kit? And her moonshine?"

"I'll get it," Sin said, heading to the kitchen in a hurry.

My throat felt like sandpaper again. Tears pricked my eyes once more.

"Jo," Clara said softly, patting the ground beside her and he came to sit. "This ward is stronger than me. I need you. We have to cut the infection out and reinforce the ward long enough for her animal to come out and shift. Do you think we can do that?"

"No," I mumbled against the floor, and I tried to shake my head. "Too much. He's only nine. He doesn't know his . . . strength. He doesn't understand . . . his limits."

"It'll be okay," he said, an innocent smile forming while he stroked my face gently. "Have faith."

Across the room, a wavy figure appeared, catching my attention.

This isn't real, I told myself. *It's another hallucination. It has to be . . .*

The same enchanting eyes I'd seen earlier glared at me; the same cruel smile curved up his lips.

The Soulless One.

Terror seized my chest. He looked right at me like he was here. It was just as real as everything happening in the room right now. The barrier was breaking completely. Realization dawned on me, and my panic surged. They were going to rip it wide open if they cut at me.

"Stop," I cried, trying to move away from them, but any strength I'd once had was long gone. "Seal it. Close . . . the ward."

"Are you insane?" Nog asked. "They'd seal the infection inside you, you dope."

Clara knocked her brother on the head. "We can't do that, Rea. As dumb as he is, he's actually right."

"Seal . . . it," I said through clenched teeth, a tear falling as I accepted my fate. "Transfer . . . ward."

"We don't know how to transfer it," my dad said. "Eres can protect you. We just need to get the infection out."

My sister returned, holding a kit we used for injuries. Whatever was in there wouldn't be enough. All of this was pointless, and they just didn't understand.

"I see him," I whispered, praying they would listen. Sin's gaze hardened as she looked at my cousin. Though the words came out mumbled, I had to keep trying. "Ward . . . breaking. Need . . . guardian . . ."

Clara chewed at her bottom lip. "Maybe she's right, Tío. We can try to transfer it to me. It would buy us time."

"What are you saying?" Nog shouted, grabbing his sister's shoulder, and turning her to face him. "We don't know how! Not really. Both of you will probably die if we do that!"

"Then I'll do it," Sin interjected.

"If the ward is breaking—" Tía Celeste began, trying to hide the pain in her eyes, but the way her words caught in her throat gave it away. "We have to, Alvaro. You know what she protects is real. We can't risk that."

Jo placed his hand on Clara's. "Me. I can carry it."

A stifled cry escaped my lips. "No . . . Not Jo."

"It's okay," he whispered, patting my hair. "I can do this."

"No. It has to be a witch. That's what Rosa said," my dad said quietly. "Clara, are you sure about this? Once it's done, there's no going back."

My cousin swallowed thickly, her throat bobbing as she gave a curt nod. "I'm sure."

"Clara, no," I cried softly. "Don't do this."

I lost your mother, Reagan. I won't lose you too," he said. "We're cutting it out. We can try to transfer it once we get there. Clara, Jo, get ready. Nog, Sin, you hold her. That's an order," he said, the command in his voice ringing in the room.

I had no ability to fight back. My bottom lip trembled just as Nog held a leather strap to my mouth, a look of fear and apprehension in his eyes. "You're gonna need this."

Hot tears fell and there was nothing to stop them.

No one was truly immortal. We all lived on borrowed time, but the moment we realized how close we were to the end, our perspective changed. Regrets. Desires. Things we wish we could have done, places we would have liked to have seen, words we knew we should have said when we had the chance all came to the forefront.

I'd only just barely learned who I was, and it was all about to be ripped away.

I was going to die, and I knew it. That wasn't what scared me. It was that *he* would come after. They just didn't believe that would be the outcome. They were holding on to hope and faith and magic with every ounce of their being.

It was all for naught.

Seconds later, my blood curdling scream rent the air. My teeth clamped down on the bite guard as moonshine poured over the wound and a rune-covered knife sliced at the decaying skin on my back.

As the end nears, the dying often call out to the gods. It doesn't matter if they were devout followers or never believed in a higher power. They ask for mercy. Pray for forgiveness. Promise anything if only they'd be saved. They beg and bargain and plead, and they apologize for their transgressions.

In my final moments, I was no different.

I just never imagined a god would answer.

CHAPTER 6
CAIUS

The perpetual pain the guardian was sending me sought an outlet, and my magic responded in kind.

Ancient power flowed through my veins, pulsing like the beat of a heart.

"Are you sure you want to open a rift between worlds here, *inside* the castle?" My brother asked in a hesitant voice, watching while I whispered the incantation in a language nearly as old as the cosmos itself.

"I don't know how long we have, Abyssian," I said, watching an iridescent orb form above the palm of my hand. As the color shifted from a brilliant purple to a deep mauve, it continued to swirl and expand in size.

The ability to create a doorway between realms was impossible for most. Only primordials and a select few greater beings were capable of such a great feat.

"It's a tear in the fabric of space and time. A true portal. What if people come through to this side?" Abyssian pressed as he watched the growing ball of light.

"Are you questioning my judgment?" I grunted, sweat forming around my temples.

"No," he said quickly.

"Yes," Pollux said at the same time.

"*No*," he repeated more sternly, shoving Pol's shoulder. "I'm just concerned. We don't know where it will open or what Earth is like now. It's a permanent gateway."

"It's only permanent until I destroy it. So, *guard* it, and if someone comes through, send them *back*." Each word was punctuated by my increasing pain and equal annoyance.

Power exploded from my fingertips, the rebound shooting through my veins and burning like wildfire. Before us stood a swirling vortex of my making, and no one in the room could escape its hypnotizing allure.

I temporarily forgot about the pain, so distracted by the blinding light. Pol closed his eyes and breathed a sigh of relief while I lifted a hand to shield mine from the intensity of its glow.

While we couldn't see on the other side, I instinctively knew it to be Earth, its unique aura calling back to one of its creators. I would know its essence anywhere. I *was* its essence.

All thoughts soon vanished as another wave of phantom pain sliced my back, and I grunted, swallowing it down.

"Oberon, Styx. With me."

"Wait, you're going to cross over without some sort of plan?" Pol said quickly, stepping forward.

"Um, we have a plan. Go through, kill the guardian, reclaim the other half of his soul, and get revenge on a few primordials, man. This isn't news," Styx said, huffing. "Let's get a move on."

"But—"

"Tartarus will be in good hands," Abyssian interjected, cutting off his counterpart. "Do what you need to do. We'll await the day that you return."

"We'll await the day? Aren't you an eager twat. You sound like you're looking forward to it." Pol glanced at him, a brow raised. "We've already been here for a few thousand years. What's a few more, right?"

"You needed more hugs as a child," Abyssian grumbled and rolled his eyes. "It's not like the elders have an address, or some castle in the sky. Can't exactly go in for an overnight coup when we don't even know where they are."

"Honestly, I hope it takes us another thousand years to find the primordials. I need a break from the bickering," Oberon muttered.

Styx snorted. "If it did take us a thousand years, I'm pretty sure they'll have killed each other by then."

Abyssian and Pollux exchanged looks, and the latter narrowed his eyes further while humming in what sounded like disappointment. Or maybe agreement.

"Shut up, for fuck's sake," I growled, massaging the side of my head. "Stay here. Don't screw it up."

Both men pressed their lips into a firm line and dipped their chins once. They'd be fine, even if they took a few swings at each other while I was gone. They were still loyal to me, and they would do the job they were tasked with. I deeply cared about Tartarus and its people, and they knew it was important.

An invisible tether pulled me toward the portal the longer I stood there. I wanted to say it was my soul, but it felt like something . . . deeper. There were no words to explain it, but I knew without question it would lead me.

I twisted my neck to the side, cracking it. "Let's go," I said, my jaw tight.

"Finally." Styx grinned, eager for action.

The portal flashed at the edges, crackling and sparkling with energy, begging to be used.

My insides burned. The secondhand pain came in waves, damn near blinding at points. With one foot forward, I stepped through the portal and instantly connected with solid ground before a flow of water rushed around our feet. The moment I'd crossed, an overwhelming sense of relief overcame me.

I couldn't help but look up. The waning moon cast its glow as it peeked around a hazy fog. Countless stars sprinkled the heavens through patches of thick clouds.

I inhaled deeply. Fresh, crisp air filled my lungs. The scent of a world teeming with life. The trees, the dirt, the nearby water: its essence enveloped me.

It was surreal. Something I'd dreamed of seeing and feeling again, though I'd often wondered if it had ever been real or if it were nothing more than a dream itself.

It was a short-lived respite, only to be rapidly replaced by a pressure so great, I wanted to split my skin open just to see if it would relieve the strain.

My hands curled into fists; the nails turned sharp, growing longer to a point that embedded in the thick pads of my palms.

I breathed heavily as I took in my surroundings. The water came from a fountain that broke where the edge of the portal had cleaved into its side. A massive, abandoned building with a cracked domed roof sat in front of an incredible white arch that towered over what appeared to be the town square. A chunk near the top of its curve was missing, leaving the center of it mangled and incomplete.

Styx stood by my side, rigid and calculating as she scanned the city, assessing our location. "Of course we'd come here at night. Haven't seen the sun in five thousand years. What's another day?"

Oberon was on alert, as always, but the reality of where we had returned hit him too. "Gods . . . we're actually here," he murmured in awe before reining it in. "Which direction?"

The invisible tether wrenched forward, pulling at what soul I had left and threatening to rip my heart out with it.

I nearly fell to my knees, growling at the searing ache.

"That way, apparently," I said, pointing and exhaling loudly, trying to ignore the pulsing discomfort coursing through my body.

"You feel your soul calling to you?" Styx asked, though I heard the skepticism in her tone.

I nodded, unable to speak. Yes. My soul. I would have believed that to be the truth if it weren't for the fire lancing through my back. Broca said it was the guardian who had reached me.

She was my compass.

We ran over the grassy knoll, the sound of our footsteps pounding the dirt and echoing in the silent night.

Our steps quickened along the stone pathway, leading onto streets with tall dwellings and eventually down to a row of houses. My heart pounded as the tether pulled me sharply to the right and down another row, until I came to an abrupt halt.

All of the houses were one and two levels tall and made of wood panels. Most of them had peeling paint. Even fewer had carved pumpkins sitting on their porches. It was sad and a far cry from what my home in Tartarus was.

"What in the . . ." Styx started. "Are those what houses look like now?"

"It would appear so," I said, scanning the line of patch-work rooftops.

A heart wrenching scream sounded, and it ripped apart my insides. The torture my body felt in Tartarus increased beyond measure.

I snarled, swallowing the transference of pain.

"There," I ground out, pointing to a dwelling on the corner of a street.

It didn't look like anyone was home. No lights were on, no windows were open. The town was asleep, but I knew without question she was in there. The tether inside heaved me toward that exact spot.

"I'm in first," Oberon said, taking the lead and darting at a full sprint. When he reached what I presumed to be the front door, he threw a small fireball of magic toward the knob. Seconds later it exploded, the door flying off its hinges as multiple screams of surprise filled the air.

Plumes of dust created a fog, and shards of wood littered the ground. Oberon was already inside, weapons drawn. Styx went in next, looking less intimidating, though she was just as deadly. They were ready to defend, but I stopped dead in my tracks the moment I crossed the threshold.

The scent of infected blood, sweat, and decay filled the room.

"Stop," I commanded. Styx and Oberon followed orders, not advancing further as I took in the scene before us.

A woman lay stomach down in the middle of the room with her cheek pressed to the floor, tears streaming down her face, and a leather strap between her bared teeth.

Some boy with dark, shaggy hair held one arm down

while a child appeared to have been stroking her hair. Two young women kneeled, one pressing her other arm to the ground, one with glowing hands hovering over her back.

A large shifter held a small dagger at her back while an older woman sat atop her legs, restricting her movement.

Everyone looked in our direction, startled, and they began shouting questions.

I didn't answer. I couldn't do anything but focus on her.

Time slowed.

The pull. The ache. The connection.

She was the woman I had been dreaming about. Her face had haunted me for years, and we never found her in Tartarus.

Everything clicked into place.

It couldn't be.

"The guardian . . ." I murmured, and Styx reached for the two sticks that held up the bun she wore on top of her head, her unassuming hidden weapons ready for the kill. Quickly grabbing her wrist, I managed to form a single word as my entire world recalibrated. "No."

"What?" she asked, her voice rising in disbelief.

"No," I repeated with urgency. "She's . . . my mate."

"Well, I didn't see that coming," Oberon muttered, twirling his sword to show off, and in a quick motion, sheathed it beside him.

"Hey! Get out of here!" the dark-haired boy screeched, shooing us away with one hand.

The young woman across from him made a loud shushing sound before redirecting her attention on me. "What do you want?" she asked, a deep tenor in her voice leaked with magic.

I narrowed my eyes in response. "Ask your questions, witch, but your magic won't work on me."

"I can see that," she snapped, but her expression gave away how deeply she was concerned. "I know The Crossroads is a bit different from the rest of No Man's Land, and you're obviously not from around here, so I'd highly suggest you get out before someone kills you." I smirked in surprise. I liked this one. She had moxie. "And the name is Clara, asshole," she added as an afterthought.

"I think not," I said simply, emitting a fraction of power into my voice.

The guardian twisted on the ground, and fire spread over me once more. I grunted, the sound deep and menacing.

The man holding the knife twisted it in his palm, his thick brows furrowing as he assessed me. The woman shifted forward while still sitting on the guardian's legs and tried to grab his arm and pull him back.

The young witch shook her head a fraction, then whispered, "Tío, I'm not so sure that's a good idea."

A battle raged inside me. Love of a mortal had led me to damnation once already. I wanted nothing to do with it, but this was different. A fated mate; a bond a primordial shouldn't be capable of having. That's not how we'd been made. Yet I knew with every fiber of my being that she was meant to be mine.

A soulmate . . . and the irony of what she guarded wasn't lost on me.

"Hold them back," I commanded. Styx grumbled, but she and Oberon rushed forward.

The guardian met my heated gaze with wide eyes. A terrified and feeble whimper escaped her throat, and she began to writhe weakly beneath the bodies holding her down.

The boy jumped up in defense, ready to attack me. I

laughed at his arrogance as I crossed the small space. While I needed her alive, the rest didn't matter. The one called Clara stood quickly, shoving her shoulder into his stomach, and knocking him backward as they tumbled onto the floor.

"Nog, don't! You're going to get yourself killed!"

"And he's going to kill Re—" As he tried to stand up, she knocked him down again, using both her magic and whatever strength she possessed. The witch was feisty.

"Your death won't save her," she snarled, sticking her knee in his back to pin him. "It's not what she would want."

At least one of them was smart.

I leaned down, brushing the hair over my mate's forehead.

While the older woman didn't struggle, accepting that this situation was beyond her control, Styx subdued a young woman with hate-filled eyes and Oberon had to shove the large shifter against a wall. "Get your hands off her!" he roared, thrashing under their hold.

After assessing the shifter's features, I then looked down at my mate. They shared similarities. Same olive skin tone. Same shade of dark brown hair. The same shape of their eyes and hands. "Knock him out if you must, but keep him alive," I instructed. Styx huffed.

Glancing at the child still crouched next to my mate, I tilted my head and considered him. His eyes . . . I'd seen them before, but never did I expect to see them again. *Impossible.* Whatever this child was, whoever he was, something old rested in him. Something ancient.

He stared at me with the appropriate amount of fear and respect, but he didn't move away. Instead, he looked at me knowingly, wise beyond his years.

"You know what I am." He swallowed thickly, nodding in a rapid motion. "Yet you stay by her side?"

"I won't leave her," he said, his small voice wavering. I bent down next to him, resting one knee on the ground.

"Jo," the older woman whisper-yelled, motioning for him to come to her arms where she thought he'd be protected. "Get away from him."

Despite all the chaos in the room, a small smile formed. "Stay, brave one. Give her comfort. She's going to need it." I held his tiny chin between my forefinger and thumb.

"Don't touch him," the woman bellowed, stomping toward us and I stood up so fast it startled her. She faltered as her steps came to an abrupt halt.

"Take another step and you die. Whether or not you survive this night means nothing to me," I said, narrowing my eyes at her. "The child is safe."

Her bottom lip trembled, and her eyes flicked back and forth between me and the boy she'd called Jo.

"It's okay, Mom," he whispered, and tears fell from her eyes as she pressed her top teeth into her bottom lip.

"You're all family?" I asked him. The witch amused me, but he was the only one worth speaking to.

"Yes," he answered, scooting toward my mate, and placing a hand on her face gently. "She's my cousin."

"Interesting."

Kneeling back down, I observed the tattoo on my mate's back as her lifeforce waned.

I felt closer and closer to my soul as each second passed, almost as though I could reach out and touch it.

As best as I could tell, they were trying to save her. Their efforts would have been wasted. She was dying, and no amount of cutting out the infection would stop it.

For as long as I had waited and for all I had endured, I was only moments away from being complete again.

All I had to do was sit and watch.

I wouldn't even have to lift a hand.

Except . . . I couldn't.

Mates protected each other, no matter how it could complicate things—and this certainly complicated *everything*. I would figure the soul situation out later. It was just as Styx said upon our arrival. It had been five thousand years. What was another day?

My mate didn't have much time left. Potent, poisonous magic had infected her, causing her skin to rot.

I glanced at Jo, inclining my head, telling him I was about to start. He pressed his lips together and did the same in acknowledgment.

Palms flat, I held my hands over her back and reached deep for a magic I hadn't used in millennia.

Fine, inky black dust misted out of the wounds, forming a small cloud over her back. It fought me, seeking her as its host and refusing to let go.

Her family's shouts filled the room, but I concentrated only on the darkness seeping out of her. Harder and harder I pulled, and louder and louder she began to scream.

The toxic mist imbedded itself in my skin, burrowing further as I absorbed all of it, and Jo's lips parted in awe. Clara and Nog had stopped fighting each other as they watched slack-jawed.

Blood poured from my mate's flesh, red and clean. Angry pink skin marred her back, finally free of what had been killing her.

With a faint cough, a small dribble of blood formed at her lips, then her eyelids fluttered closed.

"Reagan!" Jo yelled, placing his hands on her back and forcing a healing magic to coat her.

I inhaled sharply. So that was my mate's name.

Reagan. Little Royal. How fitting.

In an instant, her flesh began to knit itself back together. Her labored breathing found a steady rhythm.

As the boy began to shake in exhaustion, I took his hands off her. He struggled against me for a moment, regarding me with unbridled anger.

"So much for one so young. Save your power, Jo. She'll live. She needs her rest, as do you."

"Your *eyes* . . ." he whispered, his skin paling. He glanced at her healing wounds then back to me. "They're black. The poison . . ."

I nodded, then stood up, motioning for the older woman to come to her son. She rushed to his side, pulling him into a protective embrace.

"What did you do to her?" Nog shouted and I couldn't help but roll my eyes. Jo was something special, but this one? Obnoxious was an understatement.

Ignoring him, I approached the large shifter. "You're related. Who are you?"

"Her father," he growled. I dipped my chin and lowered my eyes to Oberon to release him. Once free, the shifter's body vibrated in fury, but he didn't shy away from staring me down. We stood eye-to-eye, a rare feat unto itself. I glanced at Styx, signaling for her to release the woman she held.

"I imagine you have questions," I said, returning my attention to the shifter.

"You could say that, starting with who the hell are you?"

"I'll answer yours if you answer mine."

"Hey! I have some questions too."

"Gods' sake, Nog. Shut up," Clara grumbled, slapping him on the arm.

"You should listen to her," I said, raising a brow.

The shifter looked me up and down. The crease in his forehead never disappeared, but he held out his hand to shake mine.

This day had taken me by surprise, and his gesture was no different. I accepted it, gripping firmly.

"I still have an overwhelming desire to kill you," he said. "But you saved my daughter, and for that, I owe you thanks first."

"Um, Tío? Apparently you were too ragey to hear the part where he casually mentioned that Reagan is *his mate*," Nog said. "I think killing is warranted. Just saying. I'd be wanting to if she were my daughter—Ow! Clara, what the hell are you hitting me for?"

Alvaro's eyes flashed with an animal I hadn't seen in a very long time.

Something told me he'd heard it just fine.

CHAPTER 7

REAGAN

My body ached.

It was different than the times I'd woken up before. Instead of weakness and gnawing pain, my limbs were stiff, and my muscles were sore. My head felt like it was in a vice.

Soft cotton graced my skin. A clean shirt. It felt nice.

I licked my chapped lips and took a deep breath, inhaling the familiar scent of fresh laundry, but there was a new scent I'd never noticed before. The earthy aromas of sweat, roasted hazelnuts, and whiskey invaded my pores and overwhelmed my senses. The smell was divine, and I felt comfort in the way it enveloped me.

Eres's curiosity reached me, and she peeked out. I'd never felt her so close to the surface before. It sent me into a panic, and my eyes shot open.

Memories of dying slammed into me. The ward failing. The Soulless One appearing. And there he was, staring back at me.

A torrent of emotions flooded my body.

I'd been curled up on *his* lap. My head had been resting

on *his* chest. It was *his* scent that had been driving me crazy. Dear gods, *why?* I scrambled back in a clumsy crab walk across the floor until I hit the couch behind me, collapsing suddenly into a sitting position.

His dark gaze tracked my every move, taking in every inch I put between us. The sinful curve of his mouth turned down into a displeased scowl. My chest seized, alarm bells screaming in my mind.

The ward had broken.

The man in my dreams was real.

A shadow stepped in between us, blocking him from view. I recognized Sin's faded, paint-splattered blue jeans. Instead of feeling secure in her strength, I was terrified for her.

"Sin, don't," I rasped, my voice sounding as weak as one would expect after everything that happened.

"No," she said, her power projecting from a single word. The chill of death touched our tiny living room, creating a frost around the windows and ceiling that hadn't been there before. "He doesn't get to just barge in here and claim he's your mate."

"Step aside," he said coolly.

"I will not." She narrowed her eyes in disgust. "We know what you are."

"Then you know what I'm capable of." He didn't look at her as he spoke. I tilted my head to see around her legs and my heart skipped in erratic beats the moment our eyes locked.

"Try me—" Sin started. I touched her leg to try to stop her, but I was too late. He didn't have to even lift a hand. My sister went flying sideways before she could even finish speaking. Her body hit the other couch and she bounced once while the woman he'd brought with him snorted.

"Stop!" I lifted both hands toward him, glancing at his two guards. "You've made your point. Just stop. Please."

Shadows danced along his forearm, over his veins, to his fingertips. It caught me off guard, and I stared for a moment, unable to speak. What little magic I possessed could do the same thing. Granted, it was more for show, and I couldn't throw someone across a room with it, but the similarities were striking.

"Tell them to leave," he said, speaking quietly. Instantly, everyone in the room began to yell and pushback against the notion.

"Let me at him! Let me at—" Clara slapped a hand over Nog's mouth to keep him from ending up on the wrong end of his magic.

Terror filled me at the idea of being alone with him and I lost my ability to speak.

The Soulless One.

My literal nightmare had been brought to life. He was the very being I was raised to prevent from escaping, and he stood in my living room.

"I'm only going to ask one more time, love. The yelling is grating on me, and I don't want to hurt them. Tell them to leave." I flinched at the supposed term of endearment, even if my core heated at the way he spoke to me. The sensation was most unwelcome.

Did I want them to go? Never. What I wanted in this case didn't matter. The need to protect my family outweighed any self-preservation.

"Go," I told them, speaking up so my voice sounded stronger than I felt.

"What? No way!" Sin demanded, trying, and failing to get off the couch. Invisible hands held her in place, not giving an inch.

"I'm with Sin. No way I'm leaving you with this—" Clara shoved a hand over her brother's mouth again.

My dad let out a roar that made my tía howl in response, and Jo winced, covering his ears.

I looked at Clara for help, trying to convey my desperation. "Are you sure about this, Rea?" she asked quietly.

I swallowed hard, trying to clear the lump in my throat with no real success, so I nodded. "You guys need to go," I croaked. "Even if it's just outside. You know how strong Sin is, and he just threw her aside without breaking a sweat. You're out of your depth." Then I looked at each of them. "All of you are. Now *go* before one of you does something stupid and dies for it."

"I'll have them removed if they don't listen, but I wouldn't kill your family," he said. I didn't believe him. Not for a second. He'd already suggested what he was capable of. I wouldn't listen to false words meant to placate me.

Nog started to struggle with Clara again. She pursed her lips in frustration. Opalescent magic gathered at her fingertips then dispersed as whatever spell she'd conjured took form. Nog stopped fighting, his body going still. She let go of him, and he walked right out the front door, forced by a will that wasn't his own.

"You," she turned to Sin. "Let's go."

Sin reared back like she'd been slapped. "Try that on me and watch what happens—"

Clara sighed and repeated it with every family member and by the end, sweat dotted her brow. That was a lot of magic use for her.

"I can't keep them contained forever," she said, glancing to the man on the floor across from me. "And when they break through, they are going to be *pissed*."

He inclined his chin. "That won't be a problem. Styx.

Oberon. Guard the house. No killing. I need to have a conversation with my mate."

Oberon, presumably, gestured for Clara to exit in front of him. The woman I assumed to be Styx hesitated. "Caius," she began, caution filling her tone. The familiarity with which she'd said his name sent a spark of jealousy through me, but the feeling wasn't my own.

It belonged to Eres.

"Keep that shit to yourself," I said, speaking to her for the first time. "You chose to lock yourself away. Don't push your emotions on me. It's weird, and it's definitely not the time."

"Don't be ungrateful. I allowed us to be bound to protect you."

"Ungrateful? Really? I can't even . . . We'll set some ground rules later, if we even survive, which isn't likely. In the meantime, he's the Soulless One. Destroyer of worlds—"

She chuffed. "And I'm a goddess of death."

"You're a bad unicorn is what you are—wait, are you really a goddess of death?"

"He won't kill you."

"Disagree. He's the bad guy."

The sound of the front door slamming pulled me back to the present.

I was alone. With him.

Knowing I didn't hold any cards in this game, the best I could do was save my family. Mustering all the inner badass I had left in me after nearly dying, I said, "If there is anything good in you, you'll spare my family. They had nothing to do with the ward. It was placed on me by witches when I was a baby. None of us had any say in it, least of all them."

His eyes were dark and unnerving. He didn't say a word, nor did he move. He just . . . sat there. Inaction on his part led to a suffocating tension in the room, and with each passing second, the wariness I felt increased.

"I know you don't care," I continued, "but they mean everything to me. I won't fight you—just let them live. And try to make it quick if you can. I have a high pain tolerance, but having almost died earlier, I can wholeheartedly say I'd rather not feel it this time."

"I don't intend to kill you."

"What?"

"Told you."

"Shut up, Eres."

"Why do you seem so surprised? You're my mate."

I laughed, and when he didn't, the sound abruptly died in my throat. Shaking my head slowly, I mouthed, "No . . ."

"Yes," he insisted.

"You're lying. I *can't* have a mate."

His brows drew together slightly. "Neither can I, yet here we both sit. Believe me, no one is more confused than I am at this moment. My kind? We don't have mates. We aren't built for it, and it goes against the laws of creation." Caius tilted his head. "Until now, it would seem."

All I could do was stare at him while I tried to process why he was saying that, but somehow ended up falling short every time.

I was the guardian. I had half his soul. The best I could guess was that he was confusing that connection to his soul for a mate bond. It's the only thing that made sense.

I opened my mouth to say as much when Eres broke into my thoughts.

"He's not killing you because he thinks he's your mate. Don't inform him of how he could be mistaken. Use it to our advantage."

"You want me to agree to being his mate? I know you and I don't exactly know each other well, but—"

Eres sighed. "I think we can agree on self-preservation."

I internally scoffed. At least I would be in on this arrangement, unlike past decisions about my supposed safety. It was worth considering that she was possibly right. If I could survive him long enough to get my family to safety, that was all that mattered.

"This is reckless."

"You know I'm right."

While Eres and I had our private conversation, I twisted my neck to move some of the stiffness. My newly healed skin pinched, and I reached up to feel the spot where Ben had bitten me. Tender skin, yes, but not inflamed. I wondered if it would scar.

Caius observed my every move, his eyes narrowing when he saw what I had touched.

"Someone tried to claim you."

"N-no . . ." I fibbed, looking away and biting the inside of my cheek.

I almost laughed at myself. Clara was right. I really was a terrible liar.

"Try again," he said, unamused by my feeble attempt. I didn't even know why I was lying. It just seemed like part of that self-preservation Eres had mentioned. "Someone tried and failed. Did you want to be claimed?"

I blanched. "No," I admitted. "But how did you know that?"

"The bite wasn't deep enough to truly mark you. It won't leave a scar. Unless they were a pathetic excuse for a shifter, something stopped them."

I gnawed on my bottom lip, considering my reply. "Why do you want to know?"

He shrugged. "I need to gage how upset you'll be when I kill him."

My lips parted. "No, you will not."

Caius lifted his brows, as if to ask, "*no?*"

"You're not killing anyone."

He hummed noncommittally and the dismissive sound made me want to slap him. Never mind that he was some sort of death deity. Apparently male arrogance surpassed species. Color me unsurprised.

"I'm serious."

"So am I, and it hasn't escaped my notice that you didn't answer. Tell me, Reagan, was it consensual?"

Once more, I opened my mouth to lie, but thought twice about it. What was the point? Instead I decided to try another tactic. "What's the truth worth to you?"

Amusement curled his lips. "You're trying to bargain with me?"

"I asked you a question." My heart pounded, sending a rush of blood to my head, making me feel fuzzy. Was I picking a fight with my executioner? Probably. So much for self-preservation.

"Very well. I want the truth—the full truth—and in return, I won't hurt your family." I blinked, hardly able to believe his words. "That's what you want, isn't it?"

"Yes," I whispered. "How do I know you'll keep your word?"

"You don't," he said simply, making me shudder as all the hope in my chest shattered. "When you're as old as I am, you know that trust is hard to come by."

"That's not exactly comforting."

"I'm immortal, Reagan. All I have is my word. I'm giving it to you. I won't let any harm come to your family." He paused, considering his words, then added, "Unless one of them gave you that."

"My family didn't do it," I said firmly. "The one who did —you can't kill him either. I won't carry the weight of that."

Caius twisted his lips in displeasure, but eventually agreed. "Fine."

I narrowed my eyes. "You can't have anyone else kill him either. He stays alive."

He smirked, winking at me once. "Smart woman."

A small part of me blushed at the flirtatious tone in his voice. The rest of me slapped that part upside the head. I blamed Eres for it.

"Do you agree to the terms of the bargain?" he asked.

I nodded once. "I do."

An invisible thread formed between us, pulling taut. My breath caught in my throat, and I looked at Caius for clarification.

"Bargains with immortals, true immortals, form a connection of sorts. One that can't be broken."

"You said all you had is your word."

"And when I give my word, the connection forms. It requires your trust." I wasn't sure I liked being tricked into a binding agreement, but at the same time, relief flooded me. It meant my family was safe. "Now tell me, who did this to you, and did you want it?"

"No," I answered quietly. I'd yet to have a conversation with my sister or cousins about what transpired between me and Ben.

Mate bonds were sacred. The claiming between them was special. Ben pissed all over that trying to take me, and when the memories of that night resurfaced, I could see his face clearly. He knew he'd screwed up.

"I had a fuck bu—uh, a friend that I was . . . friendly with," I said clumsily. Clearing the lump in my throat, I continued. "He thought I wanted more. Or at least that's what he said after the fact. I didn't want it, not because I'm waiting for true love or some stupid notion like that. I just know that I can't mate. I live a half-life as the guardian. My soul can't bond because it has your half, and my life is too complicated even if it could. Now . . ." I paused, noting Caius's tense features. His fists were clenched. Something was raging in his eyes. Anger didn't quite cover it.

"I will keep my word. He won't be killed, nor will I have someone kill him, but if he comes anywhere near you again, if I so much as catch his scent, he'll spend the rest of his days in agony for having dared to touch you."

I paled, but for all the wrong reasons. Eres perked up, even more intrigued by the man in front of us. He stirred something in her, but neither of us were willing to call it a mate bond. Lust was more like it, shameful as it was to covet someone with a murderous reputation.

Hormones were stupid.

"Let it go. I doubt he'd be stupid enough to come around again." I blew a strand of hair away from my face. I'd made a bargain for safety. Now I needed to know the rest of his intentions. "So, where do we go from here? You claim I'm your mate, but I won't stand by while you fuck over my world."

He chuckled, shaking his head. "I'm not going to destroy this world, love. Where would you get an idea like that?"

"I . . . That is what I was told growing up. The witches, the coven, they passed down stories of you. It was foretold that your return would be the end of days." He stared at me, both surprised and confused. "It sounds a little melodramatic now as I say this out loud and you look at me like that," I muttered.

"I helped create this world. Was that passed down to you as well?" He cocked his head to the side, genuinely interested in my response.

I stumbled over my thoughts, mouth opening and closing. "No. That tidbit was omitted." If it were even true.

"Figures." He sighed.

"Okay, so you don't plan to destroy Earth, so that's a win. What about me? I have half your soul, and I know that part is true. Are you going to kill me?" It was probably not the smartest thing to bring up, but I couldn't help it. This man was nothing like what I expected.

"Originally, I was going to, yes," he answered after a pregnant pause. My stomach roiled, and my head felt light. Breathing became hard, but I did my best to keep a strong face. "But that would be contradictory to my objective now." He shook his head as if trying to clear it. "If I'd been asked whether I'd wanted a mate or my soul returned, I would have laughed. There was no comparison."

"Oh, and now there is?" I was infuriated by the way he so casually laid out my worth. I was an *objective*.

"Yes. I want to know you, Reagan. You can't deny me that."

I scoffed. "I most certainly can—"

The front door flew open, slamming into the drywall. The knob would have dented it, if not for the crumbled hole in the wall from how many other times one of us opened it a little too hard. Plaster wasn't made for shifter strength, or an overly excited Nog.

"You have got to see this. There's a portal, Rea! Right smack in the middle of Old Kiener Plaza!"

I sucked in a sharp breath and shot Caius a dirty look. "You left a portal to Hell open?"

"Tartarus isn't Hell," he countered, but conveniently didn't answer my question.

"For fuck's sake," I mumbled, then looked at Caius and then jutted my chin toward the door and held my hand out. "After you, Soulless One."

He grunted in irritation, his lips twisting in distaste. It was clear that name had an effect on him. "Caius will do. Or mate. Your choice, love."

I hummed in derision. He'd just admitted he'd intended on walking through that door to end my life, and then he just changed his mind because he was stupid enough to confuse a bond with his soul reaching for him.

It would be a cold day in Tartarus before I'd call him my mate.

CHAPTER 8

CAIUS

A dozen yards away, the portal I'd created spun in mesmerizing swirls. From Tartarus's side it was a brilliant, blinding light, but from this side it was a gaping abyss. The polarity was striking, but I wasn't paying near as much attention to it as I was the woman trying her damnedest to ignore me.

I'd upset her, that much was clear. I wasn't bothered by her refusal. On the contrary, I expected nothing less from the guardian. The fact she was my mate was just a cosmic sort of irony. It was as though the universe truly didn't want me reunited with my soul.

Reagan had said she lived a half-life. I had lived one for five thousand years. Perhaps that was our destiny. Primordials were creators, but we had no control over the fates.

Fire danced in her golden-brown eyes, and I wanted little more than to taste her full lips, but I didn't need a glaistig to tell me that my kiss would be unwanted. For now.

"You're staring," Styx said, speaking Sumerian. The

world no longer spoke the language, and she felt safe having the conversation without keeping her voice down.

"I'm aware."

Ever since we'd arrived on scene, her family swarmed the portal along with two dozen onlookers. Black magic oozed from it, stopping a few feet away, except for the thin trail that led to me. I kept my eyes on it, not expecting Tartarus to cling to me in such a way.

She sighed. "I don't want to be that asshole, but one of us needs to say it before you make a decision that is going to affect us all. How do you know she's actually your mate?"

I'd been waiting for her to ask that very question from the moment we'd left Reagan's house.

"I just do, Styx. How do we know to breathe? Or to fuck, for that matter?"

Styx groaned. "Not the same, Caius. I mean how are you sure it's not just because she's the guardian? What if you only think she's your mate because she literally has your soul trapped inside her?"

My hands fisted at the reminder, but I kept my temper in check. "I can feel the difference. Yes, she has my soul. I can feel it pulling at me, but the desire to *have* her, to take her, to keep her and give her everything is just as strong, if not stronger. They're separate."

I'd once felt the overwhelming desire to destroy anything and everything. Betrayal blinded me. It morphed over time to only wanting revenge on those that damned me. All of it became an afterthought, faded into the background. I just wanted her.

"So you've chosen, then?" she asked carefully. "You're going to mate with her, regardless of your soul or what she wants."

"That's not what I said." The truth was, I didn't know

what I was going to do. Reagan was my mate, and I wouldn't let her die.

"Well you better figure it out, Caius. If you catch feelings for her, it's going to be that much harder to, well, you know."

"Kill her? That's out of the question."

"Never say never."

"Enough," I growled quietly. "She will not die. The woman I've been dreaming about? It's her. The moment we walked through that door, everything hit me. It's one thing to recognize a mate bond, and it's another to realize she's also the one you've seen every time you close your eyes at night." I wondered if Reagan ever dreamed of me too, and the thought suddenly consumed me.

"Oh, shit," Styx said, turning to look at Reagan through a new lens. "I see it now. She fits the description. The color of her eyes. I didn't pay attention, of course, coming here to kill a guardian and all. Now I understand. You already caught feelings. Damn Caius, I didn't think your life could get any more complicated."

I sighed. "You and me, both."

We watched as her cousin walked toward the portal. Around it, dead trees were blown back and frozen in a blackened state. Like the plant life somehow knew to fear the realm of death and tried to get away, only to be caught in its magic's snare. Water spilled over the cracked stones where a fountain once stood. Every part of it was stained black, despite never being alive.

"Nog! No!" Reagan yelled at the boy, not that it stopped him. He paused a couple feet away, looking at the trail of magic that led to me. I could see the wheels turning in his head.

He touched the death magic with a single finger and a

crack echoed through the plaza. The boy flew backwards a few feet, his body twisting, morphing mid-air. Nog hit the ground and yelped as he collapsed in a pile of clothes.

"Nog!" Reagan and Clara yelled simultaneously. I started moving toward her, the distraught tone of her voice instigating a primal instinct to protect her.

She ran to the pile in a panic. She wasn't the only one. Most of her family had moved in that direction as the fabric started to shuffle around, something moving beneath it.

A black snout shoved its way out of the neck hole of the boy's shirt, followed by a head.

"What in the—" the witch started, her jaw dropping.

"Is that what I think it is?" Reagan asked, stopping short.

"Yup," the witch answered after regaining her senses.

The tiny dog wiggled its way out of the shirt, showing off his pure black fur—as was to be expected of all shadow shifters. I stepped to Reagan's side.

"He's a corgi?" my mate said in disbelief, her voice rising in question.

"A what?" I asked, never having heard of one. Crossing a portal made by a primordial gave anyone the ability to speak that realm's language, but that didn't mean we understood all of it. If they came to Tartarus, it would be the same.

"A corgi. You know, the dog breed? I've never seen one in real life, but based on the pictures I've seen in books, those ears and legs are definitely all corgi."

The dog started zooming circles around his sister, his head lifted to the sky as he let out yapping barks.

"For fuck's sake, Nog!" Clara said, covering her ears. "Shut up and shift back before my ears start bleeding."

The dog did no such thing, and he yelped louder in distress.

"What happened? Why can't he shift back?" Reagan asked no one in particular, and Clara shrugged.

I watched him carefully. "I take it he's never shifted before?"

Both Reagan and her cousin shook their heads while prompting him again. "C'mon, Nog. That's enough. Shift back."

"He's a shadow shifter?" Styx whispered, looking at him while he ran around.

"It would appear so," I answered quietly.

The boy continued to run in circles, incessantly barking at absolutely nothing. I was going to force the shift, if for no other reason than to end it when Reagan commanded him, the power in her voice radiating. "*Shift.*"

Mid-run, the dog collapsed. Bones popped as a gangly human teenager took form.

"I can shift," he yelled. "You hear that Tío? Clara? Clara, did you see me? I CAN SHIFT!"

Reagan scrubbed a hand down her face. "Yes, Nog we all know you can shift now. Can you put your damn clothes on while we talk?"

He gave her a side-eye like she was being unreasonable, but he grabbed his clothes.

"And I thought he was insufferable before," Clara muttered.

There was a murmur of agreement that went through the crowd as Nog shucked his pants up one leg, then the other. "Oh, fuck all of you!"

Ignoring him, Reagan turned to me. Once again, wariness colored her features, and I could honestly say I didn't like it when she looked at me that way.

"What's a shadow shifter?"

On a heavy sigh, I answered, knowing this wasn't going to go well. "Tartarus's version of a shifter. They're very similar to your kind on Earth, except the shifting cycle coincides with our dual moons. When they're both full, it will force a shift. I'm not sure how that will impact him here . . ."

"Is that all?" Reagan said tersely.

I ran my tongue over my teeth before speaking. "There are good odds he'll inherit the savagery that all shadow creatures have. Tempers run short, and the desire to find one's mate is maddening, or so I'm told. There seems to cause a decline in humanistic characteristics as the animal within drives them to find the only thing that can stop it. Their mate."

Reagan pinched the bridge of her nose with her index finger and thumb, taking a deep breath before releasing it harshly.

"You mean to tell me, my cousin is going to go insane if he doesn't find his *fated* mate? The one that is literally a single person in the entire world—assuming she's even alive yet. There's a chance she may not have been born, or worse, she already died. Dammit!" Her hands clenched in a show of emotion I wasn't expecting. She was taking this even worse than I thought. So much for trying to soften the blow. "How is that even possible?"

"Probably when he touched the death magic," Styx blurted out, and I turned to her with wide eyes. She lifted her shoulder. "What?"

"That's death magic leaking out of the portal?" she asked, pointing to the inky tendrils reaching for me.

Pinning Styx with a side glare, and I nodded.

"Well. That settles that. You need to go."

Not without her. Returning to Tartarus wasn't as off-putting as I thought it would be, but returning without her? Impossible.

"Only if you come with me," I answered.

Her lips parted and she laughed. "To Hell? No. No way."

I took a step toward her, coming face-to-face. "I told you, Tartarus isn't Hell."

"Fine." She cleared her throat. "To Tartarus?" she began, using a mocking tone as repeated herself. "No. No way. Better?"

"Then we're staying here."

"You can't," she said, her brows furrowing . "The grass around the fountain is dead. The magic is moving toward you. Look." She waved her hands wildly over the area where blackened char was stretching toward me. "If you stay, it will spread, and it's going to kill what it touches, or turn it into a shadow shifter."

I couldn't argue her point. She was right, but that didn't mean I would just walk away from her. "So, come with me. We can—"

"I'm not going with you," she said, clenching her fists. "I don't trust you. I'm not your mate, no matter what you believe—"

"*Know*," I corrected, feeling my frustration rise.

She shook her head. "Agree to disagree. You said you weren't going to kill me, right? Then just *go*."

"If I were another man, anyone other than the twat that tried to mark you—would you tell me to leave?"

"If it was killing my world, I would!"

"And if not?"

"That doesn't matter! There is no point in discussing it because this is our reality. Right now."

Frustration turned to anger at her outright dismissal. "Our reality is that you're my mate, and you are stubborn as hell and won't listen to a word I say. If I weren't the man you've been *conditioned* to believe was here to destroy everything—you wouldn't be doing this."

That stopped her short, and silence ensued. The audience watching us didn't whisper or move as they waited for her to speak.

Finally, she spoke, and her voice was even-keeled, lacking all the fire she'd had before. "You're right," she said with a sigh. "But you are that man, regardless of what truth is in those stories. You admitted to coming here to kill me, which is why it'll never work between us."

I ran my fingers through my hair, nails scraping my scalp sharply. This was getting nowhere.

"I'm not leaving without my mate, so either we set up camp near this portal, or we go to my side."

Reagan stared at me, eyes watering with anger. It was a confusing reaction and seeing her battle this struggle made me want to reach for her, but she wanted nothing from me.

Then she said the words that shattered every bit of grace I was holding onto.

"Caius, I reject you."

Shock slapped me only a second before the pain took hold, twisting my insides. I nearly collapsed from it. She didn't just . . .

Raw emotions tore at my heart. She tried to deny herself and me by proxy, but for a bond to be rejected, I had to accept it. That much I knew.

Nothing I could say or do would make her believe me. In her eyes, I was the Soulless One, and no words could convince her of the truth.

She wanted to see me as the villain? So be it.

I'd be the villain, and she could be the savior.

I turned to Styx and Oberon, giving a final command. "Do not let a soul through, except her."

Moving swiftly, I grabbed Clara and threw her over my shoulder, then walked through the portal to Tartarus.

CHAPTER 9

REAGAN

Clara's screams echoed in my ears, drowning out the commotion.

That bastard had dragged her through before any of us could stop him. In the seconds that followed, chaos broke loose. A crowd formed around the portal, and I was at the center of it.

Reason left me, and I ran forward, shoving Oberon. He took it in stride, only budging a little but not fighting back. The look on his face was almost apologetic.

Nog, however, stormed toward it before promptly getting knocked on his ass when Styx blocked him.

"Bring her back!" I yelled, pointing, and stomping like that was somehow going to showcase my anger in a more vigorous manner.

"You heard him," Styx said, gesturing to the portal behind her. "You are welcome to go through."

Fire raged in my veins, but logic overrode the desire to lash out. It would do nothing to get Clara back. I took a deep breath, closing my eyes and trying to count slowly in my head.

If I could remain calm, I could think clearly. If I could think clearly, I could make informed decisions.

Trying not to scream, I looked at the ground and ran my fingers through my hair, yanking hard on tangles I didn't realize I had. The quick shot of pain jolted me into a momentary clear head space.

The grass. The inky black lines had stopped.

Whatever death magic was leaking out of the portal had been reaching for Caius, and now it was gone. It's path ceased shortly before the spot where he'd been standing, and it no longer moved. It wasn't seeking Styx or Oberon, in fact, if it hadn't left its black mark, there was no indication anything had ever been reaching out of the portal at all.

Well, I suppose he gave me what I wanted. Two could play that game.

"Fine," I ground out, turning on a heel and heading home at a brisk pace.

"Wait," Nog shouted, catching up and waving his hand frantically toward the old square. "Where are you going? You're just going to leave her? We have to do something!"

"Stop shouting and let me think," I said, a forceful command in my tone. I didn't ever throw out orders the way an alpha would. I wasn't an alpha, but I really needed my cousin to shut up.

It didn't work. My family followed me, yelling about anything and everything.

I flung the door to my house wide open and headed straight for my room. It took no time at all to change out of my bloodstained pants and into fresh jeans, a light sweater, and boots. I grabbed my backpack and stuffed clothes and other essentials I figured would be good to have on hand: underwear, a toothbrush, knives. After tucking my mom's necklace under my shirt, I swung the bag over my shoulder and prepared to leave my house.

When I entered the living room, the rest of my family had arrived and things were, in a word, hysterical.

My dad was trying to calm Tía Celeste as she cried in deep, hyperventilating sobs. Sin was yelling at Nog while he threw things and broadcasted every idiotic idea he had on how to get his sister back.

In complete contrast, Jo sat on the couch calmly, not partaking in any of the mayhem that filled the room. His little feet didn't even touch the ground, and he entertained himself by tapping his heels together.

He looked up, and his big eyes met mine. Jo smiled at me while I knelt beside him, and no one paid us any attention. "Hey, mijo. I haven't had the chance to say thank you."

"What for?"

"The memories are a little fuzzy, but you tried to save me. I remember feeling your magic on me at one point before I lost consciousness. I know it was you." I handed him the doll that Clara had crocheted for him.

His lips curled into a shy smile. "You told me not to, but I think you were too sick to know what you were really saying."

"Your magic is special, Jo, but it hurts you when you use it too much. Don't waste that on me again. If it's our time to go, you have to let us go. Got it?"

He tilted his head. "Do you believe that?"

"Having just come face-to-face with death, yeah, I do. We can't cheat it, and I couldn't live with myself if you got hurt trying to help me, okay? I know everyone else in the family feels that way too."

"You're telling me this 'cause you're going away, aren't

you?" he asked, and I nodded. "Good. You have to be the one to bring her back," he whispered.

"I know." Signaling to our frantic family with a tilt of my brows and a slight angling of my head, I continued, "Take care of them, okay? They won't understand."

"You have to make them understand." He shrugged. "Besides, you'll be safe."

Not an ounce of concern escaped him, and I couldn't help but wonder what that meant. He was the youngest of us all, and one would think that made him the most naïve. The truth was that he was probably smarter than anyone in the room. He'd proved it time and time again.

"You haven't happened to have read any books about Tartarus, have you?"

He smiled, shaking his head. "No. The library doesn't have any."

"Damn. Was hoping you could tell me what to expect."

"You always tell me to expect the unexpected," he said, his big, brown eyes sparkling with mirth.

"I suppose I do." I cupped his cheek. "This is more dangerous than grave digging, though. The Soulless One is . . . ruthless." I sighed. "He wants the soul I guard, but now he's claiming we're mates. I don't understand what's happening here, but I can't leave Clara there while I figure it out."

Not a damn thing made sense anymore and it made me feel uneasy. Eres stirred inside me, but I ignored her. She'd shut herself off from me for sixteen years. She could freakin' wait.

"Maybe there's more to him than you realize," he replied, picking at a loose thread on the doll.

"I seriously doubt that," I huffed.

"Why? There's a time in our lives where we're limited in

what we know just. We believe what we are told to believe, and we do because we don't know any better. It's only by opening our hearts and minds to listen are we able to experience the world around us. We need that knowledge and understanding so we can grow."

My jaw slackened at the strength of his words. It was almost as if someone else was speaking.

"Dude. You're *nine*," I said, after finding my voice again. Giving him a tiny squeeze of his shoulder, I shook my head in disbelief. "How can you be so smart?"

"It's 'cause I read all the books in the library. If you find new ones in Tartarus, bring some back for me," he whispered. A mesmerizing light flickered in his eyes, and an invisible force pressed upon my skin, enveloping me in what I could only describe as comfort. My breath caught, and before I could ask him what he was doing, my family seemed to have noticed my backpack and turned their attention to me.

"The hell you think you are doing?" my father said forcefully, crossing his arms.

After a few more seconds of staring at my youngest cousin in awe, I shook myself free of where my thoughts had taken me. Clearing my throat, I stood up and looked at my dad directly. "I'm going to get Clara."

"You can't seriously think I'm going to just let you walk through that portal with that—that monster waiting for you on the other side?"

"Um, yes, that is exactly what I am going to do. There is no way we are leaving her there, and you heard him. He told his two stooges not to let anyone else through except me, and I'm pretty sure they're good at following his orders."

Sin pinched the bridge of her nose, squeezing her eyes

shut. "For all you know, you'll cross over and he'll just kill you both."

"You know damn well he could have done that while he was here. Hell, he agreed not to hurt any of you, and technically, he didn't," I argued, irritation crawling over my skin.

"Reagan, you can't risk your life this way. You have the other half of his soul. That's all he's ever wanted. Crossing over means he could take your life at any moment. You know the stories as well as I do," my dad pleaded, talking with his hands the way he did when he was exasperated.

I glanced at Jo, and he dipped his chin, and I replayed his words in my mind.

"Do you mean the stories that Mom was told before she was sacrificed? The ones that creep and his lackeys told me?" I laughed coolly, without humor. "I know who Caius is, Dad. I *know* what I guard. The origin of the stories are real, but that doesn't mean they're the full truth. Something happened today that we can't explain. He was the one that saved me for crying out loud." I shot back. "I knew I was dying, Dad. I felt it. I was on the brink of death, but he *saved* me."

Gods, was I actually defending Caius? Add that to the list of things that didn't make sense. At least he wasn't here to hear me. I could just picture the smirk on his perfect face.

"But *why* did he do it? He wasn't exactly forthcoming with answering questions, and once you woke up, Clara had us shoved out of here before we could find out what we needed to know. He claims he's your mate, but is that it? What motive does he really have?" My dad shook his head angrily, clearly put off that I wasn't backing down. "If all the stories passed down were true, he's willing to destroy everything to get back the other half of his soul, and you aren't strong enough to protect yourself—"

"And whose fault is that?" I shouted, not realizing the hurt that was lingering beneath the surface. So much had happened so quickly that the truth of what he'd done to me had all been temporarily squashed, but that one sentence brought it right back up.

My dad winced, the words hitting him harder than any fist ever could. His shoulders sagged as all the fight he had in him left. "Reagan . . ."

"No." Tears welled in my eyes, and I clenched my fists. "Now isn't the time. You did what you did. I feel magic in me I can't even begin to understand. I now hear Eres's voice when all I've ever felt was her faint presence. I find out you bound me, and for whatever reason, you chose not to tell me until I was dying. Not when I was eighteen. Not when I was twenty. Not when I was struggling with barely *any* power while living in a magically driven world. Now the very thing I guard is attached to someone claiming to be my mate, and he has my cousin hostage. That is too much shit to deal with all at once, so this—this has to wait until I'm back."

"Rea," my sister started, reaching out to touch my arm, but I jerked away.

"You knew too. That hurts more than you could ever imagine." I swallowed down the sob that threatened to escape. "The clock is ticking and none of this compares to Clara being trapped in Tartarus. Only one of us can enter. I'm going."

My dad took a step quickly but halted. "Reagan, wait. You can't leave like this. I'm sorry I hurt you. I'm sorry I didn't tell you sooner." He stood up straight, showing his full size. It wasn't for intimidation. It was to show me he was giving his word. That everything he was saying was truthful, swearing on his honor as an alpha "But I won't apologize for saving you."

"I know." I pressed my lips together, dipping my chin once. "I love you both more than you could ever know. I even forgive you, but despite all that, I can still be mad at you—and I am, Dad. I'm pissed as hell at you for keeping Eres and my magic from me."

Tía Celeste placed her hand gently on my dad's arm, and she sniffed harshly, her nose audibly stuffy from crying. "Give her time, Alvaro. She has earned that."

"Um, what time does she have?" Nog interjected, throwing his hands out. "She's crossing through a portal, apparently, and she might never come back."

I rolled my eyes. "I'm just going to get your sister, you numbskull. Not to go live happily ever after in Hell."

"Tartarus isn't Hell," Jo said, and I tilted my head as I squinted at him. Caius had said the same thing.

"How do you know?" Nog asked, oblivious to anything going on in the room that didn't involve him. "It's not like you've ever been there."

"No, I haven't. That's true." He swung his legs innocently, his hands curled over the edge of the couch for balance.

My dad sighed. "Sin, go with her."

"No," my sister and I said in unison.

My eyebrows shot up in surprise as her refusal caught me off guard. Considering how she had always been the one to look out for me, I assumed she'd be hot on my heels. It's what big sisters did best.

"Dad, she has to go by herself. The two guards aren't going to let anyone else through. I . . . I don't think he's going to hurt her."

"You saw that death magic." I picked up the backpack

and hoisted it over my shoulder. "It was branching out, reaching for him. And it stopped the minute he left. It wants him. And he wants me. And I want Clara. We all have different goals. I just need to go there and figure out how to achieve them." *If* I even could.

Not that I wanted it to be true, but I was basically the only bargaining chip I had, and well, that sucked. Surely they had to realize that too. I wondered how it could get any worse.

My dad bit his bottom lip and glared at us, the frown between his brow shaking. Finally his features softened, and he sighed, yielding to his two daughters. "Celeste, my satchel is in the kitchen. Get the Sumerian dagger with the runes. And the book. She might need it."

She nodded, stepping into the kitchen, and grabbing his bag from a barstool.

"Tío! You're the alpha," Nog said. "Make her stay. Do . . . I don't know—something!"

Tía Celeste scoffed alongside my dad as she handed him the leather bag he'd requested. He glanced at his sister-in-law, raising a brow. "He has no idea how women work, does he?"

She shook her head. "Not even a little bit."

"What's that supposed to mean?" My cousin put his hands on his hips, offended.

Dad put his large hand firmly on Nog's shoulder, looking down to him as he spoke. "It means you have a lot to learn." He glanced up and turned his head toward me and my sister. "There's no amount of alpha that can bend a woman's will, Nog. You have to know when you won't win."

"You're kidding," he said, his jaw slackened as he stared.

My dad walked around my cousin and stopped in front of me while he reached into his satchel. He pulled out a book wrapped in a soft muslin cloth. "This belonged to your mother, Reagan. Spells. Some she learned, and some she was working on creating herself. I . . ." He paused briefly, and my heart thundered in my ears. "I can't read most of it. I should have . . . done things differently with you. Both of you. But maybe now that you have Eres again, she can help you read it and figure out how to work your own magic."

I took the book and rubbed my fingertips over the cloth. There was a scent I recognized but couldn't place. Another memory that had been locked away, just out of reach.

I walked up to him, wrapping my arms around him and squeezing. "I swear I'll bring Clara back."

"Yeah." The single word was enough to make him choke up as he hugged me in return.

Sin came out of her room with a small suitcase. Then she went into the kitchen and began putting large mason jars of my moonshine on the counter.

"Why are you getting those out?"

"Because you're taking them with you."

I huffed a laugh. "Are you seriously suggesting I head back to that portal and cross into another realm holding a bag stocked with liquor?"

She looked up, dead serious. "Yeah. It's better than being without moonshine." Then she shrugged, placing them carefully in there with some towels so they didn't clank around. "And who knows? Maybe you can learn how to make poison in that new book of yours. And if you did, I bet your moonshine would block out the taste."

Nog shuddered. "Maybe the moonshine is the poison," he muttered, eliciting a chuckle from me. He was a proven lightweight, and my homemade brew wasn't meant for the weak. Still, he hadn't truly learned his lesson despite bowing to the porcelain gods at least once a month.

Sin brought it to me. "C'mon. I'll walk you there."

"Thanks." I tried to smile, but considering where I was going, the sentiment felt forced.

After hugging Jo, my tía, and my dad one final time, I went to Nog and did the same. When I let go, I gave him a harsh look. "Don't be a dumbass while I'm gone. Help them keep people away from the portal, okay?"

He was upset, and it was written all over his face. He nodded, not making any promises. That was the best I could hope for.

"I'll keep an eye on the two he left here," Sin said as we prepared to leave. "They can't guard that portal every hour of every day. If I see a chance, I'm taking it."

"That's what you think," I muttered. "Something tells me they are more than equipped at keeping that portal guarded, or he wouldn't have left them in charge of it."

I'd been saying how much I wanted to travel, but this wasn't what I'd had in mind. How many times had I wished to be anywhere other than The Crossroads? As the saying went, ask and you shall receive. I needed to be more specific in my wishes from now on. I'd meant visiting my cousin Danni at Mt. Rainier, or going to her husband's castle in Italy, or crossing into Arcadia to see where my cousin Adora lived with her mate. Instead of traveling the world, I got to be the bride of Frankenstein, heading to Hell with rolling luggage like Tartarus was the coveted destination for a relaxing weekend getaway.

When I swung the front door open, Ben was standing on my porch. My heart almost stopped beating. The mark on my neck tingled. He was holding flowers, and his shame-filled eyes met mine.

"Reagan, I am so sorry. I don't know what happened—"

Without thinking, I reared back, my fist connecting with his face.

I'd wondered earlier how things could get any worse.

I got my answer.

CHAPTER 10

CAIUS

The woman draped over my shoulder kicked her legs forcefully, angling her heel toward my face, though she never made contact. Her fists pounded onto my back. Waves of magic rippled over my skin as she tried to use spells on me, but it was only when a sharp current of electricity passed through me that I felt the effect of her power.

I grunted in response. "That's really not necessary."

Guards came rushing toward the portal as we entered, wide-eyed and surprised I had returned.

"Your majesty, we didn't expect you—"

"I know. A young woman by the name of Reagan should be following soon. Allow her passage, and no one else," I said, then dropped the small witch on the ground in the atrium. "Bring Pol and Abyssian."

She landed on her palms and knees with a harsh thud, then pushed herself to stand quickly. Without hesitation, she brought her hands up into a defensive position to protect herself using magic.

I couldn't help but smirk at her boldness. "That's cute, but you know it's not going to work on me."

"What are you going to do to me, you asshole, because let me warn you and whatever shitheads you're bringing to torture me, I will *not* go down without a fight—"

"Relax," I said, raising my voice to speak over her. "Stop being so dramatic. I have no intention of harming you."

"I—you what?" she said, narrowing her eyes at me and not lowering her hands. "Then why am I here?" Her tone didn't change. She didn't believe me. All things considered, I understood her position.

"Come." I waved for her to follow me, but she didn't move, and I sighed. "Or don't. Suit yourself." I took a seat at the large table in my throne room. The humid air felt nice compared to the chill on Earth. "You seem smart enough. Let me ask you a question. How would bringing you here for such a vile purpose benefit me?"

"I don't know," she scoffed, raising a brow. "I've never kidnapped anyone before, so unless you have a Villainy for Beginners manual you'll let me borrow, you're going to have to clue me in."

"The answer is that it wouldn't benefit me." I leaned back in the chair and crossed my leg over the other. "How am I supposed to convince Reagan she should accept me as her mate if I killed her cousin?"

Her lips parted, and she stared at me, lost for words.

"Clara, right?" I asked.

"Yes."

"Well, Clara, Reagan wanted me gone so that death magic doesn't hurt your world, correct?" She nodded. "We can't have a constructive conversation while she's hyper-focused on that and yelling about me leaving, but on the flip side, I need her to listen to me and understand that we are, in fact, mates. So I've done what she asked of me. I've left her world, taking the magic of Tartarus back with me. Now I need her to do what I've asked, and bringing you here will accomplish that."

"So I'm your bait?" Dropping her arms to her side slowly, she considered my argument.

"Essentially, yes."

"So you'll let me go?"

"Once she agrees to my terms, you're free to leave."

"Oh, see, that means I'm actually your hostage. Got your terminology a little mixed up there."

I shrugged. "Call it whatever you wish. The fact remains that you will not be harmed."

The doors to the chambers burst open, and Abyssian and Pol ran in, flustered and confused.

"What happened?" Pollux asked, coming to an abrupt halt the moment he saw Clara. "And who—" He gasped, his nostrils flaring and his pupils dilating. "Is this the witch?"

Her hands flew up again, preparing to defend herself.

"No," I said, standing up, gesturing to them to sit at the round table. "She is a witch, yes, but she's not who you think. Please, sit."

"I think not." Clara didn't move and I struggled not to roll my eyes.

"Really, Clara, this is getting tedious. Have a seat. You can't stand like that forever. You'll burn yourself out."

After several moments of deliberating, she finally released a frustrated breath before stomping over to a seat, dropping herself on it with an audible thud, and then crossing her arms.

I forced a tight smile in thanks, and she squinted her eyes at me in return. Addressing her, I said, "These two gentlemen are Pollux, my oldest and most trusted friend, and Abyssian, my brother." I inclined my head to her. "This is Clara."

"Charmed," she said sourly. Pollux didn't take his eyes off her while he spoke.

"That doesn't tell me much of anything, Caius. Who is she?"

"It's complicated—"

"And where are Oberon and Styx?" Abyssian interjected, looking around the room.

I sighed. "That's also complicated, and—"

"Did you find—"

"Wow, you guys just keep interrupting him nonstop," Clara said, the exasperation in her tone matching exactly what I was feeling. "If you'd both just shut up for a second, he'd be able to tell you that I'm Reagan's cousin, he kidnapped me and is holding me hostage—sorry, as 'bait'—so that she'll come talk to him, while your two missing buddies are guarding your stupid portal back on Earth." Abyssian opened his mouth to speak, but she cut him off again. "And before you ask, Reagan is the guardian, who he also *claims* is his mate."

"Wait, your *what*?" Pollux yelled.

Clara ignored him completely, looking at me as she spoke. "It's really not that complicated. I don't know why you said it was."

"Did she say the guardian is your *mate*?" Abyssian repeated.

"See? They're not as stupid as they look," she quipped. "They understood just fine."

Clara really did amuse me. She'd do well in my court if she didn't hate me so much.

"Everything she said is true," I said, then proceeded to fill them in on all that happened in the short period of time

I'd been gone. I finalized the storytelling by enforcing the fact that neither she nor her cousin could be harmed.

When I finished, Abyssian lowered his voice, glancing at Clara from his periphery. "Caius, you're a"—he paused, looking back to me—"you can't have a mate. That's not possible."

"Apparently it is. And I suspect she'll be joining us soon."

With his elbows on the table, Pollux hovered over it and placed his head in his hands, running them through. "You can't be serious right now. You brought some witch—no offense—"

"Offense taken, rudeness," Clara said, giving him the middle finger. "I don't know if that gesture works here, but in case you don't know what it means—"

"I know what it means," he ground out. "I was *trying* to be nice."

"Did you have a point?" I asked, bringing the conversation back to the topic at hand.

He glared at her, then continued. "You bring *Clara* back to Tartarus, and now the guardian, the actual guardian, is coming here, with the half of your soul she still guards fully intact inside her, and you're going to . . . what? What's the plan?"

"Okay, maybe I spoke too soon. He doesn't seem to get it," Clara mumbled.

Pol exploded out of his chair and went to face her. "Gods, woman, do you always have to be so infuriating? I haven't done shit to you."

Clara slammed her palms on the table and stood up, meeting the fury in his eyes with a powerful rage of her own.

They were chest-to-chest, standing only a hairsbreadth

apart. "Look here, fucker, I was dragged through a portal to Hell by your boss over there, so while you haven't personally done shit to me, you're one of his minions, so you are one hundred percent going to take the heat with him."

"What the hell for?"

"I don't know! For existing!" she shouted in return.

I rubbed my temples and groaned, but Abyssian stood up, sliding gently between them.

"Hey," he drawled, holding his hands up in a non-threatening manner. "Can we call a truce? You're short tempered right now, and rightly so, having been dragged here and all, and me and Pol, we're just a teeny bit surprised and trying to swallow this new information. Can we get some things figured out first, then we can attack each other?" He flashed a smile, and added, "Or you can just attack Pol, which I find thoroughly entertaining."

Abyssian was charming, and always had been. Apparently his smooth words and easy looks won her over, albeit for what I assumed would be a brief time.

She crossed her arms, shifting her weight back onto one leg as she appraised him. Finally, she gave a single nod and extended her hand, accepting his offer, and they shook. I didn't miss the fact that they held on for a few seconds longer than would have been necessary.

"Great. Now that we're all acquainted and running under a temporary white flag," Pol began, pointedly ignoring Clara and only addressing me, "what in the actual hell is going on?"

Before I could answer, a crackle of energy rippled over my skin, and my lips curled into a smile.

My mate had arrived, fury and fire in her wake.

CHAPTER 11

REAGAN

I fully expected to enter Tartarus and be assaulted with the oppressive heat of fire and the overwhelming scent of brimstone.

Instead, I walked through the portal and straight into what could be best described as an atrium. Deep blue ferns lined the pathway, and ivy the color of amethysts crawled up the onyx walls. Pomegranate and persimmon trees added contrast with their pops of red and orange as fruit grew in abundance.

"What in the . . .?" I whispered to myself, raking my fingertips over the lush leaves as I trailed the walkway.

Two guards met me at the end, crossing their spears to form an ex. "No one may enter. Return back to your world."

I sighed, and Eres chuckled internally. "Your . . . whatever he's called here, is expecting me. I'm Reagan." They exchanged a quick look, dipped their chins, then moved to let me pass. "That's what I thought."

As I came around the corner slowly, I heard voices, instantly recognizing my cousin's. Ducking down, I hovered behind large fronds. No one seemed to have noticed my arrival, though I didn't see Caius. Instead, I saw Clara standing in a grand room, with two men flanked beside her.

"Stop hiding in the bushes," Eres chastised.

"No one asked you. I'm scoping this out before I just waltz in, okay?"

She huffed. *"He knows you're coming, and you're out of your element here. Learn about your environment first. Sneak later."*

I shut her out, trying to listen in on the conversation, but the moment one of them touched Clara and she slapped his hand, rage coursed through me and drowned out any form of reason.

"That mother—" I muttered, then grabbed a pomegranate, stepped out from my hiding spot, and hurled it with everything I had as I stormed toward them. It crashed against the man's head, cracking open and spilling arils on the ground as I shouted, "Get your hands off her!"

"Ow!" His voice echoed off the ceilings and he cursed loudly, rubbing the side of his head while the other man made a poor attempt at covering his laugh.

My cousin whirled around, conflicting emotions lining her features. Happiness, relief, surprise, frustration. What had she already been through? Had I taken too long? Should I have come in after her immediately?

Now that I'd come fully into view, I realized that Caius had been there the entire time, and my grand entrance came to an abrupt halt. Standing idle with hands in his pockets, his relaxed posture was not at all what you would expect from someone who had just kidnapped a woman. Another surge of fury fueled me, while a whisper in my mind told me maybe I needed to think before acting.

Between the two options, anger won.

"You!"

"Me?" he replied, much to my irritation.

"Give me back my cousin right now."

He lifted his eyebrows. An inkling of the fire I'd seen in his eyes before made itself known. It wasn't metaphorical. It seemed as though literal fire gleamed within. "I never intended to keep her," he said, keeping his tone light. "She is free to go once you agree to stay."

"No." I figured when negotiating with Caius in this matter, it was wise to go in with my absolute baseline of wants, and that was simple. I did not want to be here at all. "I'm taking her back to Earth, safely. You can send me a letter or something. We can be pen pals. How about that?"

"What's a pen pal?" one of the men asked quietly, and his counterpart shrugged while still rubbing his head.

"Request denied," he said, taking his hands from his pockets and crossing his arms.

"Look, I think you know I have no intention of staying with you—"

"Then why did you bring luggage?" he asked, gesturing to the suitcase I'd left behind.

"That's . . . a valid question," I began, thinking of an alternative explanation. As soon as one formed, Eres groaned internally, urging me to stop. "I thought I could bring you a gift. A, uh, gesture of goodwill. Give me my cousin, you get my special homemade, one-of-a-kind moonshine."

Clara smacked her palm on her forehead and shook her head. Even I cringed as the words spilled out of my mouth.

"You want to . . . trade your cousin for liquor?"

"Yeah, okay, it sounded better in my head," I admitted, twisting the end of my braid with my fingers to give my hands something to do. "Look, you took her from our realm. *Our home.* You can't just take people against their will, just like you can't demand that they stay here."

"Perhaps it's frowned upon, but I wouldn't say 'you can't' do those things." He gave an annoyingly handsome smile, tilting his head as he spoke. "You are my mate, Reagan. I gave you what you asked for—"

I barked a laugh. "No, you didn't. What have you given me other than a headache?"

"You asked me to leave. You wanted the magic leaking out of the portal to stop. You said, if I recall, you wanted to keep your world safe. So I did what you asked, and I left. You were the one that wasn't willing to return the favor in kind. I only wanted the opportunity to talk to you."

All I could do was stand stoically, stunned at his counterargument. He was in the wrong, and yet he sounded so reasonable and made me sound as though I wasn't. A cruel smirk lined his full lips, making heat gather low in my belly.

Eres snorted internally, pretending to disguise her laugh as a cough.

"Bad horse. We don't like him, remember? Soulless. One."

"I'm not the one having the physical reaction. You are."

"You're not controlling that part?"

"Afraid not."

Caius's nostrils flared, as though he could sense my response to him. My cheeks flushed and I cleared my throat.

"Well, I'm here now. So talk." I crossed my arms uncomfortably and looked at the two other men in the room. "Who are they?"

"Oh, I know the answer to this one." Clara extended her thumb to the man with long brown hair, styled in braids, with his pointed ears sticking peeking through. The piercing nature of his blue eyes caught me off guard. "This is Abyssian. He seems okay so far."

"That one is dangerous," Eres whispered in my mind.

"We're in Tartarus. They're all dangerous."

"Fair point, but I don't sense Caius as a threat."

"Pretty sure the evil soul forcibly embedded in me deems him as safe. Don't get confused here."

She hummed, not sure she agreed.

"And this one," my cousin continued, gesturing vaguely to a man with a shaved head, thick muscles, and tattoos of feathers running down both of his arms. A leather vest with drawstrings on each side prevented me from seeing if they ran down his chest as well. "His name is Pol, which sounds like he's named after a chicken. Should have aimed your pomegranate at him."

"Also dangerous." She paused. *"Very."*

"Shush. They're all dangerous. I don't need the commentary."

He scowled at Clara's assessment, and Abyssian snorted.

"Now that everyone is acquainted, find somewhere to be," Caius ordered. The bald one turned on his heel and left without another word, but he aimed a glare at Clara before leaving. "Both of you." Abyssian lingered for a moment before he then lowered his gaze in respect and followed suit.

Clara attempted to subtly walk forward as if she'd been included in his dismissal . . . until her body slammed into some sort of invisible force field that prevented her from going any further.

"You stay here, remember? Do you think I just say things to hear myself speak?"

Clara tilted her head to the side, speaking in a faux innocent tone. "You mean you don't?"

"I told you that you're not leaving until she agrees to stay," Caius said, choosing to ignore her antics.

"I was just going with the two minions, but fine. I'll stay. It's not awkward or anything," she muttered. She met my eyes with an apologetic smile.

"You promised you wouldn't hurt my family," I said.

"I haven't hurt her. Ask her yourself," Caius replied. When I looked at Clara, she twisted her lips to the side, then shook her head.

I blew out a frustrated breath. "I know what you want, but if you make me stay here, this will only ever be one-sided," I said slowly, gauging his reaction.

A slight crease formed between his brows. "One year," he said. "That's all I ask. You give me one year where you agree to stay and Clara's free to go. I'll even keep the portal open so that your family can come and go as they wish." After a pause he added, "Except Nog. He's annoying."

Despite our current circumstances, Clara cackled, and I looked at her with wide eyes, giving a look that said "really?"

So our official negotiations had begun. I knew this was coming when I made the decision to pack up and cross through that cursed portal.

"How about a week?" I countered. Caius barked a rough laugh and somehow the sound of it was welcoming. It passed through me like the warmth of moonshine easing my aching bones after a hard dig on a Friday night. I found that physical response unexpected and completely annoying.

"Ten months," he said, giving more than I thought. I'd honestly expected him to not budge.

"How about two weeks?" At this rate, I'd get him down to a month. I could last a month, right?

"Ten months," he repeated.

Well, that glimmer of hope died quickly. I lowballed him once, but it appeared he wouldn't let me do that again.

"Six weeks."

"Eight months," he countered with a tilt of his head.

"Two months."

"Seven."

"Three."

"Six," he said, "and I won't go any lower. This is meeting you halfway when I don't have to at all. Consider it, what did you say earlier? Ah yes. A gesture of goodwill." When I opened my mouth to respond, he added, "Six months, and if you still don't want to be here, I'll let you go."

"You'll . . . let me go? Just like that?" He inclined his chin, but darkness clouded his eyes.

Eres and I both felt uneasy. The next question was perhaps the most important.

"And when that day comes—"

"*If*," he growled.

"Then what of . . . what I guard? You'll let me walk away as your mate, and . . . that's it?"

"I'm still working that out," he began, sighing between his responses. "But yes, I will let you go. You have my word."

"Fine," I whispered. "Six months." I tried not to focus on how long six months felt on Earth, much less what it could feel like as a prisoner.

An invisible thread pulled taut as the bargain we'd made solidified, the universe sealing it between us. The smile he gave me was blinding.

"Shall we kiss on it, then?"

"Yeah, right. Why not?" I mumbled, but my sarcasm

was misinterpreted. Caius closed the distance between us in two strides. My lips parted at our sudden proximity, and his mouth came down on mine with a passion I didn't expect.

My blood ignited. Everything else faded away, apart from his lips on mine. His taste invaded me, earthy and deep. He licked and nipped at me, causing me to shudder. I didn't realize until our tongues twined together that I'd kissed him back, and gods, it was good.

A faraway part of me was saying this was wrong. That I shouldn't be doing this, but that voice was silenced when his teeth scraped my bottom lip. I gasped at the sensation. Heat ricocheted through my chest, down to my belly, where it settled in my throbbing center.

"Ahem."

My cousin's fake cough startled me, pulling me out of the moment. I pushed at his chest, ignoring the hard muscle that met my hands. Caius released me but didn't move an inch.

Clearing my throat, I wiped my mouth with my wrist. "That was meant to be sarcasm."

Dark, bottomless eyes followed my hand's movement, and his nostrils flared. "Whose smell is on you?" he ground out.

"I don't know what you're talking about," I said, taking a step back. "People. I live with a bunch of them, you know."

"I know the scent of those I met in your home. This isn't someone from your family."

"What are you even—" I paused, flexing the aching joints in my right fist, and I groaned when I realized what he meant.

He snatched my wrist before I could pull it away. Caius

inspected the small split in the knuckles, the healing bruise, and the slight swelling. Then he sniffed my hand, and a low growl rumbled in his chest.

"What happened?"

"It's nothing," I said, yanking my hand back and taking a step to put some distance between us. "I just took care of something before I left."

Clara exhaled in an annoyed huff. "I knew I should have put up a shocking spell in case that douchebag showed up. I'd pay good money to watch him get electrocuted."

I closed my eyes and took a breath.

"It was him, wasn't it? The one that tried to claim you."

"I said I took care of it. I don't need you trying to protect me from something that's not a threat."

"The fact that his bite almost killed you and I had to save your life says otherwise." My cheek flushed.

"He showed up as I was leaving. I punched him in the nose. Then Nog went after him while I walked away. That's the end of that story."

He hummed, clearly not believing me.

"Look, I don't have a reason to lie to you. We agreed you and your people wouldn't harm him. I expect you to hold up your part of that bargain."

He hummed again, this time more like an aggravated snarl.

"So where are we staying?" Clara said, changing the subject. The blush drained away from my face as I whipped my head in her direction.

"You're not staying anywhere," I said, looking at her incredulously. "You need to go home."

Clara snorted. "Cute. I'm not leaving you here with the Soulless One. If you stay, I stay."

I bit the inside of my cheek. "I just agreed to stay so I could get you home."

Clara shrugged. "It's six months versus forever. I'll live—and I'll make sure you do too." Her eyes narrowed on Caius who stared right back.

"I have no intention of killing her."

"That's not the same thing as *not* killing her," Clara pointed out. "We're a packaged deal."

A frown formed between his brows as he considered her. "Am I going to regret letting you stay?"

"I never have been good at telling the future." Clara flashed him a saccharine smile. "But I'm not leaving. If you force me, I will keep fighting your stooges on the outside to get back through that portal every day of every week of every month. I am a powerful witch and I'm relentless."

He sighed, muttering something under his breath that I didn't understand. I used that moment to cut in.

"Hardheadedness runs in the family. Just . . . let her stay."

"Fair enough. Having family here is . . . comforting. It helps with the transition."

"Yeah, not the word I'd use," I said, my tone flat. "With that all settled, can someone show me to my room? Today has been a lot to process."

It wasn't every day you learned most of your life had been a lie, and you almost die but end up being saved by the one entity you thought wanted to kill you. Top it off with an interdimensional field trip? Definitely fell into the category of worst days ever.

"Hey, Pol," he called out, placing a hand on his hip while he looked at the ground. He used his other hand to pinch the bridge of his nose. "I know you're eavesdropping.

Make yourself useful and send for Isobel. Have her ready their rooms."

"Plural?" Clara piped up, asking the same question that had immediately come to mind.

"Already did that about ten minutes ago," he yelled back, his voice getting further away as he spoke.

Caius chuckled, then held his hand out, gesturing for us to go in front of him as we exited. Grabbing the bags I dropped, we then headed to our rooms. I tried to keep track of the twists and turns we took, but quickly got lost. Clara's troubled frown made me think the same happened to her.

A woman stood at the end of a hallway, large black doors on each side. With a modest smile and polite curtsy, she greeted us as we approached.

"Isobel, this is my mate. Please see—"

"Not his mate," I cut in quickly. While I had no idea how I would get out of Tartarus without dying—or giving up what I guarded from him—accepting him as my mate was out of the question, and being introduced as such was a no-go from me. "Just Reagan."

The warmth of her expression quickly soured the moment I shut him down, and that caught me off guard.

"Thank you for getting their rooms prepared. I can handle it from here. Will you make sure the kitchen knows we have extra guests?"

"Of course, Your Majesty." Isobel hurried off, but I didn't miss the side-eye she gave me as she left.

Caius turned to Clara and pointed at the door across the hall. "That one is yours. Give us a moment."

She gave me a quick glance to make sure I was okay with it, and when I nodded, she went into her room muttering that he could have at least asked her nicely. Sometimes it was easy to see the resemblance between her and Nog. At the sudden thought of him, sadness began to consume me.

"Isobel is going to be one of your chambermaids, but you didn't make the greatest first impression. I don't want either of you to be uncomfortable, so call for me if you need something, or if the room isn't to your liking."

"Earth is to my liking," I replied, feeling the heaviness of the day beginning to weigh on me.

Caius hummed under his breath and closed his eyes briefly. "Do you intend on acting like this and staying in your room for six months?"

"The thought crossed my mind, yes."

"That's truly a shame," he said, taking a step past the border of my space bubble. I receded, and then bumped into the door. "If I have to, I will spend every day, of every week, of every month trying to show you who I truly am, and not what you believe me to be. I saved you because I recognize you as my mate. Not for what you guard inside you. I *will* make you understand."

Mimicking my cousin's wording was clever, and it certainly drove the point home. I never believed that I was safe, but I knew he truly believed I was his mate. For now.

"I guess we'll see about that, won't we?" Reaching behind me, I found the knob and twisted it, pushing the door open and putting some distance between us.

"Indeed." The muscle in Caius's jaw clenched, and his eyes flashed. "Get some rest. We have plenty of time to talk tomorrow."

"Goodnight, Caius." The words were forced, much like my decision to take up residency here. I'd been quick to temper for most of our interactions, and I wasn't sure how much longer he was willing to put up with me. Basic survival skills said I should be nice, but exhaustion coupled with the skeptical part of me that had been warned about him my entire life stupidly threw caution to the wind.

"Oh, and Reagan?" I paused, not shutting the door completely. "Take a bath and get that shifter's scent off you. While you're here, you belong to me." I shut the door and cupped my hand over my mouth..

You belong to me.

The words lingered long after his footsteps had faded, and another door slammed shut. The memory of his lips on mine quickly flashed in my mind. My cheeks warmed in an instant. Closing the door, I put my back to it and slid down until I landed on the floor. Scrubbing my hands down my face, I stifled a sob as hot tears fell unbidden.

"Welcome to Tartarus," I whispered to myself, the emptiness in the room already haunting me.

I was trapped in a realm created to imprison monsters, and it was just my luck I was mated to the biggest one of them all.

CHAPTER 12

CAIUS

I turned away from Reagan's door to find Abyssian leaning against the wall. Pol stood opposite of him; shrewd eyes boring into me. I sighed, then turned for my room.

They followed without needing to be told. It wasn't a long walk. Pol had correctly placed Reagan at the end of the same corridor from my suite. Creamy white doors flung open at my approach, the magic of the castle recognizing its master and responding without needing to be directed.

I approached the bar cart by the fireplace, pouring myself whiskey. They didn't even have the decency to wait for me to have my drink before starting in on the interrogation.

"For centuries all you could think about was being reunited with your soul, and now you're throwing that away for what exactly? A mate that doesn't want you?"

I made a sound in my throat. "I'm not throwing it away. I'm simply choosing to play more than one game. Reagan is my mate. She's also the guardian. Why must I pick?"

"Is he serious?" Pol asked Abyssian, making me lift my brows. It's not like they got on during the best of times.

"It appears so," my brother said with a heavy sigh.

Pollux turned back toward me, his gaze nothing short of hawkish. How fitting. "She has to die for you to get your soul back. There's no way around that. That's why."

I made another sound that I meant to be nonchalant, but it came out more as a growl. "That we know of. Maybe there is a way. It's not like we've invested much time into finding one, and with the portal to Earth, now we can."

He pressed his fists into his eyes, rubbing in frustration. "You don't even know her, Caius. And she's very obviously not all that keen on knowing you—"

"I'm well fucking aware," I said, starting to lose patience with this. Reagan wasn't the only one who'd had a long day. "Why do you think I bargained for six months? So I can get to know her."

"And what are you going to do if there's no way? Are you certain she's even your mate and that you're not confu—"

"*Don't* finish that sentence. Styx already asked, but she wasn't there that day. She wasn't there to help me pick up the broken pieces. You were. I damn well know the difference between my soul residing in a guardian versus the pull of a mate bond. I'll never forget the feeling of hopelessness when I was ripped in half, and the overwhelming loss and insurmountable grief when they forced it into Abraxia. It is forever burned into my memory, Pol. Reagan may be her descendant, but the commonalities end there."

Pol sighed. "It had to be said. On the off chance you weren't thinking clearly."

I lifted my brows at him. "Not thinking clearly?"

"He just means that Reagan is a beautiful woman. No

one could blame you if you were confused," Abyssian started.

"Fuck off. Don't try to placate me."

My brother lifted both hands in mock surrender, inclining his head. "So, you what? Plan to get to know her? Play house for the next six months? What happens if there isn't a way to remove your soul without killing her? What then?"

I grit my teeth. "I don't know. I'll deal with it then."

Pol laughed coldly and Abyssian elbowed him.

"And if she doesn't fall for your . . . charms? Are you going to kill her for it?"

"No," I snapped harshly. "And if I was that sort of god, I would hope you'd have found a way to end me eons ago, before Pious imprisoned us."

Pol lowered his gaze in agreement, acknowledging without words he went a step too far in his questioning. Abyssian flopped back on one of the loveseats, throwing an arm over the back.

"So you're going to try to woo her," my brother said, changing the subject. "I can give you some pointers if you'd like. You know how the ladies flock to me—"

"Because they think you're one of them," Pol coughed.

I took a sip of my whiskey, hiding my smirk behind the glass.

Abyssian glared at our spymaster. "For your information, ladies like the long hair. Why do you think I keep it this way?"

"I figured it was to attract Broca and other assorted barn animals."

Abyssian snatched a glass off my bar cart and threw it at Pol, who ducked, missing his cheekbone by a hairsbreadth. A booming laugh echoed through my room.

"That was one time, you fucker!"

"One time too many. She's unhinged, and she's half goat, man. Just shows you really will fuck anything with a hole."

"Better than forced abstinence."

"Nothing forced here," Pol said with self-assurance. "I choose not to stick my dick in crazy. And around here? They're all fucking their way to the top. No thank you."

Abyssian rolled his eyes skyward. "It's *fucking*, not marriage."

"Says the goat fucker."

"That's it—" Abyssian jumped to his feet.

"Sit down," I said, shoving the loveseat forward and hitting the backs of his knees to force him down. He couldn't decide whether to glare at me or Pol. "For fuck's sake, you two are worse than a married couple."

"Nah," Abyssian said, gesturing at his counterpart. "That's him and the witch. What was her name? Claire? Clara? That's it." He snapped his fingers. "She's hot too. Since Pol is waiting for marriage, I might take her to bed one night. I'm sure once they're settled in, she'll be more than happy—"

"You'll do no such thing," I said, imagining how that scenario would play out. Abyssian was an insufferable flirt and made no attempts at hiding that he liked to fuck around, but he was allergic to commitment. The last thing I needed was him to play with the witch and then discard her like a broken toy. Something told me Reagan wouldn't take kindly to that, and I would be the one who'd have to deal with it.

"Are you serious?" my brother asked.

"Dead serious. Besides, I have an assignment for you. Both of you. I need to find a way to remove my soul from

Reagan. Pol, I'd like you to cross the portal and search there. Start with her family and see what they know. Abyssian, you can search here in Tartarus."

Pol's mouth dropped open. "Why am I being sent earthside if he's the one that wants to fuck the relative?"

"Because you scare people here and that tactic won't work. Her family is angry. They aren't going to fear you, trust me, but they will do anything for Reagan. If they have any leads or information, I have a feeling they'll share it if you get to know them. For all Abyssian's faults, he's good at getting people to talk and would be better suited here." My brother started to preen, but I shut him down. "Making a pass at her sister or aunt won't win us any favors either, so he's staying, you go."

Pol snorted, and Abyssian muttered under his breath, but I chose to ignore it.

"If we're doing the legwork, what will you be doing, brother? Taking long walks on a volcanic beach with that pretty little mate of yours—"

"Call her pretty again and I'll cut out your tongue and feed it to you."

Abyssian threw his head back, laughing with ease. "Touchy, touchy."

"Possessive much?" Pol added.

I ran my fingers through my hair, looking out the window at the twin moons. "Something like that."

CHAPTER 13

REAGAN

Blinding light filled the room, making me wince.

"What the . . .?" I slurred, wiping drool from the corner of my mouth with the back of my hand. After Caius left last night, I'd collapsed into bed on the plush, comfortable mattress.

A tall woman with broad shoulders and a thick blonde braid that fell to her waist stood by the windows. The curtains had been flung open, and all the fairy lights and lanterns had been lit. I sat up quickly. "Who are you?"

"Jana," she said, giving a bland curtsy.

I hadn't heard that name yesterday, and I still had no idea what she was doing in my room. My confusion apparently came through loud and clear.

"Your chambermaid," she supplied in a flat tone.

Uneasiness swirled in my chest as nausea churned. "Hi, Jana, I'm Reagan."

"I know," she replied sharply. "You were supposed to be at breakfast with His Majesty half an hour ago."

"Oh, I didn't realize . . ." I scrubbed the sleep from my

eyes. "He didn't say anything. Guess he just expected me to read his mind."

Jana pursed her lips. "Perhaps if you had been sharing a room with him, you might have stirred when he woke." I wasn't going to touch that with a ten-foot pole, but her irritation with me was confusing.

She didn't seem to be some jealous ex, and for that I was grateful. The last thing I needed was some territorial woman mad at me for thinking I wanted to be the Queen of Monsters . Oh gods, was there a Queen of Monsters?

These were important questions I should have asked before this morning. He may think I'm his mate, but that didn't mean there wasn't someone here before me. Ugliness unfurled in my chest, and I squashed that down with emotions that I wanted to pretend weren't there, especially this early in the morning. Was it morning? I actually had no idea.

Jana sighed, clasping her hands. "I need to make your bed."

"Oh, I'm sorry," I said, swinging my legs over the side. A light bulb went off in my head. "Look, I can make my bed. It's okay. I know you're supposed to do what he tells you to, but you don't have to do his bidding here. You're safe with me."

Jana looked at me as though I had two heads. "I beg your pardon, miss?"

That little light bulb fizzled right out.

"Um, I meant . . . you don't have to be . . ." My inability to choose better words didn't help her understand me at all, and I let out a loud breath. "All I meant by it was you seemed put out that you had to take care of me. You have an entire castle. I'm sure when he made you add me to the list of responsibilities, it wasn't wanted."

Jana blinked several times, considering me. "We aren't slaves here, miss. We work here, by choice. He doesn't *make* us do anything."

"He's your . . . employer? You want to be here?" That was unexpected, and I hadn't considered the possibility.

"Yes," she answered in exasperation. "And I would like to change your sheets and make your bed now, so . . ."

"Right." I got out of bed, moving out of her way as she began to silently pull off the sheets. She wasn't outwardly aggressive, but something had clearly transpired between us, and I wanted to remedy the situation. I subtly lifted my chin and scented the air. She was a shifter, but I wasn't sure which kind. A note of pine was there, earthy, with a final sharpness that reminded me of a winter frost. I've never smelled such a combination before, which ruled out all the ordinary breeds of shifters that I was familiar with.

It was an unspoken rule back home that we didn't ask what kind of animal someone shifted into. It was considered rude, and I wondered if the same sort of rule applied in Tartarus. Jana already didn't seem to like me, so instead of potentially sticking my foot in my mouth, I thought it best to not ask.

Looking around for my satchel, it was nowhere to be found. My heart skipped a beat. "Jana, do you know where my bag went by chance?"

She lifted her eyebrows at me, seemingly unimpressed, before pointing to the bathroom door on the opposite wall. "It's by the tub."

I opened my mouth to thank her, but her frosty demeanor was too much for me to ignore. "Have I done something to offend you?"

She stopped, turning to face me. "No, miss."

I hummed. "See, I would believe you, except you seem

put out by my being here. I assure you, it's not by choice. I'm sorry for intruding on your space or whatever is happening that's caused—"

Jana scoffed, pursing her lips with a subtle shake of her head. "Unbelievable," she muttered.

"What?" I asked, caught off guard.

She schooled her features, and smoothed out the smock that covered her uniform. "Our king is a good man. He's kind, and generous, and treats his subjects well. Then there's you."

"Me?" I repeated, completely taken aback by the force of her words. "What the hell have I done? You don't even know me."

"Word travels fast here, miss. And your words? They traveled quite quickly. We all know you're his mate, and we all know you've had no problem shutting him down in public. You didn't even give him a chance." She sighed, appraising me from head to toe. "Isobel was right. He deserves so much better than you."

My jaw dropped, and I stood there, unable to defend myself. Too much had just been said for me to even process it. He came to my world with the intention of killing me. *He* was a good man? *He* deserved better? I was the shithead in their scenario?

How dare they.

I'd been dragged to Tartarus and cajoled into staying here for six months. I was being held hostage. These people had blinders on. After mentally counting to ten, I gathered my thoughts.

"Look, Jana," I began, knowing full well my voice was terse. "I actually agree with you. He deserves someone else. I understand your allegiance to Caius, or whatever it is you want to call it. There are things at play here you and Isobel and everyone else don't understand. If you don't mind, I'd like some privacy now." I pointedly gestured to the door.

Jana narrowed her eyes and her nostrils flared, but she curtsied and did as I'd asked.

I scrubbed my hands down my face and groaned, turning toward the bathroom. Last night I was too tired to do much of anything. My clothes were clean enough, but my body still had a layer of grime on it left over from my dying episode. If I could smell myself, everyone else could too.

Cold tile floors nipped at my bare feet. The bathroom was elegant, but dark, and inside a dozen candles had been lit. A large basin was already filled to the brim, with a selection of soaps and bottles on the edge. I dipped my knuckles in to find the water was as frigid as the floor.

This place just keeps getting better, I thought to myself.

Quickly scrubbing my body first, I managed to figure out which bottle was shampoo, and which was conditioner. I washed my hair as quickly as I could, not wanting to sit around here any longer than I had to. My teeth were already chattering.

Giant fluffy cream towels sat next to the silver tray of soaps and cleansers. I wrapped my hair in one and my body in the other, quickly drying myself. My bedroom was significantly warmer than the bathroom, and I had a good mind to burrow beneath the covers to regulate my body temperature.

I tucked the cream towel under my armpits, wrapping it tightly around my chest and re-entered the main suite. Only a few steps in and I felt the instant sensation that I was being watched. I looked up to find Caius leaning against the wall, one hand in his pocket.

Physically, he looked delicious. His posture was relaxed,

but it was somehow sexy, and that didn't escape my notice. I reminded myself he was my captor. I didn't want to give him that satisfaction of knowing that he affected me in any way. So instead of turning and going back into the bathroom like a pansy, I kept walking until I got to my suitcase next to the bed.

"Apparently I was late for breakfast," I said, attempting to sound nonchalant despite my pounding heart.

Caius shrugged. "You were exhausted. I told them not to wake you. Although I'm surprised your cousin's voice didn't carry from the atrium. The shouting match she had with Pol this morning could have woken the dead. Something about switching his water out with some sort of homebrew hard liquor." My lips twitched. She must have come in here and gotten a jar of my moonshine for the sole purpose of annoying him. How very Clara.

"I was exhausted. Still am. So, what are you doing here?"

I didn't want to look at him, but the silence left me with little choice. Dark eyes threatened to swallow me whole as he appraised my body, everything from my towel-wrapped hair to the ends of my chipped toenail polish.

"Jana told me that you'd woken up. I wanted to come check on you and make sure that you slept all right."

I snorted. I wondered what else Jana had told him.

"Right as rain. I can't ask for much more than that after being dragged to Hell."

"Not Hell," he supplied. "Also, I didn't drag you. You walked through that portal on your own two feet.

Were we really going to start that this morning? He and I both knew the only reason I came across at all, let alone stayed, was because of Clara. Pretending like he didn't kidnap her wasn't going to change that, and I didn't have the desire to repeat myself.

Caius just stood there, and surprisingly, it wasn't awkward. My words were clipped, and my tone was sharp, but whatever invisible current ran between us was charged. Being near the Soulless One while carrying half his soul was going to take some getting used to.

"What did you really come here for?" I said, shifting my weight and holding up my towel.

"To take you out," he answered. "The first moon cycle has already passed, and I thought you might want to have a tour. Get to know the castle."

"I'd rather be alone," I said, despite the fact he was offering exactly what I wanted.

"You know, it's not a bad place, Tartarus." Caius turned his head, looking out the window before he sighed. "You can't just spend the next six months in hiding."

I laughed. "The first thing you need to learn is never tell a woman what she can't do. We will go out of our way just to achieve it, and if spite is the only thing that drives us, so be it. So, yes, I could hide in here for six months if I wanted to." Caius inclined his head, and he waited for me to continue, but I didn't miss the way his jaw clenched.

"And the second?"

"We made a deal that I would spend six months here, but we didn't make a deal that I would spend any of it with you."

"You only see me as the villain," he said softly, taking steps toward me. I backed up, bumping into a piece of furniture. My heart was racing, but I wouldn't stand down.

"Is there any other way to see you?" I asked, holding my chin up in defiance.

"You haven't seen me be a villain, Reagan. You only

think you know who I am. Would you like me to be that man instead? Is that what you really want?" he asked softly, his eyes swirling with dark glittery threads as he advanced another step, making the space between us non-existent.

I swallowed thickly. "Do whatever you want, Caius. It'll just prove my point about you. You'd do well to remember that the villain never gets the girl."

He leaned into me, pressing his body against mine. The dresser at my back pinned me in place. Scared, vulnerable, out of my depth, and I *still* felt my traitorous core clench. He bent down, his lips near my ear as he whispered, his hot breath heating my skin.

"Depends on which story you read."

CHAPTER 14

REAGAN

Clara sat on the edge of my bed, painting her nails while I sat hunched over in an armchair in my room.

"He's right, you know," she said, after I'd told her about the exchange I'd had with Caius three days prior.

I'd holed myself up in my room, doing nothing but sleeping and basically feeling sorry for myself. I ate what Isobel and Jana brought me, and bathed only because they drew my bathwater—not that it was relaxing. They had a job to do, and even though they hated me, I let them in and just kept quiet until they left. There was no way I wanted to spend six months doing that.

"I know he's right, but there is no way I would tell him."

"You shut me out too," she said, pausing after a brush stroke to look at me. "I snuck in here while you slept just to make sure you were okay."

I sighed. "I guess I needed to have a pity party for one. No invites. I didn't mean to push you away." A tear fell, and I wiped it away.

She smiled softly. "Look, you were dealt a weird hand in

life. A ton of choices have been taken away from you, and you never had the opportunity to feel bad for yourself. You've always taken care of other people, and sort of had this giant responsibility on your shoulders that also required you keep it together for the sake of humanity. Honestly, three days to fall apart isn't that much and it's kinda overdue if you think about it."

I laughed quietly. "Clara the therapist. Who knew?"

She shushed me, making a show of looking around the room. "Keep it down, or people will hear you. They'll know I'm smart and they'll want to talk to me about stuff. Your life is enough to handle."

"Okay, okay," I said with a smile. "You can just be my advisor."

"At your service." She waved her hand in a dramatic gesture.

"All right, advisor. What do you recommend I do here?"

She shrugged. "Oh that's easy. You give him a chance."

My mouth fell open, then I shook my head. "Nope. Never mind. You're fired."

Clara's head tilted back, and she barked a laugh. "I'm serious, though, Rea. Give him a chance. You have six months. Do something with it."

"Oh my god, you are serious . . ."

She set down the polish and shuffled her body forward to give me her full attention. "Yes, I am. I've been sneaking around and listening to people talk, and I've been asking questions to anyone that will have a conversation with me."

"What's this have to do with me?"

"Everything. They love him, Reagan. Caius is revered in this place. Supposedly it was awful before he came, but he changed it, and Tartarus is definitely not Hell. The people here have nothing but good things to say about him. He visits the villages and holds townhall meetings where people get to speak up, and apparently, he even attends those. He's just and fair, a one-with-the-people-type, and . . ."

"And?" I prompted when she'd trailed off.

"And they know you've rejected him as a mate, and people are upset about it."

I sighed. "Of course they are. Butting in on something that isn't their business."

"They don't know you're the guardian or anything like that, at least not that I heard, so they think it's their business. What they know is they want their king to be happy, and the mate he found has publicly rejected him."

"I didn't reject him here. That happened in The Crossroads," I pointed out.

She shook her head. "When you told Isobel you weren't his mate, you might as well have rejected him. She told everyone in the kitchen, and it spread like wildfire."

I sat up straight, feeling defensive even though she wasn't attacking me. "So you think that because people are mad at me that I should just roll over and give him a chance?"

She scrunched her nose. "Hardly, but I do think maybe learning about him on your own terms might be worth something."

My defensiveness wilted away, and in its place was my reality. I picked at the end of my braid, tugging at little split ends. "And then what, Clara? I don't want a mate, and he could have me killed at the end of all this, agreement or not. He doesn't get his other half returned, or the person he thinks is his mate, and he's just going to let me walk away with both my heart and his soul? Not likely. He may not hold the knife, but someone else will."

"Then you've got six months to live," she said with a lift of her shoulder, like it was just easy to announce my upcoming death. "Better to spend it enjoying yourself than in self-imposed imprisonment."

"I can't believe you're advocating for this place," I muttered, dropping my braid.

"It's not home, but it's also not all that terrible here so far. The no sunlight is *weird*, but otherwise the food is good. Would be better if you cooked for me," she added with a wink. "The people have actually been really friendly, and the bathtubs are divine."

"Sure, the tubs are great, but bathing in the Mississippi River is warmer than that water."

She looked at me in confusion. "What? The water is perfect. The castle is built into the side of a volcano. I guess the water is warmed by it somehow. Natural thermals or something like that."

I blinked rapidly, processing her words. "Wait, you get hot baths?"

"You don't?"

Three short raps on the door sounded, and Jana entered. They liked to do that here, just knock and enter whether or not I invited them.

"His Majesty has requested you join him for dinner," she said flatly, a bored expression on her face.

I stared at her for a moment, realizing just how much she disliked me. Here my cousin was getting the royal treatment and hot water, while I was being shunned. I understood. So I'd obviously made a bad impression, and they wanted to make me suffer for it.

I sighed, glancing at Clara when I mouthed, "Do I have to?"

"Go on," she urged quietly, shooing me toward the bathroom. "Even Belle had dinner with the Beast."

Honestly after my cousin had mentioned Beauty having dinner with the Beast, a part of me imagined dancing teacups and a long, ornate table. The reality was quite the opposite. Rather than opulent, he'd gone with a laid-back approach to dinner. Instead of a grand dining hall, we were in a cozy room, seated at a six-seat rectangular table. A grand fireplace was centered on the wall, lit and flickering, but not creating too much heat. It was strange, as though it was a cool fire, fueled by magic. Warm furnishings accentuated the space. We sat at opposite ends of the table, eating each course in an awkward silence that had dragged on for so long, the sound of my own chewing became deafening.

Every now and then someone would come in to check on us and serve the next course. The tension in the room was palpable, and a few of the servants gave me dirty looks. Clara's words came back to mind. What I had said spread like wildfire. It seemed like the best thing that I could do was be pleasant and hope that replaced the narrative. Jana and Isobel had already been running me cold baths. Who knows what else they would do to me over the next six months?

I cleared my throat nervously but couldn't think of what to say, so I went with just. "I don't really know what to talk about."

Caius hadn't taken his eyes off me. "I wasn't sure if you were enjoying the silence. You've been dead set on avoiding me. We all wondered if you actually planned on following through with hiding away for six months."

Pushing aside the desire to be defensive, I forced a small smile. "I'd considered it. You would deserve it, you know."

He raised his brows? "Do I? I feel that I've been most accommodating, all things considered. Your cousin is here to stay with you. I've provided you with rooms across the hall from each other. Clara has even started a list of things to bring back from the other side of the portal. I understand you'd rather be home but look at this from my point of view. My mate wants to leave. I want her to stay, and I want her to want to stay."

Setting down my fork, I placed my hands in my lap and sat back. "All of that is true, yes. In that regard, I'm only kind of sorry for being bitchy, but I'm also not sorry at all. You were going to come through that door to kill me. It's hard to let go of that. First impressions, and all."

He pursed his lips dabbing his face with a napkin and setting it down he placed both hands on the table nodded quietly and looked up. "Fair enough. I think we need to lay it all out on the table, so to speak. That way we can start fresh."

I huffed. Doubtful. "Okay," I said slowly. "How do you propose we do that?"

"By being honest. You're upset because my intention walking through that door was to kill you, yes. I can't change that any more than you can change the fact you're a guardian. It wasn't personal."

"It was personal to me," I said, clenching my teeth and trying to calm my anger.

"Of course it was. Let me ask you this. If reversed, are

you telling me you wouldn't kill someone to get your soul back? Regardless of why you think it was taken. It's yours. Would you or would you not take it back?"

I wanted to protest and tell him I would never do that. I would never harm another person. That wasn't entirely accurate. We lived in a strange world. Did I want to kill anyone? Absolutely not. I hated the idea of it. Would I do it to defend our family? Yes. Would I do it to get back my soul? I sighed. Probably.

"Fair enough," I conceded, looking down to my hands and picking at my fingernails.

"I didn't know you were my mate. I didn't know you, but I would like to. I want you to give me a chance. The very little that I do know about you is from what Clara has told me."

My head snapped up. "You've been speaking to my cousin about me?"

He shrugged. "I had to. You didn't give me the opportunity to speak to you myself."

"What did she tell you about me?" Clara and I were going to have a chat. She'd failed to mention this little tidbit.

"For one, she told me that you're an incredible cook. Her favorite in the entire family, apparently. She told me that you and your cousin Jo are very close and always have been. She told me you loved to paint; that you will disappear for hours to paint whenever you're stressed. She also said you are secretive and it's hard for you to trust people."

"Can you blame me?"

"Not at all. It's hard for me to trust people as well. Once you're betrayed and thrown in a realm of your own making, it leaves a lasting mark." He drank what looked like whiskey, slamming it back before setting the glass down.

"Oh yeah? Who betrayed you?" I couldn't help but think of how my mother was murdered by the people that raised her. The people she thought loved her and only wanted the best for her. The same people that raised me and planned on doing the very same.

Any attempts at civility were soured when those thoughts flooded my mind. We were forced into guardianship. Forced to bear the burden of the ward. Betrayed by our caretakers. Whatever he did to lose half his soul was his own fault.

Caius shook his head lightly. "That's a story for another time."

His features hardened for a moment, and I studied the angles of his jaw, and the smoothness of his perfect skin. He was gorgeous—if I were into the idea of falling for my captor, of course. Which I wasn't.

"Could roll around a bed with him for fun."

Eres barged into my thoughts the moment I'd let my guard down.

"You need to knock or something first. And no, I will not do anything of the sort."

"Just a taste."

I groaned internally. *"You need a bell around your neck."*

Eres scoffed deeply. *"You need to accept that we are one now."*

It was my turn to scoff. *"Not until we sort some of our shit out, and I'm kinda busy dealing with this. You are just going to have to wait."*

Before she could respond, I closed the barrier between us, but I could still feel her seething at being pushed away. Her irritation leeched beneath my skin and made me feel itchy.

"Fine." Reaching for a glass, I took a sip of water.

"Another time, then. Anything you care to share with me now?"

"I hate radishes."

I hummed. "I was thinking of something with more substance."

"No really. They're awful. If they end up in my food, it just ruins the entire day. I forbid them in the castle. Not really a fan of turnips either."

I gave him an unimpressed glare. "So aside from your disdain for root vegetables, what else? Clara told me the people of Tartarus think you're pretty great. Must be they hate radishes too."

"I hear the note of sarcasm in your voice. Either you love those demon vegetables, and I've offended you, or you find it hard to believe that the people of this world are happy with me. I'm betting on the latter."

"Yes, if that's what you want me to say. I find it hard to believe." I wasn't sure why I was so irritable. Maybe Eres's emotions were leaking into my own.

"And why is that? Would your reasoning be based on your extensive knowledge of me?" My silence spoke for me, and he nodded, getting up from the table. "You think you know so much about me, but you know nothing, Reagan. Only what you were told. It's a shame."

I stood up as he approached me. "And why is that a shame, Caius? Do you think a dinner and some surface level conversation is going to change anything?"

"You're my mate, Reagan. I feel that in my bones. You trying to push me away won't change that." He tilted his head as he considered me. "I'll get through to you eventually. Six months is a long time."

"That's it? You'll get through to me?"

"What did you expect?"

"You aren't going to stand here and tell me you're wonderful and magnanimous and that I should just accept you as a mate and live happily ever after?"

"Would it work?"

"No."

"Then why bother?"

"I don't know. I figured you wanted me to believe you."

"And you will."

"How?" I crossed my arms, jutting my hip out to the side as I shifted my posture.

Caius traced a finger down the curve of my cheek, and my body stiffened. His touch sent tingles over my skin. Taking my hand in his, he pressed his lips to it, kissing softly before letting go. When he looked at me, he let a few seconds pass where we stared in silence and my heart pounded.

"Actions speak louder than words, love. Just wait."

He exited the room, and I ran my fingers through my hair, huffing in frustration. I picked up my glass and threw it across the table toward a painted picture of him.

It shattered just as two dinner servants walked in the room, their eyes wide in shock. Just what I needed. They'd just witnessed the only two seconds I'd lost my cool.

No doubt this incident would spread like wildfire.

I just hoped the flames wouldn't consume me as well.

CHAPTER 15

REAGAN

I lay on my side, curled and content in my slumber. The bed beneath me was warm and hard—harder than a bed could possibly be. My eyelids cracked open, then I blinked.

This wasn't my room, not from back home or the one in Caius' castle.

Panic said I should sit up and scramble away, but my body didn't move. The thought of paralysis sent a chilling fear through me. What had happened?

While my thoughts were racing, my head tilted back, as if I were controlled by someone else. I peered up at a beautiful and familiar face. A smile graced my lips as I stared up at Caius. His strong chiseled jaw was slack with sleep. No tension lined his eyes. His features were smooth and at peace. I could reach out and run my fingertips over his straight nose and high cheekbones—if I wanted. I could taste his full lips—if I were in control.

None of these actions were my own.

Instead, my hands splayed across his broad chest and his bronze arms encircled me. The short style of his hair was replaced by a long, thick braid that disappeared beneath his heavy body.

He looked different than how I'd seen him only hours before, but there was no mistaking him.

Slowly, my body sat up. My fingers trailed over his abdomen, testing to see if he stirred.

While I wasn't in control of my actions, and I could feel everything this body felt, my thoughts were still my own. Gods, I had questions. First off, what was happening and what kind of mushroom-induced nightmare was this? Was I in the body of one of his former lovers? I really hoped not. The idea made me queasy. How could I throw up if I was in someone else's body?

When Caius didn't wake, I lifted one bare leg, gliding it across his hips so that I, she—whoever she was that I was in—could straddle him. Oh, dear lord. This was really happening. I was going to have sex with Caius, and it wasn't even me.

Caius groaned as she lowered her hips, grinding against him. Nausea swirled in my gut as the nameless woman arched her back, stretching forward like a cat. I could feel her love for him, her desperate longing . . . but something about it wasn't right. It was distant.

While she grazed his lips with her own, the woman used her free hand to reach for something in the far corner. A glint of metal made my pulse quicken. She grabbed a knife from the table on the other side of him.

Oh *gods*. It was like watching a scene in a horror film where you wanted to scream and let the person know they were about to be murdered.

Only this wasn't a movie, and Caius was alive and well, not to mention he was a primordial that couldn't be killed. Even with that knowledge, fear lanced through me.

"Abraxia," he hummed against her mouth, still half-asleep. His eyes didn't open as he deepened the kiss, and she parted her lips in earnest. I was going to be sick. Not because of what they were doing, but because of her intentions. I could see them all too clearly from the passenger seat and I couldn't stop it.

Her fingers curled around the base of his braid where the hair was only a couple of inches from his skull.

"I love you," she whispered.

The knife swiftly moved with a flick of her wrist.

Confusion swirled within me, followed by agonizing pain. She'd cut his hair, not his throat—and yet somehow I knew this was worse.

This felt deeper.

This was betrayal.

I closed my eyes against the agony, or I tried to at any rate. I was still inside her head, still watching in complete shock as she shifted her gaze between the ten-inch-long braid and the balcony. Uncertainty seemed to lodge within her throat.

I wished I could scream. That I could convey the bone shattering, soul-cleaving pain inside me. That I could curse her by name.

Abraxia.

It hit me where I had heard that name before.

She was the first guardian. The first woman to bear Caius's soul.

I had no idea how or why, but I knew without a doubt that what she held in her trembling hands was his very soul. Or a piece of it.

Caius shuddered, his muscles spasming as they tightened in shock. The ground beneath her feet quaked as Abraxia leapt from the bed and began to back away.

How could she do that after saying she loved him?

Grunts of pain echoed like thunder. Who knows? Maybe it was. In the wake of a primordial's despair, the heavens broke open, and storms consumed the earth.

This was not the story I'd been told.

Abraxia ran onto the balcony just as my vision went dark. I couldn't make out what she was saying or who she was talking to. All I knew was an overwhelming ache and gut-wrenching suffering. Not even death was this terrible. It hurt, but not nearly as bad as one's essence being split in two. I'd never felt anything so all-consuming, not even on my deathbed.

"*Wake up.*" The harsh words whispered across my consciousness. I barely heard them. "*Wake up.*" The same phrase repeated; soft, yet urgent.

I couldn't listen to them when I was having trouble separating myself from the torment Abraxia had put Caius through. Somehow, the remnants of his soul inside me, the part that I carried, felt his pain. It empathized with his anguish and recognized it as its own, thereby subjecting me to the same horrors.

Maybe the piece I carried wanted to hurt me because I was the guardian. Maybe it wanted to make me feel what he went through, or maybe watching it happen all over again simply triggered the response. Despite thousands of years having passed, the soul was able to recall what happened in perfect clarity. Whatever the reasoning was, I didn't know it.

That voice, that unrelenting whisper, spoke louder. "*Wake up, you infernal human.*"

Human? I clawed for my consciousness, not sure how but trying, nonetheless.

"Eres?" I called out. *"Why are you doing this? Why are you making me relive—"*

"WAKE UP!" The power in her shout threatened to blast apart the last remainders of my mind. I held myself together—held those pieces tight—while I pushed for the surface.

My eyes flew open as I inhaled.

Air filled my lungs, but the relief was short-lived as soon as I saw the knife poised overhead.

My consciousness snapped into place like a rubber band. I thanked my lucky stars for the countless safety drills my family and I would practice. That was the world we lived in. While we had never been attacked in The Crossroads, my training would come in handy in Tartarus.

I rolled to the side, flinging my arm up to protect my neck. I was ready for it to make contact, but nothing prepared me for the searing heat of the blade when it lodged itself in my forearm. Air hissed between my teeth.

Whipping my left leg back, my abdominal muscles locked, and I caught my attacker's jaw with the curve of my ankle. She hadn't expected me to react so quickly, completely caught off guard when I used the full power of my leg and core to throw her sideways by attempting to pin her neck to the bed.

Blonde hair. Ice-blue eyes. Stockier build.

Jana?

"What are you doing?" I choked out, but the words were scratchy and raw from screaming in my nightmare.

My raspy voice triggered a flood of memories from the horrid dream, and the overwhelming sense of pain and betrayal threatened to pull me back under. I did the best I could to shake my head of them so I didn't get swallowed in the darkness.

Jana lifted my ankle and twisted, jarring me back into reality. The pain, while lesser, acted as an anchor to the present. My hands curled into fists as she said, "You don't deserve him." Her sentence was punctuated with a snap as my ankle fractured.

What. The. Actual. Hell.

I wouldn't give her the satisfaction of screaming. Through gritted teeth, I panted. "You're jealous and *this* is how you choose to handle it?" I reached across my body to grab the dagger. I really hoped that it didn't hit my radial artery, because if so, I was going to bleed out within minutes once I dislodged it.

Not that I had many options with a broken ankle.

"I'm not jealous," she scoffed, and I would have laughed if it were possible.

"Then why are you trying to"—I bent at the waist slashing the knife upward—"kill me?"

The knife made contact, cutting her arm, but I didn't want it to go too deep and risk me losing my only weapon by burying it in bone.

"If you're going to refuse him as your mate, you're better off dead. At least he'd be whole again."

Her truth, no matter how crazy or crudely stated, hit me deeper than I wanted to acknowledge. I tried to conceal how much her words shook me.

"How did you know that?" I demanded when she stepped back. I threw my legs over the edge, putting my weight on my good ankle.

"We know more than you think," she spat, then turned her neck to crack it before she stared me down.

"What the hell does that mean?"

"Neither of you should be here. Just die already and let him find another mate."

"You're attacking me in my sleep—like a fucking coward, I might add—because my life means *nothing* unless I agree to be his mate?"

Why was it that no one saw me as anything more than an object? A vessel, a guardian, a mate . . . where did it end?

Heat was rising. My face warmed and rage ignited within.

I didn't know what I was doing, only that I was done.

"*My turn*," Eres said.

CHAPTER 16

REAGAN

My back bent at an unnatural angle until it snapped. Every bone in my body seemed to be trying to torque, despite being impossible.

Every limb spasmed as I jerked unnaturally. My shoulders rotated forward then back, popping out of the sockets.

It took me too long to understand what Eres meant.

I thought she was going to pull out some fabled powers that unicorns were meant to have. In hindsight, I should have guessed.

For the first time in my life, I shifted.

Nausea roiled my belly. She pushed me to the metaphorical backseat so I couldn't act on the instinct and retch all over the bed like I wanted.

Eres let out a deep chuff worthy of a majestic warhorse. Red tinted her vision as she took control of us. She stamped her foot like a bull, then lowered her head.

She didn't detail what she planned on doing, but we were feeling each other really well for once. I withered, knowing her intent.

"We can't kill her," I said, trying to throw her off course. Eres attempted to charge, but it worked.

Our balance was a delicate thing and we wobbled on unsure legs like a newborn foal instead of an obsidian steed.

"Like hell I can't," she replied back, *"stop vying for control."*

"Like hell I won't," I said, throwing her words back at her. *"I need her alive."*

"Let go. Blame me for her death later, but we'll be alive and that's what matters."

"Eres, she said 'we' know more. I have to find out what that means and if Clara is safe! What if they go through the portal to the family? Subdue her, dammit, but don't—"

Eres let out a whinny that may as well have been a roar from her perspective.

"I am a death god," she said. *"I am superior. She is a danger to us, and we will end her. That is final."*

Jana seemed to watch us with narrowed eyes, like she was trying to understand our agenda as we thrashed back and forth. Too bad she wouldn't appreciate how much I was fighting to keep her alive. Eres thought of herself as the end all, be all but she wasn't the only one in this body. While I'd always been a shifter, I was latent. She didn't have nearly as much control as she should. For that, she only had herself to blame.

I jerked a little too hard, trying to pull her back when she got near Jana, and we went sprawling in a plume of dust. Not only was she a bitch for trying to kill me, but she was also a shitty maid if there was this much dust down here.

"If you're going to have inane thoughts, the least you could do is stop fighting," Eres insisted.

"If you're going to kill someone, the least you could do is consult me first," I shot back.

"I don't know what you're playing at, but I'm ending this," Jana said, then shifted way faster than I had. Seconds passed where Eres tried to kick her legs out from under her. It worked, sending her to the floor beside us, but it was no matter. She quickly got back to her feet in the form of a full-grown elk.

"Great. Something tells me that she's not going to suck as bad as we do."

I didn't mean to voice that at Eres, but she let out a grunt in anger.

"Because you won't listen to me!"

"I'm listening! I'm listening! There! I let go."

The time to argue was gone, and I had no plans on dying. Pulling back, I let Eres take over. She kicked her legs out, turning her body so we could stand, but just as she gained her footing, Jana lifted back on her hind legs to bring her heavy hooves down on us. Bones crunched on impact as she attacked viciously, repeatedly slamming her weight onto us.

"We have to move away from her!"

"I'm trying," she said, her voice strained. She jumped up, losing balance and toppling to the side again, but she'd managed to pierce Jana deeply on the hind leg with her horn.

Jana's elk let out a wail that shifted into a human scream, but I didn't think the injury was enough to incapacitate her.

"Maybe you shouldn't have taken over and let me handle it."

"We'd be dead already if you handled it." I wanted to

scream in frustration, but a pained whimper escaped our mouth.

"*What's happening?*"

"*This body is broken,*" she whispered. "*Needs to heal . . .*"

"*Can't death gods heal fast?*" I asked her.

Eres didn't respond and my anxiety increased tenfold. If she was doing bad enough that she couldn't respond . . . "*I'm trying to keep the worst of it from you. Ingrate.*"

All at once the pressure eased off.

Blood was dripping into my eyes and making it hard to see past the red haze. Just as my vision began to darken, a door slammed into the hard brick wall, and an invisible string tugged hard in my chest.

He was here.

Buzzing swarmed my veins like a thousand bees. Adrenaline coursed through my system in a way I'd never felt before, which meant only one person had caused it.

Reagan.

Desperation clawed at my throat.

My fists pounded against the locked dreadoak door, sending thundering echoes down the corridor. Not a sound could be heard through it, almost as if someone had intentionally tried to silence our bond.

There was no time to waste. Summoning my shadows, I broke through whatever barrier separated us and thrust the door open with a force that buried the handle in the stone wall.

Horror filled me.

Lying in the center of a destroyed room was my mate. She'd shifted into a glorious dark unicorn, but she was bleeding out everywhere. Still, she kicked weakly, not giving up the fight.

I wanted to go to her, but her attacker was still

conscious. Jana was up against the wall in her human form, mostly naked. Beside her were the shredded clothes of her uniform.

I didn't know what happened here, but I would find out.

Shadows snaked out from my hands, pulling her off the ground and holding her up by her armpits. Then they wound around her like a python, more than willing to squeeze.

"Your M-maj—"

"Save it for the dungeon," I ground out, then I knelt beside Reagan. Her heartbeat was strong, but slow. She needed to shift back to heal. Without looking away I said, "By the time I'm done, you're going to wish she'd killed you."

The things I did to traitors were famous, and yet that was *nothing* compared to what I would do to the woman who'd hurt my mate.

Regardless of how difficult she was making our situation, she was still mine. For her to be injured under my roof . . . a shudder ran through me, and more shadows poured from my skin.

Once they'd called me the light; they rejoiced at my name.

Having my soul torn before being thrown in Tartarus changed me to my very core. It changed my magic. Now I was darkness. I was shadow. I was death.

To all but *her*.

"Reagan," I said quietly, stroking my fingertips down the side of her neck. I wanted to take stock of her injuries but there were too many.

"Come on, my love," I whispered. "You need to fight it." A low whine went through her, the sound gutting me. Her eyelids blinked, slow to open, but when they did, it wasn't pain that filled them.

It was fire, vengeance, and fury.

Good. She was still fighting.

Blood vessels had popped around her iris, staining her eyes with red starbursts around the brown. In this form it was so dark, only one shade from black.

"Shift, Reagan," I said. "It's the only way you'll heal."

She stared at me but did nothing.

A terrible thought crossed my mind. She didn't know how to shift.

Fuck.

"Visualize the change," I urged, hoping I could walk her through it. "Imagine your bones breaking, rearranging until you're you again. Picture who you want to be."

She blinked again and if not for that fuck-off-stare, I might have wondered if she'd recognized me.

Instead of letting my increasing anxiety take over, I whispered low assurances and explained shifting as well as I could. While I wasn't a shifter, it was still a power I possessed. Under different circumstances, I would have felt triumphant that my mate was a dark unicorn of all things. A shadow shifter of lore, hiding amongst mortals.

Right now, I just hoped she could shift back to herself.

Fast footsteps sounded down the hall.

"What's going on—" My brother's voice broke off sharply as he crossed the threshold, his wide eyes taking in the bloody scene. "Fuck, *guards*! Pol! Where's your feathered ass when we need—"

"Get Jana to the dungeons and find Clara. In that order." I didn't need to tell him to hurry. Abyssian didn't waste a second manhandling the elk shifter out the door and dragging her down the hall as she cried out.

"Reagan, you're losing too much blood. *Shift*," I commanded again. The alpha tone should have worked on her, but all it did was seemingly piss her off. I bit the inside of my cheek. This couldn't happen. I couldn't find my mate just to lose her because she never learned to shift.

I refused.

"Fucking hell, Reagan," I cursed, rolling up my sleeves. She flinched and twisted when I laid a hand on her. "If you don't want me to touch you, then *shift*."

To my surprise, her bones began to pop and crack. Blood smeared the floor as her body broke itself all over again with such slow agony that I started to worry she wouldn't be able to finish shifting back.

But she did.

Finally.

A weight lifted from my shoulders when her naked form curled up on the floor in the fetal position. I pulled her into my lap, wrapping my arms around her to calm my own emotions.

"I'm fine," she coughed. "You don't have to—"

"This is for me. Please," I said, needing to reassure myself she was alive. I wanted to kiss her senseless, but now was not the time, so I settled for holding her tight to my chest.

The sound of people running down the corridor made its way to her room, and Reagan shifted uncomfortably. "Can you grab a blanket or something? I'm naked."

I let go of her to pull my shirt off then tug it over her head, feeding her arms through it like she was a child. "I can't believe you just dressed me," she murmured, lowering her forehead to my shoulder with a pronounced exhale. The simple act of affection was her white flag waving in the air. I didn't think I'd won the war, but that she felt comfortable enough to rest against me when she was so vulnerable . . . I would take it as a small win.

"Reagan!" Clara exclaimed, barreling through the door. Reagan's head snapped up. I instantly regretted sending for her.

Her cousin collapsed to her knees beside us and all but pulled Reagan back to try and take stock of her injuries. Other than some bruises though, her body had healed them all. I'd checked after pulling her into my arms.

"What happened?" Pollux asked, stepping into the bedroom. The hairs on the back of my neck lifted and I was severely tempted to order him away because I didn't want anyone near my mate when she was in this condition—not even him. Logically I knew it was an emotional reaction. Pollux was my oldest and most trusted friend. He'd proven himself hundreds of times over.

"Jana attacked Reagan," I said through a clenched jaw.

"What?" Pol and Clara spoke in unison, their voices rising at the end of the question.

Reagan let out a shaky breath. "I'm okay. Safety drills kicked in."

"Thank fuck," Clara said, hugging her tight.

My brain was stuck on what she'd said. "Safety drills?"

She pulled back, picking at the edge of the shirt I'd put on her. "My dad trained our entire family to react in case of an attack, day or night."

"What kind of an attack?"

"Anything. Rogue factions from other areas of No Man's Land wanting to take over The Crossroads. A House or two deciding they wanted our territory." Reagan's cheeks turned a shade of pink. Her eyes shifted, making sure to look away from me as she continued. "A coven member surviving and coming after me to finish the job they started. We all did the drills, but I think everyone was more concerned with making sure I could take care of myself in case it was the latter."

Words left me. The anger I felt on her behalf was immeasurable. Not only for what had happened to her today, but all the years prior. Nothing I could do or say would make it better. After all, at the very base of it, I was the reason she was a guardian. Even if it wasn't my doing, the fact remained that I was the cause of her suffering.

My eyes lowered to the pool of blood. "Reagan, I'm sorry—"

"Don't," she said quietly.

I sighed. We were back to where we were before. I should have known, but the reality of it stung. Rocking back on my haunches, I stood up to face Pollux. Before I could interrogate Jana, I needed his help with the magic that had sealed her room.

"Caius," Reagan whispered, "I . . ." She took a deep breath.

"Whatever you need," I said softly, crouching down.

"I don't want to be alone."

"I'll be with you every second," Clara said dutifully.

She smiled at her cousin. "I mean . . . I need to talk to Caius. Just the two of us."

Her cousin's mouth formed an "o" then she tried to hide a smile. "Maybe let me help you bathe first?" she said in a hushed voice, angling her head to all the blood.

Reagan pressed her lips together and with a scrunched nose, nodded in agreement. "Right. Probably a good idea."

We helped her stand, and Clara wrapped her arm around Reagan's waist as they walked to her bathroom.

I didn't want to let hope sneak its way in, but there was no stopping it. She wasn't pushing me away, and I was going to hold on to that.

"Wait," she said, a slight panic to her rushed statement as she turned around. "Where are you going to be? What if . . .?"

"I'm staying here. Pol and I are going to clean the blood off the floors. Take as long as you need. I'll be right here waiting."

Her chin dipped and a slight half smile of relief crossed her face before Clara whisked her away into the bathroom.

The door closed, and Pol turned to me, bewildered.

"What in the actual fuck just happened?"

Water sluiced down my skin. It hurt to move. Then again, hurting was better than dead, which is what I would be if Caius hadn't forced me to shift.

As much as it killed me to admit it, probably what I would be had Eres not taken control as well. While I was competent enough to handle myself, master assassin I was not.

Eres remained blessedly quiet in the shadows, pushed into the background while I processed things on my own. I wasn't ready to talk to her, keeping the barrier between us while I took my time to think. She accepted it, not trying to worm her way into my thoughts, and I appreciated the respite from our bickering.

"Do you want to talk about it?" Clara asked, her fingers gently scrubbing my scalp, trying to rid it of blood.

"No," I said. "But I probably should."

Clara chuckled, but it lacked any real amusement. "Internalizing is bad. Especially for you."

"Why me especially?"

"Because you blame yourself for things you have no business taking the blame for." While that was a correct assessment, this was different.

"This isn't one of those times," I said quietly. "Jana's reason for attacking me was so weird. She was pissed that I hadn't accepted the bond. That he deserved someone better. She said I was better off dead."

"Everyone knew she didn't like you, but apparently giving you cold baths wouldn't suffice."

I huffed. "I guess not."

Clara used a cup to wash the soap from my hair. "Wonder what made her think killing you was the better option?"

Water splashed and I replayed her words in my mind. "I don't know, but she knew I was the guardian."

My cousin stiffened, her eyes widening. "How?"

"I don't know, but she said 'we know more than you think,' so someone else is involved. She said neither of us should be here. I didn't know where you were or if you were okay too." The thought made me shudder.

"I was snooping in the library," she said, squeezing a bottle of a floral-scented liquid onto a loofah. "Seeing what I could find for Jo."

I smiled. "He asked me to find him new books. I've been too bent on avoiding Caius that I haven't even bothered to look around this place." Clara scrubbed my back in smooth strokes, alternating between washing and rinsing. "You were right," I finally said. "I should at least try to get to know him more. I know all the stories say he'd betrayed the other primordials, and that he'd been destructive and on the verge of eliminating mankind, but I don't think there's any truth to it."

"Damn, one dinner and that's the takeaway?"

I chuckled softly. "Hardly. I wasn't very nice to him at dinner. Honestly, I think he has the patience of a saint when you think about how I've been treating him."

"Okay . . ." She waited expectantly for me to finish. I was quiet for a minute, getting my thoughts together.

"I had a dream last night, except it wasn't a dream. It was a memory," I began, twisting around to look at Clara. Her dark eyebrows were pulled together. "You don't believe me."

Clara sighed. "It's not that, Rea. I heard your dad say what happened with your memories, and before you ask—no, I didn't know. That was a secret your dad and Sin kept from both of us."

Relief flooded me at her admission. I hadn't realized how much I needed to hear it. The desire to ask her about it was there, but I wasn't sure I could handle the answer if it had gone the other way.

"Would you have told me if you did know?"

She paused, pursing her lips in thought. "I'm not entirely sure. If I thought it truly protected you, maybe, but Jo says we can't hide from our past, no matter how much we try."

"That kid is too smart for this family."

"Tell me about it," she said in exasperated agreement. "Once you taught him how to read, he just absorbed everything and became a fountain of knowledge."

"I wonder what he would say about my dream."

She shrugged, and while the initial action irked me, I knew it was because she didn't understand all of it yet. "Now that you've shifted, it goes to reason that you'd start remembering things—"

"This wasn't *my* memory," I said, cutting her off, but keeping my voice low. Caius and Pol were supposed to be in my room. They didn't strike me as the type to press their ears to the door and eavesdrop, but this conversation was critical.

"How is that possible? What do you mean it wasn't your memory?" She dropped her voice too, following my lead.

"It felt so incredibly real, like I was stuck in the body of another woman, unable to stop anything. I couldn't even shut my eyes to what she was doing. I was the passenger. A witness, paralyzed to react."

"A witness to what?" she prompted.

"I think I saw Caius lose his soul."

When she didn't respond, I turned to look at her. Wide eyes and fingers stilled, she watched me. "What do you mean *think*?"

"I'm like ninety-nine-point nine percent certain."

"And the other point-one percent?"

"Logic telling me it's impossible for me to see the past, let alone experience it from Abraxia's perspective."

"Abraxia?" she repeated carefully, and I nodded. "Tell me everything."

By the end of it, Clara was completely stunned. At some point she'd set the cup aside and sat cross-legged by the bath, listening intently.

"That's insane," she said in a low voice.

"But?" I nudged her on, hearing it in her voice.

"Not impossible. You guard half his soul, right? And you're her descendant. Maybe something about being around him is triggering the memories of your blood. I've heard of it happening in incredibly powerful witch lines sometimes."

I sighed. "I'm only a half witch."

"So?" she replied. "Reagan you're a motherfucking dark

unicorn. It doesn't get much more special than that. Your mom was a pretty powerful witch from what my dad said. You descend from a mortal that literally stripped a primordial of their primordial . . . ness."

"Primordialness?"

"It's a word now. The point stands. You have no idea what your witch powers are because you were forced to forget. For all you know your specialty lies in something that lets you see the past."

"What do you mean specialty?"

"Well, you know, I'm a spirit witch. It means that my magic is largely centered around spirits and death. Least it was before I crossed over to Tartarus. Not that I see that changing much since this place is all death magic."

"Maybe I've got spirit magic too?" I said thoughtfully.

"Maybe," Clara shrugged. "You could be a time witch, or a seer for all I know. Specialties may be specific, but they're also broad. There are a lot of ways that one can present. Hell, you could even be a blood witch. The sky is the limit there."

While this knowledge was useful information, it didn't answer anything about if what I really saw was a memory or not.

"Why don't you ask Caius what happened?" Clara said, seeming to read my mind despite me knowing for a fact that wasn't one of her powers.

I groaned, sinking into the water. "It's my only option, but I feel so guilty for treating him like I did. I keep holding on to the fact he was going to kill me when he walked through that door."

"Well, he was. We all know that. But we would have done the same if the situation were reversed."

I scowled. "That's pretty much what he said."

"But he also saved your life. He didn't hurt anyone in the process."

"He kidnapped you," I pointed out.

"A little kidnapping is sexy under the right circumstances." My jaw dropped, and an unwanted tinge of jealousy nipped at my insides. "Relax," she said, seeing my reaction. "After I got over the initial anger of being dragged here, I could see things a little more clearly, that's all."

"How so?"

She lifted her shoulder. "I don't know how to describe it. Something here feels like it's tapping into my magic. Nothing has happened yet. It's just a feeling."

I sighed, dunking under the water for a refreshing warmth, and then resurfacing. "I don't understand any part of my magic. I wish I did. I feel like I'd have some answers, but every day here just brings more questions. I've flipped through my mom's journal and so much of it I can't understand. There are runes I recognize. Moon cycles that make sense. But spells and diary entries are all foreign. I can't decode it."

"Maybe I can?"

I perked up. "Maybe it needs a witch. That's why my dad couldn't decipher it, and I'm not in touch with any of my powers yet so it's unreadable."

"How about this," she said, propping her elbows on her thighs and leaning forward. "I'll work on translating the journal, and you talk to Caius about your dream-memory. We have six months here. Best to woman up and make the most of it."

"I don't get why he hasn't just killed me, to be honest. I have done nothing but fight him and treat him like shit."

She snorted. "Because he says you're his mate, Reagan. Why else would he put up with your moody ass? The easiest thing he could do is kill you, but he hasn't. Won't, in fact, even though he could have just watched you die. He's saved you twice. Why is that?"

Visions of the dream I'd had filtered through my thoughts. His vulnerability. His searing pain. The heart wrenching sense of betrayal.

"Because I've misjudged him," I whisper.

CHAPTER 19

REAGAN

*D*on't be a pansy.

You can do this.

It's just one conversation . . . about a topic I'd rather walk on hot coals than discuss.

Who was he really? Not the fear-mongering stories that had been passed down. The truth.

The truth . . .

His name was Caius, for starters. That was never in any of the tales. He was only known as the Soulless One; a name that sounded like some kind of monster. A creature from Hell with big teeth and a craving for flesh.

"He craves our flesh, all right," Eres said.

"Just stop."

"What? It's the truth. He's made no attempt to hide it. Now that we know he doesn't want to kill us, we should take him up on that. He's a worthy mate. Strong. He'd protect our foals—"

"Oh my god. This conversation is ending now."

"You're rather prudish for having several fuck buddies, as you call them. None of them were worthy of mating with us, but you still—"

"Can't—hear—you—it's breaking up—"

Eres snorted. "Human. I am a god. Our bond does not 'break up' like cell reception."

Interesting that she knew what cell reception meant. I wondered how much she was actually privy too, sitting in the recesses of my mind for the past sixteen years or so. Judging by her response, a fair bit.

A knock at the bathroom door startled me.

"Clara told me to knock if you didn't follow her out in a minute. Everything okay?"

Godsdammit. My cousin was totally a traitor. One hundred percent.

Knowing I would chicken out and would talk myself out of confronting him, she cut me off at the pass. Well played.

I reached for the handle to open the bathroom door. Caius leaned against the door frame; one arm braced against the trim. His sleeves were rolled up and his skin stained red from my blood.

I tucked a strand of hair behind my ear nervously.

"Listen, Reagan—"

"Caius, I—"

We both stopped, waiting for the other to continue.

"Is there somewhere we can go?" I asked after a suspended pause. "That we can be alone?" I swallowed hard on the word "alone" and it came out softer than intended. "Not here . . ." I added, glancing at the broken dresser.

If he was surprised by my request, he didn't show it. "My suite. We won't be bothered there."

I nodded, stepping around him. Caius led me out of my room and down the hall. It didn't escape my notice that the puddle of red on the floor was gone. Caius and Pol cleaned it up, as promised. Without thinking about it, I skimmed his body, focusing on his strong hands and found myself blushing before I could stop it.

"You can look."

"Excuse me?"

He chuckled. "Your hearing is just fine, but because I'm a gentleman, I'll repeat—you can look at me if you want to."

Okay, I thought I was blushing before. It was nothing compared to the inferno engulfing my face now.

"I wasn't—"

"You're not a good liar. Did you know that?" His teasing tone turned flat, emotionless. A shudder worked its way down my spine, but I suppressed it.

"Fine. I noticed the floor wasn't stained, but I was looking at your hands and saw they are."

He nodded. "Aterstone isn't porous; skin is." I didn't recognize the name, but I wasn't exactly versed in geology on Earth, let alone Tartarus. "Was that so hard?"

Pressing my lips together, I formed a thin smile. Dream or no dream, his smugness got under my skin.

The walk to his rooms was short. I realized that he was in the same hallway. No doubt intentional on his part. How had I not paid attention to any details since arriving?

Caius waved his hand and a large door opened in front of me, leading to a room that was largely black with smaller accents of white and gray. A four-poster bed was situated on the opposite side of the room, covered in midnight-colored blankets and pillows. Positioned between the bed and the door was a sitting area with two wing-backed chairs and a loveseat . They were patterned with threads of silver and cream that popped in the low firelight emitting from the hearth.

"I never thought black could be . . . comforting."

"I'll take that as a compliment," Caius said.

"It was one." The giant fur rug looked so soft, I actually squatted down to brush my fingers over it. Somehow it was even softer. "I could sleep on this."

"If you like it that much, just wait until you feel my comforter. It's made from the underbelly pelt of the same creature."

Said creature must be a mammoth for how large the rug was, and that wasn't all of it? I'd never seen anything close to this size in The Crossroads.

"Awfully presumptuous that I'll end up in your bed."

"You will," he said, completely and utterly assured. "You'll be staying with me from now on."

My fingers froze. My body stilled as my heart started to pound harder. He said what now? I wanted to talk to him; not sleep with him.

"Umm . . ."

"It's for your safety. Jana couldn't have acted alone. When you were being attacked I—" He broke off, and the emotion in his voice made me stand.

"You what?" I asked quietly.

"I tried to get to you. I could feel your panic. Your pain. But the door was warded shut. Someone put a silencer on your room. Jana may be powerful, but that takes magic she doesn't possess."

Indecision warred within me, but I couldn't argue with his logic. He was absolutely right. Jana hadn't acted alone. I wanted to fight him, argue that he couldn't tell me what to do, but for what purpose? Even if I talked him into putting me and Clara together, all that would do is put *her* in danger. I didn't offer up six months of my life for her to die for me.

"All right, I'll stay here," I said simply.

He looked surprised I had given in so easily. I couldn't blame him when basically everything he said had just given me ammunition. "That's it? No pushback?"

Where could I start? The dream, the attempt on my life, Clara giving me advice—all of it had my head in a tizzy. I wasn't all that interested in fighting him anymore. Not without good reason. For now, I would settle with facts. They were easier to deal with than emotions. "You're right that she wasn't working alone."

Caius's expression darkened, his entire mood shifting in an instant. "Tell me why you know that."

After giving him the replay of events, Caius scrubbed a hand through his hair in frustration. He paced like a caged animal, one that I couldn't stop myself from watching in fascination.

"Fuck!" Caius turned and sent a fist through the aterstone. It fractured like shale beneath his power.

"Caius . . ." I put a hand on his shoulder, and he tensed. "It's, well it's not fine, but it's over. I'll stay here. I won't fight you on this. We can figure this out—"

Caius turned, and it occurred to me just how big he was. Rough hands cupped my cheeks. The same hands that so easily broke stone held me so tenderly, and it left me speechless. "No one is going to try anything because we're going to tell them we're mated."

My lips parted. That was not what I was expecting him to say. "Um. I'm not sure that's—"

"No part of our deal has changed, Reagan, but they need to see you differently. Not a soul in this realm would dare harm their king's mate." His thumb brushed over my cheekbone, sending a shiver through me that I failed to suppress. Caius dropped his hands as if I'd burned him.

I realized he thought I was afraid.

"I'm sorry, love. I should have foreseen this when I brought you back."

"Excuse me, but I walked through on my own two feet."

He paused, taking in my words and what I was trying to say. "Is this your way of saying that you've come to your senses about us being mates?"

I really needed to woman up and quit being a pansy because that most definitely was *not* the vibes I was trying to put out.

"No," I began, sighing and thinking of how to phrase it all. "You wanted to get to know me. I want to get to know you. The real you. Your past. I'm just . . . ready to listen."

"I sense there's something you aren't saying," he said cautiously.

Cursing under my breath, my cheeks flushed, and I closed my eyes, trying to hold onto the words. What was the point? Anything else would be a lie, and there was nothing good that could come of it. The rest of it came out of me in a rush so I didn't have to think about them or get wrapped up in the potential consequences.

"I dreamed of you losing your soul." Shitdamnfuck. "That's not how I meant for that to come out. What I'm trying to say is I had a dream and I think it was a memory. When Abraxia . . ." Betrayed him? Stole half his soul? Trapped him here?

Caius froze and I followed suit, sensing the predator side of him not far off. As if the words triggered a shift, when I stared into his dark eyes, I saw an abyss—and I could have sworn something else stared back.

"It was real, wasn't it?" I whispered softly. "She cut your hair . . ."

Caius shuddered. "That was a long time ago." When he turned away from me, it hurt in a way I didn't expect. Over the last week I'd gotten used to him inserting himself in my space and part of me didn't care for the sudden distance. Which was crazy. That's exactly what I should want . . . but the truth was, I didn't. Not now that I'd learned he was someone else entirely.

"She was your lover, wasn't she?"

He nodded, unwilling to speak of her.

"You weren't at war with other primordials, were you?"

He shook his head, his nostrils flaring with heavy breaths.

"The pain she put you through—"

"Reagan, I don't think this is a good idea."

"Please," I said. Caius jaw tightened. His muscles were as tense as a bow ready to snap. But instead of dismissing me again, he waited for me to continue. Progress. I'd work with it. "I need to understand it. If that was real, I need to know why you don't just kill me for your soul. I know you believe I'm your mate, but is that *really* enough? If for some reason we completed the bond, I would live forever, and you'd never be whole again. I felt the pain of your loss, Caius. The betrayal. I felt—" It was my turn to shudder. "It was a dream, and yet I thought I'd lose myself to it. I felt like I would fracture under the weight of that unbearable sorrow."

Caius sighed deeply, his muscles relaxing a fraction. "If what you say is true, then yes. That was what Abraxia did when she cleaved my soul in two. As for why I won't kill you . . ." He tilted his head, thinking through his words. "I wish I had an explanation that felt like enough, but it really is that simple for me. As far as I'm concerned, you're also part of me, and I'm unwilling to let that go. Besides, I have Pol and Abyssian looking into ways that we might be able to separate my soul from yours without killing you."

It was my turn to sigh then. I ran a hand through my wet hair. The wavy strands were curling into ringlets under the heat of Tartarus. "And if you can't?" I asked hesitantly, playing with a frizzy lock at the base of my neck.

Caius let out a low growl. "There has to be a way. If there was a way to steal it from me, then there's a way to retrieve it. We just have to find—"

"What if there's *not*?" I asked, growing more anxious. "What if all your searching just turns up more proof that I have to die to get it back. What then?"

His lips parted, eyes meeting mine. "I've lived this long without it. I can keep going."

"You're certain about this?"

"Fuck, Reagan, how many times do you need to hear that I'm not going to kill you? I'm trying to win you over, for fuck's sake."

"Okay, so we tell everyone we're mates, and you try to win me over." I took a deep breath. "What happens if you can't?"

His eyes darkened. "Then you'll go. I gave you my word."

"Just like that?"

"Just like that," he said, taking a step toward me. Then another. The urge to back away was strong but I held my ground. "But make no mistake, Reagan, I plan to use every weapon in my arsenal to make you mine."

I shivered at his dark words and heat pooled low in my belly. That was *not* supposed to turn me on. I wasn't Clara. I wasn't into kidnapping. Or—

His index finger lifted my chin as he stepped into my personal space. His presence stole all the oxygen, making it hard to think with him this close.

"What if you're wrong?" I asked him. "What if I'm not your mate?"

Caius lowered his head slowly, lips only a hairsbreadth from mine.

"You are."

"But if I'm not?"

"Has anyone ever told you that you're infuriatingly stubborn?"

One side of my mouth quirked up. "My whole life."

Caius smirked back. "Color me unsurprised."

"You should know that stubbornness applies to everything. So if you really want me, just be aware, you'll be fighting an uphill battle—"

"Shut up," he whispered, and when I opened up to begin to protest, his mouth came down on mine. Hot and warm, he plied my lips apart with expert precision. A groan escaped me when his tongue touched mine. The scent of roasted hazelnuts and the taste of whiskey invaded my senses. He clamped a hand around my hip, fingers digging hard into the soft flesh at my sides. His other hand slid along my jaw and around the back of my head to hold the nape of my neck in a possessive gesture.

My insides quivered in ecstasy. My breasts felt heavy, aching for touch. He pulled me flush against his body, a rumble starting in his chest and echoing where his mouth met mine. Our lips battled for dominance. Even I couldn't deny that our chemistry was explosive.

Without realizing it, my hands curled inward, gripping his shirt. He nipped at my bottom lip, and I whimpered. Pushing harder into him, wanting more, demanding it without words—I kissed him back despite all the reasons I shouldn't. There were many, but the second his lips touched mine, they seemed to dissipate.

The hand at my hip shifted, fingers burrowing beneath the thin material of my t-shirt. I gasped when the rough pads of his fingers grazed my hip then waist, traveling north. I didn't stop him from cupping my breast. On the contrary, I arched into him, seeking an outlet for the heat that was suddenly burning inside me.

"Mine," he growled against my lips, breaking our kiss. He trailed his mouth across my jaw and down my neck, biting my pulse sharply, then sucking the tender skin between his lips. I jerked when his thumb brushed across my nipple. Liquid fire seemed to form and combust within me at the same time.

I slid a hand up his chest to wrap my arm around his neck. I grabbed his shoulder roughly with my other hand and bounced once on the balls of my feet, wrapping my legs around his waist in the next second. Caius caught me without breaking the suction on my neck. The hand that was on my nape, dropped to my ass, taking a generous handful.

I groaned when he flipped the cup of my bra down, pushing my breast up. His fingers rolled my nipple between them, making my back arch. The sensation sent a pleasurable ache that settled between my legs.

"Caius," I murmured, grinding myself against him. My heated center brushed up and down the length of his bulge, providing the friction I was desperate for.

"I love hearing you say my name." My body tightened, only to be found achingly hollow. But he could change that.

Caius twisted and my back pressed against the wall. Next thing I knew he rolled his hips and white flashed behind my eyes. My head tilted back, and I let out a low moan.

A series of heavy thuds banged on his bedroom door. "Caius, we've got a problem out here."

My head snapped up, my body tense as sanity rushed back to me.

Caius growled low, sensing the change. Then he sighed. I dropped my legs, but he didn't step back, instead letting me slide down every agonizingly hard inch of his body. Only when I was on my own two feet did he step back, but not before kissing me one more time. It was brief but lingering. A promise.

When Caius opened the door, I was back to looking like me, bra in place and all that. Albeit more off kilter.

Pol stood there, giving me an apologetic glance, and knowing without a doubt he'd pissed off Caius beyond measure.

"What?" Caius ground out through clenched teeth.

"This can't wait. Reagan, you should probably come with."

Caius nodded, silently taking my hand. Lacing his fingers through mine, he held me tight as we followed Pol.

To those we passed, it was a gesture indicating we were together, sending a message to everyone to spread the word.

I could hear the whispers already, and we hadn't even made it to the other side of the castle.

The king had claimed his mate.

Was that ... barking?

High-pitched yelps echoed down the hall. I glanced over at Caius. "Do you have a dog?"

"Several," he said. "But none of them sound like that. My girls are hunting dogs, trained to track down the vilest of men should they escape imprisonment. Their barks can be heard miles away. That yapping is definitely not my girls."

His word of choice gave me a sinking feeling. I hoped I was wrong. That the barking was not in fact a certain dense cousin of mine, but as we entered the atrium my hopes were dashed.

A black floof darted between one guard's legs and down one of the five paths that led away from the portal. Another guard dashed to grab him. Nog dodged smoothly, pivoting his three-inch legs, and bolting through the purple ferns, disappearing from sight. If not for the shaking plants that showed where he was, there would be no telling.

"Oh for fuck's sake," I muttered, running one hand down my face.

"Is that—" Caius started.

"Yep," I answered. "My dumbass cousin seems to have evaded your guards and slipped through the portal."

I'd say that reflected poorly on his people, except Nog could be *really* persistent when he wanted something. Knowing him, he camped out by the portal and waited for someone to go on bathroom break. While he was a bit of a klutz in real life, his corgi form seemed to be fairly agile. Given his legs were literally three inches off the ground, that wasn't surprising.

"Reagan!"

I turned toward the voice and froze before I could take even a single step. This could not be happening. It couldn't. *He* would not be that dumb—

Ben closed the gap between us, and Caius stepped directly in front of me, body checking him swiftly. Ben flipped mid-air and landed flat on his back beside me.

"Oh shit," Clara said, arriving on the scene at that exact second, practically snarling when she saw my ex. "That's Ben. He was the—"

"Clara!" I snapped her name in warning, not for her though. We all knew Ben made a massive mistake coming here and I didn't need her adding fuel to the fire. If the look on Caius's face was any indication, he'd be dead soon.

"He was what?" Caius asked, not looking at her. His entire focus was on Ben as chaos ensued, but he stood still as stone, hovering over Ben's prone form. Clara sidestepped away from us, sensing the very palpable tension.

"He *was* my frien—"

"I'm her boyfriend," Ben declared, getting to his feet. He dusted himself off as he rose to his full height—only an inch beneath Caius. He was built burly and thick, with large beefy biceps, but there was zero doubt in my mind who would win this fight. Sin was stronger than anyone I knew, and Caius put her on her ass without blinking.

"*That's offensive,*" Eres piped up.

"*This is so not the time for your ego.*"

"Boyfriend?" Caius repeated softly. I didn't miss the way the corded muscle in his arms twitched. Suddenly the blood stains on his hands seemed chilling. "I take it this is the prick that attempted to claim *my* mate."

"Nope, he's no one—"

"Yeah, that's me," Ben said, digging his own grave with a backhoe. I smacked my forehead with my palm. "And I fucked up, but that doesn't change that she's taken, buddy—" He broke off when Caius swiftly wrapped his hand around Ben's throat. He lifted him off the ground with ease.

"Caius," I said, keeping my voice soft as I put a hand on his shoulder. "He's no one—"

"Don't insult my intelligence, Reagan. I'm well fucking aware he's *no one*. The boy thought he could enter my realm and what? Win you over? Take you as his mate?" On the word 'mate' his fingers tightened. Ben started making these awful choking sounds, face turning bright red.

"He's delusional. I promised you six months and I'm keeping it—"

"Reminding me that you plan to leave is not the way to save the boy. I suggest you stop talking while you're behind."

How was it this was the same man who moments ago had me turned on, and now he had me infuriated by ignoring what I was trying to say? I ground my teeth.

"Now you," Caius said, addressing Ben, "are a liar. You told me you were her boyfriend. That wasn't true, but you are here for her. After what you did, what makes you think

I'm going to let you live, let alone walk through that portal with Reagan?"

"Res—cue—her—"

"Rescue her? From what? A man that respects her choices?" Caius laughed cruelly. "Boy, you can't even rescue yourself."

Ben didn't have a retort and not speaking was probably the smartest thing he'd done since coming through that portal. The purple shade of his face might have had something to do with it.

"Caius, please—" My words were punctuated by Nog's barking.

"Will someone shut that infernal corgi up?" Caius growled.

"Nog," I barked his name using the alpha command my father did whenever he really wanted to get the point home. Nog closed his mouth and lowered his head, giving me the biggest brown eyes as if to say he was sorry.

Clara snorted. "No one believes you're innocent. Not for a second."

Nog walked over to sit behind my legs, like he was hiding from the guards that were creeping up. They didn't dare approach Caius when he was like this. He totally knew what he was doing, but Nog wasn't my priority.

Ben's face was violet and drawing closer to blue with every passing second. Giving it one last effort, I put my hand on Caius arm and squeezed. "Please," I whispered, aiming for low enough only he could hear. "You said you were trying to win me over. You'll never have any part of me if you prove to be the monster I feared. Ben is stupid. Well intentioned, in this case, but still stupid. That isn't punishable by death. Let him go. We can talk this out."

A beat passed, then another. My heart sank. He really was going to ignore me and choke the life out of Ben.

Just as the thought crossed my mind, Caius released his grip. Ben fell to his knees, clutching his throat in the mother of all coughing fits as he tried to inhale as much oxygen as possible into his lungs at once.

Holy shit.

It worked.

Caius turned to regard me, ignoring Ben entirely. His dark eyes held mine, searching. I reached up to wrap my arms around his shoulders, hugging him. "Thank you."

Caius encircled me in his arms. "For you, my love, only you."

When he pulled away from our embrace, he lowered to a squat as he leaned over Ben, speaking to him in a menacing whisper.

"Did you hear that? For her. Just this once. Mark my words. Touch her again, and you die. Reagan is *mine*."

That word. The way he said it.

Goosebumps erupted along my arms, and my skin simultaneously flushed. The notion that he would protect me so fiercely, so openly, and without question. It was hot, to say the least.

Not that I ever wanted him to do it, but he just threatened to kill someone for touching me . . . and it turned me on.

Pretty sure that meant I was going to Hell.

Oh wait. I was already there. Guess that makes it okay.

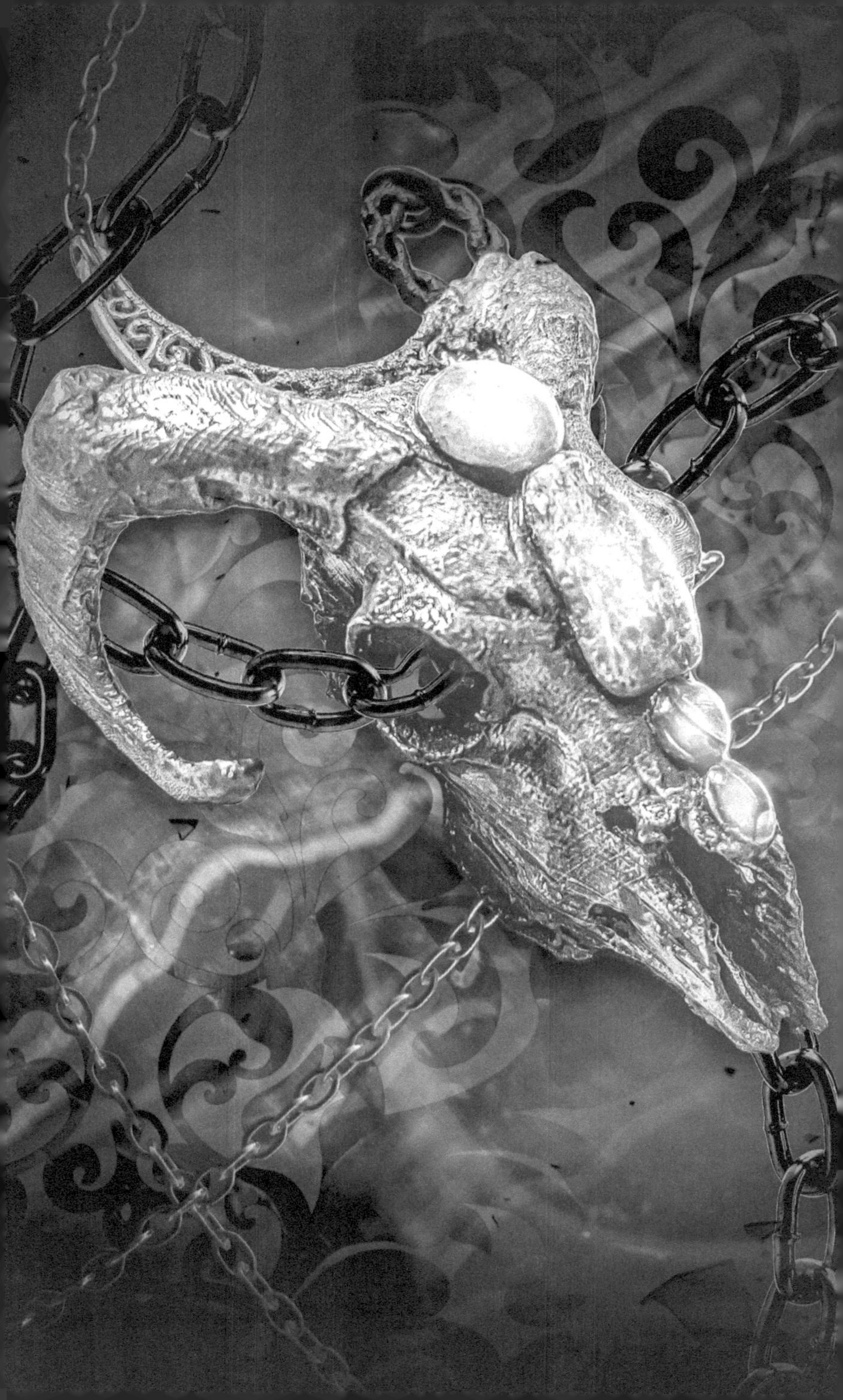

CHAPTER 21

CAIUS

Standing up, I wrapped my arms around her again. Never in my life had I felt so right, so complete, as I did when I held her. She thought I wanted what she guarded, and I had—until I found her. My soul wasn't what made me feel whole.

Only my mate.

I had always viewed myself as a good king. Fair and just, though I ruled with strength. That didn't stop the rage that coursed through me. It was true the only reason I let him live was because she had begged me to. The moment her voice softened, her words pleading, I was reminded that she was simply perfect in every way. *She* was fair. *She* was just.

Reagan would temper my fury. She didn't see it, but I did. My queen would be exactly what I needed and who she was always meant to be.

Unequivocally mine. The Queen of Tartarus.

We weren't there yet, but we would be.

A sharp bark shattered my peace.

My hand clenched in a fist as I narrowed my eyes at the monstrosity called a *dog*. More like an overgrown rat.

I peered into his dark brown eyes, and despite the cute and cuddly appearance, there was keen intelligence there. He knew exactly what he was doing.

Which meant he had to go.

"Shift," I commanded.

Bones cracked and he let out a pained yelp. A human boy appeared, not quite a child, not yet a man.

Naked as the day he was born, Nog covered his manhood and looked up at us bashfully. An apology lined his eyes, but a knowing smirk lessened the attempted contrition.

Little shit.

"Hey Rea," he croaked. "How's it going?"

Reagan released me and I instantly missed her heat. She twisted to look at her cousin and I yearned to grab her and pull her flush to me once more.

"Seriously, Nog?" She sighed, frustrated but not angry. "You put yourself *and* Ben in danger coming here. What were you thinking?"

"Hey!" He held up both hands then thought better and went back to shielding himself. "You don't know it was me—"

"Ben isn't smart enough to come up with how to bypass the two guards on the other side."

"Well, thank you, actually." Nog threw his hands up in the air again. "*Finally,* someone sees me for the genius—"

"Ugh!" Reagan scrubbed a hand down her face. "Someone get him some clothes. I can't have this conversation while he's naked. It's gross."

"Wow, Reagan," Nog said sarcastically. "There you go ruining my chances with all the hot hell babes."

"You're my cousin," she said, still not looking at him. "And you're not staying."

Thank fuck. Glad we could agree on that.

"Actually," Nog started, the first sign of uneasiness entering his expression. "About that. You see, it was my idea to come here, but it was more out of necessity. Don't get me wrong, I wanna save you"—Clara huffed a snort, earning her a glare. "But a week ago I got annoyed with Dad and shifted, but then I couldn't shift back. No matter how hard I tried, nothing worked. Tío even used his alpha command on me like you did, and nothing happened. So I got to thinking, Tartarus magic changed me, maybe I needed to be here to learn how to shift. Which led to me hunting down this loser." He hiked a thumb toward Ben, who remained on the floor recovering. "I remembered he could talk to dogs, so I figured all I had to do was sell him on saving you and suddenly I have a sidekick to do my dirty work—i.e. distracting the hot chick at the portal."

"Call me "the hot chick" again and I'll rip your fucking tongue out then feed it to a real dog."

I half turned to look over my shoulder.

Styx stood in blue jeans and a black flannel shirt. Her fingers twitched like she was itching to reach for the thin silver daggers in her hair to use on Nog. That wouldn't do.

"Hello, Styx."

"Caius." Her eyebrows lifted a fraction at Reagan's close proximity to me. "Reagan."

My mate stiffened. If I wasn't watching her, I might have missed the way her eyes seemed to glow for a brief moment. Almost like something *in* her was looking out and sizing up the other woman.

I would have found her potential jealousy cute if not for the fact that I didn't want her to be insecure about us. I was hers. Only hers. After Abraxia, I didn't get into relationships with anyone. Period. Reagan would be my only exception.

Styx was a friend, and a very good one who wasn't going anywhere. I needed them to get along. Or at least to not have to worry about that entity in Reagan lashing out in anger. While I doubted my mate would ever do such a thing, I was intimately familiar with the darker side of magic. The real question was, was it her animal, or something else looking out through those beautiful eyes?

"Well, this is awkward," Nog said.

Reagan slapped him upside the back of his head, and he grunted.

"Who's the boy?" Pol asked.

"My dumbass brother," Clara muttered, putting her face in her hand.

"Excuse me, but I'm nineteen. Thank you very much. I'm a grown ass man—"

"I've taken shits bigger than you," Styx replied.

"I sincerely doubt that," Nog said, crossing his arms over his chest.

"Can we get the child some fucking clothes?" I said, and guards snapped to attention, running around like worker ants.

"I'm not a child," Nog insisted.

"You pick your nose and eat it," Clara pointed out.

"You have a poster of Britney Spears on your ceiling," Reagan said. I had no idea who that was.

"Jesus, that was when I was five," Nog said to Clara first then turned to Reagan. "And Britney is hot. Any man will tell you."

"We know what you do with that poster. Find a fuck buddy like the rest of us," Clara said. "Even Reagan found —" Her mouth snapped shut.

My mate glared in her direction. "Does the phrase *read the fucking room* mean anything to you?" She took a step closer to me, closing the distance between us. I knew it was to protect her old flame, but I couldn't think about that now. Not if I wanted to leave him breathing, which was really in my best interest because I needed Reagan to let down those walls between us—and as much as she was softening to me, she made it clear she would have a difficult time ignoring murder. Even if the asshole deserved it.

A guard arrived with clothes, silently handing them off to the boy. I pointed at him and said, "You. Get dressed." Then I wrapped my arm around Reagan's waist, pulling her to me like I wanted. "The rest of you, follow me. I want this shit sorted. Now."

I sat on my throne. Reagan idled beside me, fidgeting with her hair in a nervous gesture. On my other side, Styx stood with her arms crossed and a bored expression on her face. I wasn't fooled by either of them.

Reaching out, I looped an arm around Reagan's waist and pulled her onto my lap. The curve of her backside fit there perfectly, like she was made for me.

It was all too easy to imagine us like this, with her turned around facing me, legs straddled on either side.

For another time. When she was ready.

Judging by the increased beating of her heart, and the sudden scent of desire, she was picturing a similar scenario.

Clara smirked, giving a nod of approval. Ben's eyes

lingered on our position, and his shoulders tensed. He looked away, uncomfortable.

Good. The possessive part of me needed to make a statement. It didn't matter where Reagan was with the bond. This woman was mine. Sharp tongue, stubborn attitude, and all. I wanted everyone to see it. Especially him.

"You already gave in?" Nog said, disbelief coloring his tone. He'd been inspecting the room and circling the table where I often sat with those close to me. We'd spent lifetimes in this room, sharing ideas, food and drink. He had the audacity to rub his grubby fingers over my furniture and then question my mate.

Disgust unfurled in me, quickly followed by anger.

As if she could sense it, Reagan touched my hand, her long fingers wrapping around my own.

"First, that's none of your business," Reagan said. I agreed wholeheartedly. "Second, it's . . . practice."

Whatever warmth that touched me fled. *Practice?* That's all this was to her? My mood darkened further but I didn't let her go.

"Practice?" Clara said, her nose scrunched.

"Yes," Reagan said, holding her head a fraction higher. "In an effort to keep me safe, Caius thinks we should tell everyone we've mated so that no one else makes an attempt on my life out of *misguided loyalty.*"

That was a remarkably kind way to put that, if not for the clear sarcasm.

"Wait, wait—attempt on your life?" Ben asked.

"What he said," Nog seconded, hooking a thumb toward the unwanted ex. "Although, what he's still doing here is beyond me. Not gonna lie. I half expected the Soulless One to kill him—"

"Nog!" Reagan admonished.

"I mean, he has a point," Clara said.

"Aww, you do love me," Nog remarked.

"Silence," I commanded. The hairs on Reagan's neck stood on end as everyone quieted. Her heart skipped a beat, then continued thumping faster than it should. Had I scared her?

My lips parted. I scented the air, but it wasn't fear that touched my tongue. It was *desire*.

She squirmed on my lap, and the pressure of her movements made me bite my tongue to keep from cursing. Gods, I wanted her. The slightest shift of her weight brought forth the fire in my veins from our kiss earlier.

Pol cleared his throat, breaking the silence that had stretched a moment too long. It focused my attention.

"First things first, why are you here?" I said to Ben. "I know why he is." I jutted my chin toward Nog who'd lowered his eyes at my command. "But if you truly came here to *save* her, then you can leave. As you can see, Reagan doesn't need saving."

"I . . ." Ben started. His hands clenched then released. "Can I talk to Reagan? Alone?"

"No."

"Excuse me," she snapped, her glare moving from him to me. "I'm right here. I can answer for myself."

"I agreed to let him live. If he wants to remain that way, I suggest he not ask to be alone with you. The answer is no."

Was I being unreasonable? Maybe.

There didn't seem to be any love lost on her end, but the longing with which he stared at her made me uncomfortable. Worse, it made me *insecure*. That was a most unwelcome feeling. Whereas Reagan's spot in my life was permanently affixed, mine was not nearly so. This boy had her before I did. Who was to say he wouldn't change her mind? I had no doubt he'd try if given the opportunity.

Reagan sighed. "I don't think that's a very good idea right now. Just say your piece and go." She waved her free hand at him in a way that was almost royal. Then she doubled back on the assertion with a quiet request. "Please."

Ben ran a hand over his short beard. "I did come here because I thought you were in trouble. I wanted to save you, and I wanted to make it up to you for—well, you know."

She crossed her arms. "You might as well say it. Everyone here already knows and omitting it is kind of a slap in the face, don't you think? Hard to be sorry if you can't even own up to it."

His face warmed in embarrassment. Making him admit what he did was so mild a punishment. The bastard deserved death for trying to mark an unwilling woman, and he deserved it slow for trying to mark *my* woman.

"To say I'm sorry for marking you. My wolf had been hounding me to do it for the last six months and I just snapped that night. I don't know if it was the full moon, or what. I really don't. That's not who I am. I fucked up, Reagan. It's no excuse, only an explanation. There's no reason he should have been able to take control. I should've been stronger. I wasn't, and you suffered for it."

My blood heated, but I kept my temper on a tight leash. Whether I wanted to deal with it or not, it was disrespectful to not let her handle this how she saw fit. I wanted a partner. If I undermined her in this, it set the precedent I wasn't all that interested in an equal. I wouldn't do that.

"Trying to mark me," she corrected. "It didn't leave a scar—thank the gods for that because I'm pretty sure my father would have killed you, if Sin didn't get to you first." She paused and he started to speak again, but Reagan wasn't having it. "I trusted you, Ben. You threw that away, and what you don't realize is all this? The reason we're even here in Tartarus?" She motioned to the room around us. "Your bite triggered the ward to break."

His face paled. "What ward? What do you mean?"

Nog laughed. "Are you kidding me? He didn't even know about the ward? Man, and everyone thinks I'm dumb. This joker didn't even *know* you."

His words were delivered in jest, but no one was laughing because they were true. It was at that moment it hit me. Whatever they once had was truly and utterly shallow. I'm glad I let this transpire. It eased that sense of insecurity.

"It's a long story I'm not interested in rehashing," Reagan said, voice tight. "The point is your actions had consequences beyond the gross breach of trust between us."

"Reagan I—I'm so fucking sorry," Ben said, his voice quiet.

The tension in her body seemed to dissipate with his apology.

"Thank you," she said softly. "It doesn't make it better, but I accept your apology all the same."

Good. Now this was settled, and—

The doors to the throne room flew open. The commander of the army in Tartarus entered; probably the last person I would have expected.

"Legion," I said his name by way of greeting.

"Your Majesty," he said, lowering his eyes in a bow before returning upright. "The prisoner is . . . resisting. We've been waiting for you in the dungeon."

"I've been tied up. It's been an *eventful* morning," I muttered, shooting a glare at Nog and Ben.

He nodded once, taking in every person present, more than half of which he'd never seen before. "I see."

"Who is with her now?"

"Abyssian."

I cursed. While few and far between, there had been futile assassination attempts in Tartarus. Abyssian was particularly brutal in killing them if I didn't myself. Call it brotherly loyalty, but for as easygoing as he could be, all that went out the window when someone tried to hurt me. Something told me that extended to my mate.

"You *left* her with him?" Pol questioned.

Legion lifted one shoulder unconcerned. "He outranks me. I wasn't going to order him to leave."

"You could have at least told him to come get Caius," Pol argued.

The commander sighed. "You have met him, right? Tall guy? Thinks he's funny? Never listens to anyone except Caius?"

I groaned. He was spot on. We needed Jana in one piece, and Abyssian would tear her to shreds if given the chance.

"I'll be back," I said to Reagan. I stood fluidly and set her on her feet. She swayed but righted herself quickly enough. I hesitated for a moment, thinking I should bring her with me, but thought better of it.

My anger was bad enough. If Jana reacted to having Reagan in the room, I might beat Abyssian to it and leave her in pieces. I didn't want my mate to see that side of me. I meant to counter the stories she'd been told of me. Not confirm them. Win her over.

"Pol, Styx, please guard the room." I started down the

steps of the dais, and Ben caught my eye. I pointed toward him. "Maim this one if he steps out of line."

"Caius, just go," Reagan said in reprimand. I hid my smile.

"Don't let anyone enter or leave until I get back. Legion, you're with me."

This day was never-ending, and I had a feeling it was only going to get worse.

CHAPTER 22

CAIUS

Shadows crawled over my skin in anticipation.

When I appeared in the dungeon with Legion, I had no question as to where she was being kept.

Abyssian leaned against the wall, next to a door. His posture was casual, legs crossed, while he ate an apple.

"Did you kill her?" I growled.

He looked at me with mild shock. "What? Of course not."

"Don't act surprised. We know how many people you've killed down here. My men clean it up," Legion said.

Abyssian shrugged. "They deserved it. Don't get me wrong. Jana does too, but I know how much you need her alive. Dead people don't talk, and we all know she wasn't working alone."

I thought back to the ward on Reagan's room, blocking her from me. Anger lingered beneath the surface, ready to lash out. "No, she wasn't."

The overwhelming scent of spells, blood, and urine hit me when I entered her cell.

She was chained to the wall with magical cuffs, binding her at her ankles and wrists. They'd already done a number on her. Lacerations lined her exposed skin. Strange marks from magic were sprinkled all over. Muscles swelled in unusual places, indicating fractured bones. I was surprised she'd endured that much without speaking.

Her eyes were puffy from crying, and the tears leaked down her face, dripping onto her chest.

The sight of her suffering should have made me happy, but instead, my blood boiled just seeing her face again.

Reagan's broken body flashed in my mind.

I didn't even bother asking a question. I walked up to her, letting shadows leak from my arms, trailing down my fingers like serpents, wrapping them around her body, squeezing.

A tendril of shadow crawled into her mouth, filling her windpipe, and cutting off her air supply. Her eyes bulged watering further. She jerked, her nervous system in panic at the sudden loss of oxygen.

I waited. When she was just on the verge of losing consciousness, I pulled a shadow back. She'd gasp, sucking in precious air only for me to do it again.

And again.

And again.

Legion stood in the corner, watching stoically. Abyssian chortled. "Damn, Caius. You're not even asking her any questions."

Without taking my eyes off Jana, I said, "She knows what question I would ask. She knows what she needs to say. I don't need to waste my breath."

"Please," she choked out, trying to suck in air. "Please stop."

"Is that what my mate asked you when you were trying to kill her?"

"I'm so sorry," she wept, sniveling sobs racking her body.

"Are you sorry because you're here, paying for your crimes, or were you sorry when you were breaking the bones in her body?" I ground out through clenched teeth.

Shadows sharpened, pressing into her skin like thousands of burning needles. She opened her mouth to scream, and another tendril of shadow snaked down, cutting her off.

Immeasurable pain silenced with no end in sight.

"You will speak to me, Jana. You will tell me what I want to know." I walked toward her; my words spoken in a low, menacing voice.

Abyssian crept closer to hear the exchange, and Legion watched with a curious expression.

"Do you know what I'm capable of? Did you know that I can keep you alive, bringing you back from death, torturing you for years to come?"

Her eyes widened in fear as she looked at Abyssian and then at Legion, as if they were somehow going to save her.

"It's true. I've seen him do it," Legion said casually, his hand resting on the hilt of his sword.

Her eyes flickered back to me she opened her mouth and closed it again.

"Don't test my patience, Jana. I will do anything for my mate."

She opened her mouth again, looking around the room, but she found that no one would help. She began to choke, as if some unknown force had wrapped its hand around her throat, but my shadows were contained.

"It was who, Jana? Say their name!"

She tried to speak again, but only a small squeak came out before she shook her head rapidly.

I jammed the shadow needles into her again, harder than before. Her scream rattled the room.

"I'm so sorry, I'm so sorry, he made me do it . . ."

"Who made you do it?" The shadows coiled around me, waiting to strike again.

Jana's eyes widened suddenly, and body convulsed. Fear filled her eyes before they rolled back into her head. She seized, a green foam drooling from her mouth.

Legion jumped toward her, but Abyssian slammed into him, holding his chest back. "Nobody touch her! We don't know what the hell that is."

We stood there, helplessly watching as Jana died a slow death, succumbing to whatever poison was pouring from her mouth, dripping like acid on the stone floor. Green ichor began to line her veins like ivy.

"What the fuck was that?" Abyssian breathed, kneeling beside her feet where she hung on the wall. He sniffed over the substance, refusing to touch it, but he shook his head, looking at me in confusion. "I've never seen anything like this before."

"Not like that, I haven't," Legion said, narrowing his eyes.

"Poison capsule in her teeth?" I asked him, and he nodded.

"Must be."

"Where would she have even found something like that? She was a chambermaid," Legion mused, scrubbing his hand down his jaw.

"Was death really the better option here?" Abyssian

asked, standing up and crossing his arms. "Whoever it was, she feared him more than you."

My mood soured further, and I turned on a heel to leave her cell.

"We'll never know," I said, my jaw tight. "It's like you said, Abyssian. Dead people don't talk."

"Sooo," Nog drawled. "You and the Soulless One, huh?"

I elbowed him sharply, hitting one of his ribs. It sent a zing through me, and I cringed, rubbing at the sore bone.

"Don't call him that."

"Why the hell not? That's what we've always called him." He scrunched his nose. "Don't tell me you have the Stockholm Syndrome thing."

"Nog!" Clara clapped her hands like she was getting a dog's attention. "You're being a dick, and you don't know what you're talking about."

"Oh, come on." He threw his hands up. "We spend a lifetime hearing how he's the worst, how he's literally out to destroy her, and I'm just supposed to suddenly call him by his name and not think she's lost her marbles?"

"That's exactly what you're going to call him," I said, folding my arms over my chest. Hearing that name for him now made me feel angry and sad on his behalf. I didn't like it, but I wasn't going to stand here and relive that dream.

"And you should trust me to know what I'm doing. I know myself. Besides, nothing is happening between us." Yet. Mostly. Except the kiss. That might not have stopped if we hadn't been interrupted.

"Lies," Nog insisted the moment he caught me shifting my eyes away. "I saw you two. You were sitting on his lap—"

"Okay, that really is practice. Like I told you, someone tried to kill me. The woman he's interrogating right now? She tried to kill me this morning."

"Why?" Ben asked.

"I didn't make a good impression around here. Caius is really loved as king, and I sort of made it known that I didn't want to be his mate. It didn't win me any favors. So she thought I was more useful dead."

Nog snorted. "Go figure you're almost murdered, not because some twat is jealous, but because you wouldn't spread your legs. That's some backwards logic."

"Right?" I nodded. "Thank you. It's bad enough he kidnapped Clara and she's been all Team Caius, but now I got the help trying to kill me too—no offense to you," I said to the beautiful woman still lurking next to the throne.

"Plenty taken," she shot back.

I paused and opened, then closed my mouth. "Okay, that's fair. It was a shitty thing to say. I'm sorry, I'm usually more, well, not eloquent, but I don't usually put my foot in my mouth like that. I'm pretty sure it's not even lunch time yet and it's already been a day."

Styx inclined her head. "That it has."

"So you're fake dating—mating—the king of Tartarus?" Nog asked, crossing his scrawny arms over his chest.

I lifted one shoulder. "Yeah, I guess that's what it is. Just for the six months, though. When time's up he said I get to go home, and he'll close the portal."

Styx made a noise in the back of her throat, something that had Pol shaking his head once as if to say *later*.

Nog's mouth dropped open. "Excuse my fucking French, but *what?!?*"

Oh, that's right.

I spent the next ten minutes catching him up. It would have been closer to thirty seconds, but Nog was allergic to being quiet. He interrupted frequently, and repeatedly. By the end I was mildly annoyed with my cousin and wanted to shove him back through the portal with Ben, who was uncharacteristically quiet by comparison.

Not that he'd ever been a chatterbox. Ben knew how to enjoy a comfortable silence, but he wasn't Caius. That man wielded silence like a weapon with the way it charged the air between us. That never happened with Ben, with any man I'd ever been with, come to think of it.

"Maybe there is more than just attraction to the god king."

"Fuck off, Eres. We're not his mate. Things can be hot and heated between two people without being tied to fate, you know."

She huffed in response. I ignored her.

After summing up the end of the story, I had one final addition. "You can go back and tell my dad that, right?"

Nog was taken aback. "Why me? Why not Clara? She's the traitor trying to get you together."

"Hey!" Clara protested. "She never said that."

"Oh yeah, but she clearly thinks it, and I think she's right. You have shit taste in men. Obviously, you think the Soulless One is hot—"

"Nog," I snapped. "I told you not to call him that."

"Just because you've grown feelings for him doesn't

mean I have to change my opinion and call him a different name," he clapped back.

"I don't have feelings for anyone," I whispered. "Stop being a prick."

The truth was, I didn't know what I felt other than confusion. I didn't have plans on sharing that with him.

My cousin released a long, slow breath, the tension melting from his shoulders. "I'm sorry. Really. I'm not trying to be an ass, but neither of you seem to be thinking clearly. You have to see this from my perspective. C'mon, Rea. Pretend mate? You can't lie. You suck at it. All someone has to do is question you and you start to clam up. You look away, your face turns all reddish-brown, and that's ignoring the fidget—"

"I do not," I said, brushing a stray lock of hair behind one ear.

"There! See! You just did it."

"Fine." I threw my hands up. "I suck at lying. Sue me. You know most people shouldn't be good at that sort of thing. It's not exactly a great quality."

Nog groaned. "That's not the point."

"He's made a good argument, though," Ben chimed in. I glared at him because *now* he decided to give his two cents?

"I third this," Clara declared.

"That's nice," I shot back with a heavy dose of sarcasm. "But it doesn't matter because it's the *only way*. Unless I want more people to start making attempts on my life, which no thank you, once is enough."

"It does matter. If you want anyone to believe this, if you want to stay safe, you have to listen to us," Ben said. "You couldn't even fake an orgasm with me. That time you tried was horrendous. What happens when you can't fake this and there *are* more attempts?"

I narrowed my eyes. "For your information, you didn't catch it the three times before then."

His face turned beat red, flushing with embarrassment and probably a little anger. It was his own fault for bringing that up.

"I did, actually," he said softly, shrugging his shoulders. "I just chose not to bring it up. You were going through something, I guess. Didn't want to share it with me, but I didn't want to make things tougher for you. Made me work a little harder, though. We got there again."

It was my turn to blush. It was awkward to have this conversation in front of my cousins, worse to have it with Styx and Pol listening and exchanging glances, and it felt terrible to know his side of it.

"Excuse me?"

And it continued to get worse. Every head turned toward Caius, who stood in the open doorway of the throne room.

"Oh, shit," Clara muttered. "Impeccable timing."

Anxiety crawled over my skin. Terrible timing was more like it.

His dark eyes blazed with unholy fire. The shadows around him seemed to grow longer. I started toward him, needing to put myself between him and Ben.

"Caius, he—"

"Needs to leave," Caius supplied. My lips pursed.

"Don't cut me off," I said, challenging him. His jaw clenched. "He is actually making points that benefit you. They all are. You can't barge in here and throw your weight around without even knowing the context."

He glared at me. "He comes into my realm, my home, the boy that tried to claim my mate, and then he speaks about . . ." His muscles vibrated in anger, and he snapped his fingers, guards coming to Ben's side to presumably get thrown through the portal.

"Wait!" he said loudly when they moved to escort him away. "Let me stay. Please. Not to be with Reagan."

"No."

"Why do you want to stay?" I asked, curious to see his reasoning.

His head hung, dejected. "I know what I did was wrong. I do. And you were wronged. I need help. You and your dad are the only people I've known more dominant than my wolf. He's been batshit crazy the last two weeks. I don't know what to do or who to go to anymore. I don't want to lose myself to him. I don't want to hurt anyone."

I sighed, looking at Caius, hoping to see some sort of sympathy. Instead, he was stoic and unyielding.

Keeping my voice in a low tone, I tried to make him understand. "His wolf can be trouble. Maybe it would be good for him to stick around a little while—"

"Out of the question."

"Caius," I said.

"Reagan," he responded, his gaze dropping from Ben to me as I came to stand before him.

"I'm not going to fuck him, Jesus Christ. He tried to mark me without my consent. He also stopped when I shoved him away. His wolf may have been riding him, that's true, but any trust we once had is gone. That doesn't change that I feel bad for him, just like I would *anyone* that struggled."

Caius stared at me, doing that thing he did with silence, filling it with tension that made me feel things I shouldn't feel.

"It is damn near impossible for you not to help others, even if they've harmed you," he grumbled.

"I'm a guardian," I shot back. "Consider that to be in your favor too."

Caius's brows lowered, his nostrils flaring with a harsh exhale. It was a low blow, but I was angry at his comment. He made it sound like a bad thing. Yes, I cared about others. Yes, Ben fucked up royally. He was also battling a wolf that was desperately trying to take over. Without help, he would lose. I'd seen it before. He didn't deserve that.

"Your Majesty, if I may," Legion said, making his presence known. I looked from Caius to the man at his side. Just past him, Abyssian stood with his arms crossed over his chest. The picture of every charming bad boy while he leaned against the stone wall.

"What?" Caius said sharply, not taking his eyes off me.

"I have experience with boys acting out. He could join my latest batch of recruits. If anyone can tame his wolf, it's me."

He looked past me then, to my ex. "Interesting proposal."

"Recruits?" Ben asked, wary as he should have been.

"In the army," Legion said. "We take boys and make men out of them."

"Or women," Styx scoffed.

"Or women," Legion said with a smirk. "That said, I'd bet good money on it that any woman in my ranks could take you. You're safer starting with the men. Less bloodthirsty."

I turned around to look at Ben. His face was ashen, but his eyes were thoughtful. Considering.

"Would that be something you're interested in?" I asked.

"Would I make it out alive?"

Everyone that was from Tartarus laughed like assholes.

"Seriously, y'all?" I muttered. "That's a legitimate question."

"You won't die, kid, but you might wish you had." I rolled my eyes at Caius.

"You're not helping things."

"Good," he responded. "I wasn't trying to."

Ben swallowed; no small amount of fear wafting off him. I could smell it, even from a few yards away. "And you'll help me tame my wolf?"

I glanced back to see Legion nod once. "You have my word. If you make it through basic, you'll be a new man—and your wolf will fall in line."

"All right, I'll do it."

"Really?" I whipped around, and Ben approached slowly. He kept several feet of distance between us.

"Funny thing. I came here to save you, and you end up saving me." He smiled sadly. "I really am sorry. I don't deserve anything you've given me, but I'm thankful for it."

Unsure how to respond, I cleared my throat of the tightness. This felt like a goodbye, and while I wasn't emotional about saying it to him, I still wasn't a fan of goodbyes in general. "Take care of yourself, Ben."

"You too, Reagan."

Legion clapped him on the shoulder. "I'm going to take this one to the barracks and show him around. You know where to find me if you need me."

Caius nodded, and then they were gone.

I wouldn't admit it, but I breathed easier without having Ben and Caius in the same space, and it felt good to know he was going to get that asshole wolf under control. "You promise you won't do anything to have him killed, right?" I whispered.

Caius' mouth curled in the corner. "Now why would I do that?"

"Say it."

He lifted both hands in mock surrender. "Fine, I promise as long as he doesn't set foot in the same room as you that I won't do anything to have him killed."

"Caius."

"What? I'd say that's more than fair."

A slight smile played on my lips, and all I could do was shake my head. He did let Ben stay with Legion. That was progress. I suppose I was making progress too.

"Sorry to interrupt . . . whatever just happened," Pol started, seemingly annoyed. "What did you learn from Jana?"

All of my warm feelings dissipated. I'd momentarily forgotten about her. Caius sighed, and tension returned, but this wasn't the sexy kind. I knew before he said anything that I wasn't going to like it.

"Nothing. Jana killed herself."

Shock ran through me.

I pressed my fingers to my lips. It's not like there was love lost. At best, I would have just said she was rude to me, then she tried to kill me and that made her a bitch, but to kill herself . . . I shuddered.

"Damn," Nog said. "I was hoping you'd let me at her."

"For the love of the gods," Clara muttered while I chastised him, saying his name in exasperation.

"I don't know why either of you are surprised. In the short time I've been around him—he's always like this. He truly is a little dog at heart," Styx said.

"Hey," Nog shouted. "I'll show you little dog—"

"I dare you. It's been a while since I drowned someone. Please. Try me."

My cousin's steps faltered, and Clara marched over grabbing his arm sharply.

"Stop being a dumbass, dumbass."

"Wow. You're *so* clever," he shot back.

They bickered between themselves, but I didn't find it as funny as I usually would, not when Caius had just delivered such a crushing blow.

She was our only shot.

Taking your own life was an act of desperation no matter how you sliced it. When she killed herself, she took whatever truths she had with her, only leaving more questions behind. I couldn't shake the quiet discomfort that wormed its way into my chest.

When she'd already been willing to kill me and suffer the consequences, what was she so afraid of that she would go to this length to keep quiet? What—or who—was she trying to escape?

CHAPTER 24

REAGAN

I swallowed hard. While I'd been in here earlier today, Caius's room suddenly felt more daunting.

My family wasn't wrong. I was terrible about lying. Which made it all the more necessary for us to be sharing a space, but that didn't mean we had to sleep in the same bed. I wasn't quite ready for that.

"I'll take the floor," I said.

Caius paused halfway across the room to grin over his shoulder. "Worried I'll bite?"

Yes. More worried I'll like it.

"No. I just don't want to sleep with you."

He chuckled, somehow finding that funny.

"Liar."

What? How dare he—"I'm not lying. I really don't want to sleep *next to* you." Fire seemed to fan across my face in anger or embarrassment. I wasn't sure which, or if it was some combination of both.

"That's not the part I think you're lying about."

I started to object when he reached for the buttons on his shirt. My mouth slipped ajar. Another kind of fire slowly filled me, one that would only burn more while sleeping in these close quarters.

"What are you doing?" I squeaked, licking my suddenly chapped lips. My mouth had gone dry. I should be protesting him undressing, but all I could seem to do was stare.

"What's it look like, love?" he quipped. "I'm getting ready for bed. You don't expect me to sleep in these clothes after I've been wearing them all day, do you?"

"I—no—never mind." A shaky breath stumbled out of me. The room was too warm, too welcoming. "It doesn't matter," I continued. "I need to change too. Where is the bathroom?"

Caius thrust his chin toward another opening door I'd missed in the low light of the room. "Scared of being naked in front of me?"

I picked up my backpack pointedly ignoring a certain tan, chiseled god as I entered a bathroom fit for a king. I tossed the bag down then knelt to dig through it. After over a week here, my clothes I brought from home were almost out. Soon I'd have to ask for more. Or I could send Nog.

We hadn't concluded what would be done about him, but for the time being, he was staying. If only because he'd shifted three times, and all three times it took me or Caius commanding him to shift back for it to be successful. I would have wondered if he was faking it were it not for the insults Clara hurled at him. There was no way he'd stay in his corgi form when he so obviously wanted to tell her off.

I sighed thinking about the bite he'd given her when he reached the end of his rope.

Clara was a witch and didn't heal the same way shifters did, but he went for her ankle anyway. Little shit.

I shook my head, grabbing a handful of soft, buttery

fabric. I pulled out my favorite sleep shorts and the cropped tank top I wore with them.

Under different circumstances I wouldn't have worn them around Caius, but my only other pair had to be thrown out after they'd been saturated with blood.

"Well," I muttered. "Guess he's getting a show."

I quickly stripped off my jeans and t-shirt, switching into the skimpy undergarments that still smelled faintly of home.

My heart panged with longing.

As much as Nog could be annoying, I was a little glad he'd come through. It was good to see him. To know he was safe and healthy. I wish the same could be said about the rest of my family. Sure, he said as much, but it was different. I wanted to see it with my own eyes. Just see my dad, even if I was still pissed with him. See my sister, even if I wanted to throttle her for lying to me. See Tía Celeste and Jo and all my other cousins.

I stepped out of the bathroom, deep in my thoughts. My feet were quiet as I padded across the smooth stone floors. If not for the heat of the volcano they would have been cold, but the hot, humid air kept everything warm and balmy.

Caius had taken my place on the velvety soft rug. He was on his side, facing away from me. The thick muscles in his back were on display where the blanket didn't cover. I swallowed hard, happy he was already asleep, as I crawled into the large bed by myself. Softer than any velvet, smoother than silk. He wasn't kidding. This comforter really did put that glorious rug to shame. I smiled to myself at his thoughtfulness. He didn't have to take the floor, but the gesture was kind.

I was still smiling when sleep claimed me only a few minutes later.

Dead leaves crunched beneath my feet.

I was startled, but my body didn't react. Instead I kept walking, moving within the shadows of the trees like I was trying to keep out of sight, hiding from someone or something.

Dread filled me.

This had to be another dream.

I was Abraxia again.

The camisole and skirt fashioned around me might be fit for a queen, but they didn't stop a chill from running down my spine. A wayward wind that didn't belong here in the hot, humid realm.

What was she doing sneaking around?

As soon as the thought took form I wanted to smack myself in the head. She'd taken Caius's soul. Of course she was sneaking around. But maybe not. Something about it all made me think this was a vision before she'd stolen from him, otherwise, what was the point in sneaking once the deed was done?

She stepped with confidence, her movements lithe and matching that wayward wind. It blew her long, dark hair around her, hiding her face like a veil. The wind was coming from her.

No wonder it felt strange and foreign. This was her witch powers at play. I scarcely remembered my own and found myself fascinated by the way she controlled the wind with such little effort. It was as second nature as breathing to her.

Abraxia stepped around a large tree at the edge of the city. Strong arms grabbed her around the middle, but instead of jumping and trying to get away—as I wanted to —she melted in his embrace.

Bergamot and lemon invaded my senses.

"I missed you," a deep voice said.

But it wasn't Caius.

Abraxia leaned back in his arms, weaving one over her head and cupping the back of his neck. She tilted her head back, a smile playing at her lips. I wanted to curse her when her eyes closed, only letting me see the curve of his jaw lined with stubble.

"I missed you more," she murmured.

Lips met hers. They both groaned, coming together like only lovers did. I tried to make out the voice she was speaking to, it sounded familiar. I just couldn't place it . . .

Hands gripped her clothes, shoving up the fabrics of her skirt. It didn't take a genius to know what was coming next and my mind revolted even if Abraxia did not.

Wake up, I told myself.

Wake up. Wake up. WAKE UP!

I gasped, my eyes flying open.

"It worked," I rasped, throat dry. I sat up, rubbing my eyes with the back of my hand. "Haha, it worked! Wait a minute . . . why am I on the floor?"

My hands bunched on the rug beneath me.

"I only just woke up myself, love. Why don't you tell me?" He rumbled in a sleep thickened voice. I turned to gape at him.

"Oh bullsh—" I stopped short. Caius was under the blankets he'd been in last night. I wasn't, and I was half on top of him. My leg was thrown over his, my bronze skin stark against the light blanket and fur. One of my hands was on his chest, but the fabric kept us separated from the mid-chest down. Beneath my palm, his heart pounded in a familiar rhythm, syncing in time with my own. My mouth went dry.

There were a few ways I could have ended up on the

floor with him, but much as I was loath to admit it—Caius carrying me here wasn't one of them.

"What was that?" he said, dark eyes roaming over my body and exposed skin. He hadn't seen my skimpy pajamas last night, but he was definitely getting a good look at them this morning.

"N-nothing."

"Uh, huh. You weren't going to say bullshit, insinuating *I* am a liar, now were you?"

"No . . . yes. Fuck. I don't know." I pulled at my hair with one hand, fingers tangling in the knots that formed in my sleep. "I don't see how else I ended up here."

"Maybe you sleepwalked?"

"What?" I said, my head whipping around so I could give him a dirty look, but it morphed into a playful glare. "I don't sleepwalk and even if I did, it would be right out the door." I might have been snarky, but I lacked conviction.

"Do you have another suggestion?" He arched an eyebrow, daring me to blame him again—except I couldn't.

"No." My entire body deflated. Caius sat up and his blanket fell to his waist. I stiffened at our close proximity when all of him was on display. No one, god or otherwise, should have abs like that, or lines of muscle, or a face that looked as though it were carved into stone then worshiped.

But he did.

Stupid god had it all, and the way he was looking at me in return did not go unnoticed.

"Perhaps you missed me."

"Unlikely," I said, trying to wet my dry lips with my tongue. "Maybe I wanted to smother you in your sleep."

He chuckled, the sound husky and sexy, and gods helped me, I liked it.

"Could be that's why you're wrapped around me. If

your idea of smothering involves my head between those lush thighs . . ." He trailed as my breath caught. His fingertips ghosted down the back of my thigh, to wrap around the underside of my knee. "Let's just say I'd happily let you do so."

"You can't say things like that to me," I protested weakly.

"Oh? Why is that?"

"Because we're not . . ." I didn't want to say it. It wasn't an argument I wanted to have. I liked whatever flirting we were doing. It was fun and didn't have strings attached to it. Saying anything in the realm of mates would ruin the moment. Maybe I needed to ruin the moment.

My face heated as he pulled me onto his lap. We sat chest-to-chest. His lips brushed against mine, a gentle caress and rational thought fled me.

"We don't have to be mates if that's what you were going to say. We're both adults. We can do whatever we want." Heat pooled in my core. With his lips on mine, he had a really good point. "I know the difference here, and I don't have any expectations."

Caius pulled back a fraction, giving me a choice. When I didn't move or speak, he loosened his hold on me, respecting the decision he thought I'd made.

This time it was me that kissed him fully. Hungrily. I nipped at his bottom lip, sucking it into my mouth. My hands curled around his bare shoulders. Caius snapped, and we crashed together like waves.

Strong, calloused fingers gripped my hips. He pulled me flush against him, guiding my hot center over his length.

The friction wasn't enough, but still I chased that feeling, rocking my hips against his.

When the lack of oxygen made my head spin, I tipped

my head back, breaking the kiss. Caius took the opportunity to trail his lips down my throat. I groaned, pressing harder against him. He rubbed a hand down my backside, grabbing a handful to better grind against me in return.

"I love your ass," he mumbled.

I chuckled, and it morphed into a sharp gasp as he teased the flesh where my neck met my shoulder, sucking hard.

I whimpered, whispering his name.

"And these sweet noises," he hummed, licking the tender skin.

Without thinking about any potential consequences, I let him twist me around, gently guiding me so that I still straddled him but instead my back was to his chest. Caius hands settled back at my hips, fingers dipping into the hem of my shorts. I rocked back against him, eliciting a sharp hiss.

His knees came up, spreading my thighs further, to the point it was obscene. My nails pricked his bicep where I clutched his arm. My other one wrapped around the back of his neck as I leaned into him, letting him take my weight.

Caius slid his hand down the front of my shorts. Blunt fingers brushed against the most sensitive parts of me.

His breathing was ragged in my ear, and the quiet rumble of his satisfied hum sent goosebumps skittering across my skin.

Caius ran a single fingertip across my wet entrance, up to my clit where he circled it slowly. My body went taut, and my legs quivered in anticipation.

"Caius," I breathed his name again, knowing how he liked hearing it on my lips.

He growled against my neck, nibbling on the skin there.

"I need . . ." I whispered, rocking back, trying to rub against him.

"What do you need?" His tone was amused, if heated. I was getting to him too.

I reached a hand between my legs, intending to do the work for him. Teasing be damned. "To finish what you started," I murmured.

"Like hell you will," he said, voice dark and serious. That single finger pushed into me, but it wasn't enough. Instead of taking the edge off it just made me crave . . .

"More," I insisted.

"Then ask for it, love."

"*Please*." The ache was building, and the effort it took to say the one word was immense.

A second finger nudged my entrance. This time there was a slight burn as he stretched me, and it was so *good*. Slowly Caius moved his fingers in and out of me, drawing my body tighter and tighter.

I tried to snap my legs together so I could grind against his palm, but his knees kept mine firmly held wide on the outside of his.

"Caius," I hissed, trying desperately to hold my hips still but struggling. I wanted to rock. To move. To pin him down and ride his face just like he talked about.

I couldn't recall a time I'd felt so needy and desperate for release.

"Ask for what you want, Reagan."

I was half a breath from telling him to go fuck himself, but I had no doubt that would backfire. So I pulled on what little courage I had, emboldened by my own desperate and immediate need, then asked for exactly what I wanted.

"*Please* make me come."

Caius let out a deep, throaty rumble of satisfaction. Two

fingers shoved into me hard, making my eyes nearly roll back in my head. His thumb circled my clit, not light but with a touch more pressure than before. It was perfect. My head fell back, and I let out a low moan and the surge of pleasure began to roll through me.

My legs shook. Muscles spasmed wildly out of control as everything in me tightened to the point of pain. Another sweep of his thumb across my clit made me jolt. Everything unlocked for a quarter of a second as the greatest euphoria hit me. I lost myself in the bliss, riding his hand shamelessly.

It seemed like minutes later when the spasms finally died down and he pulled his fingers from me. Wrapping his arm around my waist, I sagged against his hard body.

I swallowed hard, mouth dry and thighs slippery. Faint flutters were still running through me. I'd had my share of friends with benefits over the years, but none of them had done that to me with just their hand, and definitely not as quickly.

Lust waned, and reality began to settle.

"I should probably go . . . Get ready for the day, night, whatever it's called here," I said.

Caius let out a deep laugh. His hand dropped away from my hip. I clambered off of him, somewhat clumsily since my legs were still weak.

Standing in the bathroom, I ran the bathwater and looked at myself in the mirror.

Flushed skin and tangled hair. A soft afterglow on my brown skin. Absentmindedly, I traced my lips, thinking of the hunger in his kiss and how much I wanted him to kiss me that way over and over.

A pang of guilt hit me. What had I done? He said he didn't have expectations, but he claimed we were mates. Of course he had expectations. I didn't want to lead him on. What happened shouldn't happen again. It was great, but I was leaving in six months.

I was.

I was leaving.

There was no way I would fall for Caius.

I was stronger than that.

In a whisper drowned out by the sound of the running water, I only had one thing to say to the woman in the mirror.

"Liar."

CHAPTER 25

REAGAN

*C**lap!***

My butt smacked against the hard floor, the sound reverberating in the room. I thanked my genetics for giving me ample booty to cushion my fall for the hundredth time that morning.

In the week that had passed since Jana had attacked me, the quiet had been a combination of blissful and unnerving. The lingering question as to who she'd been working with remained unanswered, and that wasn't comforting, but I was thankful for the peace.

Well. It was mostly peaceful.

Caius and I had decided it would be worthwhile to have training sessions for self-defense. My dad had trained me in basic hand-to-hand combat, but that was nothing compared to fighting a five thousand-year-old shadow god. Sessions with Caius were brutal, and I knew for a fact he was going easy on me.

The truth of the matter was that I'd never actually been very good at fighting. For all my effort, I was a novice at best. I had strength and speed as a shifter, but grace and follow-through were my shortcomings.

"Your footwork still needs improvement, but you have good balance," Caius said, not for the first time.

"Wonderful," I mumbled, wiping my forehead with the back of my wrist. "Next time I'm attacked, I'll be sure to warn my opponent and tell them I'm skilled in the art of balance. Best watch out."

Caius chuckled, unbuttoning his shirt, and using it to wipe the sweat from his chest. The glistening planes of his muscles made me look away. I may be doing *stuff* with him, but I wasn't going to be some fawning schoolgirl like the kind I'd seen in The Crossroads. There was nothing wrong with it, but it wasn't me. That was more Clara's style.

"You can't land a punch while sparring with me. That's not the same case when fighting someone else."

I snorted. "If you say so."

He cocked his head, throwing the shirt to the sidelines. "Would you rather I go easy on you?"

"Aren't you already?"

"You know what I mean."

"No." I sighed while shaking my head. "That would be pointless. While this is demoralizing, the logical part of my brain reminds me fighting you isn't the same as fighting literally anyone else. I might have some demonic moose come after me, but unless there are other gods around here, I don't have to worry about going toe to toe with a real immortal, right?"

"Right." He smiled. "Now get up."

I planted my hands on either side of my hips and rocked back then forward, into a standing crouch. Bringing my hands up to protect my face, I quickly used the back of one to wipe the sweat as it dripped into my eyes. The saltiness stung, making them water more.

"I'm sweating so much it's leaving salt on my skin," I complained, blinking away the tears.

"You'd sweat in a real fight too." That earned him a huff from me. I'm not sure I'd last this long in a fight, but it wasn't worth saying so. "Now this time, focus on the steps we talked about. Duck, step in, grab me, flip. You have power in your hips and legs, more than your arms. Use it."

I nodded once.

Caius moved almost too fast for me to keep up. When a right hook came sailing for me I dropped to one knee, but that's as far as instinct got me. I was fast enough to avoid the hits, but not fast enough to capitalize on his misses.

Determined to get it right, my legs popped back up as my hand hooked his ankle. I straightened as fast as I could, releasing his ankle. Caius rolled deftly instead of landing sprawled on the ground as I had.

With the first maneuver complete, I dashed to the other side of the gym. My steps fell short when the ground was yanked out from under me. Instinctively, I wanted to catch myself on my hands, but I'd been working on softening my landing and spreading out the impact. Learning to fall correctly was our first lesson. Then we moved to more offensive things, or defensive, in my case. While Caius thought I'd stand a good shot against whoever else might attack me, there was the worry that I'd be outclassed so the priority was to get away.

Which suited me just fine. While Eres was all on board the kill-train, I'd rather maim and run than stick around and risk dying all because she wanted to be badass.

I belly flopped onto the floor, using my forearms for impact rather than my hands and elbows. Still, I miscalculated, and my head whipped back, then down, my forehead hitting the mat.

"Ow," I groaned. Caius crawled up the back of my body, reminding me we were still in the scene, and I couldn't let him get me in a headlock or it would be all over.

I twisted, bringing one knee up as I did. I planted my sneaker on his shoulder and pushed as hard as I could. While Caius didn't move, my body slid upwards and out from under him.

This was the furthest I'd gotten all week, which meant I had no idea what he'd do next. I crab walked backwards, moving fast as I could. My back bumped into something hard.

Weapons wall.

This was good. I could work with that.

Springing to my feet, I spun to grab the first thing I saw—a spear. Caius grabbed me while my back was turned.

"Got you," he breathed against my neck. Goosebumps scattered down my spine, making me all tingly.

"Did you?" I spun the spear, bringing it over the back of my head. Then using two hands I used it to bear down on the back of his neck, pushing it into my shoulder. Caius grunted.

I took a step back into him, then bent at the waist once more. My hips supported his weight as I used the spear to flip him over my shoulder in a slightly tweaked maneuver. This time he didn't roll with grace or elegance.

Caius recovered quickly, but I was ready for him. Instead of turning my back and running, I stepped back and swung my spear like a baseball bat, or in my profession, a shovel.

The hard wood connected with his head.

Wood splintered. The handle went flying.

Too much.

I fell to my knees before him. "I am so sorry," I said, reaching for his cheek where a slash marred his skin. Golden blood dripped from it.

I froze, hand raised toward him.

"It's okay," Caius said, rolling his neck. He plopped down into a sitting position and massaged the back of his neck while the cut on his cheek healed before my eyes.

Shifters healed fast, but that? I swallowed. No wonder he was unkillable. He healed like Wolverine.

"Your cheek," I said, pausing when I wasn't sure how to finish that statement. He lifted a hand to the thin trail of blood, all that was left of his wound.

Caius fingers smeared it together as he regarded it then me.

"You hit me."

"I know." I swallowed thickly. "And I am so sorry. I should have—"

"Don't apologize."

My mouth fell open. "Why not?"

"You did perfect, Reagan. Flipping me with the spear? That was a great use of what you had and using it to help implement what we've already worked on. It shows you know the moves. You also handled it like a natural. Have you fought with one before?"

I scratched the back of my head. "Not exactly. My job was unconventional." I paused for a moment, realizing this wasn't a conversation I usually had with people. In fact, it might have been the first time I said it out loud. "My family are graverobbers and it was my job to dig. I've gotten in more fights than I can count, and I have a shovel as my first line of defense."

While I didn't expect it, I wouldn't have been surprised

if he judged us. People often did. I mean, we were graverobbers. Even I judged us sometimes for the jobs we took. But Caius didn't do that. Instead he threw his head back and let out a deep, bellowing laugh.

"Are you serious?"

"As a saint," I said, cracking a smile. "I've tangoed with plenty of ghouls. Half a dozen crazy vampires. More than a few souls, though Clara mostly dealt with those since they're not hurt by anything on the living plane. But yeah, so when I grabbed the spear I just kinda treated it like I would a shovel."

He shook his head. "Every time I think I have you figured out you surprise me again."

"What can I say?" I crossed my legs and then put my elbows on my knees. "I'm a surprising kind of girl."

"Did you choose graverobbing or was it something expected of you?"

I pushed a sweaty lock of hair out of my face. "Expected to some degree. My family is big. There's a lot of kids and few adults. We all have to do our part to provide."

Caius nodded thoughtfully. "That's a lot of pressure to put on kids."

I snorted. "No, not really. Being the guardian was a lot, but working?" I shook my head. "We were all fed, clothed, educated, and had a roof over our head. That's just part of being in a family. You give back by helping out. Besides, it's not like we worked for free. We got our cut from every job. We paid our bills and did what we wanted with the rest. I usually used my extras to buy really good paints from this one woman in the market."

Caius was quiet for a moment. "You have an old soul."

"Literally," I said before I thought better of it. Thankfully, he cracked a smile.

"When did you become the guardian? I'm a bit fuzzy on the details since I was on this side of the portal the whole time." My smile waned, and Caius noticed instantly. "We don't have to talk about it if you don't want to."

"It's okay," I said slowly. "I'm just not used to talking about it. My family all knew what I was, but it wasn't exactly something casually brought up at the dinner table, you know?" I raked my hands through the sweaty, loose curls that formed around my face.,

He nodded. "I assumed as much when Nog pointed out your ex didn't even know."

"It wasn't safe to tell anyone."

"If you'd rather not—"

"It's okay," I repeated. "Really. It's normal that you'd be curious. It's your soul, after all." I rolled my shoulders and leaned back, putting my weight on my elbows. "I was a newborn when they put it in me. It was customary that it moved from mother to daughter, right after birth. Then the cult I was born into would raise the guardian, ensuring she do her duty and have a baby at twenty-five, and the cycle would begin again."

His lips parted. "The day I saved you, at your house, when you were asking me not to kill your family . . . you said witches put it on you as a baby. You were serious . . ."

"Yup. Shitty doesn't cover it, right?" I huffed a small laugh.

"You're not twenty-five," he said after a pregnant pause.

"I'm not."

"You're older."

"I am."

The quiet spread between us, his unasked question hanging there. I took pity on him and answered it. "I escaped as a child. Back then I had Eres and some pretty powerful witch magic if my memories are to be believed."

"Eres?"

"My unicorn."

"Ahh, most people here don't name their animals. I wasn't aware yours had a name."

"We were separated for a long time. That separation, well, let's just say it's made our relationship rocky at best. She and I could use some couple's therapy."

The internal grumbling of a certain death god in my psyche indicated she disagreed.

"What happened to the cult when you escaped? Are they still hunting you?" Something dangerous flashed in his eyes.

"No, Eres killed them when I escaped. Or I did. The details are a bit fuzzy." He relaxed a fraction. "Why? Planning to handle them yourself?"

"If I could, I would," he replied. "Part of me wants to bring them back just to end them again but I promised I would leave your world since it rejects my magic and therefore me. If they were still breathing, I'd send Styx and Legion to bring them here. Then I could torture them for eternity for what they did to you."

Wow. That was oddly sweet, if a little crazy. "You can do that? Bring back the dead?"

"Not exactly. When a soul leaves, it still exists. If they haven't been reborn yet I could trap them in their rotting corpse if I wanted. It would be a painful experience on their part, and that's before the torture."

I snorted. "You sound like Clara. She traps evil souls in the stuffed animals she crochets and then gives them away to kids in The Crossroads."

"She does what now?" he asked, stunned.

"Spirit witch, remember? She says it's their penance."

Caius raised his eyebrows in what appeared to be surprise coupled with approval. "That's what she's crocheting all the time?"

I nodded. "She only looks sweet and innocent, but she's ruthless."

He hummed in what sounded like agreement. "I don't mind teaming up with her should we ever find some that survived. What did you mean by that when you said if your memories are to be believed?" He questioned, laying down on the floor next to me, putting his hands behind his head.

I swallowed hard. "After I left . . ." A shudder ran through me. "I wasn't whole. The things they planned to do to me, the things they did do—it affected me. I had nightmares. Apparently during one of them I lashed out and almost killed my sister. So my dad conspired with Eres to lock away most of my past and in doing so also locked away Eres." I bit the inside of my cheek. "It's why we're so separate from one another."

"I had figured out you couldn't shift when I found you on the floor in your room. Apparently I was right," he said, quickly putting together what I told him.

I nodded. "That was the first time I shifted in seventeen years. I don't even remember shifting before unless I really think about it. Even then, everything is still murky. Like looking through muddy water to see your reflection. You know something is there, but you only see vague shapes and outlines. The ward breaking unlocked my memories, but it's not like it all came back to me with clarity. I have the memories now, but I have to actively sift through them if I want to remember, and bad as it is—I don't."

Caius frowned. "Why would that be bad?"

I lifted my shoulder. "I gave my dad and sister hell

before I left because they never told me. I feel like I don't have a right to be pissed if I'd rather not know."

"That's bullshit," he said. "You have a right to be pissed because they gave you no choice. Whether or not you want to remember doesn't matter. You weren't given the option to choose."

I sighed. "Yeah, you're preaching to the choir."

"What?"

"It's a saying. It means you're telling me exactly what I already agree with. Things with me and my family are just complicated right now. I'm still mad, but I also feel bad I left them on a bad note. Now I'm gone for six months and they're going to wonder . . ."

"Nog can take notes back and forth for you," he reminded me. Since Nog was only in Tartarus for his random shifting fits, he could go back and forth if he wished.

"That's true. Maybe I should write to them."

We fell quiet for a few minutes, both lost in our own thoughts. It was a comfortable silence. Not the kind that practically begged to be filled. I'd be lying if I said I didn't enjoy spending time with him and talking to him—once I let myself stop hating him. He was easy to get on with, and he was a surprisingly good listener. It made me feel bad that Abyssian and Pol had yet to find a way to get his soul out of me. I mean, don't get me wrong, I had no desire to die. But he wasn't what I originally thought, he might be soulless, but he wasn't evil.

"Can I ask you something?"

"Hmm?"

"I wanted to ask what your plans are if they *do* find a way to get you your soul back? You know, without killing me."

Caius didn't tense like I'd expected. "Truth be told, I have no idea. I'd go on just as I am now I suspect—albeit less pained."

Something akin to guilt touched me. "I'm sorry."

"Don't be," he said, sitting up. "It's not your fault. You were just a baby. If anything, they stole your life just like they did mine."

I'd never thought of it quite like that, but he had a point. "I wouldn't have survived having my soul cleaved like you did. The pain you went through . . ." I shuddered again. "I know it's not my fault, but I am sorry. I wish I could give it back."

His lips quirked up in a smile. "Is that affection I sense coming from you? Empathy for the Soulless One?" he said in jest. "Don't tell me you're already in love with me?"

I smacked his side playfully, and Caius laughed. "Nope, definitely not. I'm just a nice girl, which I'm sure is so surprising to you since you don't know what those look like."

He snickered, continuing to laugh at my expense. Reaching up to the spot where I hit his cheek, he grazed over it. "Still don't know what nice looks like. I'll let you know when I see her."

"I take it back. I'm not sorry for hitting you with the shovel. You deserved it, I just didn't know what for yet."

"Which one?" I asked Clara while holding up a short-sleeved tunic and three-quarter length loose knit sweater.

"Aren't you going to a barn?" she asked, cocking her head and glancing at my closet. "Maybe something a little more practical? I'm picturing you shoveling shit, and that's not the ensemble I'd imagined."

I rolled my eyes, dropping both options on the mattress and throwing a sock at her head. "We're going out to be seen in public as "mates," I said, using my fingers to make air quotes. "And it's the kennel, not a barn."

"Oh, fancy." She blew out an exaggerated breath. "Maybe in Tartarus that's a date? Kind of weird, but who am I to judge?"

Laughter escaped me. "You judge everyone." I pointed at her crochet needles and skein of yarn. "Don't pretend otherwise. You call it punishment, but it's judgment too."

Clara shrugged her shoulder, but she couldn't hide her grin. "Tomato, potato."

"That's not how the saying goes."

"It's my saying." She got up from her reading chair and walked over to the bed. Pointing to the flowy tunic, she said, "That one. It'll be warmer in the market with all the people around."

"How'd you know we're going to the market too?" I pulled my t-shirt off and slipped the tunic over my head.

"Pol and Abyssian were arguing about it not being safe for you. I was eavesdropping." She plopped back into the chair and began working on her latest crocheted doll.

"More like stalking. Which one do you have a crush on?" I pulled leggings on and laced up my boots quickly.

Clara scoffed.

"Oh, it's Pol, then? The way you two poke one another looks like two kids on the playground who don't know how to say they like each other. Just push him down already if he won't pull your hair and curse your cooties." I grinned. She absolutely had her eyes set on him.

"*Please*," she countered, scrunching her nose. "He's grouchy and annoying, and he's sketchy about everything. Abyssian is more my type." Her voice had a dreamy lilt when she spoke about the latter.

"Careful there," I said as I brushed my hair. "He's quite the ladies' man from what I hear. Charming and handsome, for sure. Maybe a bit of a player too. Besides, what about you and what's his face?"

"Crowley? We actually broke up the night of our last job."

My demeanor softened, and I turned to her. "What? You didn't say anything about that. You'd said you had a job with his crew that night."

She blew a stray hair off her face and sighed. "I did. Finished the job, got payment, and everyone left. But I went back when I realized I'd dropped a crochet hook somewhere between my truck and the location where we'd been. When I got back, I saw him with Ariel."

"His ex?" She nodded. "Could it have been a coincidence? Maybe she was working nearby?" I didn't like Crowley. Nog was right that his sister had bad taste in men and usually went for a fuckboy of the month, but I still gave people the benefit of the doubt until I had more information.

Clara barked a laugh. "Not unless it was also coincidence his pants fell off while by happenstance hers did too, so he accidentally fucked her up against a tree."

My lips parted. That was certainly enough information. "What a dick." A few moments of silence spanned between us before I said, "I hope she got a few splinters in her ass for it."

Clara laughed. "I actually thought the same thing."

"You told me you cancelled your plans with him because you suspected me of lying." I narrowed my gaze at her, humming in disapproval.

She pressed her lips together. "I said I cancelled plans. Didn't say they were plans *with* him. You just assumed."

"Isn't that some shit," I grumbled, wishing I knew how to fib that well. "Why didn't you say anything about it?"

"In front of Nog? No way!" She lifted her shoulder, trying to blow it off. "I would have said something to you later, but things went haywire pretty quickly that night if you recall." Clara glanced at my neck, then waved her hand, gesturing to the castle we were currently occupying.

I chuckled. "Can't argue that. So I guess you're a single lady." Clara waggled her eyebrows and I smiled. "Okay, but don't get your heart broken if you hop on the Abyssian train."

"Says the woman who is fake dating a king and taking a little side action," she countered.

"What? That's not—" I spluttered, feeling my cheeks warm, and she laughed at my inability to form a sentence.

A knock on my door interrupted us and I took a deep breath, knowing full well who was on the other side.

"Liar," she mouthed, grinning.

"Come in," I called out, giving my cousin a death glare to keep her sex comments to herself. She pressed her lips together tightly and made a locking motion, throwing away the imaginary key.

Caius entered, greeting my cousin politely, but it didn't escape my notice that his gaze lingered on her bag of crochet for a few seconds longer than he normally would have. Now that he knew what it was, I suppose that curiosity and skepticism was to be expected. Not every day you meet a spirit witch with homemade little devil dolls.

Grabbing a hair tie and slipping it on my wrist, I smoothed my shirt and took a few steps toward Caius. A nervous buzz filled my chest and I wanted to smack myself for it. This was for show, and I knew it, but our last conversation had somehow managed to bring a wall down for both of us—at least to some extent. As though he could sense my anticipation, his lips slightly curved up.

"Are you ready, mate?" he asked, holding his arm out, elbow crooked so I could slide mine through it.

"Yup." I slid my arm through his, preparing to parade myself around like a trophy. I could survive a few hours of showing off. I'd be fine.

"You look nice," he said softly. "I hope you're hungry."

A normal person would say yes, or where are we going, or sure. Not me. Before I could stop myself, with a flattering smile on my face, I responded with, "Thanks. You too."

My eyes widened, and my cheeks flushed again. Caius's nostrils flared slightly, his pupils dilating.

"Hungry for a little side action," Clara muttered, looking away with a wry smile.

I groaned and Clara snorted.

"That's not what I meant," I mumbled, having a hard time making eye contact with him. "I meant you look nice too."

Giving me the thumbs up, she mouthed, "Get you some."

Could I survive a few hours without making unintended sexual innuendos? I wasn't sure.

Maybe just kill me now.

The kennels where Caius's dogs were housed were nicer than the houses in The Crossroads.

It was set up similar to horse stables, but grander and more opulent than one would ever imagine. The rich red tint of the wood gleamed. Ornate carvings of canines with men and women adorned the archway above each den, along with a name encrusted in crystals. Kish. Nanna. Kai. Bau. An.

Plush beds in each stall looked as though they were made of the finest cloth. Fresh, clean hay lay on the ground. There wasn't even a scent of animals here.

I breathed out in awe. "You keep your dogs here? Their mattresses look more comfortable than mine. Hell, my Tío Amos's house isn't this nice, and he took an entire fancy apartment building in the old Clayton neighborhood."

"Is this a good thing or . . .?"

"Sorry," I began. "Just an old area of The Crossroads, before it became The Crossroads. It was a nice place once upon a time."

"And where you lived?" he asked.

I raised an eyebrow, catching his use of past tense. "Is not as fancy."

"I sense a "but" in there."

"But," I said, smiling, "I love it. It's home, and we do just fine."

"Your Majesty," a woman said, coming around the corner and doing a quick curtsy. "We weren't expecting you. The dogs are on a run. Should be back any moment."

"No problem, Izza. We were heading to the market for lunch, but I wanted to come down and show my mate the kennels, introduce her to the staff here," he said gesturing to the empty dens around us.

"Oh, gosh, why didn't you—" Izza's eyes widened, and she brushed stray hairs out of her face then tried to smooth out her shirt and work pants before she stopped and laughed. "Piss. I'm wrinkled and covered in mud and that's not going to change." Taking a deep breath, she smiled warmly and held out a dirty hand. "I'm Izza. Lead handler, head caretaker, and the boss of everything in between."

"Reagan," I said, taking her hand in a firm shake and smiling in return.

The dogs howled in the nearby distance, and thundering paws shook pebbles on the ground.

"Kish is in a mood today, so look out for her. She's bitey," Izza warned, rolling a sleeve down before buttoning the cuff. "Gild didn't pay attention to her signals earlier."

Caius shook his head and huffed. "One day that kid will listen."

"Well today isn't the day." She huffed in return. "The healer had to sew a finger back on before she could do anything else." Turning to me, she gave additional instructions. "Kish will come to us when she's ready. Leave her be until then. She's so territorial right now. Damn double new moons."

Her final words echoed in my mind.

"Th—the moons?" I stuttered over the words before clearing my voice. "What do the moons have to do with it?"

"She'll go into heat," Caius answered.

"That's an understatement," Izza muttered.

I looked at him. "Dogs do that with the moon cycles?"

He tilted his head side to side. "Not exactly. Usually just shifters go into heat with the double new moons sync, but Kish does as well."

"What?" I asked, feeling like I had swallowed sand. "Does that happen to all shifters?"

"Only mated shifters." I blew out a tiny breath of relief, but he added, "whether or not they accept the bond."

Still, I was fine. There was no mate bond, and it wasn't a conversation I wanted to have anymore. He sensed my denial in the silence, but neither of us could bring it up in front of others.

"We have time to—"

"Talk about it in private," I interjected, and he accepted my plea to stop having any part of this cryptic discussion. He nodded. "Why don't you tell me more about Kish. She's not a shifter, so how is she tied to the moons?"

Caius cupped my cheek, rubbing his thumb over it gently. "Kish is just special. As are you."

My lips parted. "Did . . . did you just compare me to a dog?" I whispered, and he stammered as he tried to recover.

"That is—That is not what I meant."

Izza snickered, but she tried to cover it with a cough as she rolled down her other sleeve. My cheeks flushed. I'd had enough of them doing that today. What the hell was going on?

"*Very* smooth, my king," she said before biting her lip. Addressing me, she added, "Don't hold it against him, milady. He's a bit rusty in romance, apparently, but he's just lovely all the same."

She winked, turning around, and heading for the main entrance to the stables.

"You know I didn't mean to compare you to my dogs— or any dogs, right?" he asked, turning to me.

"Look, all I know is you just informed me you think I'll go into heat in this place." I kept my voice low while I focused on the double doors of the grand kennels. "I can't very well leave, so if all I get is a well-aimed shovel at your head and a few jabs in public, I'll take what I can get." Even though I was certain he was wrong, it was fun to tease him. A smile curved up my lips and I could feel him staring at me.

What I should have said was "I make jokes when I'm feeling awkward and immensely uncomfortable and now seemed as good a time as any."

The thundering increased as the dogs got closer.

"Well played, my mate."

"Thank you, my king," I said, flirting back. I think. Was it flirting? I wasn't good at this.

Whatever the moment held was interrupted quickly when his dogs came barreling at full speed.

Our attention snapped over to them and he ducked down, arms open, while I took several steps to the side when I realized they weren't slowing. In fact, when they saw him, they lowered their heads, and stretched their bodies into a harder run until they plowed into him, and he went crashing to the ground in a pile of wagging tails and giant paws.

His face was covered by wet snouts as they sniffed him

and licked him, all while he mumbled that it was good to see them too.

Watching the exchange was weird. It was . . . wholesome. Unexpected, to say the least.

All but one had piled on top of Caius. A large brown dog with deep blue eyes sat by the door, regal and confident. I could feel her hardened stare and I knew without a doubt that this was Kish. Her pupils narrowed, her focus solely on me as she slowly approached, head hunched down.

Eres stirred, warning me of the danger I was putting myself in as I lowered myself to one knee.

You do not bow to a dog.

Stop it. She's the leader of her pack. I'm giving her my respect. She needs to know she can trust me. You can't just storm up to every animal and expect them to accept us just because we can shift into a unicorn.

Eres huffed in disagreement.

I remained kneeled, and the other dogs sensed their alpha moving close to them. The licking and wagging of tails ceased, and Caius sat up. Izza nervously called Kish, and when the dog ignored her, she took a step toward us, but I shook my head.

Izza looked at Caius, but he sat still, watching the exchange. Kish turned and glanced at him, and he inclined his chin as though they were having a secret conversation. She huffed, her jowls jiggling with the exhaling of air.

Did she just roll her eyes?

Kish stopped in front of me, letting out a low rumble in her chest and she pawed at the ground twice.

"She wants you to . . . pet her," Izza said, the last two words sounding as though they were a question.

"That's a friendly growly sound?" I asked, arching an eyebrow. Kish barked loudly. "Okay, okay." I reached out, finding a spot behind her suede-like ear. She grumbled her delight, closing her eyes and sighing as she leaned against me.

"Well, I didn't expect that," Izza said, clearly relieved.

"Why not?" I asked, almost falling over as she plopped herself down at my feet, knocking my balance off.

"She only likes Caius. She hates everyone. She only tolerates me for his benefit." Kish turned and grumble-barked at her in response. "Oh don't act like it's not true," Izza shot back, and Kish sighed.

Caius got up, dusting his pants off and walking to a water barrel to wash his face. "Izza is actually the only one who hasn't lost a body part when working with Kish."

My mouth fell open, and I looked at the dog whose head was in my lap. "And you didn't think to warn me?"

"No need," he said, splashing the water on his skin a few times before patting himself dry with a towel. "I'm the only one she truly answers to, but she has always indicated she'd accept my mate."

"How does she know?" I whispered, glancing at Izza, and not wanting to say anything further. I wanted to ask, what if she just recognizes the other part of his soul?

I expected Caius to answer, but Izza was the one who spoke. "Kish is his familiar. She'd recognize his mate anywhere."

"Then why were you worried?" he asked her, coming to stand beside me. Kish had passed out in my lap, snoring.

"Not worried. Just cautious. I said I didn't expect it to go so well because," she paused, lowering her voice into a whisper, "she's been a moody bitch all day and meeting someone new could tip her over the edge."

Kish's eyes snapped open, and she turned her head to Izza. She barked, getting up and stretching completely before leaning to lick my hand once. She walked by Caius, and he knelt down to kiss her nose and she gave him a single lick. Kish turned for her kennel, with fresh straw and clean water and a large, warm bed—then she glared at her lead caretaker before softening, and nudging Izza's hand with her snout in a kiss-not-kiss.

"Love you too, mama," Izza said, smirking.

"Do you want help getting them cleaned up and put away?" Caius asked.

"Nonsense. You two go off and have lunch. Gild will be back soon enough, and with any luck, he'll have all ten fingers." She smiled, then tucked her bottom lip between her teeth and whistled, calling the dogs with a sharp sound I had never heard before.

Caius bent down and rubbed their faces in a goofy way as each one went to Izza as instructed. He mumbled what could only be described as baby talk to each of them.

Growing up, I'd always heard we could judge a person by how they treated animals. As I watched him show affection, loving on his beautiful dogs, I had to assume it wasn't just a way to judge man, but primordials as well.

We left the busy markets after an hour or so. Watching Caius mingle amongst the citizens of Tartarus was interesting. He didn't lord over them or treat them as if they were lesser. He spoke with several townspeople, even asking about their family members by name. Checking in on the progress of a blacksmith's child who was learning how to ride a horse. Getting an update on the construction of a woman's second pub. Her first was a smashing success and in such high demand, they needed another location, which he helped procure.

How are the moon crops this season?

Is your grandfather well? Tell him he owes me another chance to win my money back at dice.

Why is so-n-so not in the bakery? She had her baby. Joyous news! I'll send a gift.

He knew *everyone*. Really knew them. Furthermore, he cared about their wellbeing. The warmth on his face was genuine, and it didn't disappear the moment we were alone again. These people brought him joy. Their happiness was important to him.

"What's troubling you?" he asked, breaking my train of thought as we headed back to the castle.

"Nothing is troubling me. Just processing." He raised a brow in question, while the other one lowered. Okay. He was confused. I took a breath. "No one knows what Tartarus truly is. I mean, how can we when no one has been here, and people only know the stories that get passed down on Earth? We all thought it was Hell. A place for torture and punishment. But these people . . . they're no different than the people in The Crossroads, honestly. Blacksmiths. Bakers. Generations of families just taking care of each other, trying to make a living. They look up to you. Respect you. It's just . . ."

"Not what you expected," he said, finishing my sentence for me and I nodded in agreement.

"Not even close. I saw community and a functioning society," I said, gesturing to the town behind us. After a long pause, I sighed. "Thank you for bringing me to the village. For introducing me to the people here."

Caius reached down, taking my hand in his and lacing our fingers together. "Of course."

Today was supposed to be for show. Let everyone know I was Caius's mate. *We* were mates. All to keep me safe. That was the goal. No hidden agendas. I was uncomfortable with the idea at first, surely thinking my inability to lie would be written all over my face. It ended up not even mattering. I wasn't lying when I was out there talking to people. I was just Reagan.

Every single thing I'd been told by the elders was a lie. A fabricated misrepresentation of Caius's beliefs and how he treated people. Falsehoods passed down from generation to generation.

The King of Monsters, they'd called him.

The Soulless One.

What I'd seen today was nothing of the sort. I saw the ruler of Tartarus, laying in the dirt and covered in happy, drooly, dog kisses while he laughed and smiled. I saw him carry a basket of fish from the docks to the market stand so for one trip, another man didn't have to. I saw him play with the baker's kids, letting one of them sit on his shoulders without a second thought.

Jo had said we believe what we are told to believe when we are young, and I'd believed every word, repeating it faithfully just as each of my ancestors had done.

If he wasn't the King of Monsters, and he wasn't the Soulless One, what else had I been wrong about?

Nightmares plagued me.

Dreams of fire and ash. Blood and poison. I twisted in my sleep, my legs tangling in the silky sheets. I didn't have to sleep, but I preferred to. Immortality, true immortality, was long without it. Sleep served to reset the mind as much as it did the body. After waking for the third time that night, I surrendered to being awake.

Darkness greeted me.

The fire had died to mere embers in the hearth. I sat up, the sheet pooling at my waist. My mate had insisted I keep my bed. As much as I didn't like it, I didn't want to argue over such a trivial thing. I'd rather we just slept together, but that wasn't an option yet either.

Over the top of the loveseat I could just make out Reagan's sleeping form. Her hair fanned out across her pillow, and she'd kicked the blankets away, leaving her in those ridiculously tiny pajamas that made me want to bend her over.

I scrubbed a hand down my face, trying and failing to

push that thought from my mind. Silently, I dropped my feet to the floor and padded across to the bathroom and washed my face with cool water. In the past I might have gone for a run, or even a swim if I knew Styx wasn't in her kelpie form and riled up. No good came from being in the water when she was upset. People had died from such a thing. Lightning tended to do that.

Instead, I re-entered the bedroom and gathered the documents Pol had brought me last night to look over. Most of it was monotonous. Towns asking for more land. Emissaries from provinces wanting to visit now that news of my mate had spread. One piece of parchment stood out among the rest.

Dear Caius,

I hope this letter finds you well. My name is Dannika. I am Reagan's cousin, and Queen of Blood and Beryl, one of the nine Houses that rule on Earth. We were recently informed that the portal to Tartarus has been open for several weeks, and though it remains well-guarded, there is great curiosity surrounding it.

The king and I would like to propose a meeting on neutral grounds to discuss the intentions and management of the portal.

It's my understanding you have declared Reagan as your mate and that she has crossed over with you as well. I've heard a few versions of the story so far, as you can imagine. Our family is quite large, and we are protective of each other, but Clara has assured me you are treating her like a queen. One day I hope to welcome you to the family.

Please give Reagan my love. Her father misses her terribly, as we all do.

Warmest Regards,
Dannika Laskaris, Queen of Blood and Beryl

. . .

I set the letter down and scratched at my five o'clock shadow. The stubble was thicker than I usually liked, but my days were filled with work and Reagan. I had no regrets. A beard was hardly the worst thing to happen.

As I was pouring over how to respond to the letter, Reagan appeared in front of me. Her body was shaped like she was sleeping, her eyes still closed. She hung mid-air for a brief second before she dropped onto the bed.

Her warm skin brushed against mine. Breasts pressed to one thigh and ass hanging over the other. I stiffened in shock as her eyes flew open.

"What the—"

She took one look at where she was and groaned.

"Don't tell me I sleepwalked *again*," she said, sitting up. I instantly missed the feeling of her pressed against me but kept it to myself as she shuffled up to her knees. "That's the third time this week."

"You didn't sleepwalk," I said slowly, pushing the papers together in a haphazard stack and setting them on the edge of my nightstand. I turned back, giving her my full attention. "You teleported."

"What?" Her tone was filled with doubt and her eyebrows scrunched together in confusion. "That's not possible I'm—"

"Half witch," I interrupted. "And a unicorn shifter. Both of which traditionally have magic outside of shifting into your animal."

She went quiet, her gaze distant . I recognized the look as her speaking to Eres. A moment passed. She narrowed her gaze. Another minute went by, then she blinked, refocusing on me. "I don't suppose you know how to excise Eres from me, do you?"

"Afraid not." One side of my mouth quirked up. "What did she say?"

"Apparently that *traitor* has known I've been teleporting the whole time. It's a power I had when I was younger, before my dad locked my magic away."

I scratched my stubble. "Why when you're sleeping? Was it that way before?"

"I—" she broke off. Eres must have said something else because her lips pressed together in a firm line. "I don't think so. Eres said I used to do it at will. My powers are slowly coming back, and she thinks—"

"She thinks?" I prompted when she didn't continue.

Reagan sighed. "She thinks I'm subconsciously moving to where I want to be." I couldn't help smirking any more than she could help elbowing me. "Ow," she complained. "Have I mentioned you're hard?"

"Repeatedly." My double entendre made her grin.

"Not that way. Get your head out of the gutter."

I chuckled, grabbing her by the waist and dragging her onto my lap. Reagan slapped at my hands. She was being playful, not serious, or I would have let her go instantly.

"You're insatiable," she muttered.

"When it comes to you? Always." Despite the fact I wanted to take it further, this wasn't the time. I kept my hands on her waist, turning her sideways so I could look at her. "There's nothing wrong with wanting to be in my bed. You know that, right?"

A blush fell over her cheeks, adding a rosy tint to her bronze skin. "That's not . . . that's not what's bothering me."

"Okay," I said slowly. "What is it, then? Talk to me, Reagan."

"It's me. My past. I just, ugh." She gripped her hair near

the roots and squeezed. "I hate that I don't remember. That the only way to remember is to go through my memories one by one and relive it. I hate that I had no choice, and that no one thought to educate me or even tell me about it as I got older. They let me all believe I was weak and now I have powers that I don't know how to use, and I'm relying on my unicorn—who is just as much to blame—to tell me what the hell is going on."

I sighed, rubbing her back with one hand while I held her to me with the other. "Hey, hey. It's okay. We'll figure this out. Together."

"How?" she asked, water gleaming in her eyes. It pissed me off to see her on the verge of tears over this. I was livid *for* her. The lies she'd been told were painful, but the truth hurt significantly worse.

"We take it one day at a time. If you want to go through your memories, then I'll be here to process with you. If you don't and you'd rather learn your powers without accessing the past, then we practice. Teleporting is a power I possess. I can help you learn to control it—at least when you're awake. Same for shifting."

The tears spilled over, and she wiped them angrily, almost like she was pissed for crying at all. "You promise?"

I hated the hopeful tone in her voice, as if I'd ever lie to her. Instead of saying as much I lowered my forehead to hers and whispered, "I promise."

We kissed softly and it wasn't the typical explosion of passion that occurred between us. Instead, it was quiet. Gentle. I felt something blooming for the first time, and it caused a sudden fear to settle deep in my stomach.

I swallowed hard and pulled away.

"How would you like to switch out sparring with shifter training today?" I asked, keeping my tone light.

"Really?" The most beautiful smile blossomed on her face, stretching from cheek to cheek. "I would love that."

This woman was quickly becoming more than just my mate. She was something vital, and it terrified me that my feelings were this deep, this fast, when she still had every intention of leaving me.

The loss of my soul was an immeasurable pain. The sorrow was all-consuming. I barely survived having a piece of me so brutally stolen.

Still, I made it.

This was different. If I couldn't make her stay, she would cross that threshold back to Earth. Something told me I wouldn't survive her ripping out my heart and walking away.

The weight of the grief would bury me, or worse, I would become the villain everyone had feared.

After all, what is the point of a soul when you have no heart?

"This is what people do for fun on Earth now?" Abyssian asked skeptically, glancing at the tamale assembly line I'd set up on the long table in the castle kitchen. "This just looks like a lot of work."

"I mean, it's tedious, but it can be a lot of fun," I said, setting down bowls of soaked corn husks. "We make tamales, eat, and spend time with family and friends."

Pol raised an eyebrow. "Spend time doing what?"

"Everyone is different. We like to dance, play lotería, kick Nog's ass at Mario Kart . . ." Clara answered, tucking a strand of hair behind her ear. "And drink Reagan's moonshine."

"I'm out. I don't know what those other two things are, but I didn't agree to this," he responded quickly.

"Agree to what?" I asked, bewildered. "It's not like we're skinning cats. We're just hanging out."

"I don't dance," Pol grumbled, looking at Caius and shaking his head.

"Relax, jackass," Clara shot back. "No one asked you to dance."

"Oh my god, just kiss already," I muttered, grabbing some spoons.

"Reagan!" she shouted, looking between me, Abyssian, and Pol. "Take it back!"

Pol stood up from the table, seeing the tension between my cousin and his friend. "Don't bother. I'll just leave."

I realized all too late that she had likely already made a move on Abyssian, and I'd just embarrassed the hell out of her.

Wincing, I mouthed "sorry."

"Sit down," Caius growled, pointing at the chair where Pol had been sitting. "My mate put in a lot of time and effort so we could share something she enjoys."

"Easy," I said gently, touching his shoulder as I came back to the table. "Pol, I was just giving my cousin a hard time. It was a poor choice of words. I'm sorry. Tonight is meant to be easygoing and fun. Dancing is optional. Please stay?"

He dipped his chin, taking his seat again.

"So . . . this is how you work the assembly line," I began, showing them how to open the corn husk, scoop the masa and spread it over with the back of the spoon.

"Why do you stop spreading it before you get to the end?" Caius asked, pointing to the empty part of the husk.

"Leave that part open. That's where we fold it." He nodded, watching intently.

"So now you put the meat filling in, just like this." I showed them how, adding, "I like a more meat-to-masa ratio, but some people like more masa. Do it however you think looks good."

The guys all nodded, but it was easy to tell they were completely unsure of themselves. Nevertheless, they followed instructions. Slowly. Painstakingly slow. Making tamales was a repetitive process. The entire point of the assembly line was to move things along faster, but when three newbies were at the table, it resulted in a lot of quality control. Too much masa squeezing out the side, or masa spread entirely too thin. The only one who got it well enough was Pol. He seemed to catch on quickly.

We got there eventually.

"This goes on forever," Abyssian said, gesturing to the quantity we still had left. "How many do you make?"

"There's not a way to make a small amount," I answered. That wasn't entirely true. You could make a casserole out of it, but that was not something I wanted to explain. I'd told Ben that once and he begged me for months to keep making them. It was still a pain in the ass. "So, when you want to feed about ten people—"

"You make about five thousand," Clara said through a snort. I laughed too because that's always what it felt like.

"What?" the guys all said in unison, eyes wide as they looked up from the assembly line.

"Not literally." As my cousin folded them and handed them to me, I put them in a giant pot to steam. "It just . . . that's how it goes. One, it's a lot of work to make them, so when you do, you make it count. Two, we're Hispanic. We don't cook for a small crowd."

"You should get her to cook barbacoa in a pit in the ground," Clara said, handing me more tamales. "My absolute favorite. It's to die for."

"I am pretty damn good at that." I wasn't humble about my cooking. In our family, love and food went hand in hand, and I poured my heart into it.

"If that's important to you, I'll get whatever you need. We can do it together," Caius said, and I gave him a half smile. He was genuinely trying, and I gave him credit for that.

After they were done, I put a pile on the first platter and set them on the table with bowls of salsa I'd asked Nog to bring us. He'd basically become my carrier pigeon, crossing back and forth through the portal frequently.

The guys looked at them with a healthy dose of skepticism, but have you ever smelled tamales? They speak for themselves. When I turned to grab napkins, my cousin shouted.

"Wait!"

Abyssian wasted no time and had bitten into a tamal. His mumbled yelp was partially from consuming steaming hot food, and partially from not knowing he needed to take the corn husk off first. He'd already ground his teeth in, desperately trying to tear it.

"You don't eat the leaf, dumbass." Pol laughed, showing him how to unwrap it.

"How'd you know how to do that?" Abyssian asked, pulling husk fibers from his mouth and gagging.

"That's what she said to do," he answered, putting the discards on an empty plate.

"No I didn't," I said, tilting my head to the side, platter still in hand. Only a little while before, he had done so well at making them, plus just knowing how to do that without instruction made me pause.

Pol held the tamal in his hand, eyes unblinking as he stared at me for a moment. Two.

"Hmm. That's weird. I could have sworn you did. Maybe it's just intuition." Breaking eye contact with me, he looked away before he took a bite and moaned. Pointing at it, he added, "Holy shit, this is *really* good. Caius, you should eat one."

I kept watching him, trying to figure out why that interaction made me uncomfortable, but I couldn't place it. Once Caius started eating, and Abyssian took a bite of it correctly, their reactions shook me out of my thoughts. Moans of satisfaction filled the room as the plate of empty corn husks grew in size.

"My tastebuds want me to eat more, but my stomach says stop," Caius said, leaning back in his chair and blowing out a breath.

Clara polished off her eleventh without blinking, and Pol stared. She looked up at him. "What? I have a high metabolism."

I snorted. "Whatever. If you had to pick a sin, it'd be gluttony."

"Damn straight." She smiled at me, lips sealed, her cheek bulging with a mouthful of food. "Now get the game. And the moonshine!"

Shaking my head, I placed small mason jars of moonshine on the table, handing them out individually, then grabbed the game I had Nog bring me. Lotería. Mexican bingo. The narrow yellow box was old and torn, taped together ten times over. A thin rubber band wrapped around it, holding the top on, but just barely. It was my mom and dad's, and he'd given it to me. It was the one we always used on game night. I would pay to spell that box back together if it ever truly fell apart.

Clara clapped her hands and rubbed them together as she opened the box. Taking out the tablas, she picked one and passed them around. "Choose one. That's your bingo card."

"What's a bingo? How do you know which one to pick?" Pol asked, tilting his head as he looked at it. "I can't read it."

"You just pick one with pictures you like," I said, taking

a handful of dried pinto beans and putting a pile next to everyone. Explaining the concept of bingo, and that we used the beans for markers, I chose my table and sat down. "Don't worry. Just match the picture. You'll learn the words."

Tamales. Game night. Quality time in the kitchen. For the first time since I'd arrived, Tartarus didn't feel foreign to me.

Clara called out the cards. El Mundo. La Chalupa. El Alacran. El Nopal. La Calavera. Beans started to fill the tablas, and we were getting so close.

"La Luna."

"That's my favorite one," I told Caius, putting a bean down on my tabla and looking fondly at the picture of a soft blue crescent moon.

"Why?"

I shrugged. "Always thought she looked beautiful. Just something about her felt calming."

"I like La Sirena," Abyssian said, pointing at the topless mermaid.

Pollux scoffed. "You like that her tits are showing."

Abyssian threw a bean at him, pelting him in the head.

"Nog!" Clara called the next one, holding up the card of a drunken man, leaning against a pole so he wouldn't fall.

It had become a family tradition to call the El Borracho card "Nog" and take a shot in his honor. He couldn't handle drinking very well. I'd even painted a version of the card, using the same colors and posture, but replacing the man with Nog's likeness instead. He didn't find it nearly as amusing as we did, but he still kept the picture.

Clara and I laughed, pouring a shot from our jars, and raising them up to clink a toast, and we each knocked it back. The guys followed suit, clearly not understanding the humor in it, yet still working to be an active part of our night.

"That is deliciously potent," Caius said, setting his glass down with a slight cough.

"Wow," Pol said, wiping a tear from his eye. "Is that a hint of blackberry?" I nodded in confirmation.

Abyssian blew out a breath, shaking his head. "Wasn't expecting that. You made this?"

"Best moonshine in The Crossroads, right, Clara?"

I looked at my cousin and my stomach twisted instantly. The burn of the liquor was gone. The aftertaste lingered like ash. A wave of adrenaline rushed through my body in panic.

Her jaw was slack, her body swaying slightly as though she'd lost her balance. Clara's pupils were dilated, her eyes beginning to roll into the back of her head.

"Catch her!" I yelled, jumping up and leaping over the table. Abyssian caught her before she fell backwards. Pol grabbed her legs, and they laid her on the ground.

"No, no, no, no," I whispered, cupping her face as I kneeled beside her. "Clara, look at me."

"Healer, now!" Caius's deep command shook the room, and two guards posted outside the kitchen took off, following his instruction.

My cousin's body vibrated, drool sliding out of the corner of her mouth, pooling on the floor. "Clara, stay with me," I said, panic leaking into my voice when I turned her on her side while she seized.

I felt helpless. I didn't know how to heal. I had no idea how to use my witch magic. I didn't even know what kind of magic I had. I screamed internally, reaching for Eres.

"What do I do?"

"There's nothing we can do. I don't know how to heal."

"What do you mean you don't know?"

"You're the witch, not me. Even if we shifted, there's nothing a shifter can do to heal someone who is dying."

"Don't you have some special unicorn magic?"

"You know the answer. If it were possible. I would have done that already."

"What is the point of being some mystical, rare creature if we don't even have some special magic in your godsdamned horn?"

I slammed the connection between us shut, and tears leaked out of my eyes as I whispered comforting words to my cousin, begging her to hold on.

Abyssian and Pol kneeled beside her, looking at each other. It was as though they were silently speaking to one another, but it only ended with each one shrugging their shoulders.

"What did this? Abyssian asked.

Pol leaned down near her face, sniffing. "It smells like poison."

My head shot up as soon as I heard the word. "What do you mean, poison?" I said, my mouth going dry.

Green lines formed beneath her pale skin, crawling over her body.

"What the hell poison turns someone green?" Caius asked, addressing Pol.

"Why are you asking him?" My thoughts were racing, and I didn't give him time to answer. Turning to the man in question, I changed course. "Do you know what to do to heal her?"

Pol shook his head, muttering, "Expert in poisons." He pressed his lips together, his brows furrowing as sweat dotted his brow. He placed a hand on her forehead, feeling for a fever. "I don't know. I haven't seen one like this before."

The green poison darkened her veins. A small drop of blood formed at the base of Clara's nostrils. She shook harder, and her teeth clattered. The lines crept further up her body, wrapping its deadly tendrils around her throat.

At that moment, I felt like the world stopped. The cacophony of questions and shouting for the healers was completely drowned out by the sound of my cousin gasping for air.

The tendrils tightened like ivy, wrapping their way around her airway, and squeezing. Her skin turned a shade of purple as the poison deprived her of precious oxygen.

"Someone help her," I cried, but they were all just as lost as me. I looked up and met Caius's eyes, begging. "You saved me. You can save her right? Take out the poison?"

He met my pleading gaze, and the sorrow I saw in his features nearly broke me. I knew what it meant. "I can only heal my mate," he said quietly. "I'm sorry."

A sob escaped me, and I threw myself over Clara, weeping and demanding that she stay with me.

When healers burst into the room, Caius pulled me off, giving them the space they needed. Abyssian and Pol stood back, arms crossed, never taking their eyes off her.

Whispered words and crafted spells filled the room. Glowing light covered my cousin as Caius's arms wrapped around me, holding me tightly against him. My tears flowed freely as I willed myself to breathe so I didn't faint.

What felt like a lifetime passed when a deep gasp echoed in the room. Clara's body arched, her chest filling with air. She coughed weakly and I broke out of Caius's hold to drop down beside her.

I grabbed her hand, stroking it, whispering to her

through my strangled sobs. "You're going to be okay. You're going to be okay." Maybe I was saying it to comfort her, or maybe I was saying it to comfort myself. Either way, I couldn't stop repeating it.

"We need to observe her, and she needs rest," a healer said softly, touching my back with a gentle hand.

Meeting her kind eyes, I hesitated, but nodded.

Standing back while a guard scooped his arm under her legs, and held her behind her back, I watched as the healer led the way.

"I'll go with her," Abyssian said, looking at Caius for permission.

Caius inclined his chin, then gestured to Pol as well. "You too. Find out everything and report back to me." He tried to remain neutral, but his jaw was tight and when I looked to his side, I saw his fists clenched.

The procession left the kitchen, and I crossed my arms around my body, cradling myself.

Styx stood in the doorway, having arrived shortly after the guards had left. She'd watched everything unfold from a distance. Her calculating gaze swept the room before she walked in with confidence and headed to the long kitchen table.

Picking up each jar of moonshine and individual glass, she sniffed.

"It wasn't my moonshine," I said, heading toward her defensively.

"I assure you; it was." She sat one down, picking up another.

"Impossible," I countered, my anger rising. "I make each of these myself. They're sealed. Furthermore, I have no reason to poison my cousin. I would *never*—"

"It was meant for you," she said, not looking up from

the jars she was inspecting. My lips parted. "Were these left in here unattended?" she asked, looking at Caius, then at me. I nodded slightly.

"I . . . I brought them in this morning when I was doing some prep work. I left them here all day."

"Were any of them unsealed?"

"I . . . don't know." It was a tough thing to admit. Had I noticed one was unsealed, what would I even have done? Nothing, probably. People snuck sips at home all the time. "We all helped setting things out and pouring glasses."

Styx and Caius stared at each other for a tense moment.

"I'm taking Reagan away. We'll leave within the hour."

She scoffed. "That isn't going to solve anything, Caius. Whoever did this would just go underground. They'll bide their time. You know they will. It's exactly what I would do, and so would you."

Caius growled, slamming his fist into a wall. A crack formed down the middle, splintering the stone.

"Keep your friends close and your enemies closer," Styx continued. "Taking her to a cottage in a different part of Tartarus isn't going to keep her safe. If they can get to her within the castle walls, you'll be sitting ducks anywhere else."

"I'd like to see them try."

"Um . . ." I stepped forward, holding up my hand. "I wouldn't. I think Styx is right. I'm already in danger. My geographical location isn't going to change that."

Caius's angry features softened, and he cupped my face rubbing his thumb over my cheek. "I don't want to risk your safety. You're my mate, and I will do everything to protect you."

I placed my hand over his, forcing a tight smile. "Then protect me here. I'm not leaving Clara."

He closed his eyes, inhaling deeply before he dropped his hand and nodded in agreement.

I wasn't sure why, but I felt the need to offer him comfort. He was struggling with rage or whatever emotion a guy experiences at a time like this, and the best I could do was lace my fingers through his and hold on tight.

"Let's say you're right, Styx. Why would somebody try to poison me? They think I've accepted the mate bond. I think we first need to figure out why I'm still a target, right?"

"They haven't seen the primal hunt ceremony," Styx said, tilting her head as she looked at Caius.

"The what?"

Before he answered me, Caius grumbled about something I couldn't understand, and it seemed directed at Styx. "The primal hunt is a tradition here for mated couples. Basically anyone who can attend does, and then the couple is officially announced in front of everyone."

"What does that have to do with us hunting?"

He hesitated. "Then I would hunt you to consummate the union."

My jaw dropped. "In public?"

"Not exactly, but sort of"

I scoffed. "How? I mean . . . When would we even do this?" I breathed out, the sound of it panicky.

The way he paused before answering me made my heart drop. "It's usually done right before the dual full moons when . . ."

My heart didn't drop anymore. I may as well have swallowed it. "A woman is in heat," I croaked, and he nodded reluctantly.

"It's just around the corner. I think it's worth considering. People like their traditions, Caius." Styx lifted a shoulder, ignoring my obvious concern. "However, I think this may go beyond the mate bond, but I don't know why. The real question isn't why she's the target, but *who* would benefit from Reagan's death?"

My entire body tensed. The obvious answer was Caius. It was also the answer that didn't make sense. If he wanted me dead, he'd just do it.

It didn't escape him that I'd physically reacted, if only for a fraction of a second. His eyes darkened momentarily before sadness took over, and I gave him an apologetic look and a gentle squeeze of the hand.

Caius cleared his throat. "Reagan needs weapons training. We've been working together, but she'd do well to learn from you."

Styx frowned. "That's not going to protect her from being poisoned."

"Obviously," he said dryly. "Jana attacked her, now this. If someone is going to attack her directly again, she needs to be ready to defend herself."

"And if someone tries to poison her again?"

"I'm taking care of it." He let go of my hand and headed for the door.

I stepped forward, reaching for him. "Wait, where are you going?"

Caius paused, looking over his shoulder. "I have someone I need to see. Or rather I need to know what she sees."

"What?" I was so confused.

He left without another word and Styx groaned, rolling her eyes. "Why he trusts the goat lady, I'll never know."

"What goat lady?"

CHAPTER 29

CAIUS

"Are we there yet?" Reagan asked with a nervous laugh.

My hands cupped over her eyes to keep her from seeing where we were going. We walked awkwardly at a slow pace, her arms oscillating from outstretched to feel in front of her, to touching my arms and holding on for balance.

"Shhh, we're almost there."

She groaned, not truly frustrated, but impatient all the same. "Can I just look? I feel like I'm going to fall."

"I won't let you."

"That's not how that works." Her protests were cute. They also had no impact. "You can't control gravity . . . unless there's some god-power you possess, and you haven't told me about it yet."

I chuckled to myself.

She paused, turning her head as if she were able to look at me. "Wait, can you?"

"No. Now pay attention, or you're going to fall," I said, giving her a nudge forward.

"You literally just said you won't let me!"

"I won't but you gotta help out. I can't do all the work," I teased. I felt Reagan's mouth lift in a smirk.

"Guess you're not all that powerful."

I snorted. "Nice try, but goading me won't work either, mate."

I led her through the propped open door and nudged the door stopper out of the way with my foot. It swung shut behind us, closing with a soft click. I navigated her to the center of the studio.

"Are we there?" she asked excitedly.

"Yes, but keep them closed," I said, removing my hands from her eyes. Taking a step back, I angled myself so that I could watch her face. "Okay, now."

Reagan slowly opened her eyes and took in the room. A moment of awe struck her before a thousand-watt smile formed, and I knew in that moment it was all worth it.

In the tallest tower that we'd mostly used for storage, I'd had all the furniture taken out. In its place was an artist's studio. Small tables filled with supplies sat near easels and rows of canvases I'd lined along the walls. A large cloth lined the floor beneath it all. Letting out a stuttered breath, she turned to me for an explanation.

"This room is yours. It has the best moonlight," I said, pointing to a natural skylight in the rock. "Everything you need should be here, but if I missed something, just tell me."

"Where did you get all this?"

"I had it all made. Clara said you liked painting, so I went to the best tradespersons in the nearest village. I don't know at all what I'm doing, but I think you'll find that they're extremely high quality."

"And the brushes? The canvases?" she asked, touching the bristles lightly.

"All made in town. Remember the blacksmith's wife?" She hummed in acknowledgment. "She made them. Do you like it?"

When she didn't speak I started to feel nervous. Maybe this wasn't as good a surprise as I hoped. Maybe she didn't like to paint as much as Clara thought she did? Surely that wasn't the case. I probably should have sent someone through the portal and brought in items from Earth.

"You don't have to paint on the canvases if you don't want," I began hastily. "Clara said you like to paint murals. You can do that too. Here or any other room. The castle is yours. And if the brushes don't meet your standards, I can have new brushes made or we can send Nog to get brushes—"

Reagan wrapped her arms around my neck, standing on her tiptoes and squeezing tight. "It's perfect," she breathed. "Thank you."

My heart started to beat harder, and I placed my hand at the small of her back, holding her to me. "I thought maybe it wasn't what you wanted."

"I'm not good with surprises," she said, releasing me. "In my experience, they're usually a bad thing."

"Not with me," I said, kissing the top of her head and taking a step back.

"Where are you going?" she asked.

"I was going to leave you to paint. Clara said you usually do it by yourself. She called it 'self-care,' or something like that. Therapeutic, maybe? Either way."

Reagan raised her eyebrows slightly before asking hesitantly, "Will you stay and paint with me?"

"I . . . I've never painted before," I answered, completely caught off guard.

"Never?" she asked. "How is that possible that you've never painted in all the years you've been alive?"

"Honestly? I'm not entirely sure. It's never been a hobby I tried." Her face fell slightly, and I realized she was expecting me to say no, and that wasn't the case. "But I would love for you to teach me."

Excitement filled her features, and knowing I did that pleased a part of me I couldn't explain. Kicking off her shoes, she kept them to the side of the cloth. I did the same but gave a questioning look.

"I hate dropping paint on my shoes. Normally I have this old pair of boots I'll wear while I work. They're already destroyed, so I don't care what gets on them."

I nodded, making a mental note to have her annoying corgi-cousin bring those to her. Reagan smoothed over her hair, pulling it back into a messy bun and tying it off with a band she had around her wrist. Her tight pants and tiny tank top hugged her body. My blood heated at the view before me.

"What about clothes?" I asked.

Looking down, she tilted her head to the side. "It's okay. I just train in this. They can be messed up. You might want to remove your shirt though. I tend to be messy and there's no telling how much will get on you."

I reached behind my head, tugging the shirt up over myself. Mentally I added painting clothes to the growing list of things to get her. I considered doing the same for myself. If this became an activity she wanted to include me in, I would never deny her. Then again, painting shirtless could be appealing if she kept staring at me.

I reached over and tapped her chin. "You can pick your jaw up off the floor, mate."

She opened and closed her mouth, cheeks flushing. "I was no—oh fine, I totally was objectifying you. Can you blame me when you have muscles like that?"

I shrugged. "I mean, I wouldn't be opposed if you also wanted to go shirtless."

Reagan smirked, shaking her head as she picked up a palette and chose an assortment of colors. Staring at a blank canvas, she pursed her lips and tilted her head to one side, then the other. Finally, her eyes lit up and she began. Standing next to her, I watched her work and listened to her instructions. The way she talked about each stroke. How to keep it in your wrist and not have a stiff hand. How to use the bristles in different ways, creating a different result and pattern.

"Do you paint with your family much?" I asked, breaking my silent streak.

"Not really, no," she answered, keeping her eyes on the canvas. "I'm pretty much the only artist in the family. Nog doesn't know anything about himself yet, outside of being an annoying shit. Jo reads every book he can get his hands on. Clara crochets. Sin does her own thing too."

"I sense that bothers you some."

"A little," she admitted, turning to face me. "I just wanted someone to talk about art with. Ben and I did, and he would sketch with me some. He was the only one who really—"

My muscles stiffened. The desire to have Legion bring her ex to me so I could beat the shit out of him was overwhelming. It wasn't his fault, necessarily. If dating my mate could be considered that. He didn't even know the truth about her, I reminded myself. Still, shadows formed around my fingertips, begging to be unleashed. She immediately realized the effect his name had on me.

"Sorry," she said, wincing. "Weird timing to bring him up."

"You don't need to apologize," I said, feeling my jaw clench. "You had a life before you came here."

"That apparently doesn't stop you from wanting to kill Ben."

"I hate that your life involved . . . other people." Truthfully, yes. It enraged me that it was Ben. The idea that he'd held her and been the one she'd turned to. The fact he knew her in ways I didn't. More than anything, I struggled with what he'd done to her. He didn't deserve to breathe after he'd bitten her.

"Oh, nice recovery," Reagan said, not hiding her laugh.

"Change of subject," I said, thinking of how to veer away from her piece of shit ex. She smiled, nodding her agreement. "What is it about painting that appeals to you? If no one else in your family does it, why do you?"

Without hesitation, she answered with one word. "Control."

"Come again?"

"Earth is . . . unpredictable. My life especially. With art, I create and own all the choices. All the mistakes. I decide what to do. I'm the creator: the good, the bad, the ugly. In a world of chaos, I feel like I'm in control." Her answer was thorough and confident, but when she finished, she chuckled softly. "Does that make sense?"

"Yes, actually."

"Really?"

I nodded. "When I create . . . *things*, I understand that desire to have control in your choices. It's one of the things I miss most about being a primordial."

Reagan burst out laughing. "Wow. I'm here explaining why I like making art to a god who made realms."

"There's no comparison, but not for the reason you think," I began. "A primordial, or a god—what we have is power, and we're born with it. It doesn't take talent. Imagination and creativity aren't even required."

"It's so not the same. I'm capable of making pictures. You can make a *planet*. Painting doesn't take talent either. Anyone can do it."

"Anyone can fuck too, but it doesn't mean they're good at it."

She laughed. "I can teach you how to paint. You can't teach me how to make a planet."

"That's just a matter of power, not creativity. If I ever get my soul back, I'll show you. We can create realms together—and paint."

"My, my," she said. "That's quite the offer. I wish I could take you up on it."

I cupped her cheek with my free hand, brushing my thumb over her bottom lip when she trapped it beneath her two front teeth, playfully squeezing.

I tugged it back, and her teeth snapped together unexpectedly.

"Ouch!" Reagan snorted a laugh, then she flicked her brush in my direction. Her eyes widened as it landed on my cheek before she burst out laughing. "Oh my god, I didn't think that much was going to land on—"

Splat.

I did the same, angling my brush so little specks of paint flew and landed on her chest and face. Reagan rubbed at the specs that landed on her cheek.

Hold on," I said, stopping her before she spread it around too much. "You'll end up getting it in your eye."

Lines of cobalt blue smeared on her skin slightly and in that moment I was completely enraptured.

There was nothing I could do but stare at her. She was breathtakingly beautiful, and for the first time, she seemed fully at ease in my presence. Happy even. I wanted to capture this moment and hold onto it.

Unable to help myself I leaned in for a kiss and she didn't pull away. Our lips met. It was soft at first but that only lasted for a moment. When she kissed me back, fire erupted in my blood. I leaned in, taking her harder. My tongue traced the seam of her mouth and she opened for me with a tiny moan. I swallowed it down, my hands gripping her by the waist.

"Fuck, I love the sounds you make," I growled against her.

Reagan sighed, tilting her head back and breaking for air. I kissed down her neck, pausing when she tucked her bottom lip between her teeth and bit down slightly. Reagan took a breath as though she were going to say something and then thought better of it.

"What is it?" I asked, eyebrows creasing.

Reagan mouth twisted into a smile and before I knew it, she'd taken a handful of paint, smearing it down my abdomen.

A slew of words spluttered out of me, confused as to why she'd just done it.

A salacious smile formed on Reagan's face, and she looked at me with a heated gaze.

Oh.

"Am I your canvas now?" I asked.

My mate took several steps back, setting the palette down, and unbuttoning her pants. She kept eye contact with me as she slowly pulled them down, tossing them to the side.

Every part of me screamed to rush forward and take over, but a single word echoed in my head. *Control.* Let her have it. Let her lead.

She dipped both hands in the paint, coating them completely before walking toward me again, an eyebrow raised as she quickly glanced at the palette I held. Without words, I followed her actions, dipping my fingers in two shades of green as she approached.

Reagan placed her palms on my chest, the chill of the wet paint tickling my skin. Her hands glided up my shoulders, and over my neck, pulling me into a kiss.

I gripped her arms with green-coated fingers, grazing up until I cupped her face. Then I pulled her tank top over her head, covering her in more paint, smearing it over her skin.

Bouncing up off her toes, she wrapped her legs around my waist. I dropped the palette. My hands grabbed her luscious ass, fingers digging in.

Our bodies were completely covered as I laid her down on the cloth running my fingers through a bright red that streaked the canvas in wet globs. I traced along her collarbone, down her chest, then contour of her breast. Her stomach dipped in anticipation as my hands traveled lower. I loved that despite all her training, she was still soft here. I kissed one of her hip bones, then the other, letting my tongue linger at the indent in her skin. Reagan shuttered.

"What do you want, my queen?"

"You," she breathed. Her hands guided mine to the seam of her underwear and tucked them beyond the band. I didn't need to be told twice. As I pulled them down her legs, color smeared further. She leaned forward, her stomach contracting as she did the same. Reagan swiped her fingers through more colors then ran them over my wrists and arms. My shoulders bunched when she gripped them. Then she pushed me down, toward the heaven between her thighs.

I grinned up at her. "Eager, aren't you?" A strangled sound escaped her. "Tell me Reagan," I said in a quiet command. "You like control while painting. I like it here, with you. I want you to tell me *exactly* what you want."

She practically purred as I settled in, tossing one leg over my shoulders then the other. I kissed her inner thigh. My fingers grazed at her hips. The cool paint made her jerk.

"I want you to lick me," she whispered between whimpers.

"There, was that so hard?"

I didn't give her a chance to answer. I spread her wide with my thumbs. My tongue swept upward from her slick opening to her clit. Reagan bucked, but I held her down. With her thighs spread and my arms hooked under them she didn't get very far.

"Caius . . ."

"Mmm." I hummed against her, loving the sound of my name in that breathy tone. I leaned forward to blow on her clit, making her writhe in pleasure. "If I didn't have paint all over me, I'd make you taste yourself." Her stomach quivered and her legs tightened around my head. "Like that, do you?"

She breathed heavily again, and I flicked my tongue over her sensitive nub. Her muscles tensed. Holding her hips, I sucked her clit between my lips.

Reagan moaned loudly, begging "please" over and over while she thrashed.

I chuckled softly against her shaking body. The tension

was palpable, and I'd hardly touched her. My mate may have been with others, but something told me she was untried in many, many ways. I planned to explore everything with her.

In due time.

"Tell me you want me," I said, then lapped at her opening. My tongue sank in deep.

"You know I do," she said in a pained groan.

"But I want the words. Tell me, Reagan."

I licked again, teasing her.

"I want you!" She stifled her scream, instead pressing her lips together with a strangled growl. Her body was a taut mess of coiled tension and unbridled need. I wished I could spread her out like this forever, testing her limits.

"I'm yours," I said, wrapping my lips around her and humming against her most sensitive parts.

I lapped at her clit, alternating between sucking and stroking her with my tongue, responding to each sound she made, using her cries as a guide. Reagan's back bowed as she begged me not to stop, and I kept going until she fell over the edge.

An unintelligible cry left her lips. Reagan's hands clutched at my hair, my arms; frantically grasping any part of me she could touch as I didn't let off the pressure. Her body convulsed, then seized in ecstasy. I rode the waves with her, pulling every last drop of her pleasure from it.

When the shaking slowed, and the twitching ended I finally pulled away. I would have assumed that was all she could take, but she guided me up her body. I kissed her, letting her taste herself on my tongue. Reagan moaned, her legs wrapped around me welcomingly, knees tucked in tight at my sides.

She angled her body, rolling us on the cloth until she sat

on top of me. I could see the natural cut in the rock as the moon acted like a backlight to her curvy form.

Her hands reached between us, rubbing over my hardened length. Tucking her fingers into the hem, she began to loosen them, but I tensed, breaking the kiss.

"Wait, Reagan, if we do this, it seals the bond—"

"Mmhmmm," she hummed, leaning in to kiss me again.

I pulled back, grabbing her hips to keep her from rubbing all over me. "Is that what you want?" I asked, because anything less than yes meant this wasn't happening, no matter how much I wanted it.

"I want you." I rolled to the side and came down on top of her, taking control of our position. It was hard to think with her heat pressed against my groin. Reagan wrapped her arms around my shoulders. "Is that not enough?"

I closed my eyes and breathed out harshly through my nose. "I want you too, Reagan, but you're ignoring the fact that if we do this it seals the mate bond. Something I'm not sure you're actually ready to accept."

She pressed her lips together and stayed silent. A slow rising anger took over my body. I pushed myself up off of her and scooted over to the side, paint sticking to me, I rested my forearms on my bent knees and dragged my fingers through my hair in frustration. "You still don't believe it exists."

"I don't," she admitted quietly. "I know that upsets you and I'm not trying to. I just don't think anything is going to happen from us having sex. Except maybe you realizing it wasn't the mate bond you felt this whole time."

Rocking forward, I stood up. "Then I guess we're done here today."

Anger clouded her features and she rolled to the side and stood up. "What do you mean we're done here today? I just told you I want to be with you. Why is that not enough for you?"

"Because I'm not going to trick you into accepting the mate bond. It's shitty, and while your past fuck buddies may have gone for that, I'm not that kind of man."

Reagan reeled back. "What is that supposed to mean?"

"Exactly what I said," I snapped. Reagan ran a hand through her hair in a nervous habit.

"Okay, I upset you. That wasn't my intention. I know you believe that we're bound together, but it's just your soul calling to its other half. I'm okay with it. I can accept that. You need to as well. I know it's not your fault I'm a guardian, and I'm not sitting here worried if you're really going to kill me. I know what I feel for you is real, but beyond that, no. I'm sorry I don't believe that we're mates. I'm not meant to have a mate, and neither are you. The only logical explanation to that is that it's your soul."

"I guess we're at an impasse then."

"What the fuck is that supposed to mean? I just told you I have feelings for you and you're acting like you don't want me without the stupid mate bond. Are you for real right now?"

"It means we're going in a fucking circle, Reagan, and we keep clashing in the same spot. I know you're my mate, and you are continuously telling me that I'm feeling something that isn't really there. What am I supposed to do with that?"

"I don't know, but if that's all you're here for, then maybe you should just let me go before things get more complicated."

I laughed humorlessly. "Of course. How could I forget? You just want to go home. Was that all this was? A ploy to soften me up then ask for your way out of the bargain?" I motioned to the canvas we'd painted in passion. Now it felt like nothing more than a bitter reminder of what could have been.

"Don't be an asshole. You know I didn't—"

"No, an asshole doesn't take no for an answer. An asshole tries to claim you even when you've said you didn't want that. I'm not the asshole here, Reagan. I would never make you do something you didn't want to do. And if we fuck, that is exactly what's going to happen because you're too damn stubborn and unwilling to see any other option as truth." I got to my feet and started for the door. "I can't talk to you right now."

"Are you rejecting me?" she asked.

"How could I? You'd have to believe in the bond for me to do that."

She flinched, but I couldn't find it in me to feel bad.

"Just because you believe something doesn't make it true," she whispered.

"I know that, Reagan. Maybe take your own fucking advice."

"You know whose advice I should've taken? Nog's."

"Oh yeah? Why's that?"

"Clara always did have shit taste in men."

"We're done here," I said, slamming the door behind me as I left. The muffled sound of shattering glass and ceramics still reached me.

The bond twisted in my chest painfully, but I kept walking before I said something I couldn't take back.

CHAPTER 30

REAGAN

The wooden sword cracked across my thigh, leaving a sharp sting in its wake. My breath hissed between my teeth in pain.

"Point," Styx said.

I barely resisted the urge to rub the newly formed welt. "Did you have to do it so hard?" I asked as I sidestepped away from her next strike. Barely. Caius never went easy on me, but we'd largely practiced in hand-to-hand combat. After our little spat, we hadn't done anything at all, much less spar. My thoughts tumbled down that rabbit hole.

Another crack rent the air as she struck my bicep. I growled under my breath. "Point."

"Goddammit—"

"Your god isn't here to save you," she replied, then did a fancy move where she twirled on her feet. I backed up, stumbling over my own. Next thing I knew, the wooden sword was at my neck.

I threw my head back and groaned. "He's not my god."

At the exact same time, Styx said, "You're dead."

I dropped my chin to glare at her. "You're supposed to

be helping me, not highlighting how bad I suck with a sword."

"I'm doing both," Styx countered. "You're distracted. I'm guessing it wouldn't have anything to do with why I very suddenly took over your lessons a week ago—or why Caius is an irritable fuck to everyone right now?" I pursed my lips, to which she clicked her tongue twice. "I see. You two had a fight."

"It wasn't a fight. It was a difference of opinion," I said, my own irritability showing.

Styx put a hand to her chest. "Oh you're right, that's *so* different," she mocked. If my scowl could have gotten worse, it would have.

"I'm serious. I was fine agreeing to disagree. He's the one with the problem."

She lifted both eyebrows. "Care to enlighten me? Because that doesn't sound like him."

I sighed. "Why bother? You're his friend, you'll just defend him."

Styx snorted. "Hardly. Friendship means calling out shitty behavior too. Besides, I've known Caius for, well, almost forever. Maybe I'll have insight into where things went wrong."

I lifted a brow, skeptically. "How do I know you won't just sit here and gaslight me?"

Styx tilted her head, assessing me. "Not my style. It's up to you. You either trust me or don't."

I dropped my wooden sword to the ground and plopped down. She took them both, hanging them up on the wall before joining me for stretches. I let go of a tight breath and the tension drained away.

"Caius and I were, um, being intimate—"

"Fucking or foreplay?" she asked.

I mouthed "wow" because apparently there was no need for a filter with Styx. "Foreplay. We didn't even make it to fucking, even though I was all for it. Caius insisted that it would seal the mate bond and he said it would be tricking me, essentially."

Styx tensed, but when she noticed my reaction, she let out a deep breath. "What did you say to that?"

"I told him . . . I still don't believe in the mate bond. I know it's his soul calling to him, and he needs to understand that's all it is, but he just won't listen. But look," I added, making sure she understood my side. "I'm okay with that. Really. I was telling him I essentially have feelings for him, but then he acted like a complete asshole."

"Right. So you told him what he feels is his soul and not a mate bond. That it?" When I looked away, a frown formed between her brows. "I'm sensing there's more."

"I might have told him Clara has been championing his cause and that I should have listened to Nog because she has shit taste in men," I rattled off quickly. "Not in so many words exactly, but the point was clear."

Styx lips parted, then she snapped her mouth shut. "Anything else I should know?"

I shook my head. "After that he got pissed and stormed off. We've been avoiding each other as much as we can, but that's not very much given the whole fake mate thing. We have to be around each other, and it's awful. I just wish I could smack him upside the head and tell him he's being ridiculous. I mean, it's completely reasonable for me to feel this way."

Styx inclined her head. "It is reasonable for you to feel that way. Maybe not reasonable to completely invalidate him."

"I . . . What?"

"He says he feels the mate bond. You told him he doesn't. Right?" When I didn't answer, she continued. "Exactly. You told him what he feels isn't real because it's not the same thing you feel. His beliefs, his feelings for you, aren't valid because it's not what you believe. Reverse that and tell me how you would react."

I opened then closed my mouth.

"Ugh," I groaned, covering my face with my splayed hand. "Words are stupid. I wasn't trying to . . . invalidate him or tell him he doesn't feel what he feels. I just wanted to point out that I don't feel it, and I don't think we're mates. So if we had sex there wouldn't be any bond form-ing. Then again, maybe if that happened, he'd realize we're not mates and let me go since that's the only reason he wants me to begin with—"

Styx made a noise in her throat. "Okay first, you may not have been trying to invalidate him, but that's exactly what you did. Accept that you fucked up. But this is a tricky subject. One where you could both be right, theoretically. You could be his mate *and* the guardian. Did it ever occur to you that maybe you don't feel it because you already have half his soul? You are already bound to him, so to speak."

Well, that had some merit. Not a lot, but some. Guilt slowly formed like a lead weight, holding me down. "And second?" I dared to ask.

"Second, that's not the only reason he wants you."

"Okay, I'll give you the first one as a maybe, but I'm calling bullshit there."

Styx seemed to mull over her words before she finally spoke. "I can't explain why, but I know for a fact you being his mate isn't the only thing at play here. If you want to know more, you'll need to ask him yourself."

A knock at the door made me look up. Clara stood in leggings, a mid-thigh length black tunic, and boots. She was missing her classic black eyeliner and dark lipstick—instead, favoring a more natural approach as her makeup had run out and Nog refused to bring her more. He insisted she'd just use it to try to impress the wrong kind of guys again, and that he was "saving her from herself." It was bullshit, but instead of bitching, she took the high road and went all natural. She looked beautiful either way. Her dark brown lips contrasted nicely with tan skin and dark, wide-set eyes.

"You ready to go?" Clara said.

"Yep, just wrapping up here." I turned to Styx who watched us with casual disinterest. "Thanks for the advice."

She nodded once. "Anytime. I'll see you at the mate ceremony."

I groaned. "You mean the primal hunt?"

"That's the one." She paused, likely seeing the lovely shade of green I was likely taking over my complexion. "You know the details, don't you?"

Caius and I had barely spoken. Most of it was curt and brief. Little more than a frigid politeness in the company of others. Anxiety welled in my chest.

"I know enough," I said, not wanting to talk about any of it. Not with him, and not with her.

"So long as you know what to expect."

I wouldn't say I knew exactly, but I knew there was no getting out of it. Maybe it was better not to know. After all, I was already dreading it. Why add fuel to the fire?

I said goodbye to Styx and walked out of the training room. Gripping the bottom of my shirt, I tugged at it a few times, fanning myself, and letting the air cool me. Then I retied my hair back, getting all the stray pieces that had escaped my braid.

"You're looking good," Clara said, appraising me. "You always had muscle from digging, but they're more defined now."

I grinned. "Thanks. I'm too lazy to do it for vanity, but I won't lie; it's a nice perk."

"Can't say I blame you there." Clara chuckled as we walked into another atrium. Dark green and purple foliage crawled between the walkways and wound around the columns, trailing up the walls. Violet flowers with teeth sniffed at us as we walked by. We were careful not to take a step off the path. Those suckers wouldn't hesitate to bite, especially after Nog attacked one in his corgi form and the flower lost the fight. Its brethren were antsy now around anything that moved.

"Hey, how's the research with my mom's journal going? Have you been able to translate any of it?"

Clara froze for a second too long. One of the flowers closest to her snapped at her ankle, making her jump. I narrowed my eyes, judging her reaction. It wasn't like her.

"No, sorry," she said hurrying down the walkway.

I debated calling her out on the weird behavior, but the memory of green lines of poison coloring her veins made me pause. Who knows what kind of side effects the poison caused? That was aside from the fresh trauma of a near-death experience. Guilt churned in me. I really did have trust issues. Everything that had happened left me seeing shadows where there were none. This was Clara. She was basically my best friend. We were as close as I'd been with my sister; perhaps closer since coming to Tartarus together. She'd never lie to me, and here I was, suspecting her of what? I didn't even know.

"We still have time. No pressure." I wanted to be supportive of her. She'd been through so much. "Guess it was wishful thinking that there'd be some quick and easy super spell you were on the cusp of completing."

I tried to laugh it off. Clara followed suit, chuckling somewhat awkwardly. It was stilted and flat.

Being poisoned really had done a number on her. I paused and touched her arm. "Are you okay?" I asked.

Clara flinched. "What? I'm fine. Why?" Her eyes narrowed on me, and I smiled kindly.

"You're just kind of jumpy, that's all. I just want to make sure you're okay. You were poisoned. No one would blame you if it was affecting you, you know?" And by no one, I meant me. I didn't care about anyone else "I'm here for you. And you don't have to stay here if you don't want to. I made the deal, not you. I just want you to be okay."

She wrapped her arms around me in a fierce hug. "I love you, Rea. You know that right?"

"Of course I do." I patted her back then held her close until she released me. "I love you too."

Clara wiped the moisture from her eyes. "It was scary. I'll be okay. Might take some time."

And that was that. The weirdness was forgotten as we talked about the latest soul she trapped in a crocheted baphomet.

Still, uneasiness followed me. Tartarus was a dangerous place, and it was clear we weren't welcome. I couldn't protect her. The throbbing welts on my body reminded me I could barely protect myself.

CHAPTER 31

REAGAN

Sweat beaded at my hairline dripping down my face while I tried to control my erratic heart rate. The back of my neck was damp and clammy. It wasn't even the heat causing it.

It was my nerves.

Standing in the middle of a circle of vertical stones, I waited for Caius while a group of villagers had formed around it, holding baskets of petals. A group of healers walked around, blessing the sacred space.

There was a nice breeze at the edge of the forest, and I was dressed in what I'd been told was appropriate for the upcoming ceremony. A white cloth skirt wrapped around my waist, a slit on each side of my legs to give me room to run. The halter-style top left little to the imagination. There was no room for a bra of any kind and white was fairly transparent. I was a brown-skinned woman. My nipples were dark, and they were on full display, but no one listened when I complained about it.

Time was crawling at a glacial pace. For the hundredth

time, I tried to adjust my boobs, smooth my skirt, and brush stray hairs back.

"Stop fidgeting," Styx chastised in a quiet voice.

"You stand here in the humidity wearing this ridiculous outfit like a virgin about to be sacrificed," I grumbled, not wanting to speak too loudly.

She snorted. "You are definitely not a virgin."

"I said *like* one, dammit." I sighed, trying to distract myself from the torture of waiting and the hum of the healers' chants. "Is this even safe?" I asked her.

"It'll be perfectly safe."

"How can you guarantee that? With everything that's happened?"

"Because Caius and I took care of it."

"What does that mean?"

"Hush. You aren't supposed to be talking while the shamans are blessing the sacred circle."

A man in robes walked to where we waited, and he dipped his head in greeting. "Your Highness."

"Oh, I'm not"—I paused when Styx elbowed me, and a frown formed between the shaman's brows—"Used to being called that." I cleared my throat. "Hi."

Styx tried to stifle her groan, and in my periphery, I saw Caius approach. His ceremonial attire was black, a kilt of sorts, coming down to his knees. A white belt wrapped around his waist, and he wore a necklace I'd never seen before. While I had a skimpy top, he had none, and it didn't escape the notice of several women that had surrounded the stone circle.

A hint of jealousy tickled me, and it quickly mingled with the pain of our argument. Envy and I weren't friends, so it was a new experience. A whisper in the recesses of my mind said he was mine, and again, the heated words we'd shared questioned if we were anything at all.

He'd said we were going in circles. Maybe that's all we knew how to do . . .

When he came to stand before me, he met my gaze with a forced smile. A tightness formed around his eyes, and I looked away, feeling the slightest prick of tears. Stupid feelings.

The healer nodded, smiling gently, handing a wooden tray with small bowls of paint for Styx to hold.

My heart skipped a beat and my eyes shot up to meet his. "We're supposed to paint each other?" I asked, and he gave an apologetic nod. I mumbled under my breath. "You've got to be kidding."

"Ironic, isn't it?" he said quietly.

Cruel was more like it.

As instructed, we took paint and covered our palms, each pressing a hand onto each other. My red handprint marked the planes of his muscular chest, and his marked my sternum, reaching all the way to my collarbone.

A symbol that we had been claimed by the other.

I felt my stomach tighten as the shaman healers and Styx left the circle while the entire audience began to chant. Caius and I stood face-to-face, silent, holding each other's hands.

It felt like an eternity had passed when a steady drumbeat was added to whatever song or prayer they were saying on repeat.

"We need to talk," I whispered.

"Not right now." His voice was barely audible.

"Please." The increased speed of drumming sent fear through my veins.

Caius stayed silent, holding my gaze. His non-answer

wasn't helping my anxiety. We should have talked more before doing this. We shouldn't have ignored each other.

Squeezing my eyes shut, I tried to take deep breaths as my heart jumped into my throat.

I'd finally asked Styx to fill me in on more details. The unknown was killing me. Better to know what was coming. Knowledge was power, and all that. If I knew what to expect, I was equipped to handle anything. That was my mindset. How wrong I was. Regret was an understatement. Instead of feeling prepared, I was fucking terrified.

I was supposed to take off running into the forest. He was supposed to wait, then chase me. Stalk me. Hunt me. Mate me.

That was the tradition here. A way to announce to the people of Tartarus that you were taken.

On Earth, we had weddings or wore rings, or both. This was too much. People here go into the woods, hoping to catch a glimpse of the couple mating. I was in a realm full of voyeurs, and I didn't have an exhibition to give them. Maybe this was Hell.

What was going to happen? We weren't actually going to fuck against a tree or on the forest floor. I was a terrible liar. No . . . Oh gods, no . . . Was I supposed to fake sounds of an orgasm?

We didn't talk about this. We didn't plan this out. We'd barely spoken to each other and now we were about to put on some show, and I didn't know my lines, so to speak.

I couldn't do this.

The rapid, thunderous thumping of drums and the vociferous chanting reached a crescendo, my heart pounding in unison with the beat. I was going to throw up.

Then it abruptly stopped.

Deafening silence reigned.

Only my heartbeat and the sounds of my erratic breathing filled my mind.

I looked at Caius, not knowing what to do.

He leaned down, his lips grazing my ear, the heat of his breath sending goosebumps along my skin. Releasing my hands, he said a single word, the deep timbre of his voice reverberating.

"*Run.*"

CHAPTER 32

CAIUS

Reagan's primal instinct took over and she bolted. Her feet dug into the soft earth as she passed the throngs of people on the outside of the circle. They tossed petals over her, yelling and hollering with glee.

I stood there smiling, watching her run into the forest, doing my best to hold in a laugh. She was about as coordinated as a baby giraffe.

Styx met my gaze with a smirk, clearly seeing the same thing. She winked, then disappeared backwards into the crowd, heading to her post.

I hadn't planned on waiting that long before giving chase, and this gave me plenty of leeway. Styx would herd Reagan toward me, and I would take over from there.

Seconds ticked by, my heart pounding in anticipation.

Even knowing it wasn't real didn't change the adrenaline rush it created just being there. The beating of the drums. The chant. The fantasy that this could be real.

I began counting down, then took off, following my mate's tracks. The petals showered me as they had her, and the shouts of joy followed me into the forest. Soon, the spectators would branch out into the woods so they could track us. I only had a small window of time to find her before they would find us.

Keeping a steady pace, I headed toward the meeting spot Styx and I mapped out earlier. It was only a matter of time before Reagan would appear, right on schedule.

Leaning against a tree, I waited, thinking back on our fight for the hundredth time. Replaying it over and over again in my mind.

Wondering what I could have done differently, or if I could have said something else. The disagreement was going to happen no matter what. She didn't believe in the mate bond. I did. There was no middle ground there.

I want you. Is that not enough?

Even through all the anger, her words lingered, and they gave me hope that we'd be okay. Today I would find out.

Reagan's anxiety traveled through the bond, reaching me. She was near. Moments later, I spotted her through a copse of trees.

"Shit, shit, shit, shit." Each word was ground out with huffed breaths. She came to a stop, resting her hands on her knees for a moment of reprieve. Turning in circles, she took in her surroundings.

A twig snapped in the distance, and her eyes widened. Leaves rustled, but in a different direction. She took steps backwards, toward me, not knowing I'd been watching her.

"Oh, c'mon," she muttered, her eyes shut, and her fists clenched. "Anywhere but here. Just anywhere but here."

"Teleporting is cheating," I whispered.

A strangled cry escaped her, and she whirled around, clutching her chest while I stepped out of the shadows.

"For fuck's sake! You scared the shit out of me. This is

awful," she began, sucking in deep breaths. "Were you hiding in the shadows? That should be cheating, fucking shadow shifter horseshit. I hate this and I—"

"Shhh." I placed a finger over her lips, then took her hand and began walking. "We aren't staying here. Follow me."

A frown formed between her brows, and she followed with hesitation. "Caius, I can't do this. I have to get out of here. I—"

Stopping, I turned to face her. "Trust me. I told you I wouldn't make you do anything you don't want to do."

"Right, but—"

"*Reagan.*" She stilled, her mouth open midway through her sentence. "Trust. Me. And be quiet, or people will hear you. We're almost there."

Finally listening to me, she obliged my request and silently trailed behind me. When we came to a small clearing, I gestured for her to go ahead of me, and she looked back and forth between me and the space before us. I nudged her forward, then followed behind her.

As we crossed through a cloaking spell, the clearing was no longer empty. Instead, an animal hide had been laid out and a basket of food sat on top.

"What is this?" she asked, turning to me, then checking the surrounding trees.

"Styx got a cloaking spell, and I used it here. If anyone comes looking for us, they'll never see anything. Just an empty part of the forest. We can wait out the primal hunt in secrecy. Everyone will think we're doing what we're expected to do, but no one will end up finding us."

"Does that happen sometimes?"

I nodded. "It's a big forest. It's not unheard of."

"And if they try to walk through the clearing? They'll

just end up in here with us," she said, nervously biting her lip and glancing around the trees.

"No, they'll end up turned around, and likely confused by it. Only you and I can get in here."

She blew out a breath, sighing in relief. "How long do we wait?"

"We have a while. Styx will come get you and sneak you into the castle before the moons hit mid-sky," I said, holding out my hand for her to take a seat on the blanket.

"Where will you go?"

I hesitated to answer, but she deserved to know. "Away. I know you don't believe it will happen, but when you go into heat, it will be hard to deny you. I just want to be prepared." Ha. *Prepared.* It was going to happen, whether she liked it or not. I blew out a harsh breath. "You said we needed to talk. Here's our chance."

Reagan tucked a strand of hair behind her ear, sitting down cross-legged and tucking her skirt between her thighs, relaxing fully for the first time. I sat beside her, not knowing how to start the conversation.

"Thank you," she said, finally breaking the silence. "For this."

"Of course."

"The entire concept of the primal hunt seemed fine up until yesterday when I asked Styx for more details. It just made me really uncomfortable."

"I could tell."

"And then when we were standing in the circle, I realized we hadn't planned on how to do this, and I didn't know what I was supposed to come into the forest and do because we didn't talk about it."

"We didn't have a chance to, no."

"I suppose that's my fault."

"Sure, it can be your fault."

"Hey." She threw a grape at me, and I picked it up and ate it with a smile.

I sighed. "We are both at fault. I wasn't ready to talk to you. The anger was too close to the surface."

"I, uh, realized a few things when I was talking Styx," she said softly.

"Oh?" Great. She confided in the one person who thought mates were worse than death. This should be good.

"I invalidated your feelings." She met my gaze, and a sadness crossed her features.

I raised my brows in surprise. "Styx was talking about . . . feelings?" She hummed in response.

"Well, yes, but it was in between strikes while she was beating me up with a wooden sword."

"That sounds about right."

"Caius, I'm not ready to leave Tartarus," she began, shifting to tuck her legs underneath. "I do want to be with you. I meant what I said, and it wasn't a heat of the moment, post-orgasm, hot and heavy sex thing. I'm sorry for dismissing everything you said, and for saying your feelings aren't real. It's just . . . hard."

"I'm sorry too, but I can't apologize for believing you're my mate."

"No, I don't expect you to. I thought I'd moved past a lot. I know I mean something to you beyond the . . . soul thing, otherwise . . . you know. But maybe some of the elders and the past still influence my beliefs. I may not know jack shit about primordials, but in all reality, I don't know jack shit about myself either. Witch, unicorn shifter, guardian. The truth is, I only know what I've been told, and I was told I couldn't have a mate. I haven't experienced anything. I don't have full memories. Hell, I've never even left The Crossroads until I came here."

"Really?"

"Yup," she said, popping the P. "I wanted to, but it was safer to stay. My dad traveled all over the continent, helping abandoned and orphaned kids. He won't leave them, so he brings them back. It's partially why my family is so big."

"Are any of you related?"

"Oh, absolutely. My dad and Tío Amos are brothers. My Tía Sarah is their half-sister. She had my cousin, Danni, and adopted my other cousin, Adora. Tío has made a lot of babies with a few different women, and he brings home kids too. Once he found my Tía Celeste, though, he became a new man."

"Mates?" I asked, knowing it was still a touchy subject.

"You guessed it. They don't have any of their own, though. Nog and Clara have different moms, and Tío Amos is their father. Jo was brought home when he was a baby. He's so powerful, and we don't know anything about his birth mother or what kind of supernatural he is."

"He is a special one." I hummed, recalling the way his inquisitive eyes had assessed me the day I'd met them. Reagan looked hopeful.

"Do you know what he is?" I nodded, and her face lit up. "Well?"

"It's not my place to say. I'm not even sure he knows it yet, but I do know he'll tell you when he's ready." Her face fell a bit, but she seemed to understand. "I'm sorry I can't answer that for you."

"No, it's okay. I trust him. Both of you, actually. I'm just happy Tío brought him home. That's what matters."

I didn't want her to dwell on it, but it made me happy to

know she trusted me. "Where would you go, if you could have left The Crossroads?"

"Oh that's easy," she said with a soft smile, easily transitioning to a new subject. "Where the mountains meet the ocean."

"Where is that?"

"I don't know, actually. I think it's where my cousin Danni lives, but I'm not sure." She stared at the ground, rubbing her fingers over the soft leather of the animal hide. "I used to dream about it. It was a castle embedded in a mountain, overlooking the sea. I painted a mural of it in my old room."

"If you haven't been there, what makes you think that that's where your cousin lives?"

"I don't know where else it would be? She ended up marrying a vampire, and it does have a very vampire look to it. Danni and Elias—that's her mate—only met about four years ago. It was a big deal. But I've been dreaming about it for longer. It wasn't clear at first. Just a fuzzy picture in my head. Then it started to get clearer. The lines were sharper, and I could make out shapes. Then I could remember the details more vividly, even after long hours of being awake. I never got to see a better color palette though. It was always dark. Weirdly, it was a comforting place. Painting it felt like . . ." She chuckled, shaking her head.

"Felt like what?"

"Home? It doesn't make sense, but that's the best word I can come up with. Maybe I saw Danni's future. Could be foresight is a power I have, but I just don't know it yet. It's not like anything I can do makes sense anyway." After a moment's pause, she huffed a humorless laugh.

"What's funny?"

"When my ward was breaking, and the infection was

starting to—you know. I saw you in a hallucination. It was like you were there, somehow built into the painting on my wall. I get it now that I was seeing things, but it felt so real at the time. Like you belonged there too. Have you ever had a dream like that? It sounds crazy, right?" Shaking her head, she sighed.

I ran my fingers through my hair, resting my elbows on my knees and looking up at her. "I have to tell you something."

A frown formed between her brows. "Okay . . ."

"I've been dreaming about you for ten years." She looked at me in shock and opened her mouth to speak, but I held up a hand. "Let me finish. It was different than your dream. It wasn't fuzzy. Always clear since day one. I had everyone searching Tartarus for a woman matching your description. Anyone they found didn't come close. I never knew why I dreamed of you. Didn't think it had anything to do with a mate; didn't have any attachment to my soul. I knew that whole-heartedly. The day I walked through your door, I recognized you. I had seen you every night for a decade, and I felt like I already knew you. It damn near broke me when you didn't recognize me in the same way."

It still threatened to tear me apart, but I wasn't here to make her feel guilty for it.

"Why are you telling me this now?"

"Because it's important for you to understand why I feel what I feel. It's not just the mate bond. I knew you before I met you, and I knew you were mine from the very first moment."

"I want to be with you, Caius." She looked down, not meeting my gaze as she spoke with a cracked voice. "But what would you do if you found out I wasn't your mate?"

"If you think I'd kill—" I started, feeling heat rise within me.

Her eyes widened. "That's not what I meant. I mean would you even want me? Let's say it's not real, for whatever reason. What then?"

All the anger that had so quickly arrived instantly faded.

My love needed assurances. Was I any different? She could deny fate, and deny the mate bond, and the truth was, I could let it go too. It wasn't an all or nothing. Love shouldn't be. I wanted her. She wanted me. Did it matter how it was classified? No. It didn't.

"Reagan, I will always choose you," I said quietly, stroking her cheek. "Mate bond or not. I would rather have you, however that looks, than live any more of my life without you by my side. You're all I've ever wanted."

Her eyes filled with shiny tears, and she smiled. "Do you mean it?"

"Every word. Always." I smiled, but it was tight. I swallowed thickly, preparing myself to say the very thing that went against all that I believed, but I would do it for her. "Reagan, I reject—"

She pressed her hand over my mouth before I could finish speaking. "Don't," she whispered. "Don't say it."

My brows furrowed, not understanding why she'd stopped me.

"I thought that's what you wanted?" I asked, holding her wrist after she took her hand away.

"Don't reject me. I know that's not what *you* want, and I won't ask you to go against your beliefs."

Hearing the words meant everything to me. Still, a problem remained if I didn't. I held her hands in mine.

"Let's say, for argument's sake, the mate bond is real. If

I don't reject you, we will seal the bond. I can't do that to you. That goes against my beliefs as well."

"I choose you, Caius," she said slowly, taking a breath before adding, "Mate bond or not. However that looks. Just claim me as yours."

Something in the air electrified. That was all we needed from each other. A confirmation we wanted the same thing, no matter what it was called.

We were on each other in a heartbeat. Her lips pressed against mine as she straddled my lap. She fisted one hand in my hair and cupped the back of my neck with the other.

"I love you," she said against my mouth.

My chest squeezed, savoring the words I'd so longed to hear.

"I love you more," I said, nipping her bottom lip. Her mouth parted, and our tongues twined, entering a dance with no end in sight. Chest-to-chest, we kissed like it was the first time. I gripped her hips in my hands, toying with the waist of her skirt.

"You can't possibly know that." She chuckled against me.

"Oh, but I can." I skimmed my lips down her throat. There was a soft patch right where her neck met her shoulder, and I kissed it gently.

I flipped us, putting Reagan on her back. Grass crinkled beneath the blanket.

Her warm brown eyes were heavy lidded with lust. She gazed at me as I leaned down and kissed her bare stomach. She quivered in anticipation.

"I've lived countless lifetimes without you, Reagan. I know I love you more because I can't imagine continuing on that way. I can't lose you. I won't." I punctuated my statement with a kiss, and she moaned against me.

A growl rumbled through my chest. I was trying for sweet. Gentle. She made it hard to do when her legs came up and wrapped around my hips. Her back arched off the ground so she could grind against me. With only the fabric of my outfit between us, it was all too easy to envision the things I wanted to do to her.

"Who says I can't imagine a future without you?" Her voice was low and husky. Sexy wasn't a good enough description. "But right now I'm imagining it with you *in* me."

I groaned. "You know, you make it hard for a man to do the right thing. I'm trying to go slow—"

"I don't want slow."

Fire heated my blood. Desire coursed through me so swiftly that I had to watch my strength as I pinned her hips to the ground and rubbed my hard length against her wet center. Reagan writhed, arms and legs a twitching mess of carnal hunger.

"Are you sure about that?" I asked, teasing her.

"*Yes*." I pulled back and flipped her over.

She moved fluidly without hesitation. I pulled her skirt off with one hard tug. The fabric ripped all too easily, revealing her to me. I shuffled back and knelt forward pressing my nose into her as I licked from clit to ass. Reagan cried out.

I hummed against her, and her hands fisted the blanket in response.

She whined, wiggling her hips against me. "Please."

"Please what?" I asked, wanting to make her say it. I loved hearing it. I loved the sound of her voice when it was needy and breathy, and I loved that I was the one that made it happen.

She reached around and grabbed at my side, trying, and failing to make me move.

"Please fuck me," she begged.

I lined up at her entrance, and Reagan arched her back, dragging my tip through her wetness. I thrust into her and damn near convulsed from the blissful heat that enveloped me.

She was perfect.

Reagan whimpered when I settled in her and held myself there. I brushed her hand away and grabbed hold of her hips. The all-consuming need to claim her was practically painful.

Pulling back, I thrust forward into her welcoming body. Her channel clenched around me, greedy for more.

Reagan cried out in ecstasy.

"Do you want me to fuck you like this?" I punctuated my question with an agonizingly slow withdrawal where I pulled out completely, followed by a deep thrust where I buried myself to the hilt.

Reagan gasped, her delicate muscles clinging to me with fervor. "Or would you like it like this?" I pulled out again, thrusting with a fast and hard pace that had her all but mewling for me as she writhed. I fucking loved it.

"Both, fast, I don't know," Reagan groaned. "Please."

Reagan's words washed over me. My lips curved into a smile at the thought that I could so easily bring her to this point. Her muscles rippled around me.

I started slowly with shallowing, entering only a fraction and then pulling back, repeatedly teasing her and building her up. She stayed perfectly still, handing over control of this movement. Her inner walls constricted in little flutters, bringing her closer and closer to the edge as I kept the slow and steady pace. When her breathing hitched, and her body tightened, I slammed harder, changing speed to fill her up completely.

All too soon, she let out a low keening noise. Her back arched into me, her hips desperately trying to match my thrusts. Reagan shuddered, her legs stiffening as her body quaked.

I wanted more, but only if she'd let me. Leaning over her, licking the soft spot against her neck, I asked the question, hoping she'd say yes. "Can I claim you, Reagan?"

"Do it," she gasped, nodding her head fervently.

Her orgasm rippled through her, and I let my release build as she spasmed around me, squeezing in rapid contractions.

My teeth shifted to the fangs of my shadow beast form. I sank them into her skin, tasting blood. Reagan screamed in ecstasy, her body now convulsing in full scale shudders that left me hurtling into my own orgasm. I shoved deep inside her as I came, and continued thrusting in slow, shallow pumps until Reagan's form relaxed beneath me. My teeth unlocked from her shoulder, and I pulled out slowly, when the last of the twitching subsided.

"Are you okay?" I asked. "I didn't hurt you, did I?"

Reagan rolled over, and her eyes opened.

My breath hitched, and in that moment we both knew.

"You're my mate," she choked out, and my entire body tensed. Her eyes flashed with hunger. The whiskey shade had always enticed me, but in lust—in love—threads of gold appeared, matching my own.

"I know," I whispered, leaning down and kissing her. "Tell me this is still what you want."

"You are still what I want," she said softly, reaching between us, rubbing my hardened length. "And I want *all* of you."

I leaned down into her, and a possessive growl rumbled in her throat. Pulling back, I looked at her in surprise. Moonlight filtered through the trees, and we both looked up. Clouds had dispersed to display what looked like a dark, moonless sky. In the distance, Kish's long howl pierced the air.

"How long does this cloaking spell work for?" she asked, placing her palms on my shoulders, and encouraging me to lay on my back. I did, pulling her with me.

"Another hour or so. It was meant to be temporary," I answered through ragged breaths as she stroked me with her hand.

"Oh well. Guess someone might get a show after all." She straddled me, reaching between her legs to guide me into her again.

My head tilted back, and my mouth fell open as her heat enveloped me.

The mating heat had begun.

CHAPTER 33
REAGAN

My mate led the way through the castle, turning corners and winding down hallways, holding my hand as I trailed behind him. After days spent in the forest, the bedroom, and well, pretty much everywhere, the heat had subsided. Whatever feral hunger had taken over me was sated, for now at least.

"Why are we in the throne room?" I asked, my steps faltering as we entered through a door I didn't know existed.

"To get to the staircase we need."

"How many secret passages do you have in this place? It's like playing a game of Clue." When he looked at me in question, I shook my head. "Never mind. Not important."

An unassuming door was across the room, and we headed straight for it. I would have guessed it was a broom closet, but as soon as he opened it, a long, dark stairwell came into view.

I came to a sudden stop, feeling like I was having a moment of déjà vu. Our interlaced fingers tugged, almost breaking our hold.

"What's the matter?" he asked, glancing between me and the stairwell. "It's harmless. Just a private exit."

Of course it was. Forcing a smile, I exhaled a shaky breath. The sensation that I had felt or seen this place before wouldn't dissipate, but I did my best to shake it off. "I've seen a lot of movies. Usually stairs like this led to giant spiders, or a room filled with skulls and torture devices."

"Nah," he said, walking down slowly. "Demon spiders are through a different door."

I laughed, taking each step with hesitation as I dragged my fingers along the stone walls. "And the skulls and torture devices?"

"A little bit of each in every room. Never know when the need will arise, and the last thing you want to do is travel all the way down to the dungeon. Really, Reagan, it's only practical."

I appreciated his casual humor. It made my nerves feel slightly more at ease as I started down the stairs.

Once we got to the bottom, he held my hand again, before pushing the door open.

A long, black sand beach spanned before us. The sound of waves crashing on the shore filled my ears. The salty scent of the air shocked me.

"What . . . ?" I began, but I halted when I couldn't find the words. Right before me, a black sand beach reached for a dark ocean beneath a starlit sky with two moons.

"Come," he said, urging me onto the sand. "I wanted you to see this."

My balance was off as I tried to get good footing in the sand, but with each step, I sunk a little. Running in this would be awful. After we'd walked forward, I started to turn around and Caius stopped me.

"Not yet," he said quickly. "Just a little further."

Finally, we stopped. He placed his hands on my shoulders, looking behind me and finally nodding. "Okay, turn around."

I wanted to, but I couldn't help myself from staring at him for a moment longer, wondering what he was so excited about. His smile was wide, and it met his eyes. When I turned slowly, my entire world suddenly shifted.

I wasn't prepared.

A dark castle built into the side of a mountain, merging as one unit. Two tall towers with spires complemented each other on opposite sides. The ocean splashed against the rocky cliffs, sending its spray misting into the air.

It's beauty wasn't what took my breath away. It was that I'd been here before. A hundred times. A thousand. There's no way he could have known that this was the place I'd dreamed of.

Silence stole my words for a moment before I asked, "How did I not see this? We left the castle to go into the village. It didn't look like this."

"You haven't been to this side. Also? No one can see it." He answered, a sense of happiness in his voice. "It's where I come to be alone and think. The beach is warded, so no one ever comes here except me. And Styx, sometimes, when her kelpie needs to let off steam."

"Why did you bring me here?"

"I thought you might like it," he said, each word getting slower as he began to sound unsure if he'd made the right call. "It's not Danni's castle, but I wanted to see what it looks like when the mountains meet the ocean. Or volcano, in this case."

"It's . . . amazing." What an underwhelming word for such a grand moment, but it was all I had. He breathed a short sigh of relief, and all I could do was nod. My hands were shaking, and I was trying to process what was happening.

I'd been dreaming of this place for years. Long before the wards began to weaken. Long before I passed the prophesized age of transference. It happened for the first time . . .

"My eighteenth birthday," I muttered.

"What?" Caius stood at my side, turning to face me.

"I've been dreaming about this place since my eighteenth birthday," I said a little louder, clearing my throat.

"I don't understand," he said, glancing back at the mountain. "This is what you were talking about? You dreamed of *this* castle?"

I bobbed my head, numb from the shock that still hadn't faded.

The longing to be here. The sense of completion and fulfillment. I thought it was Washington calling to me. That maybe I was meant to go live with my cousin and see what fate had in store for me there, only it wasn't Washington. It was Tartarus. This castle. *Him.*

"The day I turned eighteen," I began, swallowing thickly. "I dreamed of this place. I dreamed of you. You were the shadow. I couldn't see your face. But this . . ." I gestured to the castle in the distance. "I saw this every night, and it felt like . . ."

My own words echoed in my mind.

Dreaming of it. Painting it. It felt like home.

I'd been dreaming of Caius for almost ten years. The nameless, faceless man wasn't merely an aspiration; I was dreaming of the man I would take as my mate.

A stuttered breath escaped me as my thoughts were flooded with a memory I'd long forgotten.

"Reagan, what's the matter?" he asked, coming to stand

in front of me, his eyes focused and his brows furrowed. Cupping my face, he tried to assess what was happening. "Reagan, talk to me."

I stared blankly, losing my focus on his face, and only seeing the past flash before my eyes.

I watched through an open window of a chapel, unseen and unheard. A young version of myself sat on a chair, swinging her legs back and forth, just as Jo often did. This was before Jo was born. Before my home in The Crossroads.

"Something is wrong, Elda."

"What do you mean?" my keeper whispered.

The seer murmured, "Her future is shrouded by shadows."

"You can't see her future?" Elda said in a hushed tone. "Has that ever happened before?"

"No," the seer said, lifting a boney hand to run over her jaw in thought. "I've been alive a long time. I carry the knowledge of all seers charged before me and I've cared for four generations of guardians. Whatever powers her parents passed to her are far greater than anything I've seen. Either you've put a cloak on her or. . ." She looked at Elda for confirmation, but Elda shook her head. "That's what I feared."

"Or?"

"She has a mate bond, and it's already protecting her."

"That's not even possible," Elda scoffed. "She's ten. She doesn't have a mate. She can't. Her half soul is grafted to the Soulless One. Perhaps it's him you see."

The seer shook her head. "I've read the future of every girl before her, and they were all the same. Death. Not shadow. This isn't some faceless god, Elda. It's a shadow of a mate bond that is powerful and transcends time." The old woman tutted. "She is not yet mated, but that doesn't mean fate has not yet determined her mate. Whoever she is destined to be with, they are more powerful than we can imagine if the bond is reaching out to protect her already. If they find her—if they find us—I don't need to be a seer to tell you what will happen."

"What do we do?" Elda asked, looking at the younger Reagan. She appeared distracted, but it was obvious she was listening to every word they said, and it scared her.

"We bind her from feeling the bond and pray to the gods it works." Both women nodded.

"Reagan," Elda said, kneeling down in front of the little girl. "We need to put a spell on you to keep you safe from someone that might want to hurt you or take you away from us."

The girl's eyes widened. "I don't want to hurt . . ."

"We don't want that either. Can you stay still?"

Little Reagan whimpered but agreed.

The seer left the room, and the clanking of bottles echoed off down the hall. When she returned, she held a small bottle and an old leather-bound book, filled with parchment with frayed edges. She handed the vial to the young girl. "Drink."

Little Reagan accepted the bottle with shaking hands, but she did as she was told. Holding the elder's hand, she stayed still while the old seer began to chant. Ancient runes swirled around the young child, an invisible shield settling onto her skin as her eyes rolled into the back of her head and she passed out, landing on Elda's lap.

Confusion settled over me. If my younger self was asleep, I shouldn't see this memory, but the scene continued to show me pieces of my past I didn't know existed.

The seer placed a wrinkled hand on the child's forehead and nodded. "There."

"Can you see her future? Are the shadows gone?"

"No, but the darkness that shrouds her has been hidden behind a wall of light. It won't hold forever. We must hope it's long enough to transfer the ward to her offspring when the time comes."

"How long do we have?"

"I truly can't say. I've never felt magic that strong before, but it's best for her to believe that guardians don't have mates. If she doesn't believe in it, she won't make the mistakes her mother did. No reason to search for something that doesn't exist. In the meantime, let us pray to the primordials who charged us with the soul's keeping that her mate doesn't come looking for her."

"What kind of bond could even conceal their mate as a child, Zona?" Elda whispered as she stroked the little's girl's hair softly. "What kind of supernatural is capable of that?"

The elder's question mimicked my own.

The old woman shuddered, then turned to look out the window of the cabin. She stared straight into my eyes as though I were there and not seeing this moment as a memory. In a barely audible voice, she answered. "A shadow shifter."

The memory exploded, my vision blurring as fragments of my past shattered like glass.

My eyes shot open, and I came to, gasping for air and bolting upright to find myself no longer on the beach, but in my bed. Our bed. Caius sat beside it; worry etched in his features.

"Reagan," he breathed. "What happened? The healers said you were . . . fine. They said there was nothing they could do. I thought—"

"I'm fine." I swallowed, the dryness of my throat evident with each word. "How long was I out?"

"Hours," he said painfully. "Tell me what happened."

"I don't know? A memory resurfaced."

"One of mine?" His eyes darkened, but they cleared when I shook my head.

"Mine. The mate bond," I began, and his face fell, probably waiting for me to try and back out. I shoved the covers off, tucking my legs beneath me so I could sit up better. "It was always there."

He looked at me, confused. "How is the mate bond a memory?"

"It was never your soul. It wasn't *because* I'm the guardian. It's *despite* me being the guardian." I shook my head, trying to make sense of what I saw. "This pull I've had to you, the dreams of this place; it's because I'm meant to be here. The bond. The shadows. All of it." Something cold flashed through me as I remembered what they did. They'd taken him away from me for so long. "The coven bound me from feeling it. From feeling you."

Caius sat on the edge of the bed, one leg hanging down and the other bent on the mattress holding my hands in his. He squeezed my hand, a small smile on his face. "All this time, I figured you were just obstinate."

I laughed because what else could we do?

"Our bond"—I swallowed, taking another deep breath. "I felt it when I was young. The elders couldn't see my future anymore. Your shadows were protecting me. They put a binding light over me, hoping it would hold you off. But it started to fracture when I was eighteen. That's why you dreamed of me. The shadows crept in through those cracks. I didn't know what it was. My dreams, my visions of shadows and safety and *home*. But I do now," I said, my voice dropping to a whisper toward the end. I squeezed his hands back. "It was always you."

"Your dreams are part of the past. They can't ever hurt you again. I'll always be here if you want to talk about them." He leaned in to kiss me, and I smiled against his lips before a sudden sense of guilt swept over me. I still hadn't told him about my second dream. I at least had the choice to tell him about mine. It felt like I was being sneaky knowing some of his past without his permission. What if he wasn't ready to talk about those things? He sensed that I was upset and pulled away.

"What's wrong?" he asked.

"I have a confession," I began, fidgeting with my hands while I sat back. "I had another dream-memory that wasn't mine. But it was a while ago. It was with Abra—" I cut myself off when I saw anger flash in his eyes. "Her. I didn't tell you because I don't want to cause you any more pain than you've already experienced. It feels intrusive, even if I can't control it."

He shook his head. "It doesn't matter anymore. There's nothing she can do to hurt me again. It might take me time to not feel hatred when I hear her name, but you're all that matters." He took a deep breath, letting the silence comfort us before he spoke again. "I actually have a confession as well."

"Oh really?"

He hummed. "Dannika sent me a letter." My jaw dropped. "She wants to meet on neutral ground to talk about the portal, and she hopes to welcome me to the family. I've written her back, but not sent it. I won't send it until you're ready. I figured we could make that trip together. King and Queen of Tartarus . . ."

My heart skipped a beat, and with it, a fresh wave of anxiety.

"That means . . ." I sighed, and he nodded.

"You have to tell your dad."

I groaned, scrubbing my hands down my face. "Can't I just stay here in Hell and hide?"

"Tartarus isn't Hell," he repeated.

"You're right," I muttered. "Hell is telling my dad I'm mated to you."

CHAPTER 34

REAGAN

"You can't keep avoiding your family," Caius said against the rim of his teacup before taking a sip. He peered at me, waiting for a response. "It's been two weeks, Reagan."

My feet were propped up on the edge of his desk, a sketch pad in my lap.

I sighed. "I know. I like to avoid conflict."

"Odd that your chosen profession was a gravedigger," he quipped, smirking. Setting down the cup, he straightened his posture. "Your sister has been sending letters. Nog won't stop barking about all the questions they're asking—"

"I see what you did there." I smiled.

He hummed, not skipping a beat. "And you still haven't told them we're mated. Were I a lesser man, I'd think you were ashamed."

"But you're not a lesser man. You're a god, so . . ."

"So you've reminded me every time my face is between your thighs." He winked, and warmth spread over me.

My lips twisted to the side in a smile, thinking about

our lovemaking the past two weeks. "Of course it's not *about* you. It's the act of *telling* them about you. It's hard."

"Would you like me to go with you?"

"Go with you where?" Clara asked, waltzing into the room with a book under one arm and a crochet bag under the other.

"Back home to visit Sin and Dad." She tripped, stumbling forward before she quickly recovered while mumbling about the uneven stones in the castle and the least they could do was put a rug over it.

"So, when are you going?" She took a seat next to me, setting her belongings in a chair to her other side.

I glanced at Caius, and he gave me a disapproving look. "Tomorrow," I muttered.

"Why would you want to come anyway?" I asked my mate, reaching for the platter of assorted breads, cheeses, and fruits sitting in the middle of the table. I popped a strawberry in my mouth.

"To be supportive, for one."

"And two?"

"It's your family. I should probably speak with Alvaro as well. He's the alpha of his pack, and he's your father. It only seems respectful that I officially ask for your hand in marriage."

A brief moment passed in silence where I waited for him to say more. When I realized that he was waiting for my reply, a giggle bubbled up and Clara joined in with my laughter.

"I'm sorry, I didn't realize you were serious," I said. "We don't do that anymore. I mean, I'm sure some people do, but that tradition got squashed a long time ago. He doesn't own me. He can't give me away."

"That is . . . an excellent point," he said, taking a stack of papers and shuffling them into a pile. "I don't think I ever considered it from that perspective."

"Men usually don't, but to be fair, that isn't unique to men. There are women who don't realize they're treated like possessions, and they just stupidly go along with it," Clara said, rolling her eyes.

"Hmm. So I suppose I shouldn't be expecting a dowry of goats and fine linens in exchange, then?" I looked at him and my mouth fell open, then he cracked a smile.

"Hey," I said, throwing a piece of piece of bread at him, and he laughed. "How many goats do you think I'd be worth, Clara?"

"Maybe ten? You're pretty hot. Good cook. You have a booty, which means you have good birthin' hips, right?"

"Ten? That's it? What an insult. I'm worth ten little lawnmowers that chew on hair and anything else they can get their teeth on."

"Personally, I think we should get the dowry for taking on a husband. Unless they come already trained." Her snark was on point today.

A knock on the door interrupted us, and a porter came in. "Excuse me, Your Majesty. Your afternoon appointment has arrived."

Caius nodded, then picked up the documents he'd been working on. He got up from the table, coming to stand next to me. I craned my neck back, expecting a goodbye peck and nothing more. Leaning down, he whispered, "I'm trained where it counts." Then his lips brushed mine in a tease before he kissed me deeply, stealing my breath away. My cheeks flushed and I clenched my thighs together. "I'll see you tonight." His final words made my skin tingle long after he left.

"I would say get a room, but I'm afraid you'd just get up

and leave," Clara said, looping yarn around her finger. She stopped, tilting her head, and looking at the table. "Or maybe just kick me out and go for it here. But if you do, I'm taking the food with me. Be a shame to waste good cheese."

I snorted. "I won't lie. I'm torn. A short break would be good. My lady parts are sore as hell. But the other part of me can't stop craving him."

My cousin lifted a shoulder and hummed. "Maybe you shouldn't go yet. Get it out of your system. You're in that honeymoon period of the relationship where everything just feels phenomenal."

I sighed, leaning back in my chair, placing my arm on the rests on either side. "I can't. Two weeks isn't long, but it's a long time when you're avoiding having a conversation with someone. Dad doesn't even know that I'm mated, unless Nog told him, but I'm pretty sure he didn't because I threatened him with a shock collar if he even breathed a word to anyone."

Clara huffed a small laugh. "Finally found a way to keep his mouth shut."

"I figured out how to make him stop yapping too."

"Really?"

"Shake a cup full of coins. He really hates that. You just see a ball of fluff, bolting into another room. To be fair, he peed on my shoes afterward, so it's not a win-win."

Clara groaned. "Figures. He needs to learn how to shift on his own without being in Tartarus."

"Hey, why don't you come with me tomorrow? It would be good for you to see your mom. Spend some time with Jo."

Something sad passed over her features. "I kind of like it here. I'm not sure I want to go back."

"Really?" My face contorted into a grimace. "Because

you don't look like it right now. You look like you're about to cry."

"Allergies, probably. Can't escape them in The Crossroads, can't escape them here. I think it's the yellow biting flowers in the atriums." She rubbed her nose. "I think you should wait a little bit longer. I'm not really sure if Tío is ready to hear that you're mated."

"It's par for the course. Were supernaturals. We find mates."

Clara barked a laugh. "That doesn't mean that an alpha is gonna accept his daughter running off with somebody and getting married, to Caius of all people."

"It'll be hard for him. Honestly, I think it's going to be harder for Sin. Sometimes I feel like she's more protective than Dad."

"Why don't you just have them come visit here?"

"Are you crazy? They'd try to bring the whole family. I couldn't do that to anyone in the castle. Not Caius. Not the staff. Pol would probably lose his mind. It would be absolute chaos, and who knows what kind of drama would get started. No, it's best if I go home."

"You won't be gone long, will you?

"No, not long. Couple of days at most. When I cross over, I won't be able to feel the bond with Caius. I don't know how to describe it, but now that I know what it feels like, the idea of losing it, even for a temporary period of time, feels awful. Like part of me won't be able to breath, or I'll be stretched too thin or something." My cousin frowned. "Why are you looking at me like that?"

"No reason." She schooled her features. "I was just wondering."

"Clara, are you okay? I know it was really scary with

what happened, and I know you said you were fine, but I'm worried about you."

"I really am fine. I have a lot of dreams about it still and it freaks me out. The way that I tried to speak but it was like this invisible pressure on my throat and in my chest preventing the words from coming out. I couldn't ask for help. I couldn't even tell you something was wrong." She stared at me her eyes wide. "Does that make sense?"

"God that must have been awful."

Clara twisted her lips and sighed, glancing off to the other side of the room. "Yeah, pretty awful when you want to say something and can't."

"I won't be gone long. When I get back, we can work through this together. I'm sorry I haven't been around. Going into the heat with Caius and completing the mate bond has been a little time consuming, for lack of a better word."

"Ohh, I know. We *all* know. It would do you some good to soundproof that room." She scrunched her nose, adding, "It would do *me* some good."

"Maybe we'll do that before we get married," I said, chuckling at her expression. "It'll be my gift to you."

Clara tilted her head back and laughed. "Isn't that the other way around? I'm supposed to get you a gift, right? I wouldn't even know where to start."

"You're trying to decode my mom's journal. That means the world to me—" I stopped when her face fell, and I realized what it meant. "You still haven't found anything . . ."

Claire's lips pressed together tight with disappointment, and she shook her head. "I'm so sorry."

I released a tense breath. "It's okay. It's just that it would be nice to be able to give that part of him back. My gift to him. But it's not the end of the world." I could tell how much it bothered her that she hadn't found anything yet. It was wishful thinking anyway on my part.

She reached over, patting my hand with a gentle squeeze. "I'll keep trying, I promise. I'm still the queen's personal advisor, right? I can add royal translator to my list of talents."

"Queen," I repeated with sarcasm. Blowing a strand of loose hair off my face, I sighed. "Clara, I have *no* idea what I'm going to do here. I feel like I'm going to have to learn how to be a whole new person. How do you learn to be a queen?"

She pursed her lips in thought before an "ah ha" look crossed her face. "What about going to see Danni?"

"That seems kind of weird, doesn't it?"

"Weird seeing a cousin?"

"No, weird because I haven't seen her since she came to visit when we were little. I don't feel like I know her well enough to be asking her for advice on how to not totally screw up being a royal."

She waved me off. "You guys have written letters to each other since we were kids. She and Adora always said they wished you would come see them."

I smiled. "She wrote to Caius, welcoming him to the family." I picked at a piece of bread, recalling her most recent letter. "Actually, we're going to see her and Elias. We're going to meet and talk about the portal and stuff. It's official business. I just don't know how to be official."

"See? No better time than the present."

"Like, right now? Nooo," I drawled, shaking my head. "I figure maybe I should send a letter first before showing up on their doorstep like some weirdo."

"Yeah, I suppose you're right."

"Besides, if I told Danni and she told Tía Sarah and Tía

Abbey before I told my dad? He's already going to lose his mind. I just need to bite the bullet and go see him."

She frowned, nodding in agreement. "Just promise me you'll take care of yourself, okay?"

"Jesus, Clara, I'm just going home." For the first time, that word felt wrong. Home had always been where my family was, but Tartarus was also home. What a strange and conflicted feeling to feel equal parts of yourself pulled in two different directions.

Clara looked like she wanted to say something more substantial but changed her mind. "Give Jo and my mom a hug from me, okay?"

"Of course. And I'll bring back all the family gossip. I have to go pack an overnight bag. I figure the sooner I get this over the better." I got up from the table and walked to the other side, wrapping my arms around her shoulders in a hug.

She opened her mouth, and nothing came out, a slight tear developing in the corner of her eye.

"I love you, Reagan."

"I love you too, Clara."

She'd told me she was fine, but I wasn't so sure. I had to take her at her word. Pressing further wouldn't do any good, but worry consumed me. I'd never seen her this scared before.

I figured I'd needed to cut my trip short. She needed me, but she was struggling too much to admit it. I'd tell my dad and Sin about being mated, listen to the fallout and rage, give Jo a giant squeeze, spend one night there and come back.

As I walked down the hallway toward my room, Pol and Abyssian were heading toward the dining hall. "Abyssian, can I talk to you for a minute?"

He raised his brows in surprise, giving me a warm smile. "Sure."

He shooed Pol away, and as usual, his counterpart looked on with a healthy dose of suspicion. Still, he left us, which I appreciated.

When I figured he was out of earshot, I spoke quickly, keeping quiet, just in case. "Clara's been acting really weird. I know the entire experience of being poisoned really freaked her out, and rightly so, but I'm worried about her."

Abyssian glanced up, looking behind me briefly, his jaw clenching. When he met my gaze, he softened. "I know. I hate how much she's hurting."

"Can you do me a favor?"

"Of course."

"I don't know how serious you guys are, or how serious you are about her, but will you keep an eye on her for me while I'm gone?"

He took a quick step back. "Gone? You can't leave. You and Caius accepted the mate bond—"

"It's just for the day." I smiled at his immediate concern. "I'm gonna go visit my family. Clara was having a really hard time letting me leave. I haven't spent enough time with her, so if you could just stay with her until I get back, it would be appreciated."

Understanding crossed his features. "Absolutely. I won't leave her side."

"Thanks, Abyssian."

I squeezed the side of his bicep as a small gesture of gratitude and kept walking. Moments later, a shiver ran up my spine, and I shuddered. I could not shake the feeling of unease as I headed to our bedroom.

It was the indescribable feeling of being watched.

Or hunted.

CHAPTER 35
REAGAN

A light breeze lifted the strands of my hair, making them blow across my face. I smiled up at the old house that had been my family's home for generations. While I now had my place with Sin and Clara, this was my dad's home base. Tío Amos and Tía Celeste, and a ton of their children lived here now. It wasn't as grand as it was before the shifter portal opened. Time and the elements had taken their toll, but even with peeling paint and loose shutters that creaked incessantly in a strong wind, it was a comforting place to be. Familiar scents, mismatched plates and repaired furniture; everyone was loved behind these walls.

The new ache pulsed inside me. Both places felt like home.

So much had changed since Ben tried to mark me. That simple action was the catalyst, forcing me to face new challenges. The infection that tried to kill me. The ward breaking. Chasing Caius into Tartarus and discovering he was my mate. While my life had changed, I also knew that deep down, I had changed. These events altered me irrevocably.

No matter how much I changed, this was still my first home. My dad was still my dad. Sin was still my sister.

The wooden steps let out a groan as I started up them. My fingers trailed over the rough wooden railing. My backpack was slung over my shoulder, and my hair was braided back and secured with a simple leather tie. The tunic I wore was loose, but form fitting. All the training had honed my body and shed softness from the most visible parts of me. It would always cling to my ass and thighs to some extent. That was just me, and frankly, I loved it. Even though I still felt like myself, there was no doubt in my mind that I looked different.

I counted to ten and opened the door. The wood panel swung back on slick hinges, hitting the wall protector Tía Celeste installed after someone made a hole in the sheetrock one too many times.

"Dad? Sin? Anyone?" I called out while strolling into the foyer. I caught the door edge with the tip of my boot and nudged it closed.

Sin was the first to appear. Dark circles lined her eyes. I barely had time to look at her before she threw herself at me, arms wrapping around my upper half and squeezing tight.

"Hey," I said softly, hugging her back. Her familiar scent triggered childhood memories to resurface. Playing tag until I accidentally knocked over a lamp and Tía made us stop. Rainy days spent inside with board games and pizza. One after another flashed through me, and it made me cling to her more.

"I'm never letting you leave again," she said.

"Right," I said quietly, knowing I'd need to explain the situation at some point real soon, but now wasn't the time.

"Reagan?" My father's voice made my head snap up. He

filled the doorway with his massive frame only a second before Sin and I were lifted off the ground in a bear hug. His wolf let out a low growl, happy to have its pack back in one place.

It was like a dam broke. Cousins flooded the foyer, each wanting to hug me or give me a fist bump. Tía Celeste sobbed as she clung to me, but thankfully Dad saved me from too much of that by dragging me under his huge arm, wrapping it around my shoulders.

It was the light thumping of little feet that caught my attention, and I waited.

Jo came bursting from between two others, running straight for me. I ducked down, opening my arms for him. He crashed into me, arms flying around my neck, and it was everything I could do to hold back tears.

"Hey, mijo," I cooed, stroking his hair. "I missed you."

"You're back," he whispered, smiling into my shoulder. "I knew you'd be okay."

"I'm back," I whispered.

He let go, stepping back to look at me. "Did you bring me any books?" His eyes sparkled with hope.

I winked, patting my backpack behind me. "You bet I did."

Jo was giddy was excitement. We traded for new books when we could, but we hadn't gotten any in a long time.

"Okay, okay, let's give her some space guys," my dad rumbled. Several of my cousins disappeared, not testing the waters with their alpha. The rest loitered around, waiting to hear me talk about what had happened.

Jo reached over, holding my hand. He gave me strength and he didn't even know it.

"Sooo," I drawled. "I'll be honest. I don't know where to start or how much Nog has actually told you."

"Infuriatingly little," Sin griped. One corner of my mouth tugged up.

Glancing at the number of family members watching me, I angled my head toward the other room. "Let's go into the den."

Faded couches and patched bean bag chairs covered every wall except the one with Jo's personal collection of floor-to-ceiling bookshelves. I took a seat on one of the couches between my dad and sister, pulling Jo onto my lap.

Then I briefed them with the tale of me entering Tartarus and learning the price for Clara's safety was six months. My cousins interrupted frequently, but we got through it—skipping over the parts where I was almost killed, Clara's poisoning, and my mating Caius a month ago.

"So he just let you go?" Sin asked, nose scrunching in disbelief. I couldn't blame her for not trusting it. They didn't know him like I did.

"Not exactly." I spoke carefully, seeing an in for how I could broach the subject of my mating, then I realized I had danced around for half an hour trying to soften the blow. It wasn't possible. Nothing could prepare them for the truth. Might as well just rip off the band-aid. "We mated."

It went about as well as I expected. The room exploded into chaos and only calmed after my dad let out an alpha bark, hushing them like they were all pups. Jo kept quiet, and he patted my hand, silently encouraging me.

"Now, Reagan," my dad said with a tight jaw. "I'm going to need you to repeat that."

I sighed. "I know it's hard to believe, and I definitely didn't believe it for the longest time. Despite me being the guardian, we are actually mates. It's too long of a story to rehash right now, but you have to trust me. We completed the bond, and it was my choice. I wasn't forced or tricked into anything."

"Wait," Sin interrupted. "I don't understand."

Getting a little irked at having to repeat myself, I said, "We're mates. Caius is my mate. I came back to visit, but I won't be staying indefinitely. Caius is going to keep the portal open so we can visit each other whenever we want. We're even going to see Danni and Elias about it."

Instead of more questions, they gave me silence. It was actually worse.

My dad rubbed his jaw with his free hand and motioned for the door. "All right everyone, I need to talk Reagan alone. Now. Out with ya. Sin, Celeste, Jo, you can all stay."

"Thanks for your permission in my own house," my tía said. I choked on a laugh as Dad sighed heavily. There was a lot of that going on.

"I need a snack." Jo scooted off my lap, then paused before leaving. "You changed, Reagan. But it's a good change. It's obvious he's good for you."

He ignored the baffled stares from our family, and when he'd left.

"That little boy never ceases to amaze me." Tía shook her head, smiling.

Sin mimicked her actions. "He doesn't act like a normal nine-year-old, that's for sure."

"That's because he's not," I said. "I'm not sure what he is exactly, but Caius recognized it. When I asked about it he said we'll have to wait till Jo wants to tell us."

"Wait, Caius knows? Jo knows?" Celeste's eyes were wide, and she looked at the door where he'd exited.

"Jo may not know yet, but he will. We just have to wait."

"But—" she began before quickly getting cut off.

"Jo isn't the subject of this conversation," my dad said.

I groaned internally. "What do you want me to say, Dad? That I'm going to forsake my mate and stay in The Crossroads forever?"

"Well . . ." Sin said, trailing off as she obviously agreed.

I whipped around to glare at her. "You can't be serious."

Sin grumbled and her shoulders fell. "I'm not, it's just a lot to take in. I knew I was losing you for six months, but I didn't think that you'd go and fall in love with the bastard."

The pain in her voice made me flinch.

"You have to understand, Sin. Everything we knew about him was based on lies. Nothing about him was true. And Tartarus? It's not at all a bad place. It might have been long ago, but under his rule, it's thriving. I know it's hard to see past what we've believed for almost twenty years—I struggled with it too—but I have no reason to deceive you. You just have to trust me."

My dad squeezed my shoulder gently. "You do love him, right? It's not just because he's your mate?"

"I do love him. I fell in love with him before I accepted the mate bond." I chose to leave out some of the details leading up to it. Less was more in this case. "Caius is . . . I don't even know how to simplify him. He's funny and smart. He gets me even when I don't get myself, and he doesn't let me lie to myself either. And he doesn't judge me. He supports me and my choices. Hell, even Clara loves him."

"That doesn't mean much," Sin said. Dad chuckled under his breath.

"She has a history of finding every pendejo in a ten-mile radius," Dad said.

"Can't disagree there," Tía said. "I wouldn't be

surprised if that girl was rooting for him right after he kidnapped her."

I stifled my laugh with a smile. "My point is, he's not perfect, no, but he is *my* choice."

Dad pulled me in tight for a side hug. "Then I guess the only thing left to say is that I'm happy for you, kiddo. All I ever wanted for my girls was a happy life. I hoped you lived long enough to find what your mom and I had." I hugged him back, inhaling his signature piney scent. "You're safe, and you have a mate. I can't ask for much more than that."

Tía raised her brows in surprise. "Alvaro, I'm shocked. You don't want to kill him for mating with Reagan?"

"Oh, I didn't say that," he answered with a laugh. "I just said I'm happy for my daughter, and I'm leaving it at that."

"There's something else," I said, wanting to get the most important piece off my chest.

"Oh, gods. You're pregnant, aren't you?" Sin said. From the hallway there was a hushed *"pay up!"* as my shit-for-brains cousins eavesdropped and took bets.

"No!" I said vehemently, shaking my head. "It's nothing like that."

"Thank the gods," my dad muttered.

"It's abuela's tonics you should thank. She's looking out for all our girls," Tía Celeste said. "She knew what it was like to be saddled with a child too young."

"Okay, so if you're not pregnant, what is it?" Sin asked, bringing the conversation back around. I laughed lightly under my breath because this was just so *us*. The chaos. My cousins. Tía and Dad going back and forth on who we should be praying to.

"The way I left things when I went to Tartarus . . ." I sighed heavily, and my dad and sister tensed at the new subject. Guilt lined my father's eyes, and Sin looked down at her feet.

"Reagan," my dad said softly, but I held up my hand for him to stop.

"I forgive you for not telling me the truth. Really forgive you. Not the way I sort of shouted that I forgave you when I was storming off. I'm still upset, but I know you aren't perfect. You wanted to protect me, and that was the only way you knew how." Sin looked up at me, eyes brimming with unshed tears. "I don't ever want to walk away from the people I love with so much anger lingering between us. No more lies, okay? Me included. We all tell each other the truth. About everything."

They both nodded fervently.

The rest of the day went by in a blur. Jo got his book, tracing the pieces of parchment delicately with his fingertips before he lowered his nose to it and inhaled. A huge grin and a giant hug were my thanks. Sin begged me to make dinner, claiming how much she missed my green chile enchiladas, and echoes of agreement filled the air. How could I say no?

We played dominoes. Told stories. Laughed. It was an almost perfect evening. The only thing that would have made it better was if Caius could have been there too. Before I'd left, he offered to come again as support, but I declined. Not only was this something I needed to do on my own, but we needed to test his magic spreading outside the portal again, but first I needed to drop the mate bomb on my family. One thing at a time.

That night, when everyone had drifted off, I laid in a cousin cuddle pile in the back living room, thinking about leaving this place again. I stretched out on the floor with Jo curled into my side. The book I'd brought him had toppled off him when he'd fallen asleep. His soft breathing calmed me. I missed this. Nights where we'd all sleep over, sprawling out on couches and blankets, camping out in the middle of a big room.

My thoughts drifted to my house and the mural painted on my wall. The portrait of Tartarus and the castle that was now my home. I smiled. I didn't believe in destiny, but I couldn't argue with fate.

Caius and I belonged to each other, as one. Our future was entwined.

He loved me. My family would get used to it, and they would learn to love him as well.

That knowledge should have been enough to keep the nightmares away.

But like many things of late, I was dead wrong.

I woke in Caius's arms. His fingertips trailed down my naked back. I lifted my head and smiled at him, but the smile felt forced somehow. This wasn't my body, I realized with a startle. I was reliving Abraxia's life.

Again.

"Must you go so soon?" he rumbled, and my heart stuttered because I recognized the drowsy quality of his voice all too well.

"Afraid so," she said, then leaned in to kiss one of his muscular pecs. "But I won't be long, darling."

The endearment tasted like ash on her tongue. I could sense love, but I also picked up on guilt. Denial. She was so conflicted. I wondered where we were in the timeline of her betrayal. One day before her heinous act? Ten? There was no way for me to know.

Abraxia shifted away from him, and relief filled her.

It confused me.

She got to her feet, not bothering to cover herself. His eyes were on her, and she felt them. She liked that. The way his gaze followed her as she dressed in a simple skirt with glass beads dangling from the ends and bandeau top with gold pieces lining the seams.

Abraxia kissed him goodbye, flashing a flirtatious smile, before dancing out of his arms on swift feet. The skirt swished with her movements, drawing his eyes to her hips. That's where they stayed as she waved goodbye and exited his chambers.

At first her movements were easygoing, but the further she walked, the more hurried they became. Abraxia exited the castle, waving at the guards as she went, before pulling on a thin cloak. It was made of some sort of gauzy beige material. Light enough she wouldn't overheat, but just heavy enough not to be blown right off her. She tugged the drawstrings at the neck, pulling the hood down as she crossed through the town. The further she got from Caius, the more impoverished the buildings were. Dilapidated homes gave way to ramshackle huts just before she entered the woods. With a cloak that matched so many others, no one bothered to see who she was or why she was here.

Dread formed in my gut as she stepped into the same forest as before. A warm breeze greeted her, playing around her ankles and making the glass beads on the skirt clink together.

She rounded a particularly large tree trunk and her heart surged. I felt her joy alongside her guilt as she threw her arms around the broad shoulders of . . . *Abyssian.*

Shock paralyzed my thoughts for a moment as they kissed passionately, and it was decidedly *not* a familial greeting but something more.

Something like betrayal.

Nothing could have prepared me for it. His hands gripped her in all the places one would a lover. She was a two-timing hussy, but he was Caius's half-brother, so that was worse.

"Did he suspect?" Abyssian asked.

"N-no," she stumbled over her words, running her fingertips along his bearded jaw. It wasn't the clean cut look he wore now, but I recognized him, nonetheless.

Gods.

Abraxia betrayed Caius with Abyssian.

Abyssian betrayed Caius with Abraxia.

Abraxia betrayed them both, damning them to Tartarus.

It was like watching my abuela's novelas.

"Good girl," he praised. They kissed a while longer and my nausea built with every stolen touch and forbidden sweep of lips. At this point I was just hoping they didn't fuck. Gods, it wasn't me, but it would feel like a shadow betrayal all the same.

I had to get out of this dream. Just as I tried pushing at the barriers, willing myself to wake up, Abyssian thrust something into her hands. Abraxia looked down.

I'd seen this once before, and I would never forget the details of the jewel encrusted dagger she now held.

My heart stopped.

"Use this. A normal weapon won't work, not against his kind. This has been spelled to hide its true identity. If you give it to him as a gift, he won't suspect it."

The smile he gave her was relaxed but nothing could mask the sinister edge in his gaze. He'd always been watchful. Involved. Ever-present. I'd assumed he was just protective. The first time I'd seen him, Eres warned me of danger. Now that I recognized him for what he was, there was no unseeing it, and for five thousand years he'd kept this secret.

He didn't just betray his brother.

He fucking destroyed him.

Something in me snapped. Rage overwhelmed my senses. I tried to lash out, to shift, to strike, to turn that fucking blade on him instead. He's the one who deserved it. To my utter surprise, Abraxia stared down at the weapon in her hand, then gripped the handle harder, just as I imagined doing it myself.

She pulled the blade free of its sheath, again, just as I wanted.

"Xia?" Abyssian asked. Abraxia angled the blade so that the edge acted as a mirror, and a thin sliver of her face appeared. In the reflection of the steel, I saw *my* eyes staring back.

I reacted without thinking further, plunging the blade into Abyssian's traitorous chest. It slid between his ribs, just as Styx taught me, the silver tip finding his heart, if the bastard had one.

"Xia?" he said again, this time in a hushed whisper. I took a step back as he stumbled. Then, all at once, righted himself as though nothing had happened.

Abyssian reached up and grabbed the dagger by its hilt, wrenching it from his chest. He observed it for a moment, turning it over in his hands and inspecting the dagger.

My lips parted.

Shit. Fuck. Dammit.

He looked up at Abraxia, and a menacing smile formed on his face, a dangerous sparkle in his vile, glacial eyes.

"Hello, Reagan."

My eyes flew open. I sat up, gasping hard and then panting heavily. I pressed a hand to my chest while I looked around. My cousins were none the wiser, all sprawled out in various positions, deep in sleep. Jo had rolled over, cuddling his book instead of me, and I was thankful I hadn't woken him. Weak sunlight streamed through the drapes of the living room window. It wasn't quite dawn.

I carefully tucked the blanket around him, then tiptoed to get my things so I could change in the bathroom closer to the front of the house. My hands were hurried as I undressed and redressed for the day.

The dream wasn't real, but it sure as hell felt real. My rage was real, that much I knew. The two other dreams were part of his past. One confirmed, and the other . . . I didn't know. He couldn't say. It didn't involve him. But this? If there was even an ounce of truth to it, I had to tell Caius, and it couldn't wait.

I donned black jeans and a sports bra, then grabbed a thin tank top to put over it. Tartarus would be warmer than Earth.

An unwanted thought barged into my mind, making me question if I was doing the right thing. Abyssian was his half-brother. They'd been locked in Tartarus for five thousand years, and how long had they been alive before then? I'd known Caius for all of a few months? Maybe? I didn't even know what day it was anymore. Would he believe me, his girlfriend, over his own flesh and blood? It was a dream, and I was essentially accusing his brother of an incredibly heinous act.

Eres chastised me immediately, and she was right to.

"You're not his girlfriend or some tryst. You are his mate."

"I know that. It's just . . ."

"Just nothing. The terms of the bond are beyond what you can understand. A mate doesn't deceive."

I nodded, silently accepting her admonishment, but I questioned if that could be true. People were still people, and shitty people ended up with mates too. I wasn't a bad person, and Caius knew that. He would listen to me.

Not bothering to repack my backpack with anything, I grabbed my socks and boots, then walked through the house and into the kitchen where I thought I'd be alone. Instead, I found a small light was on. Sin was leaning against the counter, seemingly deep in thought. That wasn't odd for her given she frequently slept like shit. That'll happen when your dead mother returns as a talking ghost you can't get rid of. I'd probably be up at the crack of dawn if I had to constantly hear a lady berate me and my life choices.

Sin startled when I stepped toward the barstools.

"Where you are headed off to at this hour?" she asked, glancing at the clock on the wall. "I didn't think you were leaving until lunch."

I shook my head, slipping on my socks and lacing up my boots.

"I'm sorry. I'll be back soon, though, okay? Or you can come over anytime. The guards at the portal will let you through."

She looked at me with a disapproving scowl. "You're sneaking out before the sunrises without so much as a goodbye? I thought you said no more lies, Reagan."

"You're right, I did say that," I breathed harshly in annoyance. This isn't what I was talking about why I said no lying. This was me in a hurry and not having the time to list off everything I'd omitted in front of the entire family last night. "I need to get back to Caius and tell him something. It can't wait."

"Why?" she asked, rounding the counter. "What happened that you have to get to him right now?"

"I had a dream. It's more like a memory. I saw who gave

her the dagger. It's Abyssian. I have to warn Caius." This wasn't going to make any sense to her, and I just didn't have the time to spell it all out.

"Whoa, whoa, slow down there. Gave who what dagger? And who is Abyssian?" Sin grabbed my forearms and winced. "Rea, are you sure you're okay? You're burning up . . ."

"I'm fine," I muttered, reaching for my pack. "Does Tía still keep the baseball bat in the front closet?" I asked, heading to the hallway without waiting for a response. Sin's old baseball bat was indeed in the same spot. I grabbed the Louisville slugger by the handle and propped it over my shoulder.

"Yeah, but—"

"I have to get back to him, Sin. His brother betrayed him. He—"

"How do you know? You said you dreamed it. Since when did you start having psychic dreams?" she asked.

I sighed. "Since I got my powers back. Since I went to Tartarus. Since Caius. Take your pick. Either way, my dreams are real. What happened is real. I just know it. At the end, he saw me, Sin. Abyssian. Saw. Me. He said my name while he looked right at me, and it felt worse than any dream has ever felt because it was real. Which means he knows that I know what he did. I think something bad is going to happen, and I don't even know what it could be, but I have to get back to Caius."

"Okay, okay," Sin said. "I believe you, but I'm coming with you this time. If this guy is trouble, you're going to need back up."

"I don't—" I paused. While I'd expected her to try to stop me, I never planned on her offering to join. And you know what? She was right. Abyssian was lethal, and Caius was in danger now that I knew. "Never mind. You're right. Just get dressed quickly. I'm worried with the portal between us that I won't feel it if something happens to him."

"Yeah," she said, running a hand through her hair. "Okay just give me five. I'll be ready."

"I'll be outside waiting. Keep quiet and don't wake the others. I don't need a parade of cousins thinking they can fight against gods like this is some back-alley brawl." She nodded, moving silently and swiftly.

I chewed at my thumbnail while I waited, ignoring the growl in my empty stomach.

"We are stronger than a fae god. Stop fretting."

"Are we? I'm not so sure. We couldn't beat the elk."

She huffed. "Because you wouldn't let me take over."

"We still haven't mastered that yet. Last time we crashed into a tree when we tried to run."

"You keep saying 'we.' I don't run into trees like a newborn foal. We look bad because you won't let go. If it's time to shift, just let me do the work."

"Got it." I nodded. Easier said than done, but still got it, loud and clear. *"Any other advice?"*

"Don't fuck it up."

Thanks, Eres. Real supportive.

CHAPTER 37
REAGAN

It was eerily quiet in The Crossroads as we approached Old Kiener Plaza. No birds were sharing their morning songs. There was no chittering of raccoons; no pitter-patters of nocturnal scavengers looking to end their evening escapades in a hidey hole. Survival instincts were strong in animals. When they went silent, danger was present.

Sin and I exchanged knowing glances. She noticed it as well. The absence of sound set me on edge, more so than I already had been. Still, it could be explained. If some wild dog had just taken down a smaller creature, it would be eating nearby, and it would be a while before any others felt safe to come out. That is what I told myself to slow my frantic heartrate, but it didn't stop the unwelcomed foreboding that something bad was going to happen at any minute.

We slowed our steps, hunching down and keeping vigilant as we moved closer to the plaza. If we somehow hadn't noticed the deafening silence, red flag number two would have stopped us dead in our tracks.

The portal was just ahead, a swirling mass sitting on the edge of the broken fountain, and there were no guards.

"Bathroom break?" Sin whispered, shrugging her shoulder in question.

I shook my head, trying to listen for any sound. "No, once Nog gave Styx the slip, they put two to three guards on it around the clock. Oberon is lead, but I don't know his rotation." And Styx was no longer involved here. Once she had returned to Tartarus, she resisted coming back to this side. Resisted was a nice way of putting it. She flat out refused and told Caius she'd rather die. "I don't know who is supposed to be there right now, but *someone* is supposed to be there."

"Well, it's not a shift change," she said, considering other options.

Sin and I ducked down, positioning ourselves behind overgrown bushes, waiting to see if something happened. If someone returned after sneaking away for an unsanctioned rendezvous with a local, or even sneaking off together. Two guards in love. It could happen. Hell, I waited for a buzzard to fly over and pick at a guard's dead body if there was one. That would at least have given me some information to go on.

We got nothing. Not a sound. No movement. Not a cricket chirp.

"Something is very wrong," I said in a barely audible whisper, peering over the hedge.

"This place is like a ghost town. I don't even hear bugs." She scanned the park, looking for signs of life. "What do you want to do?"

I struggled with the knowledge Caius may be in trouble, but I wasn't going to run through the portal, guns blazing.

Not when my better judgment was telling me to stop. To wait. Assess the situation and make a plan.

Squeezing my eyes closed, I pinched the bridge of my nose and cursed.

"What?" Sin whispered.

"I don't know who is on Abyssian's side. Is Pol part of it? Legion?" Not Styx. She wouldn't . . . I hoped not. "If the guards were his, he had them pulled."

"Well," she said, pressing her lips together and raising her brows. "Then that means there's an ambush on the other side and that's kind of a problem."

"Okay, look. When you go through, you end up in this atrium. There's a lot of plant life. Giant ferns with big fronds. If we go in low, maybe we can hide and observe before making any other moves.

She raised her brows again like I'd lost my mind. "They set a trap for you. What's your plan if they're just waiting on the other side when we come crawling through on our bellies?"

"Tuck and roll?" I tried to smile, and she did too, but neither of us pulled it off well.

"Wait, you just said they set a trap for me."

She stared at me. "Yeah?"

"He would think I'd be coming alone." The wheels began to turn as I tried to form a plan.

"So?"

"So, I go through, get captured, but then you come through right after. They won't be expecting two of us. As long as their backs are turned, they won't see you coming."

My sister looked at me like I was crazed. "Have you lost your mind?"

Eres shoved herself forward, interjecting no matter how

hard I tried to keep a wall between us. *"Don't concern your-self with what's on the other side—"*

"Why wouldn't I? We can't just waltz in there. I'm guessing strategic warfare wasn't a skill the god of death needed."

"Infernal human. What do prey do when a predator is close by?" she ground out.

"We already noticed." I mentally tried to bat her way, but she persisted. *"That's not important right now."*

"On the contrary, it's of the utmost importance."

"They stay silent and hide. Happy?"

"Why do they do that?"

"So whatever is hunting them doesn't find them, Eres, for fu—"

"And what are you doing right now?" Her tone was harsh as she punctuated her statement, but somehow, even she was whispering.

I swallowed hard. In the stillness of the early morning hours, the blood rushing to my pounding heart echoed so loudly in my ears, I thought I'd given away our position.

No guards. No witnesses to a struggle.

This wasn't about getting to the other side and warning Caius. It wasn't about saving him.

This was about *me.*

I turned my head to Sin, feeling the color drain from my face. "We're being hunted."

A slow clapping started. It sounded like it came from everywhere and nowhere at once. Abyssian strode forth from the shadows, the early rays of the dawn casting a warm glow around him. His dark hair was braided back like Caius's had been in my dreams.

"Smart girl," he said, the voice coming from every direc-tion. He wasn't one lone figure, but one of a dozen exact replicas. Slowly, the small army of Abyssians exited the shadows. From behind the trees. From inside a building. From behind the fountain.

"I take it this is the asshole you saw in your dream?" my sister muttered.

"Yup."

She nodded once. "Got it."

Abyssian drifted closer and I narrowed my eyes at him in disgust.

"You were right, Reagan. You were supposed to come alone." He tutted, shaking his head in disappointment. One hand was clenched in a fist at his side. The other hung loose. "No matter."

I lifted the baseball bat and cracked my neck. Sin automatically moved so we were back-to-back, close enough to guard each other, not so close I would end up striking her with the bat. I positioned my weapon of choice and my sister kept her hands up, ready to use her magic.

The dozen Abyssians converged on us, effortlessly moving like wraiths. I swung the bat and went spinning as it passed completely through him. Stumbling, I quickly caught my balance, whipping around in time to see Sin throw a shot of pure death magic at another illusion.

We weren't bad fighters, but not knowing which Abyssian was an apparition and which of them wasn't proved to be a huge disadvantage. Logically I knew I could swing hard and keep my stance, but my brain couldn't comprehend the message that the bat might swing through the air and miss its target. Instead of keeping steady, my mind said, "prepare for impact" and when there was no impact, my body said, "maybe you should fall down instead."

My lack of coordination made my movements stiff and

clumsy. Eres pressed against the barriers, ready to shift and take over.

"Not yet," I warned.

"Let me—"

"Do what, Eres? If you can tell which one is which, share with the class, dammit! If I shift, Sin can't have your back. You're too big. You're a giant fucking unicorn-shaped target with blind spots that are worse than mine, and in case you haven't noticed, we are surrounded. It's not safe! When I find out which one is him, by all means, shift and take over because this sucks!"

Movement in my periphery caught my attention. Turning my head a fraction, I saw a small figure peering around the edge of a building. Shaggy brown hair, sweet brown eyes, with an oversized t-shirt swallowing his frame.

Jo. He'd followed us.

A new fear had unlocked inside me.

None of the Abyssians had noticed and I sent a silent thank you to the gods.

"Go get help!" I shouted, knowing he would hear me, but if they didn't know he was there, they would assume I was talking to my sister.

"What? There's no way I'm leaving you," Sin replied, and I stayed silent. Jo's little shadow disappeared, and I felt a moment of relief knowing he wasn't seen. Maybe we could hold them off long enough for our entire family to arrive.

The relief was short-lived when all of the Abyssian's lifted a clenched fist. Their fingers uncurled, revealing a small pile of sparkly dust. Their lips formed an "o" as they blew a puff of air.

"Hold your breath!" I shouted to my sister, reaching back blindly to feel for her.

We didn't know which way to turn. When they were

surrounding us, performing the same movement, it was disorienting, and I didn't know which of them was real.

Panic increased my heart rate. My increased heart rate pumped my blood harder, faster. My lungs screamed for more oxygen.

We ducked low to the ground, trying to avoid the glittery cloud. The dust spread rapidly, a fine powder shimmering in the morning light. We waved our hands like we could make it disperse, the way you would when it was smoky or to waft away a bad smell. Instead, it settled on our skin, burrowing, and absorbing through our pores.

My vision swam. The world shifted under me.

"Reagan," Eres croaked weakly. She sounded so far away. It took everything I had just to muster the strength to whisper her name in my mind. Give her a small piece of comfort as we drifted into darkness.

"Eres . . ."

"You fucked up . . ."

Stupid unicorn.

What an asshole.

Tartarus was created to house monsters. Soon it became a Hell, of sorts—a place to banish criminals, murderers, and the worst of those on Earth. No matter how many times I had reiterated it's not actually Hell, the truth was it was treated that way for a time.

When we arrived, it was bloodshed, terror, and chaos.

Pollux, Abyssian, and I were determined to change this realm. With Styx and Oberon at our side, we did. Too often they attributed that change to me, never taking credit for their part, but I knew they were integral to the creation of a better world.

Not all crimes are created equal, and not all crimes make someone a monster. Styx had certainly done her share of damage, and she was nothing of the sort. So were thousands of other people. They were allowed to live.

The rest were not so fortunate.

An entire island within Tartarus, devoid of life, was transformed into a rocky prison where the worst of the monsters were locked away. Their powers stripped, when possible. All cells warded with the strongest of magic—a massive gemstone mine, used to create the network of wards to guard the Titans.

They were kept there for almost five thousand years. No one had ever escaped.

Until today.

The wards were tripped, sending me and my men into a frantic search for who it could have been. We'd found nothing.

After I sealed the ward behind me, the ancient rock rumbled as it shifted into place, closing the prison for the Titan, Kronos. I'd rushed here first, believing Kronos had escaped, but he was still deep in his slumber—the only escape he'd ever have from this captivity.

Pollux rounded the corner, coming to a stop before me. His face was grim as he shook his head. "No other prison was disturbed."

"Who all has reported in?"

"Legion, the guards on this shift, and me. Legion called in half the army to be on standby. The rest of them are searching the outer isle in case we missed something."

"Where's Abyssian?" I asked, rubbing my hand over the stone, and feeling the hum of the ward beneath it.

"Reagan charged him with taking care of Clara while she's gone. He's not to leave her side, apparently." Pol crossed his arms, looking down at his feet in thought.

Legion appeared, directing two guards at his side as a group of soldiers followed him in formation.

"Anything?" I asked him as he approached.

"No one was found."

We were missing something. Some small detail. Some clue. That's what he didn't say, but we were all thinking it.

The guards around us looked between each other, eyes round and brows raised.

I shook my head, biting back a curse.

"Continue your watch," I told every man in the corridor. "If anyone is spotted, report to me. Do not engage."

My orders might seem strange, but no one here outside Pollux, myself, and Legion possessed enough power to actually set off a ward. If one of these prisoners had escaped, these men would be outmatched in every way. Legion was a great military leader, and he trained his men well, but it was no easy feat to imprison the monsters residing on this island. I'd rather not have an entire squadron dead on arrival, which is likely what would result if they tried to apprehend our mysterious escape artist.

I turned to Pol and extended my arm, then to Legion.

"I'm going to stay," the commander said. "I want to see if there's anything we overlooked."

A silent exchange reaffirmed his uneasiness. He wanted to find the missing detail. We'd been searching for the better part of a day and come up short.

He and I both knew if the Titans did escape, it would be disastrous. A war would break out—and it would be worse than before. Incomprehensible in size. This time they'd have been stewing for eons, and they'd be out for revenge. I knew all too well what the need for bloodshed and vengeance felt like. It was unlikely it would be quelled by finding a mate. I had been lucky. She centered me in ways I never knew possible. That desire for recompense had been replaced with the desire to simply be with her.

I inclined my chin in a firm nod, acknowledging the commander's request. "Pol?" He touched my arm and we dissipated into shadow, reappearing in the castle only a moment later.

Pol stepped away, rubbing at his temples. From a small credenza, I poured myself a glass of whiskey. Nothing as strong as my mate's moonshine. She certainly knew how to brew, but I had a taste for something more refined. White liquor could never match the dark chocolate and peaty undertones I preferred. I sipped my drink, deep in thought.

"I don't understand, Caius. There aren't many beings on Tartarus that can set off the wardstones. Not without escaping," Pol said. I looked over to see him standing with his back to me, facing the fireplace instead. One hand was in a fist and the other holding his wrist where they locked behind his back. To someone unfamiliar with Pol's magic, it would appear as if the fire were playing tricks and the feather tattoos on his arms were dancing. In reality, they were shifting. It was just another sign of his agitation.

"And even fewer that can escape without getting caught," I added, taking another sip as I sat in the wingback chair.

"And fewer still that can disguise themselves," Pol continued. "If it's not someone trying to get out, it's someone trying to get in. Someone powerful wanted to free them. Someone wanted to start a war here. What are we missing?"

"It's not only the who. It's the why," I said, thinking through it out loud. "Why try to free them when you know you can't? What is the purpose when all they're capable of is setting off the wardstones?"

A prickling of awareness traveled up my spine. The hairs on the back of my neck rose as I felt a sliver of *something,* but I couldn't discern what.

"Do you feel that?" I asked.

"Feel what?" He questioned, turning back to glance at me. "What are you talking about?"

"I . . ." My fingers wrapped around the end of the armrest, nails biting into the wood. "It's almost like, anticipation, maybe? Anxiety?"

Pol squinted at me. "What the fuck are you going on about?"

"It's right there," I said between clenched teeth. "Like it's in the air somehow, seeping in." I paused as an uncomfortable sensation ran through me, bordering on pain. A sweat broke out over my forehead. " Seeping in below the surface. Like it's in the—"

Pol and I looked at each other as we came to the same conclusion.

"Bond," we said at once.

I jumped to my feet, the glass slipping from my fingers, shattering against the stone floor. My feet were already carrying me away from my rooms. Pollux kept his running pace beside me, his steps equally hurried as we crossed the palace quickly.

"Something's wrong," I breathed, looking around the atrium outside the throne room. It was empty, sans portal guards, who looked at me quizzically. "She's not here."

"Has Reagan returned?" My tone was aggressive, and the room rumbled with its volume.

"N-no, Your Majesty," one of the guards stuttered in response.

Pol turned to me. "I thought you said you wouldn't be able to feel the bond when she crossed over."

"We feel it in the sense that we know it exists, but it's stretched so thin, it feels out of reach."

Which made the fact I was feeling it on this level all the more terrifying. I was sleep deprived and running on fumes, but my body was wired awake like someone had hooked me up to an energy source and forced its power into me.

"Nothing about this godsdamned day makes any sense," he ground out. "We've spent all day checking wards, and the minute you come back here, this happens."

"What'd you just say?" I asked slowly, lowering my tone.

"I said we've spent all day . . ." He trailed off, his eyes widening as he understood the weight of his words.

All day.

I'd been working on wards all day. Far from the portal. Expending my energy and resources to keep Tartarus safe. A sense of foreboding pressing against me, but it was nothing more than misplaced worry . . . misplaced focus . . .

I snapped. Power lashed out of me, plunging the room into utter darkness before I pulled back. Pol let out a hiss. When the moonlight returned and torches relit, I saw one of the yellow flowers clamped around his ankle, its teeth burrowed deep. He bent at the waist and ripped it from the soil, pulling it out at the root. The flower released him with a wail that we both ignored.

"It was all a distraction," he grunted.

"All of it," I bit out.

I'd encouraged Reagan to go visit her family. When I'd offered her bodyguards, she insisted it was a short walk. Not only was it her home, but it was filled with dozens of Santiagos, all of whom had been protecting each other their entire lives. The Crossroads was safe for her, and I had a hard time disagreeing with that.

I should have.

It wasn't a coincidence that the moment I let her out of my sight was when the wards tripped. It wasn't a coincidence that I could feel the bond, could feel it all day when I really thought about it, except I hadn't been able to separate the energy from my own until now.

None of it was a mistake.

It was planned.

We hadn't tested whether our bond would control the death magic of Tartarus leaking into her world. We'd planned on waiting until she'd told her family about us. Wait until my crossing wasn't seen as a threat.

Now there was no question of waiting. Her desire to protect Earth was null and void. My mate's wellbeing came before anything else.

"Stay here," I commanded. Before Pol could resist, I stepped through the portal.

Its power buzzed, coating my skin as I crossed. A slight chill in the morning air greeted me, and immediately the scent of the air was amiss. A hint of decay lingered. Death was nearby. Fear coiled in my gut.

I should have felt the bond. It should have been stronger, but it wasn't. It still felt like it was just out of reach. Scanning my surroundings, I realized the portal was unguarded, but the park wasn't empty.

Half a dozen yards from me, Reagan's sister lay in the grass. Her clothes were rumpled, and grass stained her knees. A soft moan escaped her, and I ran to her side.

"Where is she? Where is Reagan?"

Sin blinked a few times, then squinted up at me while groaning.

"What . . ." Her voice was scratchy, parched. Wracking coughs woke her up more. She cursed in Spanish before springing to her feet, unsteady at best. I braced her with a hand on her shoulder to keep her from falling.

"Where is she?" I repeated. I didn't want to ask again.

"He took her." Her pupils were dilated, and the words were thick, like her tongue was in the way. She'd been drugged, but with what, I didn't know.

"He?" I growled. "Who is he?"

Even I didn't recognize the terrifying tenor in my voice. If Sin was afraid, she didn't show it. My world was fracturing without my mate, but nothing could have prepared me for her answer.

Drip.

Drip.

Drip.

The sound was already grating my nerves and I hadn't been awake for five seconds. Who left the faucet on?

My neck ached, my arms hurt, and my shoulders were cramped. I tried to move, but my body didn't cooperate. It was almost like I was tied up.

My eyes flew open.

I hung like a slaughtered animal, dangling from the ceiling by a hook and rope bound at my wrists. A couple of tugs told me those bindings weren't going anywhere.

Everything came back to me in a hazy whoosh. The dream. The fight with a dozen Abyssians. The cloud of powder that had enveloped us before I passed out. I stopped struggling to take stock of my surroundings, trying to clear my blurry vision so I could search for anything that could help me.

The dingy hotel room was not a comforting sight. Unknown substances coated the walls. My bare feet dragged against the scratchy and *sticky* floor. That was just disgusting. Abyssian was sprawled on the couch, both his arms behind his head and his eyes closed.

"W-where's Sin?" I croaked, my voice scratchy and dry. I felt like I had licked sand.

"Your sister? I imagine she's still in the park where I left her."

"She's alive," I breathed softly, really only speaking to myself. It was a relief. My situation was bad, but at least she wasn't hurt.

"She wasn't a threat," he answered casually, though I hadn't formed it as a question. He opened his eyes, turning to me as he spoke. "There was no need to kill her. I'm not wasteful."

"You killed the guards." I had no proof, but it wasn't hard to figure out. At first I thought they were on his side. Now, I sincerely doubted it.

"Ah, see, they were a threat. They would tattle, and I couldn't have that."

I hummed, clicking my tongue against the roof of my mouth while I smacked my lips, trying to move some sort of moisture around. "Where am I?"

"I would have thought that was obvious." He took a lazy look around. "One of the old hotels downtown."

That was just grand.

Functioning hotels didn't exist in The Crossroads. We didn't have embassies for the Houses. We were a No Man's Land. If we had visitors, it was a short trade and they went on their way, or it was someone to see their family, and they stayed with them. Any other outsider was up to no good, so they weren't welcome. The unease settled further. I could scream all I wanted, but these hotels were all condemned before they became abandoned in the aftermath of the shifter portal opening in Portland. No one even tried living in them. There were a mere afterthought.

Drip.

Drip.

Drip.

I angled my head down, following the sound to just beneath me where a bowl sat gathering my blood. He'd cut my arms and legs in whirling patterns that caused thin streams of blood to run down my body.

Reaching mentally for Eres, I found a terrible silence. In all the years she'd bound herself from me, I still felt her presence in the background. A sliver of her existence had always been there. Now there was nothing, like our connection was completely severed.

Drip.

Drip.

Drip.

I could barely process what it meant to lose her when Abyssian said, "Relax, it's not midnight yet. I need the new moon for the spell to take. Earth's new moon. What timing, huh? I was still working out how to best hide you from Caius if you came early, but you put it off until now and it's perfection, really. I have you to thank for that."

One word in all his rambling was what I focused on.

"Spell?" My lips formed the word, but no sound came out. Abyssian was watching, though, and he liked to hear himself talk.

"C'mon, Reagan. I know you're drugged but try to keep up. I'm going to take his soul out of you"—he gestured in my direction—"and put it in me." He pointed to his chest. "Which is where it should have gone five thousand years ago."

He was deranged. Forceful shudders racked my body.

"Have fun with that." My voice was still weak, but at least I was able to speak more clearly than before. "Only a witch—" Abyssian smirked, and I stopped myself short.

He waved a book around teasingly, and bile rose in my throat when I realized it was my mom's journal. "See, that's what I thought too. But your mom figured a few things out. Smart woman, she was. Awful shame."

My eyes welled with tears. He said he wasn't wasteful, but my cousin had that book. What had he done to get it? I swallowed a thick lump forming, not wanting to ask. I couldn't bear the answer.

"Turns out, anyone can do it . . ." He stood up, walking toward me and spinning me slightly to see the other side of the room. Clara sat on the edge of a decaying mattress, gagged, but unbound. "Though it's much easier when you have a witch's extra set of hands."

Adrenaline shot through me, and with it, a tiny crack appeared in the blockage to Eres. I felt her again, and I felt a hint of her rage.

"Clara would never help you," I said. It sounded more like a question than I would have preferred. My cousin shot a look of exasperation at me, that said "really?"

"She won't have a choice. Did you think I would let her make that decision? Hardly. I have control over her, the same way I did Jana. The only difference is that Clara hasn't failed me."

I sighed. Jana. The weird reason for attacking me. She didn't kill herself when questioned. It was all Abyssian "You poisoned Jana."

"Not the way you think, but yes. I didn't kill her. She'd still be alive if she'd decided to shut her mouth. Tricky how some spells work. Try to tell the truth, and you'd dug your own grave." His eyes lit up. "Hey, you're both gravediggers, right? Is that a pun?"

I scrunched my nose, looking at Clara while she rolled her eyes. If we ever got out of this alive, I was going to veto every man she ever found worthy of dating.

"No one was trying to poison me," I surmised. "You hit your target the first time, and there was no way she could tell me a damned thing."

Drip.

Drip.

Drip.

"Catching on, I see." He checked the bowl collecting my blood. "Turns out Jana not killing you worked out in my favor. Having Caius's soul returned and starting over from square one was going to be tedious. Instead, dear Clara brought the book to me thinking I could help with some of the ancient runes. Don't be mad at her. She had no way of knowing she handed me the key to everything I'd worked toward for five thousand years. It was almost like destiny. Or fate." He shrugged. "Either way, Clara will help because I'll make her. You'll die from the separation, same as every other guardian that came before you. It's not personal, if that's any consolation."

I tried to work my wrist again and maybe see if I could slip it from the rope that bound them over my head, but it was no good.

"Agree to disagree. It feels pretty personal right now." Things were still a little fuzzy from the magic he'd used on me, but more of Eres was peeking through. The downside was I could feel my blood pressure dropping from all the blood loss. By the time I got access to her, it might be too late. "So that's your big bad plan in a nutshell. Kidnap me and bring me to a dirty hotel where you can do the ceremony and become the guardian," I frowned, shaking my head. "Why would you even want to be one? It's not that great."

"You don't know?" he asked, then scratched idly at his jaw. "Mortals aren't meant to hold a primordial soul. It slowly kills them. A primordial can't hold another primordial's soul. It corrupts them. But me? I can do it."

"Why? Why do you want it?"

"I thought it would be obvious. Caius is my half-brother. He was born a primordial, but thanks to my bastard father, I'm simply a lesser fae god. With his soul, I'll be elevated to a primordial—as I should have been before."

My eyebrows rose. "Power? You're doing this for *power*?" He heard the disbelief in my voice, and it confused him.

"Why else would I?"

"Villains are so unoriginal," I muttered, shaking my head as best I could. There was no point explaining to him how fucking basic he was. Or stupid. He was born a *god,* and he was immortal, but it wasn't enough? Boo—fricken—hoo. "Why now? Why didn't you just kill me yourself?"

"After Jana failed to kill you, Caius wouldn't let you out of his sight until now." Abyssian sighed. "I figured I'd have to wait until your six months was up, but once it was clear you were falling for him, I knew there was nothing I could do to stop it. So I sped up my timeline. A few well-timed thought insertions—a good mate would encourage her to go visit her family—and poof! Here you are. With the portal between you, he can't feel the bond or what I'm doing, but he will feel it breaking. It's actually perfect this way. Here you are. Alone and defenseless. Almost like the universe planned for it."

Alone? Maybe. If what he'd said about Clara was true, she wouldn't be able to help. Defenseless? Not so much.

Even with all the blood he'd drained and the magical drug in my system, I still felt Eres. I just needed a way to free myself from my bindings and then I'd shift and let Eres handle him.

"Solid plan, human. How are we going to do it?" she said to me.

"Oh my god, I can't believe how happy I am to hear your voice. I don't care how you do it. Suffocate him. Stab him with your horn. Anything. You have full control. Just shift and fucking kill him the minute we can break through this drug."

"Yes. I'm liking this plan more."

"You underestimate me," I bluffed. "I have Caius's soul. I'm stronger than you."

"Oh, you most certainly are," Abyssian said with a laugh. "But you don't know the first thing about how to use that power. All of that strength is just wasted on you. Much like your dark unicorn. It's a shame I can't take her too."

"He can fucking try," Eres growled.

"You deserved to get thrown in Tartarus with all the other fucking monsters," I said with disgust.

"They betrayed me. Just goes to show you that you really can't ever trust someone." Abyssian said with a sigh, and I could not figure out if he was being serious. "Caius and the other primordials made a bargain. Caius, sap as always, took Abraxia as a lover. A witch. *A no one.* He meant to make her his bride. That didn't sit well with Pious at all. Most of them thought it gave the mortals delusions of grandeur. That mortals would use them for an elevation of status. My brother, being the arrogant prick he is, thought otherwise. Caius was so sure Abraxia would never betray him, they struck a deal where they set out to prove if she could be trusted. He agreed, and the idiot was willing to tell her his secret. His weak spot. You see, when primordials take a body, they also have to take on a singular liability. Like Achilles and his blasted heel."

I thought back to the first dream-memory when she cut his braid and a sadness consumed me. The level of betrayal was so multifaceted, it was remarkable.

"He'd picked the weakest part of the body to be his, and he told Abraxia that if she cut his hair, she'd sever his soul. Some of the primordials and I had made a deal as well. They weren't willing to lose. Pious, especially. If I corrupted Abraxia and persuaded her to betray him, I'd receive the half she stole and be elevated to their status."

It all came together to form a sickening picture. How did someone throw away their family that way? Did he feel *nothing*? I couldn't grasp it because I'd do anything for mine, even die.

Drip.

Drip.

Drip.

"Except they threw you in Tartarus alongside him." I pressed my eyes together, trying to focus my vision. "I can't believe they abandoned you," I said, but I was certain he missed the sarcasm. He was too busy listening to himself. And he cursed *Caius* for arrogance.

"I know, right? Fucking pricks." He came up to me and cupped my cheek, running his thumb over my chapped lips. "You know, it really is a shame you'll die from this. I liked you; you know? You're not Caius's type, but you're mine. Maybe if things had been different, it could have been you and me . . . I so wanted a taste of you."

"Oh gods," I said, my stomach roiling with nausea. I was so thankful I managed to get out of the dream before he fucked Abraxia in the woods.

"I'm a god of many talents," he said, his voice low. He

leaned in, holding my face tight as he kissed me. With his thumb pressed into my jaw, I couldn't bite. With my arms strung above me, pressing to the sides of my head, I couldn't even pull away. I was stuck as he licked the inside of mouth with his serpent tongue.

Please throw up. Please throw up. My stomach heaved once, but nothing came. He released the kiss, but still held my jaw with one hand.

My eyes watered with the overwhelming emotions swirling inside me.

"Don't cry," he whispered, using his fingertips to wipe my tears away. "Your death will be quick."

"Promise?" I asked, reaching for Eres. I felt her presence coursing through me. The drug was becoming less in my system, but it was getting harder to focus as I continued to lose blood. All she needed to do was take over, kill him, and we could get the hell out of this dump.

"I promise."

Just past him, Clara sat wide-eyed watching the exchange. When our eyes locked, hers narrowed in question.

"Eres, I really need you to shift right about now!"

"I can't shift yet!"

His hand dropped away from my face. Thinking quickly, I asked, "What will happen to Clara after . . . you know?"

Abyssian paused. "That depends on her." He glanced over his shoulder at her. "I'm certainly not above killing her, but what purpose would it serve? So much talent would go to waste."

Glancing out the window, I couldn't guess the hour. There was no clock on the walls of the old hotel. All I knew was we didn't have time. The longer I waited, the weaker I would become.

I struck.

Swinging my legs forward and up, my core muscles clenched tight as I rocked. I caught him around the neck and brought my thighs together, squeezing, trying to crush his windpipe. I wasn't sure if he healed like Caius, but I couldn't just sit back and wait for him to kill me.

"Anytime would be great."

"I can't! Give me control!"

"You have it, just do it, I am literally handing you the keys, so fucking shift already!"

Using every ounce of strength I possessed, I brought my legs together even tighter. Abyssian choked, but he still managed to call me a bitch.

"Oh don't be surprised," I ground out. He thrashed, trying, and failing to escape my grip.

"I'll—kill—you—"

My body was trembling. My abs wanted to give out and were straining from how hard I was working them, but I wouldn't stop. I wouldn't let up until he was dead.

Abyssian jerked, losing consciousness. Only when the burden of holding his massive body was too much to handle did I finally give out, releasing him.

He dropped to the floor like a lead weight.

"Clara," I panted. "You need to get the knife. Cut me down."

My cousin stayed still. Water formed in her eyes. A sinking sense of dread coiled in my gut. She couldn't move.

"Clara?" I coughed.

She shook her head, trying to tell me something. It was hard to make out with the gag, but it almost sounded like, *"He's not dead."*

Abyssian gasped.

Fuck me.

It was the only thought I had time to process as he got to his feet. Bloodshot, angry eyes glared at me. He wrapped a hand around my throat and squeezed.

"Trouble shifting?" he croaked. He pressed against my windpipe, a cruel smile on his face. "I need you alive to do the spell, Reagan, but the book said nothing about needing you to be awake."

He gripped me tighter and tighter until spots appeared in my vision and the only thing I could hear was the sound of my blood.

Drip.

Drip.

Drip.

Voices drifted in and out.

"... cut her hair..."

"... give me the athame..."

Some unintelligible mish mash of gibberish words I couldn't understand.

"*He said 'soul becomes mine'...*" Eres translated for me, but even she sounded far away.

That same phrase repeated over and over again. A knife grazed my back. Then fire erupted in my blood.

Pain became me. Or rather, I became pain.

Somewhere along the way I lost my sense of self in the suffering. Darkness shrouded my gaze. I fought to clear it, but that did little good.

In the midst of the torture, I recognized what was happening. I'd felt it before.

My soul was separating, being ripped apart at the seams, the stitches popping slowly one by one. Except it wasn't my soul he was taking. It was my mates. The piece of him that I had guarded since birth. It was never mine to have anyway. It was definitely not his asshole brothers.

That fire turned to anger as I thought about all Abyssian had done. What he put Caius through. What he was putting me through. All for his own selfish gain.

Power.

Not even power, when it really came down to it.

Status.

He wanted power and status.

It was just so shallow. So basic. So fucking . . . infuriating.

I grabbed hold of my rage, and I used it to ground me. Pain was an assault on my physical self, so it took something strong to combat it.

Rage would do.

I settled into it, wrapping it around me like a cloak to keep me warm in the winter—and then I fought.

"Where do you want to be?" Eres asked, *her voice sounding closer than it had before.*

I didn't answer. Right now I just wanted to fight.

"Teleport, Reagan. Take the rage, let it fuel you. End him."

"With what magic?"

"Mine."

We both knew what it meant.

I clawed my way out of the darkness. My hands fisted, nails digging into my palms, likely leaving little crescent shapes. That was good. My rage almost slipped but I held it tight, damn near strangling it.

Sweat beaded on the back of my neck, dripping down, and mixing with my blood. The sting was lost in the fire that seemed to consume me, but it was there. I focused on it —the shaking of my arms—the cramping of my abdomen —the dryness of my mouth.

And I felt it all.

My eyes flew open.

Abyssian knelt before me, Clara behind him, forcibly painting his back in my blood. She looked up, sorrow and terror in her eyes. She faltered, her trembling fingers making an errant brush stroke.

Abyssian's head snapped up. Shock colored his features.

"Impossible," he whispered. I shouldn't have heard it, but I did. That anger, that rage that I held so tight? I became it. It empowered me. I felt strong. Unbeatable. Unchained.

"You may succeed in killing me," I said. My voice didn't sound like me. It was deeper. Darker. *Eres*. "But you will not control my mate's soul. I will not allow it."

He blinked twice. A shadow of fear crossing his features. Then he took stock of my arms, still tied and hanging from the ceiling.

My position didn't lend credence to my threat.

"You can't stop me," he said. It's almost done.

I still had one thing. One thing I could do.

I felt Eres step up and look out through my eyes, but we spoke together. "We can't stop our death, but we can take you with us."

Everything in me seemed to boil and build. It was as if my skin heated to a thousand degrees. I arched my back. In the blink of an eye, I disappeared, teleporting as I reappeared next to him. He had no time to react. I pressed my hand to his chest as Eres opened a gateway between us. Her power lashed out, blinding in its darkness.

Pure black, obsidian magic arced from me into him.

I cried out, and Abyssian joined me.

It was a beautiful and terrible thing.

"Eres . . ."

"I'm with you, Reagan . . ."

Our screams reached a crescendo, and I could have sworn I heard Caius's roar of fury beside us. His face in my thoughts. The way he smiled at me and caressed my cheek with his thumb. The scent of him. His love. It gave me strength to push through, to do what needed to be done.

In the end, there was only Caius.

In the end, there was only silence.

CHAPTER 40
CAIUS

I felt her soul leave her body right as I crossed the threshold of the hotel room. My shadows had unlocked the warded door and then blasted it open. I rushed forward, getting there only in time to catch her body as it fell straight into my waiting arms.

Eyes open and unblinking, she stared at nothing at all. Her chest didn't rise or fall. Her pulse didn't hammer at my touch.

She was just . . . empty.

A shell.

I dropped to my knees, head hanging forward. "Reagan, come back. Come back to me." I begged her to stay, to live, even though she was already gone.

"I need you, my love."

Her pulse didn't restart.

"I only just found you . . ."

Her chest didn't rise.

"Please . . ."

Her eyes remained unseeing.

And something in me cracked wide open. Shadows

swarmed the room and beyond. It was pure darkness. It was what I would become without my mate.

Despair would pull me under, and I would let it.

Clara was wrapped around Jo, the young boy who found me outside the portal and led me here.

I didn't know what had transpired in this shithole. I didn't know much of anything. All I knew was Reagan was gone, and Abyssian had taken her from me.

A soft hand touched my shoulder, I tensed.

"Caius, I'm here." Jo addressed me directly in the voice of a nine-year-old but with the wisdom of someone far older.

"She's gone," I whispered. "I've only just found her, and she's gone."

"Caius," the boy said gently. "Look."

Fingers touched my chin, lifting my head. He pointed, and I followed.

Bloody ropes hung from a hook in the ceiling. Glancing down, I saw her wrists were rubbed raw and stained red. But that's not what Jo was pointing at.

There, right in front of me, was a floating orb of brilliant white light. It was the only light in the darkness. The only source of purity. Or joy.

It was my soul.

But I didn't want it.

Because *it* was the reason for her demise. My soul had been attached to hers, by no choice of her own, and the loss of it is what had killed her.

"I don't care," I said.

"What was taken can be returned," the boy continued in a patient voice. "Her soul is lingering because of your bond, but it won't stay forever. There's not much time."

I stilled.

"You can put it back?"

Jo nodded. His expressive brown eyes were full of understanding and empathy. "I can."

"Jo," Clara said, her brows furrowing, a deep crease forming. She hugged herself, rubbing her arms. "I want her back too, but this kind of magic isn't . . . it's not possible."

"Do it," I said, ignoring Clara's protests. I didn't hesitate at the thought of saving Reagan.

If the choice was between having my soul or having my mate, there was no question. I would *always* choose her.

Jo knelt on the opposite side of her body and laid one hand on her chest. His smile was sad and sweet. "She fought so hard for you. She stripped Abyssian of his soul as she died. His body is as much a husk as hers—except he still lives."

"How do you know that?" Clara asked him.

"I can see it," he answered simply, nodding toward Abyssian's prone body. "It's whole. Not split like yours, Caius. It's hovering, but the veil hasn't opened for him since he's not truly dead."

Clara cursed in Spanish, her eyes narrowing.

He shook his head. "I'll bring her back for you, Caius."

"Wait," Clara said, kneeling and putting a hand on Jo's back. Confusion and fear filled her features.

He smiled at her. "It's okay," he whispered. "I know what I'm doing."

With one hand still on her chest, he extended his other toward my soul, coaxing it to him. It floated effortlessly, then the orb slowly touched his fingertips, the glowing light pouring into him. It moved through Jo's body, down one arm, and into his chest. He tilted his head back, his eyes shining a brilliant white. Blinding light emitted from his mouth as he gasped harshly, fissures developing on his skin, light seeping through the cracks. Clara shouted his name, putting her hands on him, trying to absorb magic and help him, but nothing happened. Tears streamed down her face, matching my own—but for very different reasons.

Jo's fingertips began to shimmer, pushing the light into Reagan. Time moved slowly, but I didn't dare take my eyes off her.

I'd seen loss a thousand times over, but now it was my own. In the end, loved ones called out to the gods. It didn't matter which god they believed in. They asked for mercy. Prayed for forgiveness, as if somehow this was their punishment. They promised anything, if only the dying would be saved. They would beg and bargain and plead. They apologized for their transgressions, offering their life instead.

With Reagan's death, I was no different.

I just never imagined a god would answer.

CHAPTER 41

REAGAN

D eath wasn't that terrible. The pain leading to it was, but my rage had shrouded me in a protective blanket, shielding me from the worst of it.

Caius was safe. I felt Abyssian's soul rip from his being moments before I felt nothing at all.

Still, here, wherever I was, alone and hollow, I still felt love.

Caius.

My mate.

In the darkness, I waited, but for what, I didn't know.

A small, angelic figure in the distant void called my name.

Whoever it was seemed to be cocooned in a glowing white light, extending their arm, beckoning me forward.

"Reagan."

Surprise. Fear. Confusion. They consumed me.

"Jo?" I asked, running toward him. "Jo?" I screamed his name, crossing the emptiness of space until I crashed into him, scooping him in my arms.

"Hello, Reagan," he said softly, curling into me.

Tears streamed down my face, or at least I imagined they did.

"What are you doing here?" I asked.

"You'll be back with him soon," he answered.

"What do you mean?" I sat him down, kneeling before him while he stood, looking at me with his warm, brown eyes. A strange jolt rippled through me, but I couldn't understand what was happening. I had no body, yet I knew without a doubt, what I felt was real.

I would cross the veil soon.

"We don't have much time. His soul will save you."

I shook my head. "It can't. Clara and Caius can't put it back in me. I'm dead, Jo."

"No, they can't," he whispered. "But I can."

It took a moment to process it. The How. But it all made sense. "Your magic. Everything we never understood about you. Your powers. This was it, wasn't it?" He nodded, and I smiled, pulling him into a hug. "We're going back?"

"You'll be with him again," he said weakly. I pulled away, holding his shoulders, looking him in the eyes.

"What are you not saying?"

"I won't be with you anymore, Reagan."

"No . . ." I choked on a sob. "No, you have to be there, Jo. You have to."

He smiled softly, cupping my cheek with his tiny hand. "This is what I'm meant to do."

Another jolt rippled through me, and then I understood it for what it was. Fissures appeared on his skin, light peeking through the cracks. Looking down, I saw my chest beginning to glow.

"You're going to die!"

"Yes."

"No," I screamed, trying to brush it away. "Don't do this. Stop it!"

"Reagan." He gasped. The voice he used to say my name was foreign. Changing it back, he spoke like the Jo I knew. "This is what I am meant to do. It's my purpose."

I shook my head fervidly, hiccupping as I cried. "I don't know what that means."

My arms began to glow, and the light was leaving my precious cousin.

"I chose this existence. For five thousand years I have accepted life in a mortal body, waiting. Waiting for you." He closed his eyes, taking a deep breath before opening them again. "It was my atonement."

"For what, Jo? I don't understand." My words were rushed and barely understandable through my sniffles.

"For banishing Caius. The weight of my actions was too much to bear. I owed him more than what I gave my friend on that day. He was my brother, and I failed him."

"Who are you?" I whispered.

"I am Ru'than. A primordial reborn, again and again, waiting for the day I could right my wrong."

I could barely process his words before he collapsed, the light around him dimming, but I knew one thing, I couldn't lose him. Not my Jo. He would always be my Jo.

"Don't leave me, mijo. You can't do this," I choked out. "Please, Jo."

His beautiful brown eyes, always so gentle and kind, gazed at me with deep, profound love.

I held his hand to my face, begging him. "I can't live in this world without you, mijo." I choked on a sob, hyperventilating between my cries. "None of us can."

"I can't die, Reagan. Not truly." A weak smile formed as

the last of the light faded from him, his eyes closing for a final time. "We'll meet again one day. I promise."

The darkness consumed him, and the blinding light exploded around me.

I screamed into the void, the desperate cry transferring into the world, before I took in a heaving gasp, and my back arched off the ground.

"Reagan!" Caius shouted, pulling me up and enclosing me in his arms.

"Caius," I breathed, wrapping my arms around him, never wanting to let go. When I looked over his shoulder, the crushing pain of loss instantly hit me.

Clara sat rocking Jo's lifeless body, cradling him in her embrace while she whispered in his ear.

Caius released me, and I crawled over to them, the tears of my time in the void appearing for real.

"He saved you," she whispered with a shaky voice. "Jo saved you . . ."

"Ru'than," I said softly, looking at Caius. His mouth fell open in shock. "He was Ru'than."

"How?"

"He chose an existence in a mortal body, waiting to atone for his actions. For your banishment."

Eres left the edge of my mind, for once, giving me privacy while I told them everything, not skipping a single detail. The dream of Abyssian. Everything he told me, and all that Jo had shared. Caius had scooted next to me, his hand on my back while we huddled around my cousin.

"What did he mean when he said he can't die?" I asked Caius, stroking Jo's hair.

"He gave up his primordial powers. He'll live as a god," he whispered. "Forever."

"How will I see him again?"

With sad eyes, he shook his head. "I don't know."

I nodded, knowing that was the only answer I would ever get. Leaning over him, I kissed his forehead, saying my goodbye. Softly, I sang to him, Arrorró mi niño, the lullaby Tía Celeste sang to him every night.

> Arrorró mi niño, /Hush-a-bye, my child,
> arrorró mi sol, /Hush-a-bye, my sun,
> arrorró pedazo, /Hush-a-bye, oh piece
> de mi corazón./ Of my heart

> Este niño lindo / This pretty child
> se quiere dormir / Wants to sleep
> háganle la cuna / Make him a cradle
> de rosa y jazmín / of rose and jasmine.

> Este lindo niño / This lovely boy
> se quiere dormir... / wants to sleep
> cierra los ojitos / He closes his eyes
> y los vuelve a abrir. / and opens them again.

Clara's breath stuttered through her coughs and tears, and I sniffled as my voice gave out at the end. "You'll always be my Jo, Ru'than. *Always.*"

As though he'd waited for me to say goodbye, his body shimmered, breaking apart into gold particles that drifted on an errant wind that had no business being in a room. They swirled almost playfully around me first, then Clara, then Caius—lingering there while he closed his eyes whispering his thank you—then it disappeared.

Heaving sobs wracked Clara's body, and she hugged herself, shaking her head. I held her, while Caius held me.

Time passed, though I didn't know how long, and eventually a numbness settled in.

"I thought you knew what he was," I said, facing Caius, wiping tears from my face.

He pulled me close, resting his chin on my head. "His eyes were familiar. I thought he was a descendant of Ru'than's. Primordials can sire children or birth them. The day I met him was the day I walked through the door and saw you. He knew what I was, and he obviously cared for you. In my mind, whoever he descended from didn't matter. I had no idea . . ."

"He was always so special. So calm and filled with wisdom that none of us could ever understand," Clara said, then blowing her nose on her shirt and not caring at all. "Now we know why."

"I wonder if he knew about Abyssian's betrayal," I said, glancing at the bastard's body.

"If he did, he wasn't able to say it, for whatever reason. The laws of the universe that governed his transition from primordial to god is unknown. It varies. He obviously retained the knowledge throughout countless reincarnations. Maybe he wasn't able to speak on it, or maybe he didn't know, and his regret formed in not standing on my side that day," Caius answered, and he looked off in the room, focusing on something that wasn't there. A memory, perhaps. One day I would ask him.

I kicked my leg out, my foot making contact with Abyssian's arm with a hard whack. "What do we do with him? Burn him? Bury him? Dump him in shallow grave? I happen to know a few."

"He's not technically dead yet," Caius said, his voice low.

"*What?*"

"He hasn't crossed the veil. His soul is lingering."

Clara scoffed. "Not for long."

Electricity sparked in the room, and I snapped my attention to her. Hatred flashed in her eyes, the loss of her little brother filling her with what I assumed to be rage. Rage and I were well acquainted today.

Just as mine had been, her rage was directed at him.

I had never seen this side of her before.

Magic swirled around her hands—spirit magic.

Throwing her arm out, she pulled at Abyssian's soul, urging it to come to her. An orb of gray and swampy green shadows pulsed with palpable fear. It tugged back, trying to escape her clutches, but she weaved her spells, muttering under her breath.

A muffled cry, barely audible, and completely inexplicable, sounded as the last of the misty colors entered the orb.

With a grin of venomous satisfaction, she held it over her palm.

"What are you going to do with that?" I asked, having a pretty good idea already of what her answer might be.

"Oh, I have plans for him."

"Good. I hope he suffers." I nodded, curling into Caius's side. He engulfed me in his arms once more, whispering against my hair.

"I thought I lost you."

"I thought I was gone too. That I wouldn't see you again or say goodbye, but I wasn't going to let him have your soul," I said, lowering my eyes. "I'm so sorry you still aren't whole."

"I'm whole because of you, Reagan. Soul or no soul, you already had my heart." He kissed me gently, holding my face and cradling me like he never wanted to let go.

"Let's go home," I said with a heavy sigh.

"Which one?" Clara asked, standing up, poking at her orb with a malicious grin.

"Tía's first. We have to tell your mom about Jo." Clara's eyes filled with grief, and she nodded.

It would be hard walking home without him, but I had a feeling that despite the loss, there would be a measure of comfort knowing more about him. I had the answers to questions we'd all asked, and finally, they would know too.

Turning to Caius, I gave him a sad smile. "C'mon, mate. We have a wake and a funeral to attend. No better time than now to get to know my family. This is as real as it gets."

"Is that acceptable for me to be a part of it?" he asked, a crease between his brows.

"It is. We do it a little backwards in my family. Funeral first. We're going to cry a lot and tell stories that will make us cry more. Then we are going to have the wake. We're going to be loud, eat too much food, tell stories about Jo—you can share yours too—and we get drunk. That's the Santiago way. And if you're mated to me, my love—god, primordial, or king—you're a Santiago." I held his hand in mine, lacing my fingers and holding him tight. "I hope you don't mind."

He smiled softly. "I will always choose you, my love, and that includes your family."

Raindrops pattered on the window while I paced the room in front of the fireplace. A knock at the door set my heart jumping into my throat.

"Reagan can I come in?" Clara's soft voice filtered in from the other side.

"Come in."

When she entered, the warm smile on her face fell and she came to an abrupt halt as she stared at me.

"What are you doing? It's almost time." She took in the white outfit I was supposed to be wearing—but it was sprawled on the bed. It was the same one I'd worn during our faux primal hunt. "You're not even dressed yet!"

"I'm freaking out here, Clara." I stepped toward her, fidgeting with my hands.

She blew out a breath and put her hands on hips to think. "Okay, well he's your mate, and you love him, so I know you're not having second thoughts. You have the full support of the family. Everyone is safe. What's going on?"

"I don't know how to be queen."

"This again?" she asked, relief spreading across her features.

"I don't know the first thing about leading people. I barely know how to be Reagan. The grave robber. The guardian. You said so yourself, I've never had a chance to just live my life without fear. Everything that I've ever known was basically a lie, and I still don't even know how to harness all my power. So not only do I have to figure out who I am, now I also have to figure out how to be queen," I said, blurting it out in a long, quick huff of words. I ran my hands over my face and through my hair. "I'm going to have a panic attack."

Clara rushed forward, pulling me into a hug and brushing my back with gentle strokes while shushing me in soothing tones. "Who do you want to be?" she asked.

"What?" I asked, completely taken off guard.

She sat down on my bed and took my hands, pulling me to sit on the edge of with her. "You're still Reagan. Reagan who loves to paint. Who knows how to swing a shovel better than anybody I've ever met. Reagan who taught Jo how to read. Reagan who uses her cousins as guinea pigs when she writes new recipes. Reagan who was willing to die to save everyone she loved. Reagan, a woman approaching thirty, who would rather sneak out the window than argue with her favorite cousin—that's me now. I've declared it." I huffed a small laugh, and she continued. "You are still *you*. The only difference is now you'll be able to know new parts of yourself. Parts that aren't limited by fear and some clock ticking toward your death or world destruction. That love you have for your family? That willingness to protect everyone at all costs? You were made a guardian by fate, but you guard and protect the ones you love by choice. That's imbedded in your soul. That wasn't a spell, or a cursed bloodline. You can't make someone care. That is just who you are. Just be the person you want to be, and you'll make a great queen," she said.

My jaw quivered and my lip trembled as I pulled it between my teeth to make it stop. With a heavy exhale, I was finally able to speak. "Do you really believe that?"

"Of course I do. When have I ever lied to make someone feel better about themselves?" She pulled me deep into a tight hug and said, "Jo brought you back because he loved Caius, and he loved you. Whenever you want to fall into some sort of despair, just remember he gave you the chance to have the life you always deserved."

"I miss Jo," I said through my sniffles. "I wish he could be here today, though I'd venture to say maybe he passed on some of his wisdom to you. That was the kind of feel-good pep-talk Jo would give."

She smiled, but it didn't quite reach her eyes. "I miss him so much. Ru'than or not, he was my little brother. The world feels less without him. He wasn't much for big crowds, though. And today, that crowd is something else."

"Well, you made me cry, and my mascara is smearing. That's your fault, favorite cousin. So help me fix it so I don't look like a raccoon out there."

Clara did a little dance at being called my favorite and headed to the dresser to grab my makeup and some tissues while I changed.

Another knock at the door sounded, and I called for them to come in.

Nog came flying into the room in his corgi form, a crocheted doll between his teeth. His muffled barks were consistent with his sounds of impatience. Pol followed him, and began to speak, but quickly cut himself off when he saw Clara was present. The tension in the room shifted the moment they began to exchange words. How could they not see how badly they wanted each other? I'd be damned if I let that one slip by her.

She rolled her eyes, looking away from him. "What do you want?"

"I came to see if Reagan needed anything before I escort the two of you down there."

"I don't need you to be my escort."

"Damn, woman. I didn't say you *needed* one. It's customary."

She whirled, facing him. "Who the hell do you think you are calling me *woman*?"

I groaned. "Seriously, you two. Get a room." Nog exhaled loudly through his nose, making sounds amounting to a laugh.

"I do *not* need a room with him," Clara said defiantly. "He's moody, and abrasive—"

"And incredibly hot. Quite like you. Everyone here knows you have a thing for him," I interjected, quickly looking to Pol. "I don't mean to objectify you, but you know you're a pretty man."

He inclined his chin. "I am."

Clara grumbled. "We aren't even each other's types."

"Oh, don't I know it." For a moment she looked smug, happy that I had sided with her. Until I finished my thought. "Your type sucks."

Her mouth popped open, and her cheeks flushed pink.

"Seriously, Clara. Your last boyfriend stole your autonomy with poison, tried to kill me, and planned on killing Pol and Caius and probably a slew of other people."

She glanced at the crocheted doll on the floor as Nog bit down on it, shaking it between his teeth with a heavy growl. With a saccharine sweet voice, she said, "And now he can live as a chew toy for eternity."

"Maybe it's because her last boyfriend was a power-hungry, arrogant piece of shit? Too bad he didn't bother to get to know her or respect her powers," he said, approaching her with his hands behind his back. Even though he was speaking to me, it was as if he were addressing my cousin.

"Oh? And what would you know about respect? Hmm? I get dragged into Tartarus and you instantly question me and my motives." She put her hands on her hips, glaring at him.

He slowed, tilting his head. "Can you blame me for being skeptical? I'd lived with Abyssian for *five thousand years* and I knew something was wrong but could never figure it out."

"You called me woman."

"You called me Pollito."

I tried to muffle my snort-laugh.

"Wait, you said you liked the sound of it?" Her voice changed slightly toward the end of her question. She was actually worried . . .

"And you care about what I like?"

"I . . . no. Maybe, but it's not like you care about—"

"You like sunsets."

Clara released a small gasp. "How did you know that?"

"You like the smell of fresh baked bread, but especially anything with cinnamon. Romance books are your preferred reading, simply because you want to find that kind of love even if you don't believe it exists. You favor the orange crochet needle over the blue. The one your little brother gave you because it's your favorite color."

"Damn, Pol. Well played," I whispered, giving him a

thumbs up, but neither of them looked at me. The corgi and I were just witnesses to whatever was happening.

"How could you even know all that?" she said, her features softening. "How could you possibly . . ."

"Because I made it a priority to learn about you."

"But you acted like I didn't belong here . . ."

"I'm an immortal being, and it's my job to keep my king safe. Skepticism runs with the territory, but regardless of my abrasiveness, I've always been a good judge of charac-ter. It would seem, according to Reagan—" Nog barked around the toy in his mouth— "and your brother, you historically have not. Maybe try something new. You might find you like it."

Clara's arms dropped to her side, and for once, she was speechless. He leaned in, just hovering over her lips, and I was about to start screaming for him to kiss her. But he didn't. Instead, he whispered, "I would take all your ire and all your curses. I could give you what you desire; everything you've been missing." Then he lightly brushed his lips over hers. "Try me."

"If you hurt me, I'll put your soul in a doll and give it to a dog," she said through stuttered breath, but there was no conviction behind it.

"For you? I'd risk it."

Clara nodded, giving him the okay with a coy smile curving upward. Pol smirked, brushing his lips over hers slightly.

"Also?" he added, winking at her. "Your family loves me."

"Wait, what?" Clara and I said in unison.

Nog tossed the doll, and it smacked into the wall where he chased it. We all turned our attention to him when the thud echoed in the room. He pounced on it, growling and arching his back as he hovered over it and began humping its face. If you listened carefully, you could almost hear a soul crying in agony.

"I've been waiting millennia for that weasel to get his just deserts, and I never imagined it would be so incredibly satisfying to watch a dog fuck him in the ear for eternity," Pol said, a wide grin on his face.

When I arrived at the ceremonial circle, my heart skipped a beat. If I'd thought the crowd for the primal hunt was big, that was nothing compared to the attendance of their king's wedding.

A warm presence cloaked me, and I knew my love was near.

"My queen," he whispered, nipping my ear ever so slightly.

I turned around, wrapping my arms around his waist and tilting my head up to look at him.

"Not a queen yet," I said, half smirking. "I thought I was supposed to go there and wait for your grand entrance into the circle while the shamans did all their chanting."

"Change of plans," he said, kissing my nose and taking my hand. "We're walking in together."

"But I thought . . . tradition?"

"Fuck tradition. We're doing it our way." He paused, tilting his head to the side momentarily. "Unless you want me to go ask your dad for ten goats as dowry?"

I smacked his arm playfully.

The throng of people parted as we walked through, heading to our appointed spots within the circle. The shamans smiled, each of them inclining their heads to bow in respect. My dad stood next to Sin and Tía Celeste. Tío Amos had even made it. We kept the list small for my family. I'm not sure Tartarus was ready for that.

Standing before each other, Clara and Styx approached silently, each holding a tray of paint.

"Again?" I whispered.

"This time is slightly different."

A beautiful, shapely woman with a cascade of braided red hair and emerald-green eyes approached, tracing her fingers down the curve of my jaw, and placing her other hand on Caius's biceps.

Her eyes flashed, and a bright smile appeared on her face. "I see a baby in your future, Reagan. The love you feel for them is otherworldly. They will bring you great joy."

My mouth fell open, and Caius's gaze shot to mine. "Are you?"

"Uh, no. Definitely not. I'm not saying never, but just . . . not right now, and kind of a weird place to talk about this," I whispered, turning to the seer, and snapping while I spoke. "See *anything* else there?"

"I said what I said."

"Cryptic old goat," Styx muttered, rolling her eyes, and huffing loudly.

The seer grinned. "Oh, Styx." She kissed her teeth. "You cannot run forever. You know what awaits you on the other side."

Styx's jaw clenched, and her gaze hardened. The woman winked, then turned away and walked to the edge of the crowd.

"Stupid goat lady. Why couldn't she have been a villain and ended up locked in a chew toy alongside Abyssian?" she grumbled, blowing out a frustrated breath.

"Wait, *that's* Broca? The glaistig?" I said, my lips parting as I watched the beautiful woman loop her arm through a happy man standing beside her. With great affection, she rested her head on the side of his arm, and he stroked her hand that rested there. He grinned at me stupidly, tilting his head to the side.

"Yes, why?" my mate asked, trying to follow my gaze and see what I was gawking at.

"Because right now she's *very* cozied up to Ben, and I'm just curious if he knows he's fucking a goat."

Clara snorted and Styx elbowed her. I wiggled my fingers in a wave at my ex, and Caius grunted, holding back a laugh.

A shaman approached, giving the look of disapproval for all our talking. After saying a few words, Styx held out the paint tray, standing beside us.

I blinked several times. "I don't know what I'm supposed to do."

"Follow me, my love."

Caius dipped both thumbs in green, then he drew two lines on my cheekbones. "For prosperity," he said, never breaking eye contact.

With his index fingers, he dipped them in orange, and dragged them slowly beneath my bellybutton, sending goosebumps over my skin. I released a stuttered breath. "For fertility."

Clearing his throat, he dipped his middle fingers in red, drawing a line down my throat, over my breastbone, and into my cleavage. My skin flushed, heat pulsing between my thighs. "For passion."

The anticipation was killing me.

Styx whispered, "Hold out your hands, palm down."

I obliged, and with his ring fingers he dipped them in purple, drawing a line down my ring fingers on the tops of my hands. "For unity."

He coated his pinkies in black, marking a line across my forehead. "Until eternal darkness."

Jagged breaths punctuated my pounding heart. I wanted nothing more than to kiss him right at that moment, but I had a feeling I had to do the same to him before the ceremony would end.

"It's your turn," he said quietly, a slight rumble in his tone.

My hands were shaking as I traced the lines over his skin, repeating as he had.

For prosperity, across his sharp cheekbones.

For fertility, tracing along the edge of his hardened, muscular abdomen.

For passion, down the column of his throat, over his sternum, to the middle of his chest.

For unity, marking down the symbolic ring finger.

On his forehead, from one temple to the other. "Until eternal darkness," I murmured.

An iridescent shimmer coated Caius's body. My lips parted, and I looked down, realizing the same had happened to me. Something deep in my chest tightened, the sensation filling me with a warm glow.

"That's the bond," he whispered, leaning down to kiss me softly. Amidst the roaring crowd and flying petals, it was just me and Caius existing in that moment. The way he looked at me drowned out everything and everyone. "It's tying the knot, so to speak."

"Then I guess there's only one thing left for me to do," I said, my heart fluttering, sending the pending anxiety through my veins for what I was about to do.

His brows creased together, and he tilted his head slightly in question.

"*Run*," I whispered.

My footsteps pounded against the stone floor. Excitement sang in my blood. My dark brown hair flew behind me, whipping my face when I took a corner too sharp. I could feel Caius getting closer through our bond and it only spurred me on.

I ascended the stairs to the tallest tower taking two at a time, stripping my clothes along the way. My chest heaved. My heartbeat drummed. I burst through the open doorway into my painting studio.

Caius grabbed me from behind. His lips kissed my claiming mark and he let out a dark chuckle.

"I should have known," he said.

"I want to finish our painting," I breathed.

His hands skimmed my waist, up my ribcage. He cupped my heavy breasts, tweaking my nipples between his forefinger and thumb.

I arched my back into him, and Caius groaned, nipping at my neck.

Pleasure shot through me, the sensation traveling to the heat between my legs. I writhed against him, biting out a single word. "Paint."

Caius chuckled against my skin, sending his shadows to grab bottles off the table and uncap them. They loomed closer, those phantom hands carrying them toward us. He dumped the contents of a bright cerulean blue over one breast and a sunflower yellow down my arm.

It was going to be a work of art by the time we were done.

.

A bottle of fuchsia appeared in front of me. I held out my hands. His shadows tipped the contents over, covering my fingers and palms. I reached behind me with my painted hands, cupping the back of his neck with one and running the other through his hair.

Caressing our hands over each other's bodies, we created swirls and lines of vivid colors, breaking only to kiss. Facing each other while we painted, looking deeply into his eyes, created a desperate yearning I'd never felt.

It was electric.

We dragged it out, savoring the moment. Increasing the desire. Escalating the tension.

Each touch, each stroke, elicited thrilling tingles. Intensifying the anticipation.

The silence between us as we moved our hands, only hearing the sounds of hitched breathing and sensual sighs, deepened the erotic nature of the experience.

When I whispered his name, Caius twirled me around again, then sucked on a particularly sensitive patch of flesh beneath my ear. His fingers laced through mine. He gently nudged the back of my knee with his and guided me to the canvas tarp beneath us, his body curling over mine in the descent.

I braced myself on all fours, and he trailed kisses down my spine, placing his hand on my upper back and directing me to lay down.

The cold canvas covered my skin, goosebumps erupting over me.

He chuckled, and I rolled over, accepting his weight, relishing the heat of his body on mine. Caius supported himself on his forearm, staring down at me with a look I couldn't read.

His tip brushed my entrance, and I angled my hips, widening my legs, waiting for him, but he just watched me.

"Why are you looking at me like that?" I whispered, my hands wrapped around his neck, my fingers toying with strands of hair.

He waited a moment, smiling. "I want you to say it."

"I want you to fuck me," I breathed, wiggling, and trying to get the friction I so desperately craved.

"Say that you're *mine*." The final was spoken so deeply, so possessively, it vibrated against me.

"I'm yours, Caius," I breathed in a shaky voice. "I'll always be yours."

Caius hummed in satisfaction, lowering to kiss me, drinking me in. Then he thrust inside me, filling me up. My back bowed as we rolled against each other, meeting each other's rhythm in perfect time. He rocked into me, and I pulled my knees up higher, countering his thrusts.

We slipped across the canvas, smearing paint.

Creating art.

Dropping a leg down, I rocked to the side, communicating without words that I wanted to be on top.

I took a measure of control in directing our position, and it was empowering the way he gave it so willingly, releasing a gratified growl as we rolled smoothly.

We fit together in every way.

I settled on top, placing my hands on his chest and rocking on top of him. Paint smeared on untouched spaces. Caius gripped my thighs, encouraging our pace, speeding up when the muscles in his jaw clenched.

As the pressure built inside me, threatening to pull me under, I sat up, reaching a hand back to balance on his muscular thigh while I rode him harder. My fingers found my clit, eagerly massaging as I climbed higher and higher.

I tilted my head back, tipping over the edge.

Ecstasy devoured me. Waves of pleasure shot through my body as I kept moving. Wild flutters pulsed inside me; wave after wave crashed. Caius's muscles contracted, his hands clenching me tight, and he roared, spilling into me.

I fell forward, spent, resting on top of him while our breaths turned even, and our heartrates steadied. He traced his fingers along my back in long strokes.

"You know," he murmured. "We still get to wash the paint off each other."

With my cheek pressed against his chest, I smiled. "I like the sound of that."

We both climbed to our feet and regarded the abstract work of art. A multitude of colors smeared together into something oddly beautiful.

"I love it," I said, a smile forming. I couldn't wait to get it stretched and framed.

Curling into Caius's side, I wrapped my arms around his body. He wrapped his arm around my shoulder and rested his chin on top of my head. "I think we could make several of them."

"We could have an art show and let Pol be the judge. Not tell him what they are until he's picked a favorite." I smirked at the thought, and Caius chortled.

"Could hang them in every room in the castle as well."

"That's an awful lot of space to cover," I mused, turning to look up at him. "Think we can do it?"

He cupped my face, brushing his lips over mine. "We have all the time in the world."

EPILOGUE: REAGAN

"So this is where the mountains meet the ocean," I breathed, taking in the view of Cape Flattery off the coast in a small section of Blood and Beryl territory. A whale sung to its pod in the distance. The biting wind nipped at my exposed skin, cutting through the layers I wore to keep warm.

Patches of blue skies scattered behind large, gray clouds. The dark churning waters splashed against the cliff sides and protruding rocks.

"I told you I'll take you anywhere in the world," Caius said, wrapping his arms around my waist as he stood behind me.

"It's more beautiful than I could ever imagined." I inhaled the salty, crisp air, closing my eyes briefly to drink in the magic of this place.

Caius looked not at the ocean, but at me. "I couldn't agree more."

We stood in silence, nuzzled against each other while I committed every detail of this place to memory. I couldn't wait to paint it when we got home. A year had passed since we'd married, and I had barely made a dent in covering the castle in my art. In some cases, it was *our* art—though it wasn't for lack of trying. There was just a lot of space to cover.

In that time, I worked on myself and continued to learn how to be queen. I spoke with Danni frequently, and her patience with my questions was kind and unending. She became my royal mentor. My confidant. We'd grown closer than expected—but Clara was still my favorite cousin, and she made sure to remind me as such.

Eres and I were still working on communication. She was a remarkably arrogant unicorn, but on that fateful day, we formed a trust. We'd get there, even if she was hard to deal with sometimes. I felt her stir within me, grumpy over my assessment.

Every day I worked at continuing to find myself, to make Jo proud, never taking for granted the gift he'd given me. Sometimes I missed him so much it hurt. Grief had a way of creeping in at the most unexpected times, like when I'd finished a book in the castle library and felt the instant need to share it with him. Then the weight of his loss came crashing down on me again. It wasn't just me. My entire family felt the chasm he'd left in our hearts. While his death reminded all of us to cherish those we love while we have them, we also came to understand he was never really ours to begin with.

Clara's voice startled me as she came through a portal behind us. "I'm really . . . sorry . . . to interrupt you," she said, clearly out of breath, and her cheeks-tinged pink.

"What the matter?" I said, running up to her while she rested her hands on her knees.

"I'm fine," she answered, waving me off. "Just in a rush

to get the portal here. You have to come back to Mount Rainier."

"Is Danni . . . is it happening?" I began, waiting for her to finish the sentence.

She smiled, nodding quickly. "Her labor came on fast, and it's progressing even faster. It's almost time."

We rushed down the hallway, coming to a stop amongst a crowd that had formed outside Danni and Elias's bedroom. The king's second, Ysabeau, dipped her chin in greeting, her dark sunglasses blocking out any readable expression.

Caius placed his splayed palm at the small of my back, gently rubbing in a soothing motion. I clasped my hands, twirling my thumbs. "Any news?"

My Tía Abbey rushed forward, throwing her arms around me. "Elias, Adora, and her mom are in there with her. She's almost there. She's pushing."

Strangled moans filtered from the room, followed by the sounds of heavy exhalations as Danni took deep breaths and prepared to push with the next contraction.

"You're going to be a grandma," I said to her, barely containing my excitement.

Babies in my family were frequent, but we celebrated the event like it was a rarity. Life was precious. Tonight there would be parties all over Blood and Beryl, naturally. A new heir would be born. But that joy extended to The Crossroads—not only for our newly formed alliance with the House and Tartarus—but because Danni was one of ours. We were family.

"I'm going to be a Gigi," she said proudly. "That's the name I'm going with. Unless the baby gives me another name. They could call me Grumpy, and I would still be happy. Sarah is going to me Mimi."

I chuckled. "Well, Tío Amos wanted to be called Pappy. But when his oldest had her first, and Miguel learned to speak, he called him Happy. It stuck." It was certainly not the word I would use to describe him, but even he found it funny.

Clara nudged me with her shoulder, jutting her chin toward the closed door. "Do you think this was what Broca meant when she said there was a baby in your future?"

"Good gods, it has to be. I take my tonic like clockwork. I'm just not ready to be a mom yet. I need to take care of myself and deal with my trauma before I add a little one into my life." I'd spoken so quickly; I didn't consider how I'd worded it. Turning to Caius, I winced, and whispered, "That was an abrupt answer. Does it bother you that we're here to celebrate Danni's baby, and I'm not even willing to consider it right now?"

He put his arm around me, pulling my closer and kissing the top of my head. "Of course not, my love."

A sudden cry broke out. Little lungs filling with air, and releasing tiny, rapid wails was music to our ears.

My heart jumped and I felt like crying. Clara squealed, clenching her fists and shaking them in the air with a big, toothy smile on her face.

"He's here!" Elias burst out the door, barely recognizable. His usual stoic features were replaced with the beaming pride of a new dad.

"Is she okay? How's the baby?" Tía Abbey blurted, throwing her arms around Elias in a hug.

"They're great, everyone is great. They're ready for you to come in." He stepped out of the way so we could pass.

Caius walked up to Elias and shook his hand clapping him on the shoulder with his other. "Congratulations, Your Majesty."

Sometimes I couldn't believe the turn my life had taken. Danni had been an outcast; a shifter that couldn't shift. Now she was a hybrid vampire. I had been a guardian; forced to guard the soul of a dethroned primordial. A dark unicorn; unable to shift. Somehow, two quirky girls from one extended family ended up queens. I smiled, winking at my mate before entering Danni's room.

As soon as we crossed the threshold, my tías ran to each other and embraced in a flurry of tears and happiness. Nova laid near Danni's feet, her head down as she watched them. My cousin Adora sat on the bed, leaning against the head-board as she stroked Danni's silvery waves. Her ombre blue hair framed her face beautifully while she looked down on her nephew with admiration. A little bundle pressed to Danni's chest, gently suckling, his teeny fingers flexing.

Danni met my gaze, and we shared a quiet exchange.

"Do you want to hold him?" she asked.

"Oh my god, yes," I said, making sure to keep my voice low so I wouldn't startle my newest cousin. Danni held him out to me swaddled in a beautiful burgundy blanket. I scooped him up, holding him to me as I gently rocked. "He's beautiful," I whispered.

"Everyone says babies are beautiful, even when they look like potatoes," Adora began, and Danni gave her sister a side glance. "But in this case, he's my nephew so he's the most beautiful baby ever."

"Damn straight," Clara said, nodding once as she

peered over my shoulder, watching the newest member of our family sleep.

I looked at Dannika, and it was true what they said. She was glowing. The perspiration from labor left its mark on her wet hairline, and her eyes were filled with exhaustion that would surely be there for months to come, but a genuine happiness lined her features, and I couldn't help but think that everything was just as it should be. I smiled, content, and looked down at the baby swaddled in my arms.

Softly I sang the only lullaby I knew. The baby stirred, letting out a little coo as his little eyelids fluttered open.

Clara gasped, grabbing my upper arm and squeezing tight in disbelief. "Reagan, look," she hissed in a barely audible voice.

My lips parted; my jaw slack.

A lump formed in my throat.

Warm brown eyes stared back at me. Sweet, kind eyes I never thought I'd see again. I would know them anywhere. My heart filled with joy and ached all at once. A single tear escaped, leaving a trail down my cheek.

"Hey, mijo," I whispered through a watery smile.

The End.

Thank you for reading MATE ME! We hope you enjoyed Reagan and Caius' love store. To read a special extended epilogue of Reagan and Caius, join our newsletter HERE. The following is a list of character's we saw in Mate Me and their book's.
Danni and Elias is REJECT ME.
Adora is WORSHIP ME.

Styx is SHADOW ME.
Legion is HUNT ME.
Oberon and Sin is SPURN ME.

I'm thrilled to offer a sneak peek of our bestselling paranormal romance, REJECT ME. **Perfect for fans of Immortals After Dark, Black Dagger Brotherhood, and the Demonica series.**

"Reject Me has everything I crave in a good book—a unique world, captivating characters, and heat! I loved every second I spent between the pages." —Ivy Asher, International Bestselling Author of *The Bone Witch*

"Paranormal romance at its best. Reject Me is action-packed, spicy perfection!"

—Jessica Wayne, USA Today Bestselling Author of *Savage Wolf*

"Reject Me was a wild ride filled with twists and turns that kept me reading all night. But it was the relationship between Elias and Danni that I loved the most. Their depth and connection made this paranormal romance one I'll remember for many years to come." —Lexi C Foss, USA Today Bestselling Author of *Carnage Island*

Sneak Peek of Reject Me

Elias

Blood dripped slowly from my fingertips, each droplet hitting the ground with a sickening splat. In the fireplace, flickering red and orange flames died down to smoldering embers, the black coals glowing with the last remnants of life.

My bedroom was silent.

The Blood and Beryl grounds were in a hushed state.

If only the echoes in my head would quiet down, but after what I'd done . . . all I heard was noise. The screams of shifters, vampires, and witches dying. The singing of a blade as it sliced through the air. The dull thud as it came into contact with an enemy's head. The squelching sound as weapons cut through bodies.

Thousands died because of the choices we made.

Choices *I* made.

While the blood rage was still pulsing through my veins, and the violent desire to kill was begging for release, it was the witch's words that haunted me.

Her soft brown skin glowed, and her eyes had been as pale as moonlight, yet looking into them . . . I had the feeling she could see into my soul. And what she saw . . .

Dahlia Renfrew had pointed a finger at my chest, uttering her prophecy in a melodic voice.

"You have rage in your heart, Elias Laskaris," she'd said. "But also guilt. Both will guide you as you seek your revenge, but your heart will be lost. On the anniversary of this night in twenty-four years' time, while you mourn, you will find your mate. She will be the greatest vampire queen Blood and Beryl has ever seen. You will *know* she is yours . . . and you will be too late. Her future is marked by death."

Dahlia was never wrong.

What she didn't know was that I had no interest in finding my mate. I'd just lost my sister. I wasn't strong enough to save her. I had no interest in opening myself to that vulnerability ever again. I wouldn't lose someone I loved.

No. If I ever found this supposed mate . . .

I'd reject her.

Dannika

They say I was born on a cursed moon.

A night when the sky glowed red as the blood spilled in Portland. Later, we'd call it "the Great Sacrifice"—because somehow, on those blood-soaked streets, peace was found.

Order had been restored.

Or some form of it, perhaps. That was what we were told. It was certainly how the leaders presented it.

I wasn't sure who believed it. I wasn't sure what the truth was. Even with a truce, there was an undeniable strain between the Great Houses. But no one ever mentioned that underlying tension. Not in public, anyway. What I did know was that the world had been irrevocably changed that day.

I'd probably heard the story more times than I could count, because that night was twenty-four years ago today.

"Cheer up," Adora said. I guessed the firm line of my mouth gave away my gloomy mood, despite the Spice Girls album blasting through my room. Her choice, not mine.

"It's not like I want to go to this stupid party," I groused. "Our birthday is literally the day millions of people died. It's not exactly a day people should be celebrating."

But they did. Every year. They focused on the peace forged instead of the lives lost that day. Lives like my father's.

He'd had to defend the pack while my mother had gone

into labor, but he'd never come home. She'd found his body. Brutalized. Claw marks had been gouged deep into his chest. There was no doubt it had been another shifter, but there was also no way to know who—not that we could do much about it even if we *had* identified his killer. What had happened before the Great Sacrifice was supposed to be left in the past.

Even murder.

"It's also the last massacre we've had in twenty-four years," Rowe pointed out. She sat cross-legged on my bed, her wild, red hair falling out of the ponytail that bound it. "That's gotta be worth something."

No. It really wasn't. Not when shifters had only walked this realm for fifty years, ever since the portal opened in Portland. After that happened, the human governments fell apart. As expected, the people revolted and then *they* fell apart. Turns out there was a whole other world no one had known about. The supernatural one. Nowadays, that was the only one that existed. All over the world, six giant portals had opened up over the past few thousand years, but they had remained closely guarded. Unseen by humans. Each one led somewhere different.

Ours?

It led to a land of beasts.

Shifters crossed over from it and mingled with the population. My parents were both products of that merging. There were other ways people had turned into shifters. Those that lingered too close to portals sometimes changed, absorbing bits of magic. It leaked into our world like a radioactive hazard. The result? Thousands of shifters basically popped up overnight.

So no, considering our kind had only been on this earth for fifty or so years, the last massacre being twenty-four years ago didn't impress me. Not when it had all been senseless violence.

The Houses may rule, but that didn't make them any less corrupt than previous governments.

My silence told them my opinion, and Adora snorted. "Dannika's a Debbie Downer, Rowe, you know that. When has she ever looked on the bright side?"

At my sister's jesting, my lips twisted, trying to hide my amusement. Not the easiest thing to do when she was all of a foot from my face, pointing liquid eyeliner toward my lids, flicking it about like a black magic wand.

"I'm not a downer, asshole. I just don't like to commemorate the day my dad died as one giant party. You know how much Mom has suffered because of it." Her lips pressed together, and she looked away. Shame turned her cheeks a shade pinker.

With the exception of Adora, all the peacock shifters had been wiped out in the Great Sacrifice. My sister had been found the same night I'd been born, abandoned in the woods but unharmed. No one knew what she was, and that secret stayed safe in our family.

My mom had kept her, knowing she wouldn't have survived otherwise. Then she'd stepped down as the Alpha Female of the pack to raise us. While Adora was probably older than I was by a few days, we considered today our joint birthday, since we didn't know hers.

"You know I didn't mean it like that," she whispered.

I sighed. "I know." Now I *did* feel like a downer, and a jackass to boot. "I just hate that we're being forced to go to the commemoration because the Alpha Supreme's son still hasn't found his mate. It's ridiculous he's forcing all unmated shifters to attend when it's not like he's stepping down anytime soon. I get that Markus needs to have a kid

—the heir having an heir, and all that—but there's still plenty of time."

"It only takes a moment for things to change," Adora said softly. Not somberly, but she was thoughtful in her answer. "You never know what the future holds. It sucks for us, but if something happened to the Alpha Supreme, Markus would need to be ready to take his father's place— or we'd all be in deep shit." The ruler of the House of Fire and Fluorite had to be prepared for anything. There were always schemes in play to take that power away. The Alpha Supreme used to fight a dozen challenges every year or so until it had become clear he'd always win. If something *did* happen, and Markus took over, things would be chaos. But by Markus having an heir—and by extension, a mate—it meant he could actually be powerful enough to handle the transition. If he didn't, no one in our House would be safe, let alone our pack. The scramble for control would end in bloodshed. I hated that she was right, but I nodded anyway. She frowned, pinching my chin with one hand to hold me still. Oops.

"I wouldn't be as annoyed if he weren't such a douche," I muttered.

"Yes, you would," Adora said, calling me out. From the bed, Rowe laughed, the sound like a witch's cackle. "But he *is* a douche. You won't hear an argument from me. I feel bad for whoever ends up stuck with him."

"You and me both."

Adora capped the eyeliner and gave my shoulder a squeeze.

"It's one night. Just a couple of hours, then we can come back and watch some episodes of *The Vampire Diaries*. 'Kay?" She smiled, and it was brilliant. My sister was absolutely stunning with hair that changed in the light, morphing with shades of blues and greens. People often noticed her small, curvy frame or big, brown eyes. It was her smile I liked best, though.

"'Kay," I repeated, taking a deep breath.

I checked my appearance in the full-length mirror, appraising my outfit. The night was a celebration, but the dress code was never formal, at least not for shifters. Black leggings with a nice tunic and boots were simple and tasteful—and it allowed me to be a wallflower. I applied a quick coat of mascara and swiped my phone off the bathroom counter. Rowe reclined back on my bed, kicking her feet up.

"You good if I hang out here?" she asked. "I can head back to my room if you prefer." Rowe was the only human in our pack, and part of a very small number that our House accepted. At the bottom of the totem pole in the new world order, she existed as the pack janitor—and punching bag on more than one occasion.

It was total bullshit that the others could treat her that way just because she didn't have magic, and almost everyone overlooked it. More than once, Adora and I had taken a hit meant for her. We might have been outcasts too, but at least we had magic. We could heal fast. Rowe? Not so much.

"Go for it. If I'm not back until late, feel free to just crash here. I wouldn't want to be out tonight if I were you."

Drunk shifters? Wayward magic? Loose morals because everyone was too preoccupied with the commemoration downtown?

Yeah, no. It was a recipe for disaster if one of the pack assholes found her on a night like tonight. She was way safer here with my mom and stepmom, Abbey.

"Thanks, Dannika. You're the best," Rowen said with a wink, reaching for the remote.

"No, she's not," Adora called from across the house. We both rolled our eyes, and I flashed her a smile before closing the bedroom door behind me. "I don't know why Rowe inflates her ego like that," she continued, speaking loudly, so her voice carried. The humor in her tone made me smile. "We all know who the best *really* is."

My moms' laughter greeted me as I walked around the corner and into our living room. It was modest, but it was just what we needed for our family. A navy-blue sofa and coal-colored recliner were the only furniture in the common space. We couldn't fit more. Not with Nova, my wolf.

She lifted her head when I walked in. Her icy-blue eyes were exactly the same shade as my own, and her fur was just as silver as my hair. Eight feet long, from the tip of her nose to the end of her tail, and nearly four feet tall, she was a true Alpha Wolf and the rightful heir of this pack—if not for one little problem.

I couldn't shift.

When other toddlers had been turning into cubs, I'd been cut off from her. I'd known she was there, but not how to bring her forward. Our bond was broken somehow.

But we'd found a way to fix it, however unconventional it may have been.

I still couldn't shift, but she was with me always. The other half of my soul, brought forth with the help of a witch. I wouldn't have had it any other way, even if it made me a freak.

"Oh, honey," Mom said. "You look so grown up now." I sensed the sadness in her voice as she walked up and embraced me with strong arms. Behind her, Adora and Abbey stood at the kitchen counter, watching us.

"No more than I did yesterday," I reminded her. She was always very emotional on her daughters' birthday. I hated leaving her when I knew the grief had resurfaced. I was so thankful that she'd found the strength to love again when she'd mated with Abbey. It made it easier, knowing that my stepmom was here for her when I couldn't be.

"I love you, baby girl."

"I love you too."

Mom lifted her hand, cupping it around my jaw as she pulled back a few inches. Her dark-brown eyes looked over me like she was committing my face to memory. She always did. It was part of why I hated leaving her for any reason on my birthday. While many years had gone by, this day seemed to take her back in time every year. The pain became fresh. Raw.

It made me even more pissed off about being forced to attend this year's commemoration.

"You get that from your daddy," she said wistfully.

"What?"

"Your steadfastness." She patted my cheek. "He was loyal to a fault, but also fair. Never seemed to have an issue figuring out right from wrong, despite how much the rest of us could struggle with it. He would have been so proud of the woman you've become . . . at how much you've taken care of me, even when you shouldn't have needed to."

I frowned at the water pooling in her eyes.

This was exactly what I'd wanted to avoid, not because I didn't care—but because I hated seeing her like this.

"Mom," I said quietly, shaking my head. I brought my hand up to cup around her fingers, squeezing gently. "You did the best you could."

Abbey came up behind her, wrapping her arms tightly around my mom. "And you did a damn good job," she said. "Look how well our girls turned out. Scott would have been proud as hell if he were here to see this now." While she spoke to my mom, she made eye contact with me, letting me know she had her. Reminding me it would be okay.

"I just miss him so much sometimes," my mom said apologetically. She turned to hug Abbey back.

"And that's okay. Missing someone when they're gone is the price we pay for love."

Adora came up, wrapping one arm around Mom and one around Abbey. She leaned up on her tiptoes to kiss our moms' cheeks.

"We'll be back late. Don't wait up for us," she said, though we both knew they would.

"You two watch out for each other tonight," Abbey said, speaking to us over my mom's shoulder. While my mother wasn't exactly short, Abbey was quite tall. Just a smidge over six feet, she could easily look at us while embracing my mom. "Stay in No Man's Land. Don't even think about heading northside—"

"We know," Adora said.

"Don't accept anything from strangers—"

"We know." My sister sighed while I squinted at our stepmom. It wasn't like we didn't know any of this. They'd been giving us this talk for over a decade now.

"Use protection, and don't forget your fluorite stones—"

"We *know!*" we both said in exasperation. The fluorite ring on my finger had never left my hand since the day my mom had given it to me. It signified our House, our pack within it, our protection. Shitty as my pack may have been at times, it was better than being without one. "Seriously,

Abbey. We'll be safe. I promise," I added. She gave us both a smile and then nodded.

"Then have fun, and happy birthday, baby girls."

I grabbed my keys off the hanger by the front door while Adora held it open for Nova to go out. My wolf brushed up against my side as she did, a comforting graze that conveyed she knew how much I didn't like leaving, and she sympathized with it.

"Rowe's in my room. If any assholes show up looking for her tonight . . ." I trailed off, but they got the gist.

My mom sniffled and lifted her head. "I might not be our pack's Alpha Female anymore, but I can still put a wolf in their place."

I glanced up at Abbey. "I'll make sure she doesn't kill some stupid punk," she said.

Adora snorted, and I just nodded in thanks.

While Abbey would have been the more intimidating of the two if someone met them in an alley, my mom was crazy when it came to protecting her own. Her temper flared the second someone looked at us wrong, and that extended to Rowe since the first night we'd brought her over. It was half the reason I loved Abbey so much. She knew how to bring my mom down with her "calm juju," as we called it. She exuded the peace of a still lake and tempered my mom's fiery personality when needed.

"All right, let's gooooo," Adora said, gently pushing me toward the door. "We'll never leave if I don't make you, and I am *not* getting punished by the Alpha Supreme for disobeying a direct command."

"Yep," I said, following behind her. She dropped the tailgate open on my truck and Nova jumped in, tucking herself under the canvas canopy. I slid into the driver's seat just as Adora closed it up. We were backing out of the driveway in no time, but as we were headed down the road, I couldn't help a feeling that overcame me when I looked in the rearview mirror. The full moon skimmed just above the treetops, painting our house in an eerie light.

They said I'd been born on a cursed moon . . . but they never said what that had looked like. Had it glowed the same as the moon did tonight? What had been different about it? Had it been the color? The size?

Or had it been cursed because of a feeling in the air? An uneasiness that had settled in the blood, gradually seeping in like a potent poison? Or had it violently riled up the magic within us, stirring it into a frenzy that couldn't be denied?

Between the options, I hoped it was simply the way the moon had looked, but something told me it wasn't.

It was the same "something" that had been eating at me all week, ever since the day the attendance order had gone out. It was telling me not to go. To stay home. To run. To be anywhere except the commemoration on the full moon.

I'd ignored the voice, even as it whispered through me that soon it would be time to fight. To disobey. To rise.

Maybe I was crazy . . . or maybe it was a feeling in the air, sending me a warning sign.

Something like a cursed moon.

START READING REJECT ME NOW

9 781957 953328